BLACK TORTOISE WINTER

Jan Pearson

Jan Pearson lived in Hong Kong for several years during the 1960s, leaving to attend university in Sydney in her native Australia. She married and led a busy professional and family life until leaving the city for a more leisurely rural lifestyle on the New South Wales north coast. She now visits Hong Kong annually, taking in the new and searching out old haunts. Jan is an excellent speaker and in demand to talk about her books.

Black Tortoise Winter, set in Hong Kong in 1979 at the time when China was opening up to foreign investment, is the third in Pearson's series of Hong Kong-based mystery novels. The first published, *Red Bird Summer*, had a most successful book launch both in Hong Kong and in Australia. The second, *Tiger Autumn*, was praised in Hong Kong's *Sunday Morning Post* as "one of the best Hong Kong novels for years" (William Wadsworth). Like the other two, *Black Tortoise Winter* was shortlisted for the international Proverse Prize, winning a supplementary prize. *Black Tortoise Winter* continues the story of Pearl Green, her father British spook Sir James Gates, her friend Karen Henderson, her father's friend Yip Yee Koon, businessman and triad head, and her late mother's former lover, Peter Benson. We also meet innocent abroad Marcus Brown, on a unique mission to set up an investment project on behalf of his affluent Native American community in Florida, USA and Belinda Jones, celebrity wife of rock legend Smut Jones. It takes all the qualities that the mythological turtle can harness – wisdom and the valour of a warrior – for James, Pearl, Peter Benson and Yip Yee Koon to overcome the criminal forces that enter their lives in this dark and dangerous winter – a Black Tortoise Winter.

BLACK TORTOISE WINTER

Jan Pearson

The third book in the

Celestial Symbols Series

Proverse Hong Kong

Black Tortoise Winter
by Jan Pearson
Copyright © Jan Pearson April 2016.
Published in Hong Kong by Proverse Hong Kong, April 2016
under sole & exclusive licence.
ISBN: 978-988-8228-06-5
Printed by CreateSpace.

Distribution (Hong Kong and worldwide):
The Chinese University Press of Hong Kong,
The Chinese University of Hong Kong,
Shatin, New Territories, Hong Kong SAR.
E-mail: cup-bus@cuhk.edu.hk; Web: www.chineseupress.com

Distribution (United Kingdom):
Christine Penney, Stratford-upon-Avon, Warwickshire CV37 6DN, UK.
Email: chrisp@proversepublishing.com

Distribution and other enquiries to:
Proverse Hong Kong, P.O. Box 259, Tung Chung Post Office, Tung
Chung, Lantau Island, NT, Hong Kong SAR, China.
E-mail: proverse@netvigator.com; Web: www.proversepublishing.com

British Library Cataloguing in Publication Data.
A catalogue record for this book is available
from the British Library.

Author's Notes

The setting for Black Tortoise Winter

An unusual state of anxiety affected Hong Kong in 1979, as China began to invite foreign investment in its push to become a developed, industrialised nation. As Hong Kong pondered its future in these new economic times, the history books tell us that triad activity stepped up to unprecedented levels; extreme weather conditions struck and even a film featuring Hong Kong (*Meteor*) caught up in an (unlikely) natural disaster struck an uneasy chord in the public mind.

Towards the end of this twitchy year, Pearl Green returns to Hong Kong after a three year absence, on the same day that Marcus Brown arrives on a unique mission to set up an investment project on behalf of his Native American Indian community in Florida. It is the first time that a Seminole Indian has journeyed out of America and Marcus is an uneasy ambassador for his people, who are enjoying unprecedented wealth after earning the right before the Federal Courts to use their lands as they wish.

Pearl has returned to resume management of the June Bowen Foundation after the death of her husband Ben, but she is still restless. For his part, Marcus' sense of unease is ramped up to an extreme height when, on his first full day in Hong Kong he is framed for the murder of the well-known business tycoon Dennis Childs in the Hong Kong Hilton Hotel.

Pearl's old friend Belinda Jones returns to bury her father but disappears from the Hilton whilst on her way to visit Pearl. Peter Benson from the Bowen Foundation senses that it is Pearl who is really in danger and that Belinda's disappearance is connected with Pearl's return. He contacts Pearl's father for advice and when James Gates subsequently announces to Pearl that he will be in Hong Kong on a flying visit during the first week of winter, and James's old friend Yip Yee Koon also contacts her and warns her of trouble, Pearl knows that the atmosphere of what Yip would describe as *strangeness* in and around Hong Kong heralds the arrival of a dark winter – a Black Tortoise Winter.

The Symbols of the Four Directions

The celestial symbol from Chinese mythology chosen for this story is the tortoise. It is said that a giant turtle, with one eye located in its abdomen, lives in the depths of the ocean. Once every three thousand years it rises to the surface and turns over on its back so that it may see the sun.

The tortoise symbolises The Warrior and has powers of divination. The early winter of 1979 will be remembered by Pearl, her friends and associates as a time when the warrior needed all of these skills to overcome the evil that emerged during Black Tortoise Winter.

Use of the Terms *turtle and tortoise*

The appearance of a "sea-going tortoise" in the book can be challenged because if this were not a work of fiction, the animal would very likely be a "sea-going turtle".

I chose to use the term "tortoise" because it has a more elegant ring to it than "turtle" and perhaps with more luck than good management Wikipedia confirms there is much confusion in the terminology. Strictly speaking, tortoises usually pursue terrestrial existences.

In Australia further confusion about the "correct" usage of the terms has arisen because freshwater turtles are traditionally referred to as "freshwater tortoises". This tempts me to claim some cultural leniency in the matter. The names "tortoise" and "turtle" have not been biologically determined.

It is interesting to note that the turtle is a sacred figure in Native American symbolism and represents Mother Earth. (*www/warepipes2peacepipes.com*)

Fake Triad Name

Mr Tony Carroll is thanked for providing a suitable name (和聯勝 = WO LUEN SHING (United to Win)) for the fictional triad society that plays a part in this book.

I

Divining The Tortoise Universe

CHAPTER ONE

Friday 30 November 1979: 1.30pm
Kai Tai Airport, Hong Kong

Terry picked Browne out of the crowd easily with only the bare description given by his step-brother. From behind his newspaper, Terry eyed Browne off: the chap was an American Indian and couldn't be more identifiable if he walked through Arrivals with his face painted and with a wigwam tucked under his arm. But even though he was certainly a most exceptional looking fellow, he still had the dazed expression of most first-time travellers to Hong Kong after experiencing the bone-shaking, brain-aching virgin touch-down at Kai Tak. He joined the crowd heading for the exit doors and Terry folded his paper and was about to follow when an airport attendant took him aside and with *a sir, please stand aside sir,* he turned in time to see a well-dressed, gorgeous woman sweep by, followed by a crowd of photographers, reporters and two porters.

A female reporter in the first press of press called out, "Lady Green! Pearl! Welcome home. Are you in Hong Kong to stay?" The woman smiled tightly and nodded and the whole flock followed her in a stream of snapping shutters and rustling notebooks. One of the attendants ushered her into a waiting vehicle and with a newspaper shielding her face, she was gone in a flash. Marcus Browne watched the incident with interest and wondered who she was to create such a media stir. Not for her the tedium of having to queue for a cab. He flexed and straightened his body, which was beginning to complain about the cramped flying conditions as much as the landing he had just endured. If he'd known that arriving in Hong Kong involved almost literally dropping out of the sky, he would have refused to leave home. It was his first trip abroad and he felt surrounded by an unfamiliarity that carried a clear air of chaos with it. Every available surface was plastered with highly coloured signage. Bamboo poles protruded from windows and balconies, festooned with washing and wires or strung with yet more posters or bunting and at ground level, most of the buildings were old, but newer structures had seemingly been dumped on top of many of them. This curious construction technique resulted in the walls of many of the newer buildings leaning at odd, intimate angles to their neighbours.

A continuous stream of people poured in and out of the airport terminal, dragging or carrying overladen suitcases, talking loudly over one another, gesturing, laughing, frowning, all at top speed. Marcus had always imagined Asians as a still, calm people, but this place was packed with men and women all living life at full throttle, whether standing still, walking or reading a newspaper. A horn sounded and someone spoke to him impatiently; he hadn't noticed it was his turn to grab a taxi and he was holding up the queue, wasting time, and no-one was impressed. He smiled weakly, leant through the window and asked the driver to take him to the Hilton Hotel. The driver nodded abruptly and Marcus climbed into the back seat and by the time they got there he was in love, with Hong Kong; the views across the harbour to the Peak, the innumerable boats of all descriptions and the tangle of tall buildings reaching for the sky in Hong Kong Central.

After check-in he admired the views again from his room, made a coffee and picked his way through a newspaper and some tourist brochures before putting through a call to Derek Wong at the Seminole Council's office. Even though he'd only been in Hong Kong for ten minutes, it would be just Derek's style to start quizzing him as though he'd been born here. Marcus shook off the familiar flush of irritation that thinking about his cousin produced and read two pieces about China's push to encourage more foreign investment. Hong Kong seemed to be rubbing its hands together, obviously expecting further wealth to be generated from the new wave of economic activity promised for the region and as Marcus was in Hong Kong on business, this was exactly the sort of news he wanted to pass on to Derek.

The idea for that business had originated with Derek who was quietly relieved to hear Marcus sounding so positive so soon after arriving in Hong Kong. Marcus wound up the call. "It's time to eat here man, and one of the brochures I picked up is for a restaurant called Stormy's. The food is sensational by all accounts. Give Granny Browne a kiss for me won't you? See you, cousin, I'll ring again in a day or two." He hung up. If the papers were even half right, the Council Elders couldn't have hand-picked a better time in history to make an expansionary push into corporate business. China was fast mobilizing as an industrial nation and Hong Kong was booming in its own right as the major centre of financial power in south-east Asia. He remembered his original opposition to the plan and smiled. It now seemed that the question he had put to Derek – *like, who buys stuff from Asia, man?* – was way off beam. Everyone was buying stuff from Asia.

It was nearly seven o'clock when he left the hotel and the cool evening air was beginning to surrender to the heat and hiss of the emerging Hong Kong night show. After paying off the cab on Kowloon side he walked for a while and by the time he found Stormy's, he knew there was something else that he would have to deal with. He would have to get used to being the odd man out in these parts. The way people stared at him – even in the hotel he'd noticed it – you'd think they'd never seen a North American Indian before. He'd have to work at getting used to it though because he'd felt the prickle of being observed ever since he left the hotel. He wondered how Derek would go down here, a Seminole Indian with direct Chinese ancestry on his grandmother's side of the family. It would probably blow the locals away.

*

Pearl Green checked in to the Hilton and after a hurried shower, she called Drew Pierson – her friend, her best friend's husband and the man who had managed the June Bowen Foundation for the past four years. Pearl dreaded the meeting, and after he arrived at the hotel coffee shop and ordered, she found that she didn't have much to say to him. She twiddled her spoon around in the coffee crystals in the bottom of the cup whilst he thoughtfully ate her rejected slice of chocolate cake. The silence between them became awkward.

"Well Drew," she finally said, "let's get down to it. Are you happy running the show or do you want out?" Her tone was as abrupt as the question and it took Drew by surprise. "Out, Pearl, I want out." Pearl was equally surprised by his sharp tone. "Running the foundation has been a great experience but I'm academic by nature, you know that. Kaz has been offered the Directorship of the museum for another three years and there's a Lectureship on offer in the Political Science Department at Hong Kong University. I've been encouraged to apply. But it depends on you. Are you ready to get back into it all? Pearl?" But Pearl wasn't listening. She was gazing out into the street through the coffee shop's floor-to-ceiling windows.

"I thought I would have had Ben's babies by now and be living in the home I was brought up in with the man I love." Her voice had become a whisper. "That's what about me, Drew. None of that is ever going to happen. No husband. No children." She let out a small, involuntary noise that was nearly a sob. Drew put his cake fork carefully back on the plate and looked at her intently: this was not right. It got worse. "I've spent most of this past year in retreat on the edge of a village near to the monastery where Peter Benson studied, you know, after he quit the Civil Service and left Hong Kong. Like Peter, I had a breakdown. The monks and the villagers cobbled me back together enough to function, but I still haven't tested out my new shell in the real world. So I don't know, Drew. I don't know about me."

Drew blinked. He didn't know what to say. Not even when Pearl's mother died had she ever been like this. Setting up the June Bowen Foundation had been her solution to coping with the grief of June's death and when she discovered that James Gates was her biological father they slowly developed a solid relationship, until eventually she met and married Ben Sanders. But after Ben's death, the Pearl they all knew fell apart and a few months later she left Hong Kong and had not been back since. Drew assumed that she would be in some sort of shape again by the time she returned, but she was still a mess. He patted her shoulder and said, "Well, you know that we will all support you and if you don't feel like taking over just yet I'm sure we can ...."

But Pearl wasn't listening. "I want to do something, Drew."

"Like what?"

"You mean, like how, Drew. Like how. Maybe it will come to me over dinner."

CHAPTER TWO

Friday 30 November 1979: 9.00pm

Pearl sighed happily and placed her chopsticks neatly across the top of the bowl. It was impossible to get this sort of food anywhere else in the world and if she had doubted the wisdom of coming home, all reservations dissipated as she sat with her friends for the first time in years, eating the food she had been reared on. "At least my tastebuds aren't dead," she said to Drew. "I've ached for this." He tried to smile, caught Kaz's eye and arched his brow at her. Kaz had observed Pearl intently all evening and as she put her chopsticks down Kaz pushed some of her own food at her, urging another helping. "Don't fuss Kaz," said Pearl. "I'm not ill and I haven't been starved. You're being such a mother."

"Just have another oyster and forget the mother stuff Pearl. You're my best friend and I've missed you, Drew will vouch for that, I drove him mad sometimes worrying about you. We've *all* missed you but now that you're really here," Kaz squeezed Pearl's hand as if needing reassurance that she really was there, "We all want to know" – she crunched on a piece of lotus root as she searched for a diplomatic way to ask if Pearl was back from hell yet, couldn't find the words, gave up and ploughed in – "We all want to know how you will cope with picking up your old life, going back to work and ... everything."

Pearl was silent and Judith Sung, the Bowen Foundation's Administrator, took an agonised sidelong look at her boss. Tonight was the first time Judith had met her employer and they were yet to speak beyond introductions. Judith wasn't sure she should even be here. What they were talking about was so personal! Lady Green – who didn't like to be addressed as Lady Green – was so lovely to look at with that long beautiful golden brown hair and her glorious complexion, and the dress she wore was out of this world, but she wasn't really with them, she was somewhere else, anyone could see that. "Sorry, Judith," said Pearl, catching the young woman's look, "I know this is very personal stuff but there is a lot of shared history around this table and you are part of the family now." Judith reddened across the top of her cheeks and Pearl turned to Kaz and said, "I'm sort of coping, Kazza. I went past the old building this afternoon, and it hit me, really hit me for the first time, that I had sold my family home. I was shattered for the first time since Ben died – about something other than losing him, that is. I call that coping, of sorts, don't you?"

Judith became even more uncomfortable and longed to leave. Pearl felt a small rush of irritation with her – they were all friends here and for God's sake surely she had been told about Ben? Maybe Judith needed to hear it from her directly, maybe she was embarrassed about knowing about it all second hand, so she said, "My husband was killed in a boating accident three months after we were married, Judith. Nearly four years ago. The old Fire Services HQ on Connaught Road was my home until then." Judith flushed and could not look directly at Pearl. But Pearl had brightened. "It was very painful looking at the old place again but not in the way I expected. I lived there for more than thirty years, it's the only place I have any memory of calling home. So maybe I am on the mend. I'm going to buy it back."

She had their undivided attention. Even Peter Benson, her former boss, was listening.

Drew spluttered, "You can't. How can you afford it? Hong Kong is booming; real estate prices are going through the roof and with China opening up to trade and investment, who knows how our futures will be affected? Pearl, please be careful."

"Too late, Drew. I've already been in touch with James Williams at Robertson & Kovacks and he has submitted my offer to the owners. Let's face it, the building itself is not everyone's idea of prime real estate and with the hottest summer on record its proximity to the fish markets may be too much for even the most dedicated pescatarian types." Peter Benson nodded approvingly at her choice of words but carried on jotting in his notebook, his brief interest in her outrageous decision to buy back the family palace already gone.

"Then there's the movie about a giant tsunami hitting Hong Kong, which is about to be released, that's a jolly little rendition of waterfront calamity, I believe," she continued, "and don't forget the recent typhoon, Hope, was the worst blow since 1971." She smiled. "I may get the place at a bargain basement price at this rate. If I *can* do it, the Bowen Foundation will move back to Connaught Road again too. Everyone will be home. It must be a bit of a squash at Upper Albert Road. She was careful not to look at Peter and careful not to say *my Upper Albert Road apartment,* partly because it had once belonged to him and partly because when he owned it he had been her boss. He now worked in his old apartment as her employee. There were very fine eggshells to navigate here, as light as turtle eggs.

Drew was still not satisfied. "Well, at least it seems that you are planning on staying in Hong Kong at any rate, which is great. There's other things that could affect Hong Kong beginning to surface now that we need to know more about – the most important being the expiry of the lease with mainland China in 1997. It's a way off but people are already starting to worry about what may happen there and outmigration is increasing every year. We need to do our research and work out how the Foundation intends to position itself in the future. It needs careful thought and probably more expertise than I have to address those sorts of issues, Pearl. Are you up for it?"

Pearl wasn't sure what she was up for but she wasn't ready to be drawn into a conversation like this, not yet, not tonight. "The handover in 1997 is just another reason why I might get a bargain with Connaught Road, Drew." She ignored the rest of his question and looked longingly at a dish of prawn-stuffed rice noodles that reclined untouched in a silky sesame and soy sauce. "I think I can just about manage that. Does anyone mind? It's too good to leave."

*

When Marcus reached the top of the steep staircase that led from the footpath into Stormy's and found himself in a restaurant where the kitchen was open to the eating area he immediately felt uncomfortable and the sensation increased when he was seated without consultation at a table with another man, who did not acknowledge his presence. Two other men arrived shortly afterwards and joined them and when he tried to explain that he wished to eat alone the waiter just shook his head impatiently. He didn't seem to understand the concept. Marcus had no idea that he had happened on one of Hong Kong's finest restaurants and as the courses rolled by, he ate his way into a world that challenged his notions of what food was about. There were no menu choices, except *take it* or *leave it*. He left the dish that offered the strangest crustacean he had ever seen. It seemed the done thing to eat the spines because there certainly didn't appear to be any flesh on it or in it that he could see.

A table for eight had been set up in the centre of the room by pushing two smaller tables together and he noticed that the chef slammed things around and frowned every time the waiter picked up a dish for that table. The dining-room was small and conversations were muted but at the big table the decibels were up and Chef didn't appear to like it. Marcus recognised the woman in the centre of the group. She was the one he had seen leaving the airport, followed, and obviously not much to her liking, by a bunch of press people. She had been in an almighty hurry to leave, just like everyone else, but tonight she looked relaxed, if not exactly cheery. She ate as though she hadn't seen food in years and seemed to dominate the conversation without appearing to want to. Her companions hung on her every word, except for an elegant greying guy, who continually jotted in a notebook. He nodded his head from time to time but kept pretty much on the fringe of the chat and although the conversation was very animated, there were moments when the smiles would fade and the woman would dab at her mouth with a napkin and Marcus could see that above all else that might be going on in her life, she was deeply unhappy. He was busy wondering how he could find out who she was when one of his fellow diners, a man with a clipped and rather military voice, spoke to him. "Sir? Are you in Hong Kong for business or pleasure?"

"If I can find what I'm looking for, sir, business." He turned to the guy and introduced himself. "Marcus Browne, Corporate Manager, Seminole Council Trust, Florida, America." The man very deliberately raised an eyebrow.

"A most unusual title, Mr Browne. ... Terence Shaw." Terry offered his hand rather awkwardly across the small plate-strewn table. "In Hong Kong as you will soon learn, most people find most things eminently possible. I hope you have started by finding a comfortable hotel." Terry watched Browne's face for signs that he might somehow have spotted him lounging around in Reception, waiting to tag along the moment he left the Hilton.

But Marcus simply nodded and said, "I'm staying at the Hilton Hotel and it seems fine, thank you." The Chinese gentleman who joined the table at the same time as the guy who was speaking to him nodded approval and introduced himself as Tsiu Wah-Yeung, Business Agent. His voice was soft and fluid and each word tended to slur into the next.

"My card, Mr Browne," he said. "Tsiu Wah-Yeung. Pardon me if I seem intrusive, please." He bowed his head and placed a plain business card on the table.

Marcus didn't find the gesture intrusive at all. In America if you were in the market for something you just put your cards on the table and got on with it, but this wasn't America. Maybe he should be careful, maybe there were different rules here.

The English guy, who could have been reading his mind, said, "You need to be careful who you deal with, Mr Browne, especially at the present time, with everything changing so quickly and the yuan behaving the way it is." Mr Tsiu nodded. "Of course everyone in Hong Kong knows Mr Tsiu to be a very good Business Agent and I would not hesitate to consult him if I needed advice. My own credentials, sir."

*

The man who had addressed Marcus was of slim build and middling height, possibly about forty-five years old. He had thin black hair and a thin black moustache and was smartly turned out. He placed an impressive card on the table, a heavy white card bordered with a thick gold border. It announced that Marcus was in the company of Terence Shaw, Senior Diplomat, Her Majesty's Diplomatic Corps, South East Asian Region. The fourth man at the table, who had not joined in the conversation, waved away the final course, looked very deliberately at Marcus and excused himself. Marcus and his two new chums were left alone.

*

"Well gentlemen," said Marcus, "Perhaps you know that there has been something of a revolution happening on Native American Indian reservations in the USA?" He wasn't surprised to be met with two blank expressions. "It started after the US Federal Court made a ruling in the early seventies that upheld my people's right – I'm from the Seminole Nation – to use our reservation land however we choose. The Elders came up with the unique idea of making money by setting up a small gambling operation and the Federal ruling meant that no-one could stop us. At first it was treated as a joke until a few years later when we built a casino. The venture has been very successful.

"Now we want to expand and we plan on manufacturing our own gambling machines to supply our brother tribes who have followed our lead and set up casinos on their own reservations. The money generated by this sub-economy of American Indians will circulate in its own little universe and most of the profits will be used to establish a national philanthropic organisation which will help fund health and education for future generations of American Indians."

Terry raised an eyebrow again and nodded. He knew much more than he could let on about all this, of course. His step-brother Sol Lewis was a member of Mr Browne's governing Council and had made Terry an interesting proposition concerning Mr Browne's business in Hong Kong. Terry feigned interest in hearing the story but he knew very well that for many American Indian Reservations, freed from mainstream legal and financial constraints imposed by the American legal system, the future was bright, especially for those communities which had languished in a torpor of defeat and poverty following successive waves of invasion and colonisation by European powers in the nineteenth century.

"The scheme is called The Tortoise Universe," said Marcus, "which comes from the old stories that respect the wisdom of the tortoise. When things get rough, the tortoise rolls over and holds the universe in its shell, protecting it, creating an alternative universe and that is exactly what my people are doing with our reservation – building an alternative universe.

Tsiu Yah Weung looked puzzled. Why did this man talk of reservations and tortoises? Reservations were made over the telephone or by one's travel agent, surely? What had they to do with tortoises?

"Simply, I'm in Hong Kong to set the business up."

"That's completely extraordinary, old man. What is your opinion, Mr Tsiu?" said Shaw.

Mr Tsiu did not fully understood Mr Browne's mission but one thing was sure, he smelt money, lots of money and he said, "Mr Browne, Hong Kong is declining as a manufacturing centre and to commission the building of such machinery here will be much more costly now compared to say, ten years ago. Hong Kong now specialises as a financial rather than a manufacturing centre. My advice is that you consider China. China is beginning to seek foreign investment and trade and manufacturing can be done very cheaply there. At the moment the currency is very strong but generally this is not the case. There are opportunities for those who have the capital and the contacts. I urge you to investigate China, Mr Browne."

"I'm very grateful to both of you gentlemen for the generosity of your time and advice", said Marcus, "but I have a major problem with China."

"How so?" said Shaw.

"How to get there for a start, where to go, who to see, Mr Shaw. The place is huge. The language. Just getting around. I don't see how I could do it. My brief is to get the plan off the ground here, in Hong Kong. Nearly everyone here speaks English and it is smaller and in the time I've got should be achievable, whereas in China…."

"Quite right old man, but look here, whilst I don't like to push this good gentleman's interests too much, Mr Tsiu may still be of help to you. What do you say Wah-Heung?"

Mr Tsiu said nothing for at least a minute. Although he had not followed everything Marcus had said, he could see that Mr

Shaw was interested in cultivating him. That was enough for Wah-Heung Tsiu. "I understand your concerns, sir. China is indeed a difficult country to negotiate but I have contacts in Shenzhen, immediately north of Hong Kong. As for getting there, it is not so difficult. Call me if you are interested and I will discuss fees with you if you decide to use my services. I have the language and the contacts. I can even accompany you."

*

Kaz saw Pearl's gaze wander off across the restaurant and she turned to see who or what had her attention. Ah, a man, a stunning looking man too, in earnest conversation with two other diners. She took a sip of beer and a sidelong glance at Pearl who was *still* looking at him. He would notice, any minute. Now that could be interesting. She said, "See that gorgeous man at table 3?" Pearl jumped. "Gotcha. Want to meet him? I'll organise it for you – I'll go to the loo, bump his chair, chat him up, invite him over."

"Save yourself the grief, Kaz. I don't want to meet him. I just had the feeling I'd seen him somewhere. I agree with you though, he is very distinctive looking." Pearl shrugged. "I can't remember where it could have been, that's all." Peter Benson stopped jotting in his notebook and calmly announced that if she couldn't remember, then it was during a flight or at an airport where the common objective of travel made people less observant of one another than usual.

Peter was right, Pearl thought with a touch of irritation. She had noticed him briefly at the airport as she had hurried to get into the hotel car and shake off the press who had somehow been alerted to her arrival. She had intended to drift back to Hong Kong unannounced but it had turned into a camera-clicking fest. She yawned and signalled to the waiter for the bill. It was good to be home and wonderful to be with her friends again, but everyone was absorbed in their own lives and she was three years out of touch and had to find a way of fitting in again and that couldn't be rushed. Drew wanted to hand back the Foundation's business to her as soon as possible and how could she begrudge him the right to move on? She felt slightly claustrophobic as she thought about the years ahead, turning up to the office every day, having an occasional bright idea for a new project, always taking care to look after the Foundation's core values.

She already felt trapped.

She began to gather her things together, stopped, and blurted out, "I can't do it. I can't come back to work. I'm sorry, everyone. What the hell are we going to do?"

*

There was nothing to do but sleep on the dilemma. *Don't get stressed over it, Pearl,* everyone had said, all anxious to comfort her. You're tired, home for the first time in a long time. Feeling overwhelmed is natural.

"Go back to the hotel tonight and tomorrow, for god's sake come and stay with Drew and me will you?" Kaz had shouted after her as Pearl left the restaurant. Kaz was worried about Pearl all over again. She seemed as aimless as she had when they had put her on her flight to London three and a half years ago. She had looked at her ticket absently then, having even forgotten where she was going before she stepped on board. Kaz had fretted for a year, until eventually a postcard arrived from Luxor, after which came an intermittent burst of cards until they stopped altogether.

With Drew in overall control of the June Bowen Foundation and Danny Chiu in charge of finances, the organisation had maintained healthy growth during Pearl's absence. Then in August just this year, when Kaz had gone into another frenzy of worry about her friend, Drew hired a private detective to try to find her. He drew a blank and eventually Kaz managed to get in touch with Pearl's father, James Gates. James hadn't heard from his daughter for nearly a year at that time either but didn't seem worried about her. In his breezy way he had said that Pearl had looked fabulous when they holidayed at his house in the Dordogne in southern France the previous year. Kaz gradually let her concerns subside and life went on as she and Drew worked at breakneck speed at their careers. Pearl slowly faded from their immediate thoughts, until today, without notice, here she was. But after the initial excitement, Kaz was distressed to find that Pearl was still so obviously in grief. Or was this just a hiccup in her recovery, the result of coming back to face old memories?

It was Saturday morning when Kaz said, "Ah Drew, what do we do?"

"Whatever we do, my dear love, we are not going to prop Pearl up. She's got to come to terms with her responsibilities as well as her grief and we are certainly not going to help her stay in that shell she seems so fond of. Did you see Danny's face? All he wants is his old boss back, to read his balance sheets and praise his financial dissections, but she's gone, that woman is totally gone."

*

Pearl lay in bed and wondered again how she could have made such a fool of herself by publicly rejecting the work to which she had devoted her adult life and on her first day back home too, when everyone was expecting to see the old Pearl, the committed Pearl, the passionate Pearl. What must they all think of her? She sipped coffee and watched, almost lovingly, Hong Kong harbour pull itself into shape for the morning show. Boats and more boats, some skittish, some stodgy, others brazenly or aggressively slicing open water into wakes that jiggled little sampans and caused one Star Ferry Master to sound the alert alarm. It was the first day of winter, with a clearing early-morning haze promising later sunlight.

She ordered breakfast and despite the eight courses she had put away the previous evening, she ate the lot, drew breath after a second cup of tea and went to collect the paper. The *South China Morning Post* was in a rack outside the room and she stood in the hall, browsing the headlines: nothing of much note, a French gangster shot by police in Paris and the British PM on another rant. As she turned to go back into the room, a movement caught her eye. All was quiet in the wide, carpeted corridor but she was sure she had caught a flash of white; she looked at the lift bank but all the lifts were on other floors.

She frowned. That was odd. She strolled along the corridor, ashamed of herself for snooping, and saw that a door further along from hers was open. She peered in. A man was bent over one of the big linen trolleys and when he saw her he stopped, obviously startled. She smiled, said "sorry, I thought you were someone else" and scurried back to her room, feeling a little foolish. She did not see the man's face settle into a worried frown, nor did she see him hurriedly push the big trolley from the room, his duties incomplete.

Pearl read the paper in depth. Hong Kong seemed very quiet. There was a small article about China's increasing industrialisation and the plans that were rapidly changing Shenhzen from a small town into an industrialised Special Economic Zone. It all appeared to be happening at breakneck speed. When she turned to page four she felt a small jolt at seeing her photograph, captioned with the question, *Millionaire philanthropist back in Hong Kong to stay?*

Am I? She dismissed the thought. She tried to focus on some of the things giving Drew pause for thought – infrastructure development on the mainland, a continuing decline in manufacturing in Hong Kong and the Chinese official currency, the yuan, soaring on the world markets. In all that surely, there must be something she could get her teeth into. She sighed and got off the couch and uttered a loud *hmmmph* of impatience. There was a knock at the door. She stacked the breakfast dishes on the trolley and went to answer it. She would have a shower and write out a plan for the next week, starting with buying back her old home. That was one way of occupying herself even if nothing came of it. She'd visit Kaz at the museum too and see if her long quenched desire to study Archaeology could be revived. She opened the door, expecting to see a hotel staffer there for the breakfast things, but instead she was face to face with the man she had noticed last night in Stormy's. He was immaculately dressed in a suit and blindingly white shirt, but what impressed Pearl more was how hard his hands were clenched at his sides and how rather threatening it made him look.

"I'm sorry, very sorry to disturb you, ma'am. Umm, I'm staying on this floor. Further along." It occurred to Pearl that she hadn't combed her hair. He looked back over his shoulder towards the lifts. "I seem to be in some trouble, ma'am. I had breakfast and went out for, ah, a walk. When I came back ... Well, there are police all over the hotel, Ma'am. I can't go back to my room.

What if they...? To be truthful, I'm panicking. Have you seen *Midnight Express* ...?"

In the corridor, the light above lift Number 5 glowed and he looked at her a little wildly. "Someone's coming ...."

*

Pearl pulled him into the generous lobby that divided the bedroom and sitting room of the suite from the bathroom, just as three men moved briskly from the lift into the corridor. One was a hotel employee and the other two men were police officers. She stepped out into the corridor and was immediately hailed by one of the officers.

"Madam, have you seen anyone leave any of the rooms along this corridor in the past five to twenty minutes?" She stepped back into the lobby and without thinking why, silently pushed Marcus into the bathroom and grabbed the handle of the breakfast trolley.

"No officer, or rather, yes," she called out. "The linen man was in a room further along when I came out to pick up the paper." She pushed the trolley towards the door and as the officers arrived she said, "I'm jet-lagged and still need some more sleep. Not much help to you, I'm afraid." By the time the third man arrived, she had effectively blocked the entrance to the suite.

"Exactly how long ago would that have been, madam? You haven't seen anyone else about? A very tall man, apparently, quite striking to look at?" Pearl yawned.

"I'm sorry officer." She stretched. "Very tired. I saw the chap who collects the linen about twenty minutes ago now. What's the problem?" The more senior of the two officers removed his hat and said that the police had received a report that a man of unusual appearance had broken into another guest's room about half an hour earlier.

"May I suggest that you fasten the safety chain madam? Good morning. I am sorry to disturb you. May I have your name and usual address?"

"I'm Pearl Green, Officer. This hotel is my only address at present. "You may have heard of the June Bowen Foundation? I work for it and have just returned to Hong Kong after being on extended leave."

Sergeant Thornton was impressed. He certainly had heard of her ladyship. "Thank you, Lady Green. Please take care and by the way, Your Ladyship?"

"Please don't call me Your Ladyship. I never use my title, officer.''

"Pardon me, but I remember seeing a big spread about you in the *South China Morning Post* a few years back. Your wedding, I think?" Pearl smiled. There was no doubt that she was back in Hong Kong, where social affairs ran neck and neck with the popular sport of making money.

"Yes officer. That would have been it. Good morning."

*

"Kaz you can't ring Pearl at this hour. Let her sleep."

"I want to make sure she managed to *get* some sleep Drew. If she adds sleep deprivation to depression, I shudder to think. Do the rooms in the Hilton have fixed windows?"

"Oh for Christ's sake, Kazza, will you please drop it?"

*

Peter Benson looked at his old service watch – a Cartier Tank, and the only material possession to which he attached even the remotest sentimentality. He should ring Pearl. There was more to her mental and emotional state than straightforward grief. Grief is like everything else. The body absorbs it well or badly, but eventually tolerates it. Pearl's wounds were still open and clearly there was something else going on with her, beyond Ben's death. He thought some more before deciding to take a stroll over to her hotel.

*

"Well?" said Pearl to Marcus. "Did you hear what the officer said?"

"No ma'am, this bathroom is just about sound-proof. Not a word. What's going on?"

"They are looking for a man who broke into a guest room on the sixth floor. They said the intruder was tall and striking to look at. Your definition of a walk, I take it? The police seem very keen to talk to you and I suggest you put their minds at ease. I can't imagine what I was thinking when I stashed you in my bathroom. Please leave."

"I can assure you ma'am that I have done nothing to harm or hurt anyone. Can I please explain?" It was a long time since Pearl had bothered much with the affairs of others but he looked so worried and seemed so sincere. She pointed to the couch and he obediently sat whilst she set about making coffee.

"I'm listening," she said.

"I saw you at Stormy's Restaurant last night, ma'am."

She nodded acknowledgement. "Who were your dinner companions?"

"I haven't met them before. We seemed to have no choice but share a table. I wanted to dine alone but the waiter wouldn't have it." Pearl's mouth relaxed. That at least was true. No-one in Stormy's could have a table to themselves even if they paid. The restaurant was full every night, and empty places were an insult to the chef. Stormy's food performed nightly and the jealous genius in the kitchen demanded the applause of a full house of adoring patrons.

"One gentleman introduced himself as Mr" – he drew a card from his pocket – "Tsiu. Tsiu Wah-Yeung, and the other man" – he drew a second card from his pocket – "is Terence Shaw, who is with Her Majesty's Diplomatic Corps, South East Asian Region."

"Is he now? May I see that? Anything else?"

"Yes, Ma'am." He handed her the card. "Oh, and there was a fourth man at the table, but he left soon after the other two started talking to me."

"Mr Browne, we don't refer directly to the number four in Hong Kong. It represents death. This man", she waved Terence Shaw's card at Marcus, "This man who said he is with Her Majesty's Diplomatic Corps. Can you describe him?"

Marcus steadied himself: *the fourth man. The death card. Was she serious or was she having him on or was she a witch?* Marcus had seen the fourth man less than half an hour earlier and he was dead all right, very dead. Should he tell this woman about that or did she already know? He concentrated on the question, concentrated on looking at her. "He looked to be, ma'am, mid-forties, thinning dark hair, moustache, excellently turned out, fine manners, English accent – a bit different to any I've heard before – but that's only ever been at the movies. He sort of didn't move his mouth much and talked more through his nose."

"You mean, he definitely wasn't from your part of the woods, Mr Browne?"

"Never been in and around the Everglades, Ma'am, I'd be willing to bet." He sipped the instant coffee Pearl handed him.

He looked more like a banker than someone whose more familiar domain was the Everglades, even given that physique, that hair ….

"So, Mr Browne, you simply went for a walk. Is that true?" He nodded between gulps of coffee.

"Ma'am, maybe I'm over-reacting, but well, I'm not ashamed to say that I was very cautious about making this trip to Hong Kong. It's the first time I've travelled out of America and I don't know anyone and you hear stories and the thought of being caught up in something criminal, I don't …."

"I hear you. However, it appears that another guest in this hotel has reported that a man answering your description came into their room uninvited."

He was defensive and avoided eye contact. "Why would anyone say *I* was in their room?"

"I don't know, Mr Browne. But really, the simplest thing for you to do is tell your story to the hotel management. I'm more interested in why you knocked on my door instead of returning to your own room after your – your walk." She said bluntly, "You *were* on the sixth floor, weren't you?"

He looked at her, too embarrassed to speak. She said, "I'm right, aren't I?" She judged the distance from her chair to the door. *What a fool I am. He's a weirdo.*

He recovered himself and striving to be conversational said, "I arrived from London on the 10am flight yesterday ma'am."

"As did I and I recognized you at Stormy's last night and now you are here." *Three strikes and you are out* said a clear and annoying little voice in her head. "How did you spend the rest of yesterday? And by the way, will you please drop the ma'am? We only call the Queen ma'am, in my part of the Everglades. My name is Pearl." She had started edging towards the door, talking smoothly, eyes glued to him.

Marcus nodded. "Well, I slept of course, had a meal, had a beer, read the papers, decided to eat out and one of the brochures in the room was for Stormy's Restaurant. I've been looking forward to trying the food here more than anything, I guess."

"So you went to Stormy's, dined with three strangers and now you seem to be involved in something a touch murky." She had a sudden flash, "Did you get a phone call this morning? Is that why you went to the sixth floor?" He nodded twice, the second time reluctantly. "Right. That's much clearer." She had it. "I'll bet my winnings from the 2.30 Novice Stakes at Happy Valley this afternoon that you've been set up. Mr Browne, are you very rich?"

There was a knock at the door. Marcus kept his eyes on her and she noticed them for the first time, the greenest eyes that could actually be imagined in a frame of coal black eyelashes. They were absolutely compelling eyes, even more so as they widened in alarm. She held his gaze.

"Bathroom again. Quick."

*

"Pearl. I confess to being worried about you. May I come in?" Peter Benson thought Pearl looked more relieved to see him than he could have expected, given their highly chequered personal history.

"Please do. Peter? I have a problem."

"You certainly have. What happened to you, Pearl? You were such a gutsy kid and then a cool-headed woman who became a trail-blazing philanthropist. You were an inspiration to people you know. It was tragic that Ben died so soon after you two married, but you've plastered a coat of grief over yourself that is so thick it will never chip off. You must know how Ben would hate that."

She stared at him, dumbstruck. "Well, I suppose I had that bottled up," he said. "Mind if I sit down?" Pearl looked at him hard. They had a complex history going back to when she was fresh from school and he had been her boss. But long before all that, he had been her mother's much younger lover. He had owned the apartment on Upper Albert Road that Pearl bought after he left Hong Kong simply because there was a framed picture of her mother on the sideboard … but he was also the man who these days selflessly helped Kaz with her post-doctoral research and worked part-time for the June Bowen Foundation. *Dr* Peter Benson, she reminded herself, double PhDs in Political Science and Marine Archaeology, not to mention being former Head of the Hong Kong arm of the covert branch of the British Home Office, of which her own father was still the UK Chief. But the Peter Benson who had once been her father's top operative in Hong Kong no longer existed, subsumed by the calm *persona* of the man in this room now; a man who had spent seven years in a Japanese Buddhist monastery after having a nervous breakdown. It seemed their relationship had shifted yet again, for he had just read her as clearly as one of the eternal entries he made in his journal.

She could now add *martyr* to the list of personas *she* must represent to *him* ….

*

"I had a baby, Peter. A daughter. And by the way, there's a man in the bathroom who seems to have intruded in another guest's room on the sixth floor. The police are looking for him."

"Tell me about the baby. The man in the bathroom can wait."

"Fine. You must know, everyone knows, that after Ben died I went a bit mad and went in for the whole package: travel, sex, booze, drugs, the lot. About a year after leaving Hong Kong I woke up in Luxor one morning, with no idea how I'd got there. It turned out that I was at Carstair's Hotel, you know, the posh expat hang-out and I was in bed with a man I could not recall ever having seen before. I got dressed and cleared out. It turned out that I had booked myself in; my signature was in the register. I was booked into room sixty-five and woke up in room sixty-three. That's all I could remember.

"I was shaken up, really badly, and I realised that I had to do something useful, anything. I visited the archaeological dig area – the Theban Road Dig." Benson nodded. He knew it. "I volunteered and spent three months there. I'd long given up the idea of studying Archaeology but was still quite interested in it, in so far as I was interested in anything.

"I lived in another hotel until I met an American woman on site and ended up sharing a house with her. At the end of three months I had to admit I was pregnant." She shrugged.

"Pearl? ... The man in the bathroom?"

"He's an American Indian, I think."

"You would think that. ... The baby?"

"I gave birth to her in Sydney but I'd made up my mind to have her adopted before the birth. Australia's a great place – it has a small population and a brilliant lifestyle and the number of people waiting to adopt a child is long. My daughter will have a fine life. I just knew that I couldn't bring her up, conceived in such a way so soon after losing the man I love, the man I wanted to have babies with. I know how cruel that is, Peter. I also know how very very much my mother's daughter I am in denying my child knowledge of her parentage. Even so mum only ever refused to name James as being my father – I went a lot further than that and it still haunts me but I did it and can't change it. I travelled up and down the east coast of Australia before going to France for six months. I met up with Dad in the south and by then I had finally started to find some peace, or so I thought."

Benson nodded in his calm, wise way. Everyone knew how June Bowen had always refused to tell Pearl the identity of her biological father and Pearl was left to discover the truth after her mother's death, but at least Pearl had been brought up by one of her parents and in adulthood had reunited with the other. The true tragedy of it was, that just like her mother, she obviously was unable to forgive herself for conceiving the child at all. Peter shook his head gently. It was entirely tragic ....

"But it wasn't peace, Peter. I was numb, that's all. It wore off and guilt about what I had done started getting to me again and I ended up in Japan, in a small house near your old monastery. They let me stay in a little villa on the fringe of the community. I couldn't see what else I could do, where else I could go ... then after eleven months I came to two conclusions – first, I have no right ever to fully heal after what I did, and second, Hong Kong is home and I need to be here where at least I can pretend to function on a day to day basis."

"Have you settled the books on this yet?"

"I've paid the ultimate price, Peter. I can't bear more children."

"And still for all that pain, your conscience wants more from you Pearl. You had better find out what it is. Now, about this bloke in the bathroom ... is that the door?" Pearl shrugged, she hadn't heard it. "Didn't you say that the police were here earlier? That will be them again. I'll have been reported as being the corridor creeper by now. I'll get it."

CHAPTER THREE

Saturday 1 December 1979: 10.00am

The sampan was small but had a surprisingly powerful motor and Kaz and Drew sat unsteadily on two small splintery wooden seats as they headed full pelt for the Sai Kung Peninsula, north of Hong Kong. Po Pin Chau Island, an outlier of splintered basalt separated from the northern point of the peninsula by a channel, was fringed by caves, and Kaz had come across some notes in the museum's archive room that described some fragments of Neolithic pottery found in one of them some sixty years earlier. It was a perfect morning for the first day of winter. She and Drew intended to have a look around before returning to Sai Kung via Sharp Island, where they would have lunch cooked by the family who lived there and prepared heavenly seafood dishes for those fortunate enough to be in on the secret.

"At least this makes a change from Hei Ling Chau", said Drew, a little caustically. He spent a considerable amount of his spare time bouncing around the waters of Hong Kong with his wife, whose marine archaeological research took her to Hei Ling Chau Island, where they spent most weekends cataloguing the week's finds, with Peter Benson's help. Today he felt as though he'd been let off the leash and treated himself to a beer for morning tea on the strength of it.

*

Saturday morning was business as usual for Danny Chiu and Judith Sung. Danny studied his columns of figures with the same concentration that he applied to them every other morning of the working week, when he turned up to the apartment at Upper Albert Road to administer the funds of the June Bowen Foundation. Judith worked in an alcove that had once been a small morning room off the kitchen and from her vantage point she could see the crowded harbour where splintered sunlight caught on a million intersecting ripples. It all looked so alive. Judith found it difficult to concentrate on Saturday mornings. By the time the office closed there were too many other things to do for her to enjoy much leisure and she often felt that Monday morning arrived before she'd had a decent break from the stresses of the previous week.

Although the job of administering the foundation was a challenge she was well qualified to meet, she felt that she had never really fitted in because the woman she had replaced – Miss Anne Cheung – was like a ghost, always looking over her shoulder. Judith never felt quite up to the mark. With her background and education, perhaps she should be doing something else? Teaching perhaps. There was flexibility in a teacher's hours and if she ever had children it could be a part-time career as well ... she forced her eyes back to the pile of papers that waited her attention and started sorting out the general June Bowen Foundation matters from the business of the grants scheme. Last night's dinner with her colleagues had been a rare treat and meeting the woman who was her official boss, for the first time, well .... Pearl – she didn't like to be called Lady Green, as Judith thought of her – seemed okay, if perhaps a little eccentric. That outburst at the end of the meal! It was all so personal. It was as if she really did think of them all as family. Judith pulled the sides of her mouth down with a conscious grimace: it was not a family she would ever feel at home with.

*

The sampan edged its way through the gap between the end of the peninsula and into a little tidal basin scraped by erosion into the rock shelf at the seaward south-east flank of Po Pin Chau. "Hey" said Drew, "Look. Kaz, a turtle!" Sure enough a large black sea-going turtle swam lazily in the small tidal makeshift harbour, feasting on the lush weed that abounded there. The water was clear and everything happening on the bottom of the pool was clearly visible.

"*Hai dan, hai dan*", the boat-woman said, pointing to the water. She made a smacking noise with her mouth. Clearly something that lived in there – and Kaz hoped it excluded the turtle – was absolutely delicious to eat. Neither Drew nor Kaz had much Cantonese between them so they entered into a pantomime of pointing at their watches and making eating and drinking and walking gestures and left the woman to watch the animal enjoy its tidal respite from the open ocean, whilst they walked the rocky circuit of the island.

"This island looks like a turtle too, when you look at it from this angle", said Kaz. "It looks as though it is rising from the ocean. Isn't there a legend about how the tortoise god comes to the surface of the ocean every so often and rolls over and looks at the sky?"

"Yes, quite true. Legend has it that the turtle is hanging around for a San Mig or a Tiger Beer", said Drew, already feeling that the effort of clambering over the uneven surface entitled him to a second beer. "Saturday's for drinking beer, Kaz, and this is thirsty work. You're right about the legend. When the natural order of the universe is sufficiently threatened, the tortoise turns over and holds the universe steady in his upturned shell until the celestial disturbance is over. Then he blinks through the progress of an aeon or two before returning to his watery world. And not only that but the poor celestial bugger has to carry the earth *and* hold up the sky. He doesn't even have his own constellation for all that effort, as the other celestial symbols do – he's master of the void."

"I think it's you who are master of the void; what happens whilst he is turning over? It sounds like a metaphor for a seismic event to me. Here Drew, have an egg and lettuce sandwich before the egg goes off. Give or take the odd celestial tortoise, this is a beautiful place. You would never think we are just a few miles from the centre of Hong Kong. I hope wilderness areas like this never become built out." Drew took the sandwich and looked at the egg filling suspiciously. Lunch was only a couple of hours away but he *was* peckish and perhaps if he had another beer it would neutralise the effects of the egg if it had already gone to its own eggy god.

*

Benson shut the door. "No-one there. People are so impatient."

"Peter, have you forgotten there's a man in the bathroom? His name's Browne, by the way."

"I forgot about him. He's very patient, isn't he? Incidentally, you know how you are of the opinion that he went into another guest's room?"

"What about it?" said Pearl.

"If he was seen, wouldn't the police have him identified by now? If he is so distinctive to look at, finding out which room he's in shouldn't take long, unless they haven't considered that the intruder could have been a guest. In any event, how do you intend to handle this matter if they come back and you are sprung with him in your bathroom?"

"I don't know, Peter. The police will sort it all out. I have no intention of going out of my way for him any further."

"You've become hard, Pearl."

"Bathroom."

Benson knocked quietly. "Mr Browne? So sorry to keep you." He knocked again, then opened the door.

"There's no-one in here, Pearl. Look for yourself." She did. The room was empty. "You are off the drugs?"

"Clean as a whistle. Except for the drink. Did you check the medicine cabinet?"

"Stop being frivolous and forgive me for harping on about it, but *what* are you going to do now if the police come back and question you?"

"I told you. I don't know. Nothing?"

"Right. Look, if you feel you are quite safe here, I'm off. Lock the door. About our conversation, your confidence is safe with me, you know that. You have the power, more than most people, to do something to mend this, Pearl, if that's what's holding up your recovery. Think about it. It's pretty bloody obvious, you know."

"Thank you for that insight, Peter. I wish I could share it. We've had a strange, motley history, haven't we?"

"You could say testudinarious. Goodbye."

*

Pearl felt unsettled again after he left. The whole morning had been unsettling. Is that what had made her spit out the story of the last few years to him? She had thought about talking to Kaz about the baby, always hesitant because Kaz was unable to have children of her own but never dreaming that in the end she would confide in Peter Benson. She thought about the times when he had come back into her life over the years; how she would initially get a thrill from hearing from him, how her long-gone girlhood would spill back into her mind. But somehow deceit always entered the picture, so why this morning had she sat here and told him things that she had shared with no-one else, not even her father? She put the kettle on and stared out of the window, aware of a dawning and stirring restlessness that felt different to the restless aimlessness she was used to.

*

The corridor was empty when Marcus slipped out of Pearl's room and he was about to do what he should have done initially – call hotel management and report that he was the man seen in the room on the sixth floor. But his resolve was brief: wasn't it better that he just leave? All he had to do was pack his cabin bag and grab his briefcase. He had done nothing and had a perfect right to go whenever it suited him to do so and besides there were police all over the place and the woman whose help he had sought and who seemed so wise thought that the answer to his problem was to remain in her bathroom – that's after informing him that he'd probably been set up somehow – what sort of juice did Hong Kong run on? He stared at the phone. Dammit, no, he was going to get on a plane and O-U-T to the nearest anywhere and then hike it on home to the States. The Council would have to figure out its next move without his involvement.

He paced around his room and stepped on a small object lying on the carpet, near the bed. He stooped and picked it up: it was curiously heavy, a small round clip with four delicately carved animals poised on each compass point on the flat edge which protected a central convex orb. He tossed it from palm to palm and wondered what it was made of; it felt as heavy as lead and was much the same colour as lead but had the patina of burnished steel. It must have been dropped by the former room occupant.

He packed his toiletries and looked at his reflection in the bathroom mirror, slicked his hair back, secured his tribal band, whipped some toothpaste across his teeth and donned the pair of sunglasses he'd bought the previous day. He had hoped that people wouldn't stare at him so much if they couldn't see his eyes. He propped the glasses up on the top of his long mane of black hair but as he gave his reflection a parting glance it mocked him: almost as soon as arriving in Hong Kong he'd been set up, hot on the heels of having been given the greatest opportunity any non-Elder in his tribe had ever been handed. What an easy target he'd been and how he'd stuffed it up! The eyes that looked back at him were filled with guilt and doubt. *Take a deep breath* he told himself, *and pick up the phone.* But he couldn't.

*

"Drew! Drew! Look out!" Drew heard the sound of falling rock fractionally after Kaz, who was looking at the cliff face at the precise moment when a slab of basalt gave way. They were on the seaward side of the island where sharp columns of tabular basalt formed sheer cliffs, at the base of which they had already found a few shallow caves. The rock face looked as though it could hold up the world, but within its lithology was a fatal flaw: It fractured horizontally across the face in a zig-zag pattern of cracks that the effects of wind, rain and water would cause to shear off from time to time; to tumble to the boulder-strewn rock shelf below.

Kaz yelped, tripped and fell over. The rocks that started to spatter around them missed her with the exception of one splinter that cut her right ankle nastily. Not so lucky, Drew was pinned to the platform by a relatively solid piece of displaced terra firma which probably weighed in at more than forty kilograms and was quite sufficient to break, very neatly, the tibia of his left leg.

Drew screamed.

*

Marcus knocked on Pearl's door. "I came back to say that I'm sorry that I inconvenienced you so much, ma'am." Pearl looked at him carefully. He turned and started to walk away immediately, obviously not expecting a response from her.

"Went for another walk, did you?" she called out to his retreating back. "Mr Browne? Rather than apologise for inconveniencing me perhaps you should think about how you *inconvenienced* that other guest."

Marcus stopped and turned around, stung by the sharpness of her tone. "I'm sorry. I won't bother you any further. Good morning."

"Not so fast, Mr Browne. I want to know more about your so-called walk."

"Ma'am?"

"The phone call, the walk you took. Why exactly did you intrude, uninvited, into another guest's room?" Her voice was all Earl's grand-daughter.

"As you say, I had a phone call. But this is not my concern now, ma'am. I'm going home. I didn't come to Hong Kong to be made the patsy for some scammers."

"You won't get past Reception, Mr Browne. Your description will be with all of the staff, and forgive the observation, but you are a little difficult to overlook." Pearl gestured for him to follow her and Marcus obliged. He took his wallet out of his jacket and began picking out wads of Hong Kong currency with the air of a man about to go to execution.

"Ma'am? If I gave you enough cash to settle my bill...?"

"Sorry, Mr Browne. Please remember, I've just arrived in Hong Kong too. The difference between us is that I'm home and I know exactly where I am and what the go is around here. My paying your bill would not only be social death – which bothers me not at all – but it may stop further flows of funds to my charitable works if I am subsequently found to have assisted a – pardon me – a possible criminal. I have in the past been erroneously associated with criminality in Hong Kong. I don't need to give my detractors further ammunition in that regard."

Marcus removed his sunglasses, looked at her and smiled. Pearl straightened her hair, which was still uncombed. *Why hadn't they thought of this back home? It would have saved coming half way across the world. A Hong Kong based charitable foundation could set up the project.* Marcus had the quick mind of those accustomed to looking for benefits and costs in the same package. This was exactly what was needed. A locally based foundation could be financed to set up the operation – one charity helping another even though they were a good ocean apart – and she knew this part of the world. Done and dusted.

The smile became a grin. "You're right, ma'am – I mean Pearl. Damned silly idea. I guess I'd better ring Reception and get this business sorted out. I got out of the room on the sixth floor double-quick because, well, because there's a body in that room and I know who it is."

Pearl sighed more theatrically than she need have done. So be it, chapter two of the morning's frolics were about to unfold ....

*

Sergeant Thornton returned to room 676 to check if the guest who had complained about finding a strange man in her room had yet established if anything was missing from the mounds of shopping that festooned the coffee table, armchairs and every other scrap of available space, but Mrs Entwhistle was still disconsolate and said it would take her some time to sort it all out. She had shopped so much the previous day it was quite possible that something new may have been taken that she had forgotten even buying.

The Sergeant nodded understandingly. He knew how shopping frenzy could seize some tourists when they were let loose in the department stores and markets of Hong Kong. Mrs Entwhistle confided that she had just telephoned her husband Mr Entwhistle, who, confined as he was by inclement weather to the sitting room of their house in the town of Whitby in Yorkshire in north England, had been quite unsympathetic. She had only just hung up on Mr Entwhistle.

"Told me that he'd never seen any sense in gallivanting off half way across the world for a bit of sight-seeing and shopping, Sergeant. *Not seeing we've never even seen all of Yorkshire, missus,* he'd said, a little too complacently for Mrs Entwhistle's liking. Mrs Entwhistle's expression took on a slightly stubborn set. "I told him it was all part of the experience of travelling, coming to an exotic location like Hong Kong. At least I'll have a story or two to tell my Maureen and her Dave's kids if they ever get around to blessing me and Mr Entwhistle with grandchildren."

"Shall we go over the incident again, madam?" The Sergeant saw signs of a long and unbridled account of the Entwhistle family history about to emerge from Mrs Entwhistle's rather thin mouth and he nipped it. "You said you came out of the bathroom …?"

"Yes, you could have knocked me over with a feather. There he was, bold as brass, standing over there" – she pointed towards the window – "and when I came into the room he turned around real quick like, muttered something and bolted for the door. I'm lucky he didn't knock me over – *and* he slammed the door. Rudeness."

"And he was …?"

"Oh, young, Sergeant, young-ish anyway. He was tall, long dark hair, oh and he was wearing a suit. His skin was an unusual colour, he looked as though he had a really deep tan and had caught a dose of the sun as well."

Sergeant Thornton nodded. It was all as she had previously stated. "I will keep you informed if there are any developments and in the meantime, please keep your door locked and on the safety chain, madam."

"But I …''

"I know you said you did, but just make very sure you do. You said the chap bolted for the door when he saw you and muttered something. It wasn't *sorry* by any chance was it?"

"Do you know, Sergeant, I do believe it was."

"It may all be a lot more innocent than it appears. Perhaps he had an appointment in the hotel, got the room number wrong, your door was open …." The woman nodded. Something else had occurred to her when the Sergeant said that, what could it be? *Something different in the room? In any event* the sensible Mrs Entwhistle informed herself, *perhaps it was an accident after all* and as a pragmatic woman she knew she'd sleep easier if there were an innocent explanation for the morning's odd event.

Whilst Sergeant Thornton talked, Mrs Entwhistle moved over to the wardrobe, there not being sufficient space on any of the chairs for either of them actually to sit down. She opened the door and absently scooped up a pile of shoes from the coffee table and was about to put them in the wardrobe for sorting out later on. As she said to Mr Entwhistle several days later, she was pleased the Sergeant had been there (*It had been a morning for men in my room, Hector*, she said, not feeling Hector's dark gaze on her dipped head) and even more pleased later, after things had settled down a bit, that, as the body of a man fell out of the cupboard, she was able to jump out of the way without dropping her new shoes.

Otherwise, as Mrs Entwhistle was pleased to inform anyone even remotely interested in the story before and after her arrival home, *I'd have had to throw them out. The sergeant caught him. The thought of that poor man falling all over me and my lovely new sandals was more than I could bear.*

*

Kaz ignored the blood that poured from the cut on her ankle and tried to rouse Drew to consciousness. She tugged at the piece of rock but it was no good, he was very neatly pinned to the rock shelf. She sobbed as it refused to budge and he remained lost to what was happening.

"Stay here, Drew", she said with complete inconsequence, "I'll get help." She struggled to her feet without taking her eyes off him and so felt the water before she saw it lapping gently over the rock shelf, breaking into gentle ripples of foam not more than a yard from where they were. A lot went through Kaz's mind; could she summon a short bout of superhuman strength? She couldn't. How long would it take to get back to the boat? How high did that water creep and did it pound across the rock shelf as the tide swelled landward? She tried to run across the maze of jumbled rock. Distress pulled the breath from her chest in jagged gasps.

Around the other side of the point and out of Kaz's sight, the boat-woman watched the sea turtle slide out of the holding pool as the mat of sea grasses stirred with a fresh influx of seawater. She looked at her watch and pulled in the fishing line she had thrown over the side of the boat and pulled up the basket of sea urchins she had dived for. Her passengers would be back soon and they wanted to be at Sharp Island by twelve-thirty. The people on Sharp Island always welcomed a fresh basket of *hai dan*. The young couple would probably be served them for lunch. *Ah.* There was one of them now. There was no need for Kaz to lament her lack of Cantonese. Her face said everything. The woman yanked the sampan's simple anchor on board, fired up the engine and within two minutes they were heading around the point with as much speed as the vessel could yield.

*

Pearl studied Marcus Browne closely. In ordinary circumstances, she would assume him to be a decent sort of man, but clearly, he was out of his depth in the present situation. Initially he had said he was in a panic because he saw police around the hotel when he came back from a walk, after which he altered his story and said that he had gone to a room on the sixth floor. After that he added that he went there in response to a phone call and now he was saying that not only was there a body in the room but he knew who it was. She glanced at the door again.

"The phone call was from the guy who was the fourth man at the dinner table last night, or at least that's who he claimed to be. He introduced himself to me over the phone this morning as being a Mr Childs, Dennis Childs. He is in a wardrobe in room 676. He's dead."

Pearl felt her skin crawl. He had known this all the time, even earlier when she had lectured him about death and the number four. "Go on Mr Browne."

"When he phoned me, he said he had heard enough of my conversation with Mr Shaw and Mr Tsiu last night to know that I was in Hong Kong to set up a business deal."

"How did he know where you are staying?"

"I mentioned it at dinner. Anyway he said I should be careful about people I meet who offer their services as readily as those two gentlemen did. Then he laughed and said that to directly contradict that comment he would be happy to talk to me and help me out if he could. He said he knew what it was like to arrive in Hong Kong alone and knowing no-one. He also said that he would be happy for me to check out his reputation before we met.

"I thought what he said sounded reasonable. I agreed to meet him in room 676 where he said he was visiting a friend who is in

Hong Kong for a stopover on his way to Los Angeles. When I arrived, the door was open. I called out but there was no reply so I walked in. Silly of me, I guess, in retrospect. I saw him straight away, in the cupboard. The door was open. I slammed it shut – I don't know why – and a woman came out of the bathroom. I don't know which of us was more scared. She screamed.

"I bolted down the fire stairs, was going to report it, but when I reached the ground floor, hotel security was all over the place and the desk staff were in an uproar. I took the lift back to my floor but panicked. What if the woman in Room 676 described me? It would be only a matter of time before they knew I was the intruder. Then I thought of you. I saw you again last night apart from at the restaurant. You were going into your room as I came out of the lift. I thought you looked like someone, someone who knew their way around this place. Someone who might help me. I....

"What *am* I supposed to do? You say I've probably been set up, but why? Guys like me must come along all the time. Why me?" His voice had taken on a panicky edge again. Pearl was very quiet. If his story was true, Dennis Childs was dead. Dennis was the father of her old friend Belinda, who Pearl knew hadn't seen her father for years. These days Belinda lived a high-powered international life with her rock-star husband and their three children and had long forgotten all her old friends and it seemed, even her father.

"She broke his heart you know. She was everything to him." Pearl talked without looking at Marcus. She wasn't even talking to him.

"You know this man?"

"Yes. Wait here. Just tell the police everything. I can at least verify that I saw you earlier and I also told Peter that you were in the bathroom. Someone has coaxed you into another room where you were taken for being an intruder so that they could ...." She finished the sentence under her breath: *frame you for murder*. Marcus nodded agreement, but he was lost in his own thoughts. He had seen *Midnight Express* last year which was a very clear depiction of just how badly foreigners could be treated when they got into trouble in overseas countries. He might be thrown into jail here, may rot here for years. His people would never be able to get him out.

"Sorry, I can't do it." She looked at him. She knew what was coming next.

"I'm *very* sorry." He left.

Pearl picked up the phone. "Reception? Is Sergeant Thornton still in the hotel? Good. Can you ask him to come and see Pearl Green please. It's rather urgent."

*

The face of Mrs Lam, the boat-woman, was set in sun-carved lines from years of living on the water. This was not the first time a visitor had been injured on Po Pin Chau. Would someone have to die before they put the area off limits? She dipped her head and took a sidelong glance at Kaz. The woman had a wound on her ankle and was heaving for every breath, but she was miles away, her own condition beyond consideration. The other thing she did not know was how quickly the tide covered the rock platform. Mrs Lam suppressed a shudder. They might not get there in time.

*

Sergeant Thornton called Division Central for back-up and Mrs Entwhistle was transferred to a room on the second floor. Room 676 was locked and guarded and the displaced guest was allowed a change of clothes and some toiletry items. The room was sealed off. The Duty Manager hurried to the sixth floor and informed Sergeant Thornton that the guest in room 359 had just reported that the guest in room 365 had come to her door, looking for help. The same man had also told the guest in 359 that he had seen a dead body in room 676. After that, he left.

"Would that be Lady Green?" The floor manager nodded and Sergeant Thornton examined his notebook. He had spoken to her ladyship at 9.48 that morning, not long after the intrusion was reported by the guest in room 676.

The young floor manager anticipated the sergeant's next question. "The guest in room 365 is a Mr Browne, sir." When Sergeant Thornton was admitted into room 365, all that was found was some money on the coffee table and a small suitcase containing a few articles of clothing. There was also a toiletries bag in the bathroom. This guest had left in a hurry.

*

It was James Williams of Robertson & Kovacks on the line. "Pearl? News for you. The Thompsons will consider selling. The hitch is that they won't start to talk under ...."

"Thirty-eight million? You're joking surely. James, my mother spent two million on the place thirty years ago to complete the initial restoration and that wasn't much less than she paid for the entire building. I spent the same again when I converted the ground floor into offices and installed a new lift. The Thompsons got a bargain basement deal for ten million. What have they done to justify a price hike like that? *Really, James? – A new Romanesque suite of verandah furniture and a rosewood bar? –* That will cost me extra to get rid of, for a start.

"I'll give them twenty percent more than they paid me for the place. Tell them the odour from the fish market won't improve if the summer Hong Kong has just sweltered through becomes the norm. Oh, and don't forget the tsunami disaster film about to be released – that won't do much for the status of waterfront properties nor will the fact that Typhoon Hope was the worst storm to hit Hong Kong for nearly ten years – all hardly auspicious for those who live near or on the harbour. Oh, and James?"

"Pearl?"

"The ghost." He laughed uneasily.

"You never mentioned a ghost when you sold, Pearl."

"Why would I? If they're keen to sell, maybe that's why. I don't want to live at the Hilton forever, James." She had only just hung up when the phone rang again. It was Sergeant Thornton.

"Ah, Sergeant, a mix-up, I need to talk to you as soon as possible. A man has not long left my room whom I believe may be involved in something – ah – that happened in the hotel this morning. Pearl found that she was clutching the hem of her bathrobe. It was now well after mid-day and she hadn't showered or in any way got ready for the day. Could you come by in fifteen minutes, Sergeant?"

*

Drew's entire body hurt and even the sun hurt his closed eyes. He lifted his head and the pain from his leg shot up into his neck and jutted into his shoulders. He saw the slab of rock sitting squarely across his left leg and felt water lapping at his right hand – had he dabbled in it playfully before he regained consciousness? Played with the little wavelets that lapped across the lip of rock to his right and now curled cheerily around him, breaking in a friendly way against his arms, his torso and his unencumbered right leg?

"Kaz?"

*

Terence Shaw glanced over the top of his newspaper and watched Marcus stride quickly and self-consciously through Reception and out of the hotel. He didn't pause and admire the fountain and garden as so many guests did but rather walked faster, as though he couldn't get away quickly enough.

He carried only a briefcase. He had left cash in the room, along with a hastily scrawled note that said the amount should cover his bill and all he had to do now was get to the airport and find a seat on the first available flight. He paused and looked around, expecting every second to be apprehended, but no-one seemed interested in him. The whole place was alive with relentlessly crawling traffic in a street thick with trams, buses and cars. There were even a few rickshaws plying their trade. There were thousands of people on the sidewalks and everyone was going somewhere and everyone was in a hurry.

"Taxi! Airport, please." The taxi was near the harbour tunnel entrance when some sense returned to him. More likely than not, he would be apprehended at the airport and things could get worse for him if he was assumed to be leaving Hong Kong after leaving a crime scene. "Driver, is there a police station around here?" Shaw, following Marcus in another taxi was exasperated by what was clearly a change of plan. He threw his cigarette out of the window impatiently and re-directed the driver to follow the other cab, but when Marcus's taxi pulled up outside Division Central Police HQ, Terence waved the driver on:

"Sheung Wan, driver. Ong Hing Terrace."

*

From the boat, Kaz saw the walkers on the cliff-top at the head of the peninsula. She waved frantically and shouted at them and curious, they gathered perilously close to the edge of the steep escarpment. She dug around in her bag for her makeup mirror and held it high above her head, manoeuvred it to reflect the sunlight and flashed it, three times, in regular succession. Did they understand what she was doing? She let it rest a minute then repeated the sequence of three flashes and pointed to where Drew was stranded. Suddenly there was action and they waved back at her with great vigour.

Kaz had a damaged lung and her voice did not carry well, but she kept shouting as much as she could and pointed again in the direction the boat was headed, near the tip of the island. But with Drew out of sight on the other side, the walkers couldn't see him, so would they go for help? As the boat-woman pushed the little craft hard through the swell, Kaz watched them hurry off. She should have felt glad. She felt sure they understood something was wrong, but as they disappeared from view, she felt abandoned. She looked into the water as the boat churned around the point. Once, the water had been a haven for her, and revealing some of its secrets, was still the focus of her work at the Squid Cove excavation site. But in recent years, water seemed to have become her enemy. She put the mirror back in her handbag. Best keep it safe. In case it had another use. She shuddered at the thought of rounding the point and coming across Drew, caught helplessly by the rock; drowned. She let out a sob. The boat-woman leant forward as if she could give the boat an additional push of speed. This was not looking good.

*

The backup request from Sergeant Thornton went to Chief Superintendent Smythe for clearance. Tommy had planned to quit the office at one o'clock and meet his wife at The Peninsula for a spot of lunch until a note arrived on his desk with the news that a body had been discovered in room 676 of the Hong Kong Hilton Hotel by Sergeant Thornton, whilst he was questioning the occupant about an earlier incident. The dead man had been tentatively identified as Dennis Childs, a prominent Hong Kong business tycoon.

Smythe sighed. Hardly necessary for him to be involved surely, but on the other hand, Dennis Childs .... He rang his wife, who expressed disappointment that he would miss out on the Carrington's famous *Lobster Americaine* but he wasn't to worry, she would phone her friend Jane. Jane was rather fond of lobster and would happily forego a round or two of bridge for a decent lunch. Tommy hung up, feeling distinctly surplus to his wife's requirements, and not for the first time. He re-read the information that had been passed to him and this time the name Pearl Green jumped out at him. That sealed the matter. If Pearl Green was involved in this business at the Hilton, the press would go mad for a story that involved one of Hong Kong's best media prizes, known also for getting herself into dodgy situations. There was a small article about her in the morning paper; the dashed woman had only just returned to Hong Kong, for pity's sake and there was trouble already. His phone rang and he absently picked it up as he completed reading the summary report on the morning's events. He'd best get moving.

"Sir! Constable Chua, sir! Sir, Sergeant Thornton has brought in a person for questioning about the Hotel Hilton matter, sir, and sir, he requests that you come to the remand cells immediately sir, please sir."

Tommy Smythe was delighted. Sergeant Thornton was on the ball. Perhaps this business wouldn't eat up all of his weekend after all. He took his cap from the hook behind the door and went at a clip to the charge desk. As he drew near he heard a familiar voice, authoritative even though ever so slightly raised:

"This is ridiculous, Sergeant. Dennis Childs is the father of one of my oldest friends. Why would I be interested in killing him and stuffing him in the wardrobe of a room occupied by some woman on the 6th floor? If I had killed him I would have stuffed him in the linen room on the third floor. Damned if I'd lug a dead body up three flights of stairs ...." Smythe felt a sinking sensation even as he smiled at the acerbic humour. He could pick up her perfume as well as her voice from here. Chanel No. 5 and a staccato glimmer of her mother's antiquated colonial accent weaved along the corridor.

"Chief Superintendent!" It was Constable Chua again. "Sir, can you come to the front desk please, sir? Chief Superintendent Smythe bit back the temptation to tell sincere and well-meaning Constable Chua that wasn't it damned obvious that he could only be in one place at one time? His quiet afternoon was going to the dogs. "A man is at the enquiry desk, sir and says he has information about the incident at the Hilton Hotel this morning, sir. I thought you might like to be informed, sir."

Smythe took one look at Marcus and knew immediately that he was the man described in Sergeant Thornton's briefing note and the man for whom an *All Alert* had just been issued. He was well over six feet tall, dressed smartly in a deep grey suit and a white shirt. The white shirt was icy white against his striking colouring which was somewhere between a deep tan and a healthy flush. His hair was all one length and reached his shoulders and it was thick, and black. He wore a wide black band around his forehead, knotted at the back of his head and when Marcus turned to him the Chief Superintendent saw the eyes of a man whose gaze went beyond what others see through their faint or faded blue or brown or hazel orbs. Chief Superintendent Smythe had the oddest feeling that questioning him would be pointless. Those eyes were eyes that could read the world. It took a few moments more before it dawned on him that he was looking at an American Indian.

*

Peter usually took a spin over to Hei Ling Chau on Saturdays to check out the site at Squid Cove that he had been excavating for Kaz since the end of 1975 when she had to give up diving. These days he did the field-work for her post-doctoral research into the two stacked layers of ancient vessels she had discovered several years earlier and which complemented his own post-doctoral work on maritime trading routes from the 15th to the 18th centuries. Between them, he and Kaz were considered *the* authorities on south-east Asian marine archaeology these days.

Kaz was unstintingly thankful that Peter had come along and offered to do so much for her, even helping her out further by taking over the job Pearl had devised for Kaz in running the JBF PhD Scholarship Scheme for financially underprivileged archaeology students. South-east Asia needed skilled archaeologists and the scheme had recently begun its third year of operation and was doing well. Kaz's role had never gone to plan because instead she had taken up the challenge to re-build the reputation of the Hong Kong Archaeological Museum after the former Director, the very corrupt Dr Albert Ho, was murdered in 1975. The job kept her desk-bound five days a week. On Saturdays she and Drew almost invariably headed to Hei Ling Chau and they and Peter would spend their time discussing the progress of the work as they recorded and stored the week's finds. Kaz relished the change of pace compared to their always-frenetic working and social life in Hong Kong. But recently, she wasn't sure that Drew shared her enthusiasm.

*

Peter realised that if he didn't get going the afternoon would be wasted. It was the first day of winter and by five-thirty daylight would be gone. He finished packing some food into an overnight bag which he then absently unpacked and put back on the kitchen bench. He couldn't get Pearl's stricken face out of his mind and there was no point thinking he could work or meditate. He picked up the phone.

It was time to call James Gates.

CHAPTER FOUR

Saturday 1 December 1979: 1.15pm

As soon as Chief Superintendent Smythe appeared, Marcus started talking very quickly, as though he wanted to get to the point of something before he forgot what it was about. "As I was starting to say to this officer, sir, I've come to make a statement about something that happened at the Hilton Hotel this morning – about a phone call I had – are you the man to speak to? I'm not about to be locked up, you must understand that, but I was on the scene. I panicked, took a cab and was heading for the airport when I realized how damned stupid I was being...."

Tommy Smythe held up his hands. "Sir, hold your horses *please*. Detective Sergeant Lee will escort you to an interview room. As for locking you up, let's see what we are dealing with first, hmmm? Personally at this hour on a Saturday afternoon I'm more interested in lunch than locking people up." Marcus thought the guy looked peeved. Maybe it was inconvenient coming by right now. That must be another British trait. No crime after close of business. *Can't you see the sign? Everyone's gone off for a pint.*

*

At last Kaz saw a blob of yellow, the linen shirt she had bought for Drew in the late summer sales in London. He loved it and wore it everywhere, even to the office. She could only see a bit of it because the rest of the garment was submerged. She couldn't see his head or any other part of him. She uttered something between a groan and a sob that was so gut-torn that the boat-woman felt tears spring to her eyes. They were only a minute or so away but perhaps they were already too late. Then both women saw something swimming near him, something big.

"Shark! Drew! Shark! Look out!" Kaz stood up in the boat and made it lurch furiously. The boat-woman shouted at her and revved the motor in an effort to stabilize it and work up more speed. Kaz sat down. If she had slowed their progress by her outburst, if it made a second's difference to whether Drew lived or not, she wouldn't be able to bear it.

"Ong Hing Terrace. Number 6, driver." The driver, Hua Leung, knew he had gone pale because his skin felt clammy around his hairline and it was not hot. Number 6, Ong Hing Terrace was a very bad luck address. A man had been killed in that house four years ago and this passenger was going there. Hua did not like this but perhaps it was part of a sight-seeing tour. Did *gweipors* go on such tours?

"You know the Sheung Wan area, sir?" he said conversationally. His passenger made a noise between a grunt and a derisory snort which Hua Leung took to be confirmation. When they reached Number 6, he shuddered. Hua lived in a tiny room in the Walled City of Kowloon and although it wasn't real estate to die for, at least living there didn't necessarily mean you had to die. But Ong Hing Terrace was clearly cursed and after the murder at Number 6, those who could afford to move away had done so and now the empty houses in the row were squats of a nature that made accommodation in the Walled City seem like luxury housing. The man got out without seeming as though he was on unfamiliar territory, paid the fare without giving a tip and walked easily up to the door of No. 6, let himself in and disappeared from Hua's view.

Hua wondered if he should tell his employer about the incident. Mr Yip might just laugh at him, but if there was anything else to make of the *gweipor* coming here, Mr Yip would want to know.

*

Drew felt a wave flick over his chest. The pain in his legs, back and head was unbearable. He concentrated on looking at his shirt, with the sleeves puffing in and out as wavelets billowed around his body. He tried to lift his head but couldn't and realised it was because there was something solid shoving him and pushing at the back of his head. He could also hear someone screaming. *That* was Kaz and there was other shouting too, from a gruff female voice.

He tried to yell but when he opened his mouth, it filled with water. But everything was all right, wasn't it? Kaz was here, she was holding him wasn't she? He stopped tensing, stopped fighting, but the shoving sensation came again and this time, his head was supported above the lapping water and he spat up the mouthful of salt water he'd swallowed and snorted more from his nose. There was just enough of his everyday mind working for him to see that although Kaz was near she wasn't in reach, before his body declared the pain unsupportable and he blacked out. He did not feel the shoving sensation stop, or Kaz's hands on him, did not hear the approach of another boat or feel the rock being eased off his battered left leg, nor did he see the ambulance that waited near the shore at Sai Kung Peninsula and took him not to the lunch that had lured him out onto the water on this fair Saturday but to the Emergency Department of the Peak Hospital.

*

Saturday 1st December, 1979: Florida, America, 8.00am. Time in Hong Kong approximately 8.00pm.

"There's still no reply from Marcus's room, Nev." Derek Wong looked at his watch and before his companion asked the question he said, "I started ringing just on daylight but we're thirteen hours behind Hong Kong. He must be out."

"Don't worry too much. He'll get back to you soon enough."

"Soon enough ain't soon enough, Neville." The two men sat in an office attached to a larger building and surrounded by beautiful gardens. A sign above the office door announced that it was the *Seminole American Indian Council Information Office*. It was a resource for people who came to use the casino facilities and wanted information about where to stay overnight, or to take a tour of the Everglades – one of the world's greatest wetland areas – buy souvenirs, that sort of thing. The souvenirs were authentic examples of tribal craft made by the community's elders and the shop sold minor items linked to the casino's core business – which was to remove as much money from their visitor's pockets and into the tribe's coffers as was either polite or possible. There were *Last Chance Instant Lottery* cards and other small, prize-linked gimmicky items. People coming here could start betting before they even reached the casino steps or spend their remaining coins as they left.

Derek broke the silence that had fallen in the room. "I'm going to go to Hong Kong. If Marcus takes this badly, as I expect, I'll have to go get him anyway. I may as well just tell him face to face what's happened here, and after that I can take over the Hong Kong operation and he can come home and bury his grandmother like he should. He can go back to Hong Kong when things settle down again."

"Of course," said Neville, "you're right. Of course Marcus has to come home to bury his grandmother. She'd pour oil in his ears if he didn't." The two men made an attempt to smile. Until the early hours of this morning, Grandmother Browne was the oldest living Seminole Indian, a woman of undisputed authority in the community. She had lived through two mighty conflicts during the 20th century and was the community's living memory of those times, even just able to recall the time when the Seminoles were close to being wiped out. Her long life had taken her from times of desperation to times when better days prevailed and she went on to live long enough to see her people win and enjoy considerable affluence.

Between the two men in the office there was nothing more to say and Derek headed off to his apartment to pack.

*

Pearl read and signed the statement. A thousand comments occurred to Chief Superintendent Smythe, none of them very diplomatic. He did consider: *back in Hong Kong for less than a day and in the middle of something dodgy already, Miss Green?* But he let the opportunity go. He counter-signed the document, checked and double checked some points and made yet more notes. He remained mystified as to why she had invited a total stranger into her room, a man who proceeded to tell her a pack of lies and who later returned and confessed that he had intruded in another guest's room in which a dead body was found not long after, and in the wardrobe of all places. Not only that but she had casually shut the fellow up in the bathroom at one point whilst she had an extended conversation with a visitor.

"He simply disappeared?"

"Yes. It was terribly thoughtless of me to leave him in the bathroom for so long but I was so caught up in talking with Dr Benson that frankly I forgot about the man. So whilst I can verify that he was in my room, when he left is a mystery to me. I'm sorry I can't be more helpful."

"But you must realize that by not telling the police of his presence in your room in the first place, you are an accessory, Miss Green, in what is undoubtedly a very serious crime." Pearl flicked at her hair in irritation.

"Chief Superintendent, you know that's rubbish. How long are you going to keep me here? I'm due to strangle a tourist myself in an hour or so and I simply must dash." She was right, of course. It was rubbish to suppose that Pearl Green would return to Hong Kong and casually harbour a murderer. She was merely the same woman she had always been – a bit eccentric and single-minded and with a knack for getting into the middle of things.

"You are free to leave" – he put up his hand before she started on him again – "but I caution you, ahem, Miss Green, that you are not to leave Hong Kong without informing me of your intentions, and that includes travel to Macau."

"Oh good, but I can wander off into the Walled City if I fancy avoiding the law, is that the case, Chief Superintendent?"

Tommy Smythe exhaled loudly. "If you insist Miss Green, but we both know that would be very foolish."

*

Marcus was in the interview room when he saw Pearl in the corridor. He called out to her and she turned on her high heeled boots smoothly and said, "Mr Browne. Have you been arrested yet?" He opened his mouth but didn't stand a chance of uttering a word. "Do you realize that I came this close" – she indicated a distance of about an inch with her thumb and forefinger – "to being arrested as an accessory in a murder, thanks to you?"

What did she mean, arrested *yet*? "I'm sorry, Pearl. I panicked, but on the way to the airport I realised how stupid I was being and turned myself in. I'm not under arrest. Did I ask you earlier, have you ever seen *Midnight Express*?"

"Tame stuff, Mr Browne, compared to *Aliens*. Have you seen *Aliens*?" He didn't answer. He didn't know what *Aliens* was about but he sure felt alien enough here. Pearl caught sight of Chief Superintendent Smythe and waved him over. Smythe, who thought he'd seen the last of her and was thankful to do so, touched his cap lightly. "Chief Superintendent. I see my friend Mr Browne has turned up. I am sure you will not take long to satisfy yourself as to his innocence in this matter, as I am equally sure you will agree that clearly, he was set up at Stormy's last night, deliberately targeted by the men Shaw and Tsiu, who obviously knew he was going to dine there, which means of course ...." She stopped talking and thoughtfully twiddled a strand of hair.

He waited. Clearly, she wasn't finished. "It means they were either having Mr Browne followed or one of them followed him to Stormy's. The idea of someone as naïve as Mr Browne arriving in Hong Kong on business and setting about murdering one of our most influential and wealthy businessmen does not stand up to scrutiny. But I'm sure you don't need *me* to point that out to *you*, Chief Superintendent."

Chief Superintendent Smythe had yet to find out what part the striking looking bloke waiting in the interview room had played in the messy little drama at the Hilton that morning. Tommy had already foregone a pleasant lunch and now his evening plans were under threat too. Privately he agreed with Pearl that it was unlikely Mr Browne was a murderer, but he had discovered the body in room 676 and failed to report it. As for being set up, why should he be? Smythe agreed to talk to her after the interview and Pearl sat down to wait, scanned the daily papers and tried to avoid looking at the photos of herself, snapped the day before as she left the airport and as she stepped gawkily into the hotel car, with a newspaper draped over her head.

Prominent philanthropist returns to Hong Kong one headline stated with great certainty but carried in its sub-title a more tentative question: *Is Lady Green still in mourning?* Pearl wondered: *is Lady Green still in mourning? Would a mourning Lady Green help out, even half-heartedly, a complete stranger?* She looked at her eyes in one of the photographs, caught for a second by the camera in a fixed, glazed stare and she wondered, not without some shock: *is this really how I look now?* But enough. She would wait for Chief Superintendent Smythe and not ruminate on things she could not change.

*

Sunday 2 December 1979: 6.00pm. Miami International Airport and Monday 3 December: 7.00am, Hong Kong

The aircraft angled sharply right after take-off from Miami International Airport and eased into the northern flight path over the port. Derek did not see the Seminole Council Community Bus screech to a halt outside the departures hall nor did he see his youngest cousin, Billy Powell, run to the immigration barrier. Billy was restrained from rushing through it by an official who was, in Billy's view, strangely unimpressed by his plea to fetch his cousin back so that he could get some urgent news to him about his cousin Marcus Browne, Billy's second cousin on his father's side. The official remained unimpressed and Derek remained uninformed that Marcus was being questioned by the Hong Kong Police in the matter of the murder of Hong Kong business tycoon Dennis Childs and would be held in the remand cells at the Central Hong Kong Police Station, pending further charges or arrest.

*

As Derek's plane flew west on its long journey to the East, Sol Lewis put in a call to his English step-brother, Stewart, who was living in Hong Kong these days and going by the name Terry Shaw. Sol's mother had died when he was a child. His father had met Terry's mother, a divorcée with a young son, Terry, when she was researching the Seminole Wars for her Anthropology degree. For some years, both boys were raised together but then the relationship between the two adults fell apart and Terry's mother returned to her native England with Terry. Sol stayed with his father but the two boys remained in contact and these days Sol was a junior Elder on the Seminole Council. He was also the only Council member who, initially, was not happy with the decision to expand into big business – too big, too visible, too accountable and it would drain money away from his own little sideline in drug dealing if the planned new casino attracted a new class of customer which in turn attracted the Florida Mafia at the expense of his own enterprise.

But Sol's initial anxiety dissolved when Derek came up with the idea that the *big business* angle should get off the ground in Asia and Hong Kong was where the new operation would be based. Terry was living there, absent without leave from the Army, unemployed and more than happy to keep an eye on Mr Browne whilst Sol figured out how to work the project to their benefit. Then good old Terry came good with an idea. It would seem as though the gambling machines were being produced in Hong Kong and Terry would see to it that Marcus was set up nice and easy, so much so that he would authorise payment before he left. The machines would never arrive in Florida. It was so good that it could almost have been legal. Terry would find a factory that would convincingly appear to manufacture tailor-made gambling machines, Marcus would see the early stages of the faked-up operation going well, would go home happy, and Sol and Terry would end up rich.

By the time the Council realised they'd been had, Terry, and – if things got dicey – Sol, would be long gone. The two men had worked together before once or twice – only on drugs stuff, sure – but they made a good team. It was perfect, and even better, the Council would keep quiet about it too, to avoid humiliation. With the successful way the casino operated these days, they'd even make their forty million back in a year or two. The more Sol thought about it, the more it sounded like philanthropy, not a con job. It was 6pm in Florida and morning in Hong Kong when he rang Terry's number for the second time. "Terry?"

"Ah, Sol. Good. Something has happened this end which will give us more time to set this thing up. Your chap is being held for questioning about a crime. Listen to this: *Tourist held for questioning over the murder of Hong Kong business tycoon: A tourist from Florida who arrived in Hong Kong on Friday morning....* Not only is he our man but I followed him to the Police Station, which must have been when he handed himself in. Good news, what? At this rate he could be locked up for at least a couple of weeks while they sort out the legal stuff. Are you interested in taking a different approach to this, Sol? One that can make us money from other casino operators as well?"

"I'm listening, brother."

"I need half a million US dollars to get going. The return from your lot can be just the start for us. When the Hong Kong end is up and going and after Mr Browne lets the Council know that the first consignment of machines is in production, I will inform him that I want to transfer the operation to China, where manufacturing is a lot cheaper than in Hong Kong. They will accept that there will be a delay with the consignment and if there are reservations at your end, well, you're on the Council...."

"Sure, Terry. I can take care of that..."

"In the meantime you have to convince the Council that it's not too early to start taking orders from other casinos. They can remit ten percent down payments on the number of machines they want produced along with their design requirements. The price will be so good it will be irresistible and by the time they all realize what has happened, we'll be long gone and a lot richer, old boy. Are you good for the stake, old man? I'm a bit short at present."

"I'm good for it."

"Send it over, phone me again in two days and I'll have some solid news for you. I've got work to do this morning – I've met a chap, someone who can help out with some premises and the equipment we'll need."

CHAPTER FIVE

Monday 3 December 1979: 7.30am

Fong took over the morning surveillance from Hua Leung. Ong Hing Terrace on Monday morning was as quiet as it had been on Saturday afternoon, when Mr Yip had listened patiently to Hua's rambling account of how he had taken a fare to the infamous Sheung Wan murder house. Mr Yip had nodded quietly and agreed that Hua and Fong should keep the house under observation. Yip's friend James Gates had discovered a body in that same house four years earlier, part of a train of events linked to a criminal case of 1975. Four years on, if there was an outbreak of what Yip thought of as *strangeness* in Hong Kong, he wanted to be in the know.

"All quiet, Fong. Perhaps this is a waste of time." Fong shrugged. He cared little about how he earned his salary and sitting in a car all day waiting for a *gweipor* to emerge from what was clearly a hovel of the worst description was better than a twelve hour driving shift. Hua Leung got out of his taxi and stretched. The front door of Number 6 opened a fraction and Hua stretched even more, in the manner of a man occupied with his early morning *tai chi* routine.

As he raised his arms in the gesture that invites the harnessing of *chi*, he looked sideways at Fong and muttered, "I will take the fare, but if he insists on going with you, I will follow you. Stay here if you can." He completed the movement, raised his head and hailed Terence Shaw as he stepped from the little house with a cheery "Good morning sir, do you want a taxi this morning?"

"Ah. Excellent. Kowloon. Beecham Road, do you know it?" Hua said he did. He was glad that so many *gweipors* seemed to think that all Asian men looked alike, just as many Asian men considered that all *gweipors* looked alike. Sometimes this misconception created an advantage, because clearly Mr Shaw did not recognise Hua Leung as the driver who had deposited him in Ong Hing Terrace on Saturday.

*

The streets were slow as the streets of Hong Kong are in the morning, after the drawn out end of each day's business makes the prospect of the next day's work slow to kindle. A few food vendors had fired up their gas cooktops, a laundress yawned as she pounded a bundle of white shirts in an old iron tub in a laundry the size of a postage stamp; strangers who shared rooms with other strangers relinquished their beds and pounded the footpaths while their room-mates took a turn to sleep and street cleaners pushed long thin fibred brooms across the footpaths.

Hua's taxi wove through Kowloon's winding streets towards the newer and wider streets that marked a new push of north-trending industry and housing. This too gave way to an area of older industrial buildings interspersed with temporary housing.

"Stop here!" Terence paid the fare.

"Will I wait for you sir?"

"No." Hua gave his most cheery smile, drove around the block and parked. Whistling gently, he pulled a dark blue cotton jacket on over his green tee-shirt, donned his narrow brimmed cotton hat and walked back to the building the man had entered. All was well in Hua's world; he had a packet of sweet dried plums for a snack, a packet of cigarettes and all the time in the world. No further entertainment was necessary to fill in the day.

*

Kaz woke up in the chair beside Drew's hospital bed, replaying the tail of a dream in which she and the Hakka boat-woman struggled against mighty seas to reach Drew on the rock shelf. Drew would be discharged from hospital in the next day or two but was not fit for much. She lectured herself: she would be upbeat and optimistic and help him to keep his spirits up. The fracture to his leg was severe and a full recovery would take time.

The boat-woman, Mrs Lam, had paid a shy visit on Sunday. Perhaps that was why the memories of the accident were washing over Kaz again, just as the waves had washed over Drew. As she smiled and nodded her thanks to Mrs Lam for her gift of lychees, in her mind, Kaz was back in the boat and it was picking up speed on the incoming tidal swell when they saw that the blackness beside Drew in the water was not a shark, but the black sea turtle they had seen grazing in the tidal lagoon earlier. With its great carapace pushed against his shoulders and neck, the animal supported Drew's head just clear of the encroaching waters and when the boat drew alongside, it swam gracefully away.

Simply, the turtle had saved Drew's life.

Kaz shifted in the chair. Drew was still in a lot of pain but at least he had slept. She looked at him, all the love she had for him showed clearly in her tired, sleep creased face – and again wondered about the turtle and what it seemed to have done so selflessly. Why was it only with difficulty that humans acknowledged altruistic behaviour in other animals? It was much easier surely, to assume that the creature simply obeyed the instincts of its own world. Yet turtles and tortoises lay their eggs and leave their young unattended and to the fates; in Chinese stories, to be called a turtle or a tortoise can be a masked form of abuse, inferring that someone so described is a bastard, a stranded illegitimate.

But Kaz felt privileged. She had witnessed something unique, beyond everyday understanding, and, if she was prepared to admit it, life-changing.

*

At ten o'clock Pearl yawned and stretched. The room was very dark and she got up and went over to the windows, drew the curtains and waited for the little sting of delight at seeing the harbour. As therapy goes, the sight of Hong Kong Harbour going into its daily act was having results and this morning, her uneasy anxiety-tossed dreams had dissipated before she could recapture and mull over them. She had made tea and settled into an armchair by the window when the phone rang.

"Lovely to hear from you, Dad. How on earth did you know I'm staying at the Hilton?"

"Oh just a feeling. Pearl, I'm in Los Angeles and due in Tokyo for a spot of business later this week and would love to squeeze in a couple of days in Hong Kong on the way. Any chance you can book me a room?"

It was well over a year since Pearl had seen her father. "If I'm still here on Wednesday; be prepared to stay somewhere else. I'm expecting a call from my real estate agent this morning. Dad, I've bid on the Connaught Road property and will move in immediately if it's accepted. I'm going home."

James Gates tried to sound jolly. She sounded so excited. "Wonderful news, my dear. You have no doubt thought about this thoroughly?" The line buzzed with a torrent of words. "Of course you have. What an old duffer for a father you have, Pearl. But I do worry about you occasionally" – James recalled his recent conversation with Peter Benson and congratulated himself on his restraint. Peter had given him cause for having more than an *occasional worry* about Pearl. James was almost in a frothing panic about his daughter's state of mind, but his voice betrayed none of it – "and going back to Connaught Road, well, that will have challenges as well as good points …."

"I hear what you are saying to me, James." James noted that he had become *James* again and considered himself reprimanded. Very well, he would comment no further. "Of course I know it will be tough. I gave it up too readily, as I said to Kaz and Drew and the others. It's my home and I belong there. I'll book you a room just in case, oh and I'll pick you up from the airport of course. What flight will you be on … and by the way Dad, could you do me a favour? I need to verify the credentials of a particular Diplomat, d'you mind? Got a pen?"

*

Pearl finalized the bid at thirty million Hong Kong dollars with the condition that the furniture she had included in the sale to Nell and Brian Thompson remain in the apartment. All she would have to do upon moving in was to rip out a hideous rosewood bar that the Thompsons had apparently installed. But she knew full well that after closing the bid at such an inflated price she had a lot more on her plate than ripping out a bar – the building would have to pay its way and the way to do that was to open up the two floors above the penthouse and convert them into luxury apartments which could be leased to overseas guests who wanted to experience life in one of Hong Kong's harbour-side precincts.

She could already see the building spilling over with happy people once again, the JBF offices on the ground floor buzzing, with affluent visitors coming and going across the great marble foyer, popping into the office to make the odd donation perhaps … she would have to install air conditioning throughout the entire building – the olfactory experience of being so close to the fish markets could be a little more local experience than some wanted.

The doorbell rang. *Breakfast and the papers. Good.*

The phone rang.

"Pearl?"

"Mr Yip!"

That was it. A phone call from her father and Yip Yee Koon all within the space of half an hour could mean only one thing. She shifted position and sat up very straight in the armchair. "Trouble, Mr Yip?"

"Perhaps. A place in which evil happened several years ago has come to my notice and I was wondering if you have heard from your father – ah, excuse me one moment please Pearl." Mrs Yip was hovering at the door to his office. Hua Leung was with her. He gestured Hua into the room and thanked his wife with a smile. Hua was clearly upset. "Pearl. I will call you back very soon. Please do not go out until then."

He hung up. "Hua Leung, sit down and tell me what I can already see in your face. You have seen our man from Ong Hing Terrace with my brother, is that not so?" Poor Hua's face creased even more. Once again his boss had proved that he had a third eye. Never would he cross him. "There is one thing I do not see. Where did they meet?"

"They met at a factory, sir, Number 44, Beecham Road." The information gave Yip pause. It was unusual for his brother to do business beyond the confines of Kowloon's Walled City.

"Describe this factory and sit down, Hua. I will ask Mrs Yip to arrange a cup of tea for you, after I make a telephone call." He quickly dialled a number. "Pearl? I am sorry if my earlier call caused you any inconvenience. This matter is after all very straightforward and there is no cause for concern. I hope we can meet for dinner when you are settled into Hong Kong life once again."

Pearl put the receiver back on its cradle very carefully and went to the door. Yip Yee Koon had just fobbed her off. It was unlike him to contact her for a trivial reason. There was something that he had wanted her to know, but now did not. What? She accepted the breakfast tray and poured a cup of tea, lifted the lid on the plate of eggs and bacon and settled in to read the papers. The headline leapt at her: *Tourist held on remand: investigation into the murder of Hong Kong business tycoon: A tourist believed to be from Florida who arrived in Hong Kong on Friday....* She put the plate of food aside and walked with forced calm into the bathroom. Not only did it seem that there was suddenly a very busy morning ahead but Pearl had just remembered something, something she should have mentioned to the police. Another visit to Chief Superintendent Smythe was regrettably going to have to be factored into her morning plans, apart from which, could she really bear the thought of poor Marcus, not only facing up to but having to live his *Midnight Express* nightmare for another day?

*

Marcus said it out loud, "Murder." The sound died against the thick walls of the remand cell. *Murder* was a word heard in news stories, something faked on screen or read about in books. It was not something that had ever touched him. The history of his people included much violence and killing during the Seminole Wars but even his detailed knowledge of those conflicts did not graze him as the word did now, with its flat, unequivocal coldness. How had he ended up in this situation?

His statement about being involved in Saturday morning's events had resulted in him being put on remand whilst the case was further investigated. He had been allowed to make a phone call and in the early hours of Sunday morning he spoke to Chief Rolling Thunder. The old man was initially shocked into silence, but he recovered and threw a volley of questions at him that Marcus could barely untangle: *I was set up, Chief, simple as that,* he had said. *What's not simple is why. I had a call offering to help with our project on Saturday morning – this was from the guy who I then supposedly killed, by the way. I had seen him before – at a restaurant on Friday night – but that's all. I need help, Chief. You have to get me out of here. Have you seen Midnight Express....?*

Chief Rolling Thunder – who preferred his tribal name to his birth name of Ferris Winton – was a nimble thinker. It was less than three hours since Derek had left for the airport. He kept Marcus on the line and sent for Billy Powell to waylay and warn Derek about what had happened to Marcus, but, as Billy later related to anyone remotely interested, he was too late, and Derek was fated to arrive in Hong Kong without knowing that his cousin was being held as a suspect in a serious crime. As far as Chief Rolling Thunder was concerned there had been no point in telling Marcus that Derek was on his way because he'd want to know why and there was no need to add to Marcus's problems any further at present. He would find out about his grandmother's passing soon enough but maybe not soon enough to get back for the funeral. That would gut Marcus.

I'll fix it Marcus, he had said wearily. *Don't worry and maintain your dignity. We're Seminoles. We don't take shit from those who would serve us unjustly. Remember that.* The slim thread of an older language discernible in the Chief's words had carried a sense of home to Marcus. The Seminoles could trace their roots back for many generations and even though most of his direct family were dead, including his own parents, Seminoles never lose their sense of identity, living not only as a community, but as a community with a common, binding purpose – freedom.

*

After the call, he had been escorted back to the cells. He was innocent. In the end, that was all that mattered and with his breakfast tray on Monday morning came the news that he was to be released, but only after he went to the police morgue to confirm that the man held there was the man he had seen in Mrs Entwhistle's room. He was not informed that the reason for his release was because the time of death had been established as being well before he arrived in Hong Kong on Friday. The Pathologist's report mentioned refrigeration, cell breakdown and other things that meant that Dennis Childs had probably died on the previous Monday or Tuesday. The finding was giving Tommy

Smythe a great deal of concern and had Marcus been aware of these circumstances, he would have been even more uncomfortable thinking about the man with whom he had briefly shared a table on Friday evening. He still had to agree to a series of release conditions however – he could be in a heap of trouble even yet. A booking was made for him at a guesthouse in Kennedy Road and when his release arrangements were complete, he stoically went through the process of identification. There was no doubt that the dead man in the mortuary was the man he had seen in room 676 and at the restaurant.

He retrieved his briefcase and by nine forty-five was outside the Hong Kong Police Division Central building, waiting for a taxi. The panic and urge to run for home had gone. He had business to do and things surely couldn't be any more difficult than these last three days had been. He didn't intend dwelling on them. The first thing he intended to do after settling in was to contact The June Bowen Foundation. He had given a lot of thought to the idea that had come to him even as the bizarre events and aftermath of Saturday morning rolled out. The more he thought about doing a business deal with a local philanthropic organization, the more he liked it and he liked it a whole lot more than dealing with the Mr Tsius and Mr Shaws of the world, who may or may not be the real deal. Philanthropy occupies its own part of the universe with its own philosophies and values and to Marcus that more than equalled the value of corporate-based business expertise.

*

Upon being informed that Pearl Green was at the enquiry desk and wanted to see him urgently, Chief Superintendent Smythe took the precaution of ordering tea. Her last words to him on Saturday were that she would help Mr Browne out if she could, and no doubt she had seen this morning's papers and was about to hurl resources from her considerable arsenal of money and influence at the entire Hong Kong Police Force to secure his release. After welcoming her unsmiling face into his office, Tommy promptly informed her that Mr Browne had been conditionally released.

But it was Tommy who ended up needing the tea. Pearl said, "That's good news about Mr Browne's release, Chief Superintendent, but I'm here for a different reason. I remembered something – Belinda and I were very close once – my apologies, that is hardly relevant," she said, seeing the Chief Superintendent reach for a pencil and paper, "Except that I'm probably one of only a few who know that Dennis Childs is an identical twin. I forgot about it until this morning." It took a few moments for the information to sink in and Pearl was already giving him the hurry-up; she had lots else to do. "You realize of course that this means that the body found in the Hilton on Saturday morning may possibly not be that of Dennis Childs, don't you?

*

Marcus was not impressed with the guesthouse that the Hong Kong Police had booked for him. He inspected the shabby room and shared bathroom facilities and walked straight back out into Kennedy Road and hailed a cab. "Peninsula Hotel, please driver!" He'd let Sergeant Thornton know where he was later. That's all that they wanted from him, and he would stay somewhere decent, not in that dump.

II

Master of the Void

CHAPTER SIX

Monday 3 December 1979: 10.00am

Terry locked the factory door and handed the key to Tony Yip. "Well, Mr Yip, do we have an agreement? I can meet your three million upfront for rent, staff hire and merchandise. I may be able to increase that figure if the budget runs over but I need notice before I can raise extra capital." There was no need for Tony Yip to know that Terry could do a lot better than three million, any more than Sol needed to know that there would most likely be some surplus remaining from his stake after the set-up. Tony Yip nodded but remained silent and Terry said, "I'll have a sign made and leave the rest to you. I want this up and running in two weeks."

*

The *South China Morning Post*'s lead story that morning concerning the murder of a Hong Kong business tycoon and the suggestion that a tourist involved in the enquiry had been arrested made Terry's morning and bought him what he needed most: time. "If my client is free to do business immediately," he said to Tony Yip, "I'll take him around to some other premises as a diversion to give you the time you need to appear production-ready. If the thing goes belly-up and the chap turns turtle, someone else from the buyer's side will come along. He's here on serious business: my sources are impeccable."

Tony scowled at the reference Mr Shaw made to *turning turtle*. This was not an expression to use lightly in his neck of the woods. He did not like Terence Shaw but that was neither here nor there because Tony Yip liked no-one. Triad bosses may have extensive *families* but they don't have friends. What Tony had was rules, but today's business was outside of his usual sphere of influence and constituted new business for him, even though he had owned the premises at 44, Beecham Road for about a year. To stray too far from the Walled City would invite unwanted attention from other triad interests, especially around the industrial back streets of Kowloon – interests that would love to get their hands on his core power base. When he acquired this particular factory it was with thoughts about the long-term future of the Walled City in mind, but if there was even so much as a whisper that he had taken his eye off his home patch, his authority would be challenged in an instant.

Tony possessed wealth that rivalled that of his brother, Yip Yee Koon, and at this stage of his life he had both the time and inclination to see what he could turn his hand to beyond the old city's confines. There were rumours that the government planned to demolish the Walled City because of the level of overcrowding and appalling living conditions that people who called it home endured. In Tony's opinion the rumours were encouraged by the increasing infiltration of *do-gooders*, as he thought of them, people who tried to educate the city's residents – his people – about health and hygiene and human rights and other things they didn't need to know about. The last thing the Walled City needed was social workers. It functioned as a densely populated organism of co-dependent citizens and he ran it. If the bulldozers ever went through, his fortune and means of making a living would be bulldozed too. Tony needed to think ahead, but as he looked up and down the street, he realized how uncomfortable he felt beyond the familiar parameters of his dark and dense city.

There were only a few people about apart from his driver and bodyguard. The bodyguard leant against the building next door, apparently absorbed in reading a paper. There was a man on the other side of the road, standing idly at the kerb, stubbing out a cigarette. None of these people seemed to take any notice of the two men who stood at the factory door, both above average height, one a fine-boned Asian man and the other a well-dressed, pale and slender Caucasian. As the guy across the road finished stubbing his cigarette and walked on, something familiar about him bothered Tony and he motioned to his bodyguard to follow the man before turning back to Terence.

"You need at least twenty five machines for it to look like the sort of operation that an overseas interest will have the confidence to invest in, Mr Shaw. I will supply ten new machines, and the others will be old models but they will be stripped back to look as though they are in production when your client inspects the factory. You can tell him that production can be increased at any time once the lines are fully operational. My people will organize the set up." He laughed and patted Terence on his shoulder in an almost friendly fashion. "Nice doing business with you. So far. We will meet at Carlo's Bar on Wednesday at five o'clock and when you pay the first million, Mr Shaw, *The Celestial Happiness Machinery Company* will be in business." He laughed again and gestured to his driver that he was ready to leave. He did not offer Terry a lift.

*

After waiting about in the empty street for several minutes, Terry gave up on the prospect of finding a taxi and began to walk. He liked walking and welcomed the time for reflection. The nature of the situation he was in was intriguing as well as risky – he was about to set up a deal between a powerful Hong Kong triad leader and his own step-brother who was recognised as a fully paid up member of the American Indian Seminole Nation. Ambitious empire builders throughout history have travelled to far flung parts of the earth chasing wealth and power and he, Terry Shaw – as he occasionally had to remind himself was his name now – was merely capitalizing on that particular type of greed, but, if he had consciously tried to dream up a more bizarre combination of interests it would not have been possible.

Triads and Indians he muttered. A passer-by gave him a wide berth. The players gave the scheme an edgy quality he would have preferred to avoid, but basically a con job was a con job. It either worked or it didn't. Terry's stocks were low. This had to work, and how many triad members would know anything about a tribe of Native American Indians and vice versa? He snorted what could have been a small laugh and flicked his cigarette butt into the gutter. Whether he was innocent or not, Browne would more likely than not be neatly stashed away for a week or two whilst the police conducted their enquiries. Terry whistled a few bars of the *Wings* hit 'With a Little Luck' as he strolled, thinking that it was a pity there was no longer any room in his plans to include Tsiu Wah-Yeung. Mr Tsiu was too keen on the Chinese solution and if

Wah-Heung set it up Terry would lose control. He would prefer to manage the China side of things when the time was right because he didn't quite trust Mr Tsiu. He didn't trust Tony Yip either, but at least there was no expectation of trust in that quarter.

Once he had the money and if he felt like taking up another venture, *then* maybe he would go in for something with Tsiu in China. In a year which had seen China abolish the position of Chairman of the People's Republic and initiate a one child per family policy, change was again sweeping across the country, reflected both in political hierarchical struggles, the new population control policy and the opening of investment doors to foreign interests. China policy was on the move again, but now, large-scale industrialisation was part of the new wave of development and Terry saw very clearly that with endless cheap labour and relaxed manufacturing standards he could provide goods quickly and cheaply to a world that each year demanded more and more mass-produced material goods. He could even do it all legitimately.

He smiled and lit up again and exhaled a cloud of smoke: he could smell money, even if for now it had a slight whiff of danger trailing it.

*

Yip dismissed Hua and gave a discreet signal to his chief house servant, Mr Kim. Hua was seen to the front gate of the Yip family mansion and whilst Mr Kim offered him a cheerful farewell, he also had an observant eye on the man watching the house from the sheltered entry of the mansion next door. Mr Kim watched him slide into a waiting taxi and casually follow Hua's cab from the cul-de-sac and with equal ease opened the front gates and slid behind the wheel of Mr Yip's new black Ford Fairlane.

*

As he waited for his afternoon cup of tea, Tommy Smythe considered his position and decided that at the very least, it was embarrassing. Pearl Green had long left the station, but before making the phone call he was putting off, he re-read all of the statements, notes and information collected after the body found in room 676 at the Hilton on Saturday afternoon was tentatively identified as that of Dennis Childs. There was no mention of a twin brother.

Childs was in the police morgue awaiting formal identification. With a sensation that his chest was filling up with something leaden – or was that merely what genuine dread actually *felt* like – Tommy realized as he combed through the pile of information that no-one had actually gone to the Childs's residence. Several attempted telephone calls were recorded as having no result, but that's all. The initial and tentative identification of the body had been made by Sergeant Thornton. Childs's only daughter Belinda had been contacted and she had stated that she wished formally to identify her father as soon as she could secure a flight.

He dialled a number and a very polite female voice said, "Mr Childs's residence. Who is speaking please?"

"Ah. Good afternoon. Chief Superintendent Smythe, Hong Kong Police Service speaking. May I speak to, ah, Mr Childs?" There was a pause and a familiar voice came on the line:

"Dennis Childs here. Chief Superintendent, a very good afternoon to you. Was it Mark Twain who said that 'Reports of my death have been greatly exaggerated'?" Smythe laid the spine of the receiver against his forehead and gulped, hard. This stuff-up could cost him his career.

"I see. Have you a twin brother Mr Childs?"

"Yes. Been wondering how long it would take for that to occur to you. Want me to come and identify him, hmm? We are identical twins, of course, information which just might get you out of any bother over this." He laughed, humourlessly.

"Thank you, sir. We will of course need you to come to the Central Division HQ but may I ask why you did not contact us, and, incidentally, did you dine at Stormy's on Friday night, oh, and did you telephone a Mr Browne at the Hong Kong Hilton Hotel on Saturday morning and arrange to meet him in Room 676?"

"I suppose I could have telephoned you, Chief Superintendent, although I didn't see why I should bail the Hong Kong Police Service out of what is obviously a colossal gaffe. On

Friday night I dined at Stormy's certainly, but I most certainly did not phone a Mr Browne or anyone else at the Hong Kong Hilton Hotel on Saturday morning. I'll be with you in about half an hour, Chief Superintendent."

*

As James packed he reflected that winter was not the time he would usually pick for a visit to Hong Kong. December is chilly and the afternoons close in remarkably early. The chestnut vendors bend over their fires and draw crowds of home goers as eager for the warmth as for the delicious, hot creamy nuts that come wrapped in cones of newspaper. He thought about his daughter. Between the loss of her husband and the intervening years, he supposed it was always certain that Pearl would return to Hong Kong one day but, *damn and blast it* – the sudden irritation surprised him – he thought by then that the old Pearl would have re-surfaced. Apparently this was far from being the case. He packed and unpacked his jacket. *How cold was it in December? Would a vest suffice?* He continued to ruminate: *Is she simply trying to buy some happiness by buying back the old place?* Pearl's business instincts were sound and he hoped she was using them. *Or does she just want to consort with her familiars, the ghosts of her mother and her husband? Or is she simply trying to re-capture a time in her own history, the familiarity of everyday movements, speech and memories, anything that will give her a way back into something that resembles an ordinary existence?*

There was no option but to find out. If she would let him, that is.

*

Even the pallor of death could not disguise that the man in Cubicle Three in the police morgue and the very much alive Dennis Childs were identical twins. Dennis looked with little sentiment at his brother's death mask and confirmed that he was Ronald Childs of address unknown. He accompanied Chief Superintendent Smythe to his office to sign the relevant documentation, produced identification and said, "I have two major concerns about this business, Chief Superintendent Smythe. The first, obviously, is for my daughter. I have already reassured her that this has been a horrible mistake. Fortunately, she was at her Monaco residence, about to leave for New York but she managed to get a flight to Hong Kong instead. She's still completely overwrought. Belinda gets thrown out of balance rather easily. She's just arrived... phoned from Kai Tak just before I left home, as a matter of fact. She's going to visit a pal of hers for an hour or so and we'll have the evening and tomorrow morning together. Welcome news for any father, Smythe assumed, but he noted that the man's expression of sour distaste did not shift at the prospect of seeing his only child. Tommy also thought it odd that the daughter, in an "overwrought" state, was to visit a pal before rushing to her father's side to commiserate with him.

"Your second concern, sir?"

"… is about my brother being in Hong Kong at all, Chief Superintendent. I paid him off four years ago, richly, for some difficulties that he was experiencing at the time. The agreement was that he never return to Hong Kong, for any reason at all. It means, I am afraid, that Ronald was up to something dodgy. You should stay alert for anything strange going on about the place. Ronald was not the most savoury person. Let me know when the body is to be released and I will have my staff make the funeral arrangements. Good day, Chief Superintendent."

After Dennis Childs left, Smythe reviewed what he had said. He didn't like that quip about Ronald Childs being up to something dodgy in Hong Kong. There were already enough signs around that all was not as should be. Smythe was near the end of a two and a half year continuous service period; he was tired, impatient with everything and everyone and in need of extended leave and would much prefer that nothing untoward was going on in Hong Kong.

*

Hua Leung was uneasy about returning to his rented room in the Walled City. Hua knew, as did most residents of the globe's most densely stacked pile of humanity, that Mr Yip's brother effectively ran the city and now he, Hua Leung, had seen Mr Yip's brother talking with the man whose house had been kept under observation in Ong Hing Terrace in Sheung Wan, on the orders of

Mr Yip Yee Koon. There was no love lost between the Yip brothers. What if against all odds Mr Tony Yip knew what he had been doing that morning? He may never leave the Walled City again. It was easy to disappear in there, easier than anywhere else in Hong Kong. There were no rules and no mercy from men such as Mr Yip's brother. Hua gripped the steering wheel, anxious and undecided and on impulse swerved sharply left into Upper Albert Road. He would sleep in the taxi, keep vigil at 6, Ong Hing Terrace and review his options tomorrow. He would ask for Mr Yip's advice about his situation and perhaps, if he spent the night watching over Mr Shaw's house, he might earn some consideration from his boss. He relaxed his grip on the wheel, happy to have a solution and a reason for staying on Hong Kong side. He did not see the car behind him follow his vehicle into Upper Albert Road, just as that driver did not notice a gleaming black Ford Fairlane make the same manoeuvre from Garden Road.

*

Derek had not booked any accommodation, assuming that he would take a room at the Hilton with Marcus, but he found upon arrival that there were no vacancies. He was advised that if he cared to make a booking for the following day, two rooms currently undergoing what was described as *deep cleaning* would be available, room 365 and room 676. He said to the desk clerk, "Not a problem. My cousin is staying here. I can share his room tonight."

Helen Kwok's brief experience on the Hilton's reception desk did not equip her to know if this was permissible hotel policy and she referred the matter to her supervisor, who said, "Possibly, for one night, at an upgraded tariff of course. What is your cousin's name, sir?"

"Browne, Mr Marcus Browne."

The supervisor's smile did not flag.

"A moment, please sir, I will need to fetch the Floor Manager."

Derek wondered why such a simple matter should set off a bout of buck-passing.

The Floor Manager, a curt Englishman who introduced himself as Mr Ward, came to the point by handing Derek a copy of that morning's newspaper. He pointed at the inset article on page one. "The suspect's name is not mentioned, but if you go to Division Central Police Station, you will find your cousin has accommodation there. Now sir, if there is nothing else we can help you with and as you have already been informed the hotel is full, good day."

Derek glared at the man but left immediately for Division Central HQ where he shoved the newspaper under the nose of the officer at the enquiry desk. Constable Chua kept his pen poised above the note he was making in the duty register, but he was startled by the aggressiveness of the gesture which did not dissipate when Derek baldly stated that his cousin had come to Hong Kong on good and honourable business for his people, only to be had-up on some cooked-up charge. "Poof, just like that, he arrives here and is spirited away by the law, like a puff of smoke, as if a void opened. What's going on?"

The thoroughly startled Constable Chua knew from the movies that American Indians communicated using smoke, but he had no idea that it was also a means of invoking spirits or voids. Whilst it was evident that the man who stood at the counter was of Asian descent, his vivid colouring, build and distinctive nose marked him unmistakably as an American Indian, as was Mr Browne, the other gentleman who had occupied considerable police time during the past two days. The woven headband tied around his head of long black hair was unnecessary to assist Constable Chua reach this conclusion.

Procedurally, Constable Chua was required to advise the Duty Sergeant of any matter that came to the enquiry desk related to active cases, but it was not a day for following procedures because just then Chief Superintendent Smythe appeared – a bit like a puff of smoke too, it occurred to Constable Chua – in company with the man Constable Chua had assumed was resting in the morgue, Mr Dennis Childs. Constable Chua and Derek Wong both literally gawped. The *SCMP* story featured inset photographs of several local prominent Caucasian business tycoons, feeding speculation about which of their number had been murdered and Dennis Childs's photo was the biggest. Derek Wong looked at the Chief Superintendent, studied the photograph of Dennis Childs again and without warning let out an almighty howl. Afterwards, as he thought about the incident, Constable Chua could liken the noise only to that which accompanies the dragon dance at Chinese New Year. But that was usually created by about twenty men and many instruments. The blood curdling cross between a yodel and a scream filled the foyer of Central Division Police HQ and spilled out into the street.

People passing by related a series of stories to their friends and families in explanation of the phenomenon and the one that eventually came to have the stamp of authenticity was that the central air-conditioning unit at Police Division Central seized up in a scream of failing machinery which collapsed in a heap of twisted metal at the base of the central core of the building.

Constable Chua was terrified, even though Dennis had not made any move, other than to open his mouth and rock Hong Kong to its basaltic foundations. He stuttered, "S-sir, this is Mr Wong, s-sir. Mr B-Browne's cousin." Dennis Childs was not amused. Nor was Chief Superintendent Smythe, who was still self-absorbed and acutely embarrassed. Marcus Browne had originally been held for questioning into the murder of an unidentified male Caucasian but had not been charged. There was no breach of legal technicalities, but that was about the best complexion Smythe could put on it. He should have picked up on the procedural anomaly that had occurred, before it was placed before him as an outright bungle.

With Dennis Childs's business with the Chief Superintendent complete, Childs shifted his attention to Derek, introduced himself, alluded to there having been an unfortunate mistake and how he, Dennis, was sure that the Chief Superintendent would put Derek's mind at rest in no time at all about what had really happened.

Smythe sighed and beckoned Derek to follow him into his office, where the Chief Superintendent delivered a highly abbreviated account of Saturday's events and ended with a rushed statement about how it gave him pleasure to be able to inform Mr Wong that his cousin had been released. But he rushed the explanation too much and should not have been surprised when Derek wanted more. He wanted to talk, explain. *Dammit*, thought Tommy, *he's going to confide in me.*

"The reason I'm here Sir, is to give Marcus the bad news that his grandmother died in the early hours of Sunday morning, Florida time. He will be very upset."

Smythe tut-tutted sympathetically.

"I arrived in Hong Kong without having any idea of what had happened to Marcus. I wanted to tell him in person about Granny Browne. When the hotel people referred me here, well, you know how I feel about that. My cousin only arrived in Hong Kong on Friday. Why would he murder someone? He was very unsure about travelling here by himself. He's not the sort of guy to go looking for trouble. He's never even been out of America before." Derek shook his head as the situation began to overwhelm him again.

Tommy saw the signs and wondered if he should block his ears but there was no need.

Derek said in grave, lowered tones. "What we are doing in coming here is for our people and we need all the help we can get. My cousin is no murderer. Whoever killed that guy set my cousin up and where I come from, that means just one thing."

Smythe looked down at his notepad where he had scribbled the address of the guesthouse that the Police Service had organised for Mr Browne. Everyone said exactly the same things in defence of their loved ones at times like this. Everyone was as pure as driven snow but even so, he was curious about Wong's last remark. "Mr Wong," he said, "this is the address of the guest house where your cousin is staying, but I'm curious, what did you mean by *where you come from, that means just one thing*, Mr Wong?"

"Where I come from, that would involve the American Mafia, Chief Superintendent. The Florida Branch, specifically."

Smythe's long experience in maintaining a neutral expression failed, and he smiled broadly. "Ah. I was momentarily worried that you were going to say that triad activity could be involved. That would be trying. Here you are." He handed over the slip of paper. "All the best and good day to you sir." He ushered Dennis to the door, returned to his desk and informed his desk calendar that although the previous two days had been trying, he had no idea that some comic relief would be provided by the American Mafia. He laughed out loud. The American Mafia popping up in Hong Kong *would* almost be a relief compared to some of the hijinks the local triad lads got up to. Derek had already cleared the station and didn't hear the Chief Superintendent's minor explosion of mirth but Constable Chau paused in his record keeping duties and noted the time in the desk registry. *Something to amuse the night shift, the* Chief Superintendent *laughing out loud behind closed doors....*

*

Pearl hung up and walked over to the window. Not even the sight of the darkening waters picking and choosing highlights from the first flares of neon lights soothed her sense of unease. She had been seen off twice today; by Mr Yip this morning, and now by the odious Thompsons.

As James Williams at Robertson & Kovacks hung up, his hands were shaking. Five o'clock. Thank God he could leave the office. Pearl was not happy and he needed a couple of stiff whiskies to restore his inner calm after the quiet bawling out she had just given him. Nell and Brian Thompson had refused her offer outright. If Lady Green is serious, they informed James with not even a hint of bravura, they would start listening at forty million Hong Kong dollars. No guarantees even at that level. Everyone knew land in Hong Kong was priceless and they had no intention of giving their property away.

When the phone rang again Pearl leapt for it. Perhaps James had made them see sense. Her offer was generous, at twenty five million, ridiculously so. Perhaps the first round of afternoon cocktails had put them in a different frame of mind.

"Pearl! It's me!" The voice was female, high-pitched, with a very effective carrying quality.

"Oh? Hello?"

"It's me! Lin. I've just arrived to identify Dad's body. Isn't that a shriek? He rang and told me all about it, just in case the story got a mention in the English press. I thought I'd come and see the old love anyway, it must be awful to almost be a murder victim."

"Ah. Belinda? If not your father, who is the victim?"

"Ghastly Uncle Ronald, darling, apparently. Haven't seen him in ages. Daddy expunged him from the family, such as we are. He was a no-gooder: swindler, con man, serial adulterer and finally, a bigamist. It would be extremely hypocritical of me to pretend to be too upset. The only thing that does upset me is that apparently the killer thought they were doing my dear daddy in. That's enough to bring a girl scuttling home, isn't it? Any chance of meeting up darling? I'm dying to see you." Pearl smiled, perhaps a little ruefully. Certainly a little of her girlish past was right there on the other end of the line, and it was a long time since Pearl had felt girlish. She and Belinda had been major players in what was dubbed by the media *The United Fashion Front of Hong Kong* during the 1960s. Pearl was always aware that it was a put-down in a Hong Kong that was less impressed by political upheaval and social revolution than by the latest fashions coming out of the European couture houses, but Belinda revelled in it.

Their friendship never made the transition into a more adult relationship however, particularly after Belinda married the Governor's Private Secretary, Toby Blake. She left him three years later for her rock star husband and became a globally famous celebrity wife. Beautiful, with a husband famous surely beyond his value to music, she followed him around the world in company with their three children. Pearl had never met the children but Kaz did once and she assured Pearl they were truly revolting. The only difference between Belinda in 1979 and Belinda in 1964 was that the contemporary edition no longer wore the false eyelashes she had been locally famous for during her heyday as a local fashion icon. She had developed severe allergies to the glue which took years and the end of a bad marriage before it cleared up.

"Will you dine with me?"

"Can't darling, got to be a quick visit. Daddy's organising dinner at home for us and besides I hardly ever eat. I loathe food. I do coffee mornings and champagne evenings, darling."

"I'm staying at the Hilton."

"So daddy said. Odd, darling, to think of you there, I mean I always associate you with your old place." Pearl tightened her mouth. "Don't mind me. I'm jet lagged. First Class is the pits sometimes. I forgot my pills and barely slept but I'd love to come and see you for an hour or so. I'm only in town overnight; have to meet Bobby in New York. He's got a concert in Times Square on Thursday. You know how it is with us...."

Pearl was sure that the whole world knew *how it was* with Belinda and Bobby, more familiar to the public as Smut Jones, front man for his band The Froth. He wouldn't do a concert without Belinda being present. A fortune teller had once told him that if she ever missed a show, he wouldn't leave the stage alive. Bobby didn't have the courage to flout the prediction and Belinda gloried in the reflected fame it brought her. Her beautiful face had appeared on the cover of every music industry magazine, including *Rolling Stone*, and once she even showed off the butterfly tattoo that adorned one of her shapely buttocks for the centre spread of *Penthouse*. When Pearl read about the curse laid on Smut Jones's head she had smiled: she knew her old friend quite well enough to imagine that Belinda would have paid the seer handsomely to predict such a dire outcome for her husband if he ever neglected her.

She hung up, relieved that Belinda was happy to come to the hotel. There was a long-standing awkwardness between Pearl and Dennis Childs and she would prefer not to be in his house, particularly after being involved in his brother's murder case, however peripherally. Pearl also welcomed the opportunity Belinda would bring with her to take her mind off her current quandary about buying back her old home. The temptation to match any price that the Thompsons wanted was almost overwhelming her, and what was worse, she could match it if she sold up her assets, without compromising her considerable financial stake in the June Bowen Foundation.

She brooded as she changed into black velvet pants and a dull gold evening shirt. She wanted her old home back like she wanted her husband back and like she had wanted her mother back for so many years. She applied some make up and creased her lips to spread a dab of lipstick. She would not include anything about babies on that list.

*

Fong was unhappy about his early relief from duty. Hua had perhaps exaggerated a little when he said he was acting under instructions from Mr Yip. Well, he was, in a way. As he manoeuvred his vehicle out of the narrow street Fong's mouth turned down further as he was forced to move over to the extreme left to allow another taxi to pass and immediately after that had to mount the narrow footpath so that a big, wide, black and obviously new Ford Fairlane could squeeze by without incident. Fong wondered why Ong Hing Terrace should suddenly be so busy. Hua Leung had the same thought. Ong Hing Terrace was only about twenty house fronts long, an east to west laneway that created a very minor connection between two wider and busier roads.

The two cars were clearly unfamiliar with the area and there was no option but to keep going as there was no room to turn around. The taxi turned left at the top of the lane and the Fairlane followed. Hua kept strict vigil but neither vehicle returned. The taxi with Tony Yip's bodyguard as passenger had no reason to: he saw where Hua Leung had parked and watched the other taxi leave after the two drivers exchanged a few hurried words. Clearly they were keeping one of the houses in the street under observation. He would report the matter to his boss.

Yip Yee Koon's driver had no reason to hang around either, being so conspicuous in the sleek black vehicle in such a rundown area. Mr Kim lost the taxi he had been following in Caine Road but a couple of minutes later, as he gave way to a gleaming Bentley that was proceeding along Garden Road from the Peak area, he saw it weaving through the lanes of traffic and followed.

*

Belinda arrived at the hotel, having allotted an hour to see Pearl. She caused a stir as she crossed the foyer and even in a hotel such as the Hilton, where people are accustomed to seeing the famous, beautiful or merely rich, Belinda stood out from the herd. She had a type of svelte, high-end seedy glamour and she was exceedingly thin.

She was dressed in black leather pants that were so tight that they seamlessly blended into a pair of knee high stiletto-heeled boots; a black tee shirt announced her rock connections and was topped with a tuxedo jacket that had a tear in the elbow. She held a pair of black metal-studded leather gloves. Her hair was a waist length mane of finely braided jet. She had curvaceous eyebrows and wore very large black sunglasses. Of skin there was little to see except for that on the expanse of her pale square jaw and she had bright red, full lips. From her ears dangled razorblade earrings, studded with precious stones. On every finger she wore a ring, each a thick gold band set with a larger version of each precious stone that adorned her ear lobes.

At thirty-eight, Belinda was a rare and spectacular beauty and an undisputed rock queen. She never failed to experience an adrenalin hit as people recognised her, which happened whether she was with Smut and the Froth, by herself, or in family mode with the kids when Smut was simply Bobby Jones.

Onlookers in the foyer parted to clear a path for her procession to the front desk and when she announced that she was here as the guest of Lady Pearl Green, her voice was a little louder than necessary and a rustle of interest reverberated from those nearest her at the edge of the crowd. She waited whilst the Receptionist rang Pearl before making her way to the lift. Even these mundane actions had a rosy air of glamour about them for the many eyes that followed the progress of the luscious Belinda Jones.

*

Pearl rang for a bucket of ice and a bottle of champagne. Belinda had not lost her taste for champagne, apparently, and Pearl intended to dull her own disappointment in not budging the Thompsons as well as celebrating what was, after all, a reunion.

She added to the order a small tub of Russian caviar and six slim slices of pale cold toast to accompany the celebratory drink. Pearl had not seen Belinda face to face for nearly ten years. Belinda's escape from her unhappy marriage to Toby Blake had come with the price tag of leaving Hong Kong at pretty much a moment's notice when she joined The Froth's entourage. Dennis Childs was initially heart-broken, but as it became obvious how happy his only child was, he resigned himself to occasional visits from her and followed her glamorous progress through the changing face of the 1970s rock music scene with as much relish as her husband's fans.

The doorbell sounded. Pearl patted at her golden brown burst of hair and went to answer it. It was room service. "Have you seen Mrs Jones?" she said. It was now at least ten minutes since the desk clerk had telephoned to say that Belinda was on her way. The waiter smilingly nodded *no*, opened the wine and arranged the caviar and toast on a small silver tray. "Probably went to the wrong floor," Pearl said by way of conversation. The waiter beamed, bowed, wished her *bon appétit* and left. The bottle lay open and inviting in a silver bucket that rapidly lost its icy coating and dribbled beads of water down the side, where it puddled on the glass topped coffee table. Pearl leant forward and poured a glass. "I will have my old home back" she said very seriously to a lump of caviar, trying to remember if one ate the caviar and swished it down with champagne or was it the other way around?

"Hang the expense."

*

Mr Kim followed the taxi to Kowloon where it eventually came to a halt in Dentist Street. He braked hard and backed up to Spring Festival Lane. The new Fairlane was out of place in this area too, just as it had been in Sheung Wan. The man who alighted crossed the narrow street and walked past the dental prosthetic shops that formed the Walled City's northern entrance and in an instant, he was out of sight. Mr Kim turned around and headed for home. He had no orders to follow the man once he left the cab. Mr Yip merely wished to know his destination. Mr Yip probably knew already.

Tony Yip listened to the bodyguard's account of events. So, the man he had noticed earlier that morning near the factory entrance was one of his brother's men. Why was Yee Koon watching him? Tony Yip and Yip Yee Koon ignored one another unless it was unavoidable. They had not had dealings for four years, when there had been a string of murders in The Emperor Inn. At that time Yee Koon had sought his brother's help in suppressing a series of death contracts, also issued from within the Walled City. He had never mentioned Tony's involvement during the police investigation that followed but paid his debt with money and honoured it with silence. Now, Yee Koon had him under observation.

Was it Mr Shaw's movements that interested his brother? Or, and Tony's eyes crossed slightly with tension, did Yee Koon have business interests in that particular part of Kowloon, exactly where he, Tony, had ambitions to expand his own interests? That was the most likely solution given the range of Yee Koon's business holdings. He gave the bodyguard curt orders. "Organise twenty-four hour observation of my brother's house. I want enough manpower on hand to follow him and anyone who enters or leaves. I want to know everything, even about domestic deliveries and where the servants go, understand?"

*

Mr Kim returned to the Yip Mansion and reported to his boss, who said, "If Hua Leung and Fong are known to be keeping observation in a street where one of my brother's business associates lives, my brother will not rest until he knows why I am interested in this matter. Mr Kim, please instruct Hua and Fong to be especially alert. In addition, I want more security in these grounds. You can ask Mr Weng at the racing stables to take care of that. Keep me informed of anything that is unusual. Anything at all."

When Mr Kim left, Yip Yee Koon studied an old framed family photograph that hung on his study wall and wondered how things had become so poisonous between them that *now brother watches brother. What would our father have made of that?*

*

Dennis arrived home and gave instructions for the chauffeur to pick Belinda up from the Hilton at 7.30pm. He summoned his Personal Assistant and arranged for dinner to be served at eight. "Lobster I think, Jane, with salad, followed by some fresh fruit." Belinda ate very little, with her place as consort to a globally famous rock star requiring that she needed to look gracefully half-starved at all times.

He relaxed with a drink and at eight-o'clock when his chauffeur George Gibson had still not returned, Dennis Childs rang Pearl. "Pearl. Dennis Childs here. Yes, fine and you? Good. I wonder, has Belinda left yet? I've ordered lobster for dinner and need to let Chef know – critical cooking time, you understand ...." Pearl's voice was audible to Jane Franks who waited to take word to Chef. Jane could hear a clear and slightly irritated voice barking from the handpiece, exactly what she expected to hear from Chef in person if he didn't get the go-ahead to start preparing dinner very soon.

"Reception rang but she didn't show up, Mr Childs. Very irritating, then after a little, I thought – possibly worrying."

"Did you ring Reception?" There was extended talk on the line. "Please don't get touchy, Pearl. I'm quite naturally concerned. You know how impulsive Belinda can be. Perhaps she changed her mind and went off somewhere else, met someone she knew in the lift, perhaps...." He inspected his glass and poured another whisky. "Security? You rang Security and Security are searching the hotel? Is that strictly necessary? She'll be furious if it results in any negative publicity, you realise. Of course you do. Thank you. Perhaps I should come around to the hotel myself."

But he didn't go to the hotel. Jane found the letter, which had been pushed under the front door. It was marked *Urgent* and contained a thick sheet of card weight paper, possibly torn from an autograph book. On one side was Belinda's familiar scrawl, "Blessings from Belinda Jones." A typewritten note was folded neatly inside: *Belinda Jones will have the blessing of continued existence only upon the receipt of fifty million Hong Kong dollars, equally divided between two different currency denominations: US dollars and Pounds Sterling. Further instructions will follow. Do not inform the police.*

Childs picked up the phone and called the Hong Kong Police at Division Central.

"Dennis Childs here. My daughter has been kidnapped."

*

Tuesday 4 December 1979: 8.00am

Chief Superintendent Smythe looked unhappy as he knocked on the door of Suite 359 and Pearl opened the door to him with an equal lack of cheer. She accepted and hung his cap with fastidious care. The flicker of eye contact between them was enough for her to understand that there was no news about Belinda.

"Tea?" He nodded. The offer of tea was inescapable. For Pearl's part it gave her a reason to leave her chair and fuss about with tea bags. The manoeuvre saved her from having to deal with him at close quarters. *Thank God it's cool,* she thought as she dipped the bag in and out of the hot water more than necessary. *At least he's in long trousers and I can't see those hairy legs. But why oh why doesn't the man do something about all of that facial hair?* Chief Superintendent Smythe was a hirsute man. Red hair grew, frantically, from every follicle in his body. It crept out of the top of his stiffly buttoned shirt, beckoned gaily from his ears and tumbled down the side of his face in cheery mutton chop sideburns that just failed to meet the forest that waved in ugly jollity from his nose.

During their occasional dealings over the years Pearl had never managed to overcome her distaste at the sheer volume of hair that the man so airily put on display. She kept the conversation flowing whilst she added extra hot water to her cup. "Odd sort of homecoming, Chief Superintendent. I seem to have seen more of you than anyone else in Hong Kong during the past three days. No news then?"

He shook his head vaguely. He certainly wasn't here to give out information about the ransom note Dennis Childs had received and he walked around the perimeter of the truth with caution. "There is no useful information about her at all, from the time she left the reception area and entered the lift, Miss Green." He said her name awkwardly. She refused to use her title and he knew she had been married briefly a few years back. Did she use her married name? Was she Mrs Sanders?" He decided to ask her. Pearl was taken aback. This was most unlike the Chief Superintendent, as English as they come with all the bells and whistles, including an inborn reluctance to appear interested in other's names unless it was absolutely unavoidable.

"I'm Pearl, Chief Superintendent. I'm too old to be Miss Green, I never invite use of my title although I tolerate it if required and I did not adopt my husband's surname. It's Pearl or *ahem*, I'm afraid."

"Ahem, Pearl, quite so. You will be required to make a formal statement of course. Your arrangement with Mrs Jones, relevant details, times. Can you recall anything of particular note in your conversation with her?"

"It was a most unremarkable conversation. Belinda and I are not close friends, Chief Superintendent. She phoned from the airport at about five, I think. I had been to the hospital to see Drew and then popped into the Foundation offices – and arrived here at about four thirty. I didn't feel like going out again and Belinda only had an hour or so to spare, so she was to come around here for a quick drink and chat on her way home.

"I ordered champagne and caviar. Will mid-day be a satisfactory time for me to come to the station?"

He nodded. There was nothing more to say. He was uncomfortable and gave up on the tea. Pearl looked away from his tired face and turned instead to contemplate the harbour.

The door closed softly.

Tuesday morning and things were a mess.

She needed to talk to Kaz.

*

From his office, Chief Superintendent Smythe saw Derek Wong slam the taxi door and run up the steps, taking them two at a time. Tommy waited. He heard the thump of a fist on the enquiry desk and shouting. "Clerk. I said Clerk. My cousin isn't at the address I was given. Where is your Chief Superintendent?"

*

Marcus ate breakfast in his modest room in the northern wing of The Peninsula Hotel. He almost wished that there had been no vacancies when he found out how steep the tariffs were and today he would have to spend time finding another hotel. The breakfast was described as *Continental* and consisted of two thin, cold pieces of toast, minute silver pots of jam and butter, a pot of tea and a silver jug half full of milk. There was a small bowl containing a half peach, sliced and garnished with three grapes. Before he set to, he took a photograph of the spread. It would amuse Granny Browne no end to see it, compared to what she considered to be a proper American breakfast. He finished eating in no time and looked around the room. It was square, solid and well furnished. He had spent nearly forty-eight hours in a cell much the same size as this, terrified that he could be held for years without being charged, never to be freed, enduring injustice and squalor. But in here, the trappings of everyday life, carpets, lamps, soft furnishings and pictures were soothing, so much so that he could not reproduce the clamour of fear that had come over him in the remand cell. The fears of a *Midnight Express* fate may still be there but it was certainly not invoked by the breakfast tray, the silverware, the solid furniture or the prints on the walls.

He took stock of his situation. He intended to call Pearl Green but before he did anything else he should let the folks at home know he was free, relatively speaking at any rate. It was evening in Florida and he could speak to Derek who would pass on the news to Chief Rolling Thunder and Granny Browne in the morning. Even though it was only eight or nine o'clock the two old people would have long gone to their beds. But there was no reply when he rang Derek's apartment. Next on his list was Pearl but he thought he should chance going to see her in person in case she refused to see him if he phoned first. He had been an unwelcome interruption and he wanted to thank her as well as talk business. He was certain that she had spoken in his favour to the Chief Superintendent, and he wanted her to think well – or in any event, better – of him.

*

Chief Superintendent Smythe referred Derek to Sergeant Thornton and the Sergeant checked the incoming call register. There was nothing from Mr Browne about a change of plan about where he was staying. It certainly hadn't taken him long to fudge his release conditions. He smiled thinly at Derek. "I'll call you at the guesthouse when I have some news, Mr Wong."

"I'm not staying there, Sergeant. The place is a dump. I expect that is what my cousin thought too. I'm at the Mandarin, Room 332."

While Derek was toying with the idea of hanging around the Police HQ to see if Marcus turned up, Kaz was in her apartment, grasping the phone intently as she listened to Pearl's account of events during the past few days. When Pearl paused for breath, Kaz looked hard at one of the potted orchids on her balcony to remind herself that she was still on terra firma.

"Pearl, this is all too much. I'll come to yours. See you about nine-thirty. I have missed out on some fun, haven't I?"

*

James settled in for the flight. With the casual assurance of the much-travelled, he removed his shoes and jacket, donned a pair of soft woollen socks, draped an airline blanket around his shoulders and pulled on a sleeping mask. He reclined the seat back as far it would go and settled in for what he thought of as a thirteen hour state of suspended animation. His body and mind would gradually ignore the range of mechanical sounds that drove the 707 screaming through the atmosphere's upper layers, seemingly drifting over the lights of the great cities below, mapping the nocturnal earthly world with their illuminations.

After they had all endured landing at Kai Tak and people had stretched and in sudden bursts of energy removed luggage and possessions from the overhead storage compartments, he would look at the rubbish tip that the plane had become overnight, the leavings of hundreds of people forced into being cooped up for many hours: their discarded newspapers, magazines, tissues, towels, toys and toiletries. When they disembarked, they would all look as usual: people who do not strew their spent possessions, do not roll empty plastic cups and bottles under other passengers' seats and definitely, oh most definitely, do not steal the soft cream and purple airline blankets as a souvenir of the ordeal of long-haul flight.

*

Pearl was in the bathroom, her hair caught back in a low ponytail which she was trying to smooth into a chignon when the doorbell went. "Come in. Kaz, *why* won't my hair behave and go into a bun?"

"Um, it's Marcus Browne. Look if you are serious about getting *your* hair into a bun you have to put some styling product in it. I know I have to." Pearl turned and it was Saturday morning again and the memory of him standing at the door washed over her as much as the waves had washed over Drew as he lay pinned to the rock shelf. She opened her mouth but promptly closed it again. He was here, it was he who had something to say, not her. "I dropped by for two reasons, Pearl," he said hurriedly, just in case she decided to offer him the hurry-up. "I know you put in a word for me on Saturday and I want to thank you. I feel very grateful for what you did for a complete stranger, and," he held up his hand for her to let him finish, "I want to talk business. Philanthropic business, to be exact."

Her face immediately relaxed. "In that case, you simply must come in, Marcus. Didn't *you* just utter the magic word! Give me one minute. Please sit down. You know where the sitting room is." She felt her hand shake just a little as she pushed yet another pin into the recalcitrant bun. She acknowledged that she had initially been attracted to him but it had fizzled out after everything that went on – so why the shakes? Was it the mere *possibility* of being attracted to a man that frightened her? She walked into the sitting room and smiled at him brightly, but it was her business smile. It was money she could smell in the room, as strongly as if it were lust.

*

Terence Shaw crossed the lobby of the Hong Kong & Shanghai Bank wearing a satisfied smile that went well with his navy-blue suit and pale blue shirt. He looked like a man who had just had good news, as indeed he had. Sol had been prompt with the telegraphic transfer of funds and Terence was now worth seven million dollars Hong Kong and The Celestial Harmony Machinery Factory was on its way to opening for business. But before anything else, he needed to establish what was happening with Marcus Browne and he thought he had that covered too: he simply needed a headband, some loud clothes and possibly a pipe. He intended to go to Police HQ posing as one of Marcus Browne's family who had rushed to Hong Kong full of concern for the well-being of his relative and fellow tribesman, when the news of his arrest became known at home. Sol had mentioned another chap's name when they first talked about who was who on the business side of things in the Seminole community. Terence pulled a notebook from his breast pocket and scanned through it as he paused on the steps of the bank. There it was: Derek Wong. He wondered about the surname – what was the story about an American Indian with a name like Wong?

He would play safe, and most definitely, a black wig would be required.

*

When Tsiu Wah-Heung read the article about the murder of a well-known local businessman at the Hilton Hotel and the apprehension of an American tourist, Wah-Heung quite rightly guessed that Mr Browne was in trouble. He tried to call Mr Shaw but all he had was his business card, which merely confirmed Wah-Heung's suspicion that the number was no more a genuine line of communication to Mr Terence Shaw than his stated occupation of Diplomat was in any way genuine, and after giving the matter further thought he concluded that if their potential target had become involved in something so attention-grabbing as murder, perhaps retreat was the best course. There would always be another opportunity to make money and one had to be careful about how it was accomplished in the shady environments in which both Tsiu Wah Heung and Terence Shaw did business. That's until he saw Mr Shaw, about to leave the bank at the same time as he, looking well pleased with life and so absorbed in reading a small notebook that he walked by without registering Wah-Heung's presence.

Mr Shaw had not contacted him again since last Friday evening when they had baited their first hook to land the American whom Terence was tailing. With Wah's help – or at least, so thought Wah – they were going to relieve the gentleman of a considerable amount of money. Wah-Heung knew how to operate in China and with Mr Browne's confidence in him would come Mr Browne's money. The tricky bit was that Mr Browne appeared to have these things called *reservations* but Mr Shaw seemed confident he could deal with that.

Still obviously pleased with himself, Terry left the bank. Wah-Heung wondered if he should follow him, at a discreet distance of course. It could be interesting to see what Mr Shaw did with his time and he might even find out where he lived. Terence and Wah-Heung only ever exchanged news at a standing appointment at the Half Moon Coffee Shop every second Tuesday at 3pm, but this was not the week they were due to meet. When the taxi he hailed to follow Terence headed deep into Sheung Wan and stopped in Ong Hing Terrace – a small street of dilapidated terraced houses – Tsiu was shocked. He scurried from the taxi and hurried out of sight into Sparrow Street, but not before he saw Terence open the door to Number 6. His erstwhile business colleague lived in one of Hong Kong's poorest districts.

Another taxi approached. The driver got out and went over to a cab parked not far from Number 6 and chatted amiably to the other driver for a moment before the man who had remained in his vehicle pulled away from the stone kerbing. The other man got back into his cab, lit a cigarette and read a newspaper. It was all very curious and Tsiu Wah-Heung wondered what would happen if he tried to hire the taxi; sure enough, without taking his head out of the newspaper, the driver flatly refused the fare, stating that he was waiting on a booking at eleven o'clock. Nodding pleasantly to the man, Wah-Heung returned to the corner of Ong Hing Terrace and Sparrow Street. He too was happy to wait. Terence Shaw was up to something and Wah-Heung intended to find out what it was.

*

Pearl had forgotten about Kaz and frowned when the doorbell rang, faintly irritated. Kaz recognized the look as she opened the door – the withdrawal from the everyday – but Pearl hugged her and drew her into the room, speaking rapidly, introductions mingling with a staccato explanation of Mr Browne's business in Hong Kong and how it could be a whole new direction for the June Bowen Foundation and did Kaz think it was genuine philanthropy given that gambling machines take money from people and maybe from people who are gambling addicts which would be tragic but what about people with more cash than they needed?

"But the end, the end result, Kaz," she said, a bit breathless, "is worth it and will benefit an entire nation, part of whose history is having to rise above almost unbelievable odds to achieve something as simple as the right to live on their traditional lands."

Kaz tried to keep up. She hadn't heard Pearl go off like this for years and even before she met Ben, Pearl was beginning to realise that the June Bowen Foundation, established as a memorial to her mother, had become her life instead of an occupation. Kaz held Pearl at arm's length and told her to slow down. She shook Marcus's hand and smiled at him, remarked that it seemed he had a story of his own to tell, listened carefully, congratulated him on his release, assured him she had seen *Midnight Express* and sympathised with his concerns but also assured him this was Hong Kong, a British Colony with a democratic legal system that was not in the business of locking up hapless tourists who got into scrapes and leaving them to rot in Victoria Jail. But again, she *had* heard of people being banged up in that place for years actually and had also heard something about how poor the conditions were. Maybe he wasn't paranoid at all. She rang room service and ordered a generous morning tea. This discussion clearly needed feeding. He had the brief, the money and the June Bowen Foundation had the contacts and project-management know-how.

*

When morning tea arrived, Pearl rang James Williams. "I *will* go higher James," she said, "But it's my final offer, and if the Thompsons refuse, tell them that I will personally see to their social ruin in Hong Kong. Fifty, and I want an immediate answer, no stringing it out." She hung up. There had been a pause in the conversation as she talked, which was relieved of any awkwardness by Kaz presiding over the tea-tray. She had taken the precaution of ordering sandwiches as well as scones and cakes and it was just as well. Marcus demolished the food in style. Clearly, the man was starving.

Kaz baulked at the figure: – *fifty*? She furrowed her brow at her friend. "Did I just hear what I thought I heard?"

"I'm going to have it, Kazza, and yes, you did and please don't nag."

The conversation was a mystery to Marcus. He finished his fourth sandwich and started on a scone lavished with butter, jam *and* cream. Fifty Hong Kong dollars didn't sound much. Why did Dr Henderson look so concerned? Maybe she meant fifty thousand. The phone rang and Pearl listened, said nothing, but her forehead relaxed and a dimple appeared, like a conjuring trick, on her left cheek. Marcus was glad he was eating because it gave him something else to concentrate on because as she smiled he remembered how she had looked in the restaurant on Friday night. He had thought she was gorgeous then, but this was a different type of smile altogether, she was beautiful. She thanked the caller and replaced the phone.

"There's just one problem." The smile, refusing to budge, had become a grin.

"And that is?" Kaz was accustomed to *this* Pearl.

"I can't move in until Thursday. That means James will have respite here for two nights when I had planned to get him onto moving furniture around straight away." She turned to Marcus. "Mr Browne, I like the sound of your venture, and I think your Turtle Universe has brought luck with you after all. We could all use some. When I first met you on Saturday and you became tangled up in your drama here, Kaz was having a pretty awful time of it too. Her husband had an accident which included being pinned to a rock shelf as the tide came in. A black sea turtle swam by and supported Drew's head above the waterline until he could be freed."

Kaz interjected. "Your project is called 'Turtle Universe'? Are you kidding, Mr Browne?" She was immediately captured.

"Do you know, if that creature hadn't come along Drew would have drowned. I know we aren't supposed to think about animal's actions and instincts in human terms but I can't help but wonder – it has been a week of so many strange events – the body found in this hotel, the mistaken identity of the body, Drew's accident, and then that business last night …."

"Kazzy…." Pearl cut her short, a warning tone in her voice: news of Belinda's disappearance had not been released. "Do you know, Kaz, for someone with your background and education you go on like a minor village sage at times."

Marcus wondered why she was having a shot at her friend. These English! What Dr Henderson was talking about made perfect sense to him. Turtles were revered by his people as symbols of wisdom and long life.

Kaz paid no attention to the criticism. "I get you, Pearl, but in his *China and Japan Myths and Legends*, Donald Mackenzie says that in China the tortoise is attributed with divine qualities, including the power of divination. A gigantic tortoise is said to live in the depths of the ocean. It has one eye situated in its abdomen. Once every three thousand years or so it rises to the surface and turns over on its back so that it can see the sun. So there. As an archaeologist I'm used to finding evidence of cultural practices that have many commonalities across cultures in relation to animals, symbols, rituals. We're all pretty much the same tribe you know, Pearl."

Marcus said, "Well, my tribe believes that when things get rough, the turtle turns over and holds the universe in its shell until things calm down again. Same. Same." He shrugged.

Pearl said caustically, "But different." Clearly she was outranked by the symbolism brigade. The phone rang again and this time it was Dennis Childs. Marcus and Kaz watched Pearl's face draw in; the lines of strain across her forehead returned and her mouth set into an even line. Chief Superintendent Smythe hadn't mentioned any note, but Dennis did now. Even with much of his security staff seconded from his dockyards and on patrol in the grounds of the Childs mansion, he said that another note had turned up.

"This one is more obscure. I think it is about you, Pearl. I haven't contacted the police yet because I want your opinion first. It says: *we seek the rare Green Pearl.* The *G* and the *P* are in capitals. It goes on: *I offer you an eye for an eye ....*"

"And I have to tell you what an effect that creature's action has had on me. I still can't think of it without ...."

"Kazzy, please." Pearl's voice was tense. She almost barked at Dennis Childs, "Well? What are you going to say? Will you accept?" The faint burr of talk on the other end of the line was the only sound in the room.

"The note stipulates that the police must not be informed but it is too late for that, at least in regard to the first one. I telephoned immediately when it arrived last night. My daughter ...."

"For another man's daughter .... Belinda Jones for Pearl Green."

"Of course it may not mean ...."

"But it probably does. Okay Mr Childs. Game on. How are you supposed to reply?"

"I simply leave the Bentley parked outside the house tonight if the answer is yes."

"Don't forget to do it then. We don't want to disappoint your correspondent. Can we leave the police out of this, at least for now?"

"I consider that to be your choice, Pearl, but I do urge you to let them in on this. You should know that I am going to meet the ransom demand for Belinda. I, ah, wondered if you might care to come and stay here. I realise we have never been very comfortable with one another, however, there is full security in place ..."

"Which doesn't seem to be very effective if you have people tripping up your garden path pushing notes under the front door. No, Mr Childs, thank you all the same. I will just get on with my current plans, which include picking up my father from the airport. You'll be able to reach me here at the Hilton until Thursday." She hung up and looked at Kaz, who was looking at her quizzically and said, "Some *strangeness* in the air, Kaz, my friend? Let's go and collect James and think about all of this some more later on."

Marcus looked from one woman to the other. "I don't know what's going on here but I smell trouble. I'm coming with you. If nothing else, we Seminoles can handle a fight."

*

The chap in front of James in the arrivals queue had obviously not done any research about the Hong Kong climate. He also seemed a little geographically confused about his destination. He wore a wickedly vibrant Hawaiian shirt, a straw fedora in a fetching shade of lime green and he even had a lei tastefully composed of frangipani flowers draped around his neck. If he planned to blend into the local scene, he had got it very wrong. James idly wondered if he had a ukulele in his luggage. When the Immigration Official asked him how long he intended to stay in Hong Kong, James was also able to conclude that as an international traveller, the chap's experience was limited:

"What's it to you, buddy?" James rolled his eyes. Judging by the official's expression, this was not going to make James's exit into the baggage claim area any speedier. He was right. In due course and after lengthy questioning, the man was escorted into the no-man's land of the Customs Office by two officials, neither of whom seemed at all moved by a stream of invective which included references to how he had heard the place was full of Try'ards and how obviously true that was.

Under his breath James said, *Triads dear man, the word is Triads, not Try Hards.* James had two passports, a British Citizen's passport and a Home Office Diplomatic Passport, the latter of which he produced just in case the official meant to give his next customer a hard time to assuage the experience he had just had at the hands of the flowered-bedecked number.

"As if", James said to Pearl fifteen minutes later, "the landing isn't bad enough with that crazy airstrip still threatening innocent lives every day, but I have the dashed bad luck to queue up behind someone who thinks they've arrived in a tropical isle full of Try Hards." He kissed her and absently handed her a parcel, "House-warming present." She kissed him back warmly, took the splendidly wrapped parcel and escorted him to a waiting taxi that idled outside Arrivals, complete with Kaz and Marcus Browne.

James was delighted to see Kaz and pumped Marcus's hand enthusiastically. "Didn't expect a welcoming committee, but delighted, absolutely delighted," he said to Marcus, who wondered why the guy should be so effusive to a perfect stranger, and once again decided it was something to do with being English. "Any particular reason for all the fuss?" James said to Pearl.

"This is the Tortoise Universe welcoming committee, Dad." James muttered *lovely* and squeezed into the back seat between Kaz and Pearl. This particular Pearl, sitting beside him and smelling exquisitely of Chanel No.5 and some sort of soap, didn't seem to line up with the Pearl that Peter Benson described to him on Saturday, a withdrawn, hopelessly sad Pearl who was still struggling to come to terms with the death of her husband.

So what the dickens was going on with the woman, or more correctly perhaps, what the dickens was going on?

*

Tsiu Wah Heung kept vigil and the taxi remained parked near Number 6. Why was a cab driver sitting idle in a street like this? Just after one o'clock, Terence Shaw emerged from his house and started walking in Tsiu's direction. Wah Heung looked around – there were no shops to take refuge in, just row after row of the same worn out boarded up shop-houses, outside of which grotesque piles of rubbish had accreted into memorials to the extreme ugliness that extreme squalor can produce. But the squalor proved to be his refuge and he crouched behind a pile of what looked like very old decomposing mattresses. Many eyes gleamed at him from the depths of the mound. Thankfully when Mr Shaw came to the end of Ong Hing Terrace he turned left into Sparrow Street, well away from Tsiu's ratty refuge. Tsiu waited until Terry was well ahead of him before following. After fifteen minutes they reached the busier, more commercial area of Sheung Wan and Wah Heung relaxed until Terence jumped on a tram just as it was pulling away from the stop. Wah Heung summoned a taxi.

The driver made heavy work of the journey, overtaking the ancient and apparently creakingly unstable tram, cutting across in front of it, back in behind it until Wah Heung began to feel quite ill; it was like being on a boat on a choppy sea. He was relieved when the tram stopped opposite the Lane Crawford department store and Terence hopped off and crossed the road. He watched Shaw enter Lane Crawford's and waited outside for more than an hour, carefully monitoring every male customer who exited, but without seeing his quarry again. An outrageously dressed tourist caught his eye and he could not help but stare at the man. He had on a loud red shirt printed with yellow swirls, tight blue jeans and boots with spurs. He wore a red bandana tied around his long black hair and a tapestry hippie bag was slung over one shoulder. Wah Heung wondered what on earth such a superior retail store as Lane Crawford's could possibly stock that would interest such a strangely presented individual.

*

Derek also wandered along Queen's Road, scanning the faces of all who hurried by, all so intent on their business. Where the hell was Marcus? There was no lingering tolerated here. If you wanted to admire the shop windows you had to press your body right up against the glass. The people flow was relentless and there was no subliminal way of understanding any rules about right of way. People wove to the right and left within the crowd, angling however they could to walk faster, get further ahead, be first.

Derek had begun to be a little critical of Marcus, who did not seem to have put a foot right since arriving in Hong Kong and now had been dumb enough to contravene his bail conditions. It was uncharacteristic of the man. That Sergeant had been very grim when he made it clear that contravention of bail conditions under Her Majesty's laws was not viewed lightly and that an Apprehension Order would be put out for Marcus. Derek figured that when the police did apprehend him, he would probably be banged up again. All the same, he hoped it happened quickly. It was the only way that he was likely ever to find him, and as if the past few days hadn't been bad enough, Marcus still had no idea that his grandmother had died and the family would not wait much longer to bury her. Derek felt, keenly, the weight of it all – being in a strange place, caught up in a situation outside the scope of his usual experience, and apparently, to boot, an object of curiosity to the locals.

He was near a big department store – Lane Crawford's – when something far more prosaic occurred to him. He needed some clothes now that it was obvious that he'd be here for more than a day or two and buying them would occupy some time. But as he chose a couple of basic outfits, thoughts about Marcus stuck with him; the way he dressed, his manners – such a refined man – Harvard educated, always so conscious of his appearance. In his role as Corporate Services Manager for the Seminole Council, he invariably turned up to work impeccably dressed in a business suit that would have fitted well into any major financial centre in a big city, and in Hong Kong, he would certainly represent his community's interests in the best possible personal and professional light. He had started out here, the way he no doubt meant to go on, in five star accommodation at the Hilton. The Mandarin, where Derek had booked a room for two nights was also five star. Hong Kong did not lack five star hotels. Which one had his cousin moved to?

He crossed the road, trying to ignore the curious glances that followed him as he walked through the afternoon throngs. People were struck by his rich colouring and general appearance, but they also saw through that to his Asian-ness. It was there in the shape and colour of his eyes, the short thick eyelashes, high cheekbones, his mouth, and particularly his eyebrows, which instead of being heavy were pointedly arched and flipped up at the ends. It was there in the way his hair grew from his hairline, even though it was long and straight and combed straight back in the traditional male Seminole style. Derek's face said loud and clear that somewhere in his lineage a man or a woman of Asian, almost certainly Chinese, origin, had contributed to his gene pool.

The Hong Kong women liked what they saw and many a covert gaze rested on the broad shoulders clad in a worn white linen shirt, Levi jeans and fine grained black leather ankle boots, but whilst Derek acknowledged the attention, his own was taken by an outlandishly dressed character who was leaving the store as he entered. In a trice, the insistent stares he felt shifted from him to the other man.

*

Hua Leung watched the man who had followed Mr Shaw. He was the same man who had asked if he would take a fare. Hua had followed him at a discreet distance and when Mr Shaw jumped onto a tram, was on the spot to pick up the pursuer. He dropped him off near Lane Crawford's and returned on foot, only to see him standing outside the store, apparently intent on reading a newspaper. The two men, observer and observed, both saw the colourfully dressed man bump into another man, and they both had the same realization in the same moment.

The man with the hippie bag was Terence Shaw. Tsiu heard the hurried "Sorry old man," when Shaw grazed shoulders with the other man. He knew that voice well and when he sized up his height and build there was no doubt that he was looking at his colleague, got up in a most spectacular disguise. Wah Heung tried to guess what Mr Shaw could be up to. Was the collision outside the department store an accident, or a set-up? Did the two men exchange something? Had Mr Shaw's sketchy plan to extract money from the tall American Indian man they had tailed to Stormy's Restaurant last Friday night developed further with another tall American Indian man now in his sights?

Keeping the colourful Mr Shaw in view was not difficult, but when he walked calmly up the steep sandstone steps to Police HQ Central Division, Wah Heung refrained from following. He would wait outside instead. Hua Leung, who was now following Mr Shaw as well as the other, unknown man, decided to do the same thing.

CHAPTER SEVEN

Tuesday 4 December 1979: 2.00pm

Drew came out of a deep sleep with a shout and this time the images that had previously blurred and melted as he woke came into the room with him. He was on the rock shelf on Po Pin Chau Island and he could hear Kaz screaming – *shark, Drew, shark* – and he could feel his head being lifted clear of the water as it began to wash into his mouth and nostrils. But there was something else – fear of the strength of whatever it was that pressed against him, fear – of what? Of being tossed and savaged before the rock that pinned his leg caused him to lie helplessly as a thrash of biting jaws lunged into his back and head?

On Sunday, in hospital, with pins and plaster immobilising him as surely as the tumbled rock had done, Drew had struggled to come to grips with it all. He and Kaz spoke in hushed tones about the giant sea turtle that had so mysteriously saved him from drowning during the minutes before Mrs Lam and Kaz reached him. The animal had slipped away as Kaz leapt from the boat, and, standing up to her knees in water, supported him until three men summoned by the cliff walkers sped in their fishing launch from the other side of Sai Kung Peninsula and heaved the giant slab of rock from his leg, fighting against the waves that by then were beginning to surge strongly across the platform of rock that lay below the cliffs of the island.

Kaz was in no doubt: the whole experience was life-changing. She considered that she had witnessed a clear display of altruism from an animal that did not even look after or guard its own young after laying its eggs. Drew agreed that his life had been spared against all the odds that morning and he talked to everyone who visited him of gratitude, mixed with disbelief in his own luck. But in his mind lurked a secret fear of the dark, strong-limbed animal that had saved him. He could still feel the edge of the turtle's carapace digging into his neck, and somewhere in his mind, when he slept, something told him that the shelly hardness would turn into teeth.

Nurse Simmons heard him and came in, concern on her kindly face. "I'm sorry nurse, I yelled out again didn't I? I really will try to behave." She smiled, wiped his forehead, offered him water, checked that his plastered leg was lying straight and re-arranged his pillows. He waited for the panic attack to subside, but it didn't. When, an hour later, during a routine check of each patient's room, Nurse Simmons found him on the floor beside the bed, moaning softly, *No, no, no*, she sent for the Consultant Physician, Dr Cleeve Robinson.

Dr Robinson helped the ward orderlies to get Drew back into bed and ordered x-rays to establish if he had done any further damage to his leg. He drew up the side panels of the bed and clamped them shut, administered a calmative drug and instructed Nurse Simmons to organize a nursing aide to keep watch at Drew's bedside until his wife could be contacted and take over the carer shift. Dr Robinson noted on the chart that the patient seemed to have fallen from bed during sleep and that some restraint was necessary until his condition was more stable. He did not record Drew's mutterings.

Yip Yee Koon listened to Hua Leung's account of his day, nodded occasionally but remained silent. Hua Leung was very excited about the afternoon's events but for Yip, it meant that someone else had to be factored into a situation which initially seemed to be the clear-cut involvement of his brother with this Mr Shaw. However it seemed there was another party involved and Yip could not even guess at the who or why of it.

Hua, who did not know or recognize Mr Tsiu from anywhere other than from his appearance in Ong Hing Terrace, had taken careful note of what he looked like. The description meant nothing to Yip Yee Koon until Hua mentioned – he was apologetic because it was so minor – that the man appeared to have a faint limp, left leg, could have had sore feet, new shoes, something like that. "When Mr Shaw came out of the Police Station...." *Did Mr Yip shudder?* Hua was certain he had.

"Tell me what happened, Hua Leung. Slowly please, and sit down. I will order tea, you need to calm yourself."

"Thank you sir. Mr Shaw ran back to Queen's Road. I saw him pull off his hair – his wig, I beg your pardon – and he also pulled off the bright shirt he wore. He threw all of these things over a wall as he ran. Almost immediately the man who had been following him walked faster and that is when I noticed him limping. A police officer ran down the steps of the police station and the limping man quickly entered a shop. The police officer looked around but by then Mr Shaw was either out of his sight or was unrecognizable. The police officer finally went back into the police station. I was not sure what to do, sir. My job was to follow Mr Shaw so I ignored the other man."

Hua did not mention to his boss that he found the pursuit of Mr Shaw extraordinarily difficult and had since decided that he needed to take some exercise to improve his general fitness. It was only by luck that he picked Mr Shaw up again. Mr Shaw stopped near the front door of the Hilton Hotel where he pretended to be tipsy. There were many people about when he arrived but they all left, quickly. "You know what it is like with drunks, sir, if you look at them they will often start to approach you so everyone at the hotel entrance hurried away without looking at him." Yip Yee Koon had little experience of dealing with drunks but did not doubt Hua's obviously greater expertise in the matter, quite possibly based on Hua's own experiences when he frequented the bars of the Walled City.

It seemed that after the display near the fountain, Mr Shaw walked steadily into the hotel and entered the Gents' toilets near the lobby. Five minutes later a very ordinary looking Terence Shaw, dressed in light grey trousers, white shirt and everyday shoes, emerged, looking unruffled. The backpack had gone as had the boots and jeans. He strolled across the hotel lobby to the street and hailed a cab. Being on foot, Hua Leung lost him at that point. By the time he had retrieved his taxi he thought it best to report what he had seen to Mr Yip.

*

James was booked into a room on Pearl's floor and Kaz, Pearl and Marcus left him to settle in and rest whilst they returned to Pearl's suite. "A drink at six, Dad?" He nodded, a little wearily, Pearl thought, and she booked him a wake-up call for five thirty. James looked his age in his fatigued state and it was something of a shock for Pearl to realise that her father was now in his mid-sixties and still worked as hard as he ever had in a job that was punishingly complex. It was fifteen years since the discovery was made that James was her biological father and she always thought of him as he was when she first met him, but now there were lines around his mouth and eyes, which no longer went away when his expression relaxed. Her father was ageing and Pearl felt unaccountably saddened by the thought.

*

Sergeant Thornton had been in Chief Superintendent Smythe's office for more than half an hour and when he came out was clearly in a very bad mood. Constable Chua was in strife. When questioned, the Constable said that yes he remembered the man who came in earlier in the day, the cousin of Mr Browne. *A Mr Derek Wong*, as he recalled. The Sergeant asked Constable Chua did he not think it strange that a different man, also identifying himself as Derek Wong, should come in later in the day with exactly the same enquiry? The Constable looked puzzled. Sergeant Thornton pressed him: did the Constable not think such an incident suspicious? Two men, of very different appearance, claiming to be Derek Wong?

When Sgt Thornton further enquired – his voice unable or unwilling to conceal an edge of sarcasm – when Constable Chua told the man that Mr Browne had been released, why had he not then thought it odd that the man ran from the station as though a thousand devils were after him? Did Constable Chua not think that the whole event was just the tiniest bit suspicious or if not suspicious, a trifle odd? "Hmm, Constable?"

Chief Superintendent Smythe made a note of the incident on the case file. Someone, for reasons unknown, had impersonated Browne's cousin in order to ascertain Browne's remand status. It certainly was odd. He called the Sergeant back into his office. "No news about Browne yet, Sergeant?"

"No sir. An Apprehension Order has been circulated and Constable Chua is ringing hotels and other guesthouses and so on, but nothing yet."

"One or the other of our Mr Wongs is an imposter, Sergeant. Have Constable Chua give a description of the second bloke to the police artist and circulate it. Let's see if we can find our third American Indian."

"There is one thing, sir. Constable Chua said the chap's accent was different from Mr Browne's and the first Mr Wong's. American, but not, somehow."

"Note that on the incident sheet, Sergeant. If I'd known that Browne was going to cause us this much bother, I'd have kept the bloke banged up for so long he would have thought he was living *Midnight Express*. Now excuse me, Sergeant but I have a kidnapping case to attend to."

*

Chief Superintendent Smythe reviewed the Jones case, as it stood: the desk staff had seen Mrs Jones enter lift Number 7 and that was that. No-one remembered seeing her give anyone in the crowd her autograph and the origin of the heavy card inscribed, "Blessings from Belinda Jones", remained a mystery. There was some disagreement between the staff as to whether anyone else was in the vicinity of the lift when Mrs Jones disappeared. A Junior Receptionist thought she had seen a man near one of the lifts but could offer no description.

Mrs Jones's disappearance took on a more sinister edge after the ransom note arrived. Jane Franks, Dennis Childs's PA, had been coming and going from his office to the kitchen regularly and had spotted the envelope, probably very shortly after its delivery. Pearl Green had stated that Reception had notified her that Belinda was on her way up to see her some short time after five-thirty and that she thought it was about fifteen minutes later, when the champagne and caviar had arrived, that she had begun to wonder why Belinda had not shown up. Before eight o'clock, when Dennis rang her, her irritation at Belinda's non-arrival had turned to worry and she had notified Hotel Security. Dennis was about to come around to the hotel when the note demanding payment for his daughter's safe return was discovered.

The ransom note was being examined. If the heavy card was an autograph that Belinda had inscribed, her prints and others might be on it and might match some of those taken from the lift. Dennis Childs's two private telephone lines were being monitored and from first thing that morning, Police Constable Sally Herron had been put on reception duty at the Childs' empire offices in Central District, where she noted the identity and nature of business of every caller.

Tommy ruminated about the Childs family and the fact that the father and now the daughter had been involved in two major crimes within the past five days, both of which had taken place at the Hilton Hotel and today, two men, both claiming to be Derek Wong, turned up looking for their cousin Mr Browne who was initially implicated in one of the crimes. Which bloke was the real Derek Wong? Tommy's money was on the shrieking one. His musings were cut short by a telephone call. Marcus Browne was on the line. Constable Chua had at least had the presence of mind to remember what *this* matter was about. Full of apologies was Mr Browne. He'd left the guesthouse and booked into the Peninsula Hotel and forgotten that he should have informed Sgt Thornton. When he remembered to do so, just a few minutes earlier, he was put through to Chief Superintendent Smythe instead of the Sergeant.

"I sincerely hope that this hasn't caused a problem, Chief Superintendent."

"Only insofar as the issue of an Apprehension Order and an All Alert Notice to every policeman or woman on foot or in a vehicle on Hong Kong Island and Kowloon Peninsula is problematical, Mr Browne."

"There is a problem."

"There is. Where are you now?"

"I'm with Miss Green and Dr Karen Henderson in room 359 at the Hilton Hotel. We are waiting for Miss Green's father to join us for a drink at six o'clock but I am actually staying at the Peninsula Hotel, sir."

Tommy felt almost jolly when he hung up. Well well, Sir James Gates was in Hong Kong. That invariably meant something else would happen, any minute. All it would take now would be for Yip Yee Koon to voluntarily walk through the doors of Central Division HQ and Tommy would go out immediately and buy tickets home to England for a holiday for Melanie and himself.

Hong Kong was oozing storm clouds.

*

Tony Yip was not a man who worried unnecessarily. Worry clouded the mind and solved little, but on this occasion the policy failed him as the observation of his brother's household revealed Hua Leung's activities and the series of events reported to him by his number one bodyguard, Li, when he returned to the Walled City in the early evening. Most worrying was the behaviour of Mr Shaw. Why did he disguise himself and enter the Hong Kong Police Department, Central Division no less, where the big-wigs of the Department had their offices? He left the building tearing off part of his disguise as he ran, only to be pursued by not one, but two men.

Although his bodyguard did not know Tsiu Wah-Heung, the general description he gave, which included that the man walked with a limp that became more pronounced as he tried to walk faster and faster, dragged the corners of Tony's mouth down and he made a derisive noise. "That is almost certainly Tsiu Wah-Heung. He is a small time crook but he has good connections on the mainland. What happened after Shaw changed clothes?"

"He returned to his home, sir. The other men watching him had gone. I stayed until it was time to report to you."

"Good. I have an appointment with Mr Shaw. He is, no doubt, working on his part of the business we are setting up, although his methods do not seem to be very clear. What of the Yip household?" With the exception of Hua Leung's movements there was nothing to report from the Yip household except the daily movements of the other domestic staff. Mr Yip had not left the house and Mrs Yip was believed only rarely to leave the family mansion. Nor were there any comings or goings of note except for Hua who had been followed back to his room in the Walled City of Kowloon. He stayed there for only a short time before going to his local, The Emperor Inn, where to the bodyguard's best knowledge he was still drinking. He would continue to be followed.

*

James worked hard to keep up with the story that Pearl and Marcus took turns to relate: the drama surrounding the death of Dennis Childs's brother and how it had involved them both in different ways, bewilderingly embroidered by Kaz as she detailed Drew's accident with references to sea-going turtles, sharks, mythological figures and stories of tortoises and turtles and all such manner of life-changing events. Then there were Pearl's negotiations with the Thompsons via James Williams at Robertson & Kovacks. He blanched when she told him the price she had eventually had to pay to regain possession of her old apartment and once again Marcus wondered why her casual reference to *fifty* seemed to produce the same shocked reaction from her father as it had from her friend.

Pearl saved Belinda's kidnapping and the call from Dennis Childs about the second note about *the rare Green Pearl* until last. James exhaled very loudly and announced that he had not had a craving for a cigarette in many years that he could remember but the last half hour had him feeling as though he had only given up yesterday.

"You have informed the police of this last matter, of course?"

"This *will* get you puffing, Dad," said Pearl. "I haven't. I wanted to talk to you first. Oh, and one last thing, Yip Yee Koon phoned and asked me not to leave the hotel until I had heard from him that it was safe to do so."

"All good saints," huffed James, "and yet you picked me up from the airport after a call like that from Yee Koon. Why?"

"Because there was no need to do otherwise. Mr Yip rang back almost immediately and said it was a family concern that had arisen after all and there was nothing for me to worry about."

Both knew Yip better than that.

CHAPTER EIGHT

Wednesday 5 December 1979: 6.00am.

Derek checked out of the Mandarin as news of Belinda's kidnapping hit the morning papers: *Rock Star's Heiress Wife Kidnapped*. It was always only a matter of time until the news leaked, especially after the police cordoned off lift 7 at the hotel. The media was in *game on* mode.

When he woke at five o'clock his first thought of the day was about money – he worked out how much it would cost to stay at the Mandarin for even a week and was shocked. Five star hotels in Hong Kong may be for Marcus but weren't for him and the sooner he checked out, the easier his conscience would be. He had travelled so light that he could easily get around with his hand luggage whilst he looked for somewhere else to stay. Then he'd let the Central Division Police guys know in case Marcus came to his senses and reported in, like he was supposed to.

*

Dennis read the article in the *South China Morning Post's* early edition, an article thin on fact and thick on Belinda's spectacular rise to celebrity-wife stardom. The story would be on the international wires by morning tea and on the BBC Television News by this evening. He put in a call to Belinda's husband, a man with whom he had only ever had the merest contact. He had always thought the man a bit of a clod, particularly when combined with all that rubbish about her being the star's good luck talisman.

It was not an easy conversation. The band was in New York, rehearsing for a concert on Thursday evening and Belinda had to fly out that day in order to make it on time. Bobby, understandably, was beside himself, but as Dennis thought later, it was about himself that he seemed most concerned – what was *he* going to do without his beloved near him at tomorrow night's concert? How was *he* going to cope without her? What could *he* possibly tell the children? And finally, if she turned up today would she be able to make it if Dennis hired a private jet? Dennis had paid particular attention to that suggestion and when mention of the ransom demand came up Bobby seemed to lose a little interest in the conversation.

"Well that's all right then ain't it, Den? You pay this geezer out smartly and she'll be back safe and sound. Have you organised it yet?" Was it mean of Dennis to suggest that perhaps as her husband, Bobby may care to contribute or even pay the entire amount? He would never know because the connection failed and the line went dead. He waited for a call back, but it didn't come.

Dennis read the article again and ordered his car for 10.00am. He had to organise the funds in the currencies demanded and in the three hours until that time he had other things to attend to.

*

James woke refreshed and immediately ordered an Asian breakfast. He considered it one of the great joys of life that when in Hong Kong he could enjoy congee and pork buns for breakfast, washed down with Earl Grey tea, a combination of exquisite subtleness appreciated by very few. Pearl dropped by and again refused to do anything cautionary at all about being under threat of harm but perfectly willing to harm James if he so much as thought of calling the police. "I don't think Dennis Childs has it right, Dad, I don't think this *Green Pearl* stuff is anything to do with me at all," she said. On that point she had been insistent and James had to be content with calling Peter Benson. The two men had a long conversation, not an easy one, but direct and insightful.

Peter was of the opinion that Pearl's mood had lifted simply because her own problems had been side-lined by other events: Drew's accident; being questioned over her role in harbouring a man initially suspected of having committed a crime; speaking up for him, all followed rapidly by the drama surrounding Belinda's disappearance. "She has spent more than three years wandering around, largely in her own company, brooding about things she can't change, James. Now she has been flung back into the unreality of everyday life."

James replied that that might be so, but that he was still puzzled about the contrast between the emotional state that Peter had observed just last Saturday and yesterday when Pearl had greeted him so cheerfully at the airport, with a taxi stuffed with others who made up a sort of welcoming committee. She had talked far into the night about the events of the last few days. He confided in Peter about Pearl buying back her old waterfront home and said that *that* worried him, her motives for it at any rate. There was silence on the line.

"She had to pay a lot for it," said James, irritated at Benson's silence, suspecting in it a criticism about his daughter throwing such a large sum of money at something for herself when there was so much suffering and disease.

"Pearl has contributed more than her share to the alleviation of suffering and disease, James."

James bridled. *Was the man reading his mind now?*

"I'm just a bit surprised at how quickly she managed it, I suppose. If she paid as much as I suspect she has, she will have to sell some of her Hong Kong assets and I hope that will include my former apartment in Upper Albert Road. That will remove some awkwardness between us, and that can only be to the good. Pearl has always felt some guilt about owning a slice of my past, much as she has about employing me, I suspect. It was a complete reversal of our earlier association. I should have ended my career as a respected public servant or academic and been comfortably off in a material sense. I achieved none of that. This will cleanse what is wrong between us in our pasts."

"Do you really believe in all that 'cleansing of your past' stuff, Pete old thing, or is it a by-product of your perhaps having spent too much time in monasteries? Never seems quite the go to me, frankly." Privately James thought it the precinct of raving lunatics but he held silent on that particular view, especially given one particular period in Peter's past when a state of raving lunacy wasn't totally off the menu.

"Whatever. James, shall I see you while you are here?"

"Of course, is there any chance we can eat at Stormy's? I've never managed it," said James "and I could do with some haute chow. 8.30 tonight suit you?" Peter wondered if Pearl had picked up the expression "haute chow" from James or was it vice versa

and for his part Peter really would have preferred something
slightly *less* haute chow, from the food markets perhaps but ....

Wednesday 4 December 1979: morning

Marcus was not offered breakfast. He was offered arrest if he reneged on his release conditions a second time. He left Police Division Central at 8.30am, then checked out of The Peninsula and made his way back to Hong Kong side on the Star Ferry. Pearl, who had flatly refused to think any further about the fact that today she was supposedly to be traded off for Belinda Jones, intended to take him to look at some serviced apartments and he was to meet her at the Hilton at ten. It was the second time he had been back to the hotel since the events of last Saturday, but this morning, he encountered one of the hotel staff, the Ground Floor Manager, Mr Kenneth Ward.

"Lady Green is not in her room at present, sir."

"I'll have a coffee and wait for her."

"You may be more comfortable waiting somewhere else, sir."

"You're telling me I can't wait for Pearl in this hotel, buddy?"

"My job is to protect the hotel's best interests, sir, and frankly, your behaviour in this establishment, followed by your cousin's arrival and bare-faced insistence on sharing the room you had vacated under very questionable circumstances, well, really, this hotel...."

"My cousin? Marcus stepped squarely into Kenneth Ward's personal space and glared at him. "Keep talking. *Well really what*, exactly?"

"This is not the sort of behaviour we encourage at the Hilton."

"Well, really? I hadn't noticed. I have noticed that you seem to encourage the somewhat ad hoc movement of corpses around the Hilton though, in *my* experience. I will wait here for Pearl and if you want me removed, buddy, call the police, they won't mind, they're keen on knowing my whereabouts. And when she turns up, maybe you should ask Pearl, pardon me, Lady Green, to vacate your hotel as she seems to keep such poor company. I left my personal possessions here when I left in such a hurry on Saturday – where is your Lost Property Office? Oh, and another thing … ” Ward glared at him. “I left cash to settle my room bill. I think I may have over-tipped. Where is my account?”

*

Terry left the house sharp on eight and walked for about fifteen minutes before picking up a cab. Hua Leung had moved his observation point from Ong Hing Terrace to Sparrow Street. He followed his quarry on foot and taxi to North Point where Mr Shaw's cab pulled up outside a shabby factory that had a most wonderfully decorative sign announcing that it was "The Perfect Picture Sign Writing Company". Shaw left after a few minutes and Hua Leung dutifully followed him back to Sheung Wan before he telephoned Mr Yip and asked if he, Hua Leung, should go back to The Perfect Picture Sign Writing Company on some pretext, to find out what Mr Shaw's business was there?

It was the first time that Mr Yip had ever congratulated Hua on his work with anything other than polite detachment, whether he had fulfilled his orders or not. Hua glowed with pleasure when Mr Yip thought that was a very fine idea, adding that Hua was to wait at Ong Hing Terrace until Fong or Yee arrived, after which he was to report the result to Mr Yip as soon as possible.

When Hua wandered into The Perfect Picture Sign Writing Company and enquired how much an additional sign would cost written in Chinese script as an addition to the order placed by the *gweipor* earlier, the operators, delighted with the extra business, said they could do the work for an additional HK$450. Hua asked them not to mention this to the *gweipor* when he called back for the English version of the sign – it was intended to be a surprise from his business partner.

Hua wondered if he might get a reward for his initiative and he did. Mr Yip smiled his broad, rare smile. "The Celestial Harmony Machinery Company. I wonder what type of machines could possibly interest my brother? Apart from money-making machines, of course." Hua had never known Mr Yip to make a joke. This was truly a propitious day. "Excellent work, Hua Leung. You have earned a bonus. Now I want you to keep The

Celestial Harmony Machinery Company under surveillance. Call in every day to report.

*

Weng, Tony Yip's second bodyguard, watched Hua Leung come and go from the Yip family mansion and followed him to Beecham Street in Kowloon. Mr Kim in turn followed Weng in the domestic staff's small van used for doing marketing and various other household related work. Hua Leung parked in a lane off Beecham Street, pulled off his blue jacket and replaced it with a heavy black cotton workman's jacket. He strolled back towards the factory.

Mr Kim was not destined to have a good day. Weng waited until Hua Leung took up his position near the factory and then departed. Mr Kim followed until Weng drew up in Dentist Street, where, hurriedly locking his vehicle, he ran across the road and disappeared without hesitation into the Walled City. Mr Kim's new instructions were to keep the man under surveillance and Mr Kim had no option but to follow. He had never been into this place before but had heard many stories about it. Even though he too hurried, by the time he had walked from the daylight of Dentist Street into the opaque, stained-ivory gloom of the main thoroughfare in the northern sector, the bodyguard was nowhere in sight.

Mr Kim walked hesitantly, trying to adjust his eyes to the gloom. The northern access to the old city was the widest thoroughfare and considered the safest entry point. Cobbled with the original paving stones that were laid when the city was built as a fort in the 12th Century, many of the ground floor buildings that abutted the alley were also original, mud brick structures. The whole place was the same colour. It was as though the very air took on the colours of the materials used to build it. An old man sat on a step smoking and he was the same colour as his house and the pathway and the smoke he exhaled was the same colour as his skin and his clothes.

Mr Kim looked up only once. That was enough for him to wonder how the stacked layers of buildings managed to remain upright. There was a maze above him, jutting buildings, flimsy walkways, bamboo scaffolding, poles festooned with washing, but oddly, there was no noise except for the faint soughing of the air, as though when it entered it despaired, knowing it would never escape. Mr Kim stood still. In front of him the yellowed gloom deepened into blackness. He had no torch but he had his instructions. But how was he to obey them in here? Where had the man gone? He looked speculatively at an old man who seemed to be smoking his pipe and asked him if he had seen anyone walk by in the past minute or two but the only response was a soundless, toothless leer.

*

Belinda woke up with the sound of machinery loud in her ears. It was totally dark and when she carefully felt around it seemed that she was lying on a pile of hessian bags on a metal floor. There was metal to the right and left of her, above and behind her. She was in a metal box. She tried to scream but her throat was so tight that she couldn't manage it. A small voice told her that she was breathing, which meant that there was a source of air, but before there was time to even think about fighting off the panic that started to set in, she dropped back into a heavy slumber.

*

Pearl was busy, and due at the Solicitor's office at nine o'clock, popped in on James first to organise a lunch date downtown and also called in at the office to see how everyone was getting on in Drew's absence. Marcus's presence had been required at Division Central overnight as payment for breaking his release conditions. Pearl and he were to meet at the Hilton at ten o'clock before taking him on a tour of some good serviced apartments that she knew of in Causeway Bay. Her inner diary had been reactivated and its insistent little voice wanted to know, rather imperiously, what would happen after all that?

What would happen after all that? Tomorrow she would be back in her own home; there were plans to make for refurbishment of the upper floors that were currently closed up and she would relocate the Bowen Foundation offices to their original home on the ground floor. Life seemed to be taking care of itself since arriving home. The solicitor was to organise the paperwork for the sale of the Upper Albert Road apartment to Peter Benson and she had four other investment apartments scattered around Hong Kong and Kowloon to contract out for sale as well. Her spare time would be occupied for quite a while. Peter did not know of her intention to sell him back his old apartment at a nominal price and that in itself would be a monumental task, convincing him it was the right and proper thing for her to do. Not to mention the Tortoise Universe Project, which just might be the elusive something she had been waiting for, to re-engage her interest in the business of the June Bowen Foundation. Suddenly she seemed to have more to do than seemed reasonable for someone supposedly easing back into mainstream life.

*

At ten o'clock, Fong stirred from reading an article about the wildly successful new television program *Jue dai shuang jiao,* which featured a short interview with one of the cast, Shek Sau, who plays the part of Fa Mo-kuet, to see the door of Number 6, Ong Hing Terrace open. Terence Shaw emerged, holding one suitcase and half lifting, half dragging another one. He saw Fong and called out, "Taxi. Taxi. Driver. Can you help here?" And so it was fortunate that Fong was able to tell Mr Yip that Mr Shaw had moved to an apartment in Caine Road.

Fong received a tip from his passenger and also received an additional bonus in his salary packet that month too because he had the presence of mind to offer to carry one of the gentleman's suitcases up to apartment 12, at 84 Caine Road, a block of well furnished, small serviced apartments.

*

Tony Yip and Weng watched Mr Kim as he walked deeper into the Walled City. "Deal with him," barked Yip and left Weng to his business. Tony Yip intended to send his brother a very strong message not to mess with him. He ran the Wo Luen Shing. He was a bigger man than Yip Yee Koon. Tony had tolerated having his business monitored for the past two days but coming on to his patch and obviously working on instructions from his brother was going too far.

"When you have finished, have the car and the driver returned to my brother's house. Do it after dark. There is no need to leave a message, his return will be clear enough."

*

Late in the morning, Dennis Childs rang Yip Yee Koon. "I have something of a problem, Mr Yip." Yip murmured the merest of *ohs*. "Yes. You know about my daughter I expect?" Yip indicated that he did. Dennis didn't find him a very talkative sort of chap and said, "I am willing to pay a considerable sum of money for her safe return and I have received a demand which the police have encouraged me to ignore. They say it will make things worse for her. But when I telephoned my bank manager to arrange the transfer – I want my daughter back, you understand – he told me that the damned Chief of Police has put a police notification on all of my accounts, including my business accounts – for any withdrawal of funds in excess of one million Hong Kong dollars."

"Ah."

"I need fifty million Hong Kong dollars in equal amounts of British and American currency and I need it today, Mr Yip."

"Yes, I see."

"I knew you would understand. I can meet your terms, of course."

Yip Yee Koon rang James. "Wondered how long it would be before I heard from you, Yip old man. There's something odd going on around the place isn't there?" Had Pearl told Yip he was due to visit, during the conversation she had with him last Saturday? "Pearl let you know I am here for a few days, I expect?"

"Not exactly, James, and yes, I think your description of what is happening in Hong Kong at the present time is more than adequate. Can we talk as a matter of some urgency?"

*

Terry unpacked his suitcases. After living in the house at Sheung Wan, his sense of appreciation for the finer things of life now included the basics of electricity and running water, so lacking in Ong Hing Terrace. He pondered his next move. Successfully moving out of that dreadful slum and acquiring Sol's half a million US dollars was a start, but he had to make the whole venture work. When he thought about how he had come close to stuffing the whole thing up with his crazy scheme to establish Marcus Browne's whereabouts, his stomach flinched in protest. The last thing he had expected when he walked into the Police HQ yesterday and identified himself as a relative of Marcus Browne was to learn that Marcus's real cousin, Derek Wong, had already beaten him to it. The enquiry desk officer must still be scratching his head. After being told that he had already been informed as to his cousin's whereabouts in reply to his *previous* enquiry about Marcus Browne's remand status, Terry ran from the station in sheer panic.

The whole incident had been potentially disastrous and worse, he was no closer to setting up Browne. He was due to meet Tony Yip at Carlo's Bar this afternoon to push the next stage of the operation along – which meant handing over three million so that Yip could come up with a working operation sufficiently convincing to persuade Browne to sign a contract.

Terry showered, relishing the torrent of hot water. Why had another member of the Seminole Tribe come to Hong Kong? With two of them around, his position was much more vulnerable – would he also have to convince Browne's cousin that his proposal was sound? What if he failed? Tony Yip would have a good slice of his ready cash which he would never recoup and that would put Sol off-side. The only cheery thing in the entire situation was that no-one knew where he was and he had just over 500,000 US dollars, a nice little stake if he decided to do nothing at all.

He towelled himself dry, trying to decide if it was all worth it. Sol and he may be family but he was one tough customer and would not hesitate to come looking for him if he became suspicious that Terry had cheated him. It had been a gift of an idea but failing to track down Marcus Browne surely heralded the end of it. The best bet was to keep the cash, come up with another scam or alternatively get out of Hong Kong and start again somewhere else with Sol's money. Regrettably, The Celestial Happiness Machinery Company seemed destined to remain in the celestial spheres.

He combed his hair and smoothed his moustache into place. What was he to do about Tony Yip? Terry did not dare stand him up. He would make his apologies and take him somewhere first rate for dinner – Stormy's would impress – by way of compensation. Perhaps there was a possibility of coming up with some other joint venture, if Terry could keep their relations cordial enough.

*

Mr Kim's death was very fast. The rush of fear when he felt an arm reach out of the darkness and seize him by the throat, was nothing worse than his mind had told him to expect. A cloth infused with a strong narcotic was thrust into his face. Like so many before him in this quiet and dangerous place, Mr Kim slipped to the ground, strangled whilst unconscious and without so much as a single sensation about the cold finality of his life.

Wednesday 5th December, 1979: 2.30 pm

The conversations of hundreds of people was a tribal roar; the rattling of glasses, plates, and trolleys continued apace in the *yum cha* palace and the demand for service from a long snaking queue of hungry customers was unabated. The waitresses were tired and it showed as they bent to fetch ever more dim sum stuffed baskets from the lower shelves of their trolleys. The one who spoke sharply to James did not get much of a look-in from Yip Yee Koon when she said, "You want *another* custard tart? I think you have had enough, sir."

"No," said James, "I don't want *another* custard tart. Make it *two*, please." Yip regarded the young woman, his mouth a thin line, eyes hard. He said one or two words to her in Cantonese. She bit her lip and smoothed the food-spotted tablecloth in what James assumed to be a gesture of apology. She would not leave her shift without reprimand or even dismissal and James was relieved that she did not notice Yip motion the maître d' over to their table where he spoke with him quietly.

Yip owned the restaurant.

James took up the thread of their conversation. "I must say that you astonish me, old boy. This Terence Shaw chap, perspicacious of you at the very least to discover that he's living in Albert Ho's old place! Must be a desperate sort of fellow, wouldn't you say?" James munched on the exquisite dual-textured pastry of a custard tart, and reflected. He had heard the name Shaw somewhere else, recently. Bloke certainly must be strapped for cash – the only reason anyone would live in a murder house would have to be for cheap rent and if the chap was broke as hell, setting up a scam might be exactly why he was in Hong Kong. James thought about Marcus's experience at Stormy's Restaurant and frowned, feeling niggled. The other time when the name had come up – *What the damnation was the context?*

"The business with the disguise at the police station – what do you make of that Yee Koon?" Yip shrugged, between spooning sauce over a small dish of marinated pork. "I could ask Tommy Smythe I suppose. There's something else I want to run by him."

"If you do, please do not expect me to accompany you, James. You know how I feel about the police, and particularly about Chief Superintendent Smythe."

"Wouldn't dream of it old man. And then to top all this off, Dennis Childs has approached *you* for a loan? His wealth is beyond calculation, surely? He must have as many spare change bowls dotted around his mansion as you..." Yip did not smile. He was familiar with his friend's banter but his friend was not so familiar with Mrs Yip. Mrs Yip would never tolerate the presence of bowls of coins dotted around her house. All money went into the bank in the Yip household, except for the occasions when Yip cellared some, much like his vintage whisky and wine collections.

"It has been a very strange week. Since the return of your daughter to Hong Kong, there does not seem to have been a peaceful moment. How do you say it, James? *Is there something untoward in the water this week?* There is also the matter of her friend, Mrs Jones." He made a gentle downward gesture with one slim hand which told James very clearly that he was not to interrupt. "I acknowledge, it is Mrs Jones who has been kidnapped, but it happened when she was on her way to meet with your daughter. Do you think Pearl is quite safe at the Hilton?"

James had to admit that because of the second note – the eye for an eye thing – he had also considered that Belinda's kidnapping was a blind of some sort, perhaps an interim strategy for someone whose primary interest was Pearl – but he said nothing. No need to. Yip seemed to know it all already. There was extra security presence at the Hilton at present but more as a salve for guests who might quite rightly resent paying top dollar to stay at a hotel which so far this week had produced a murder victim on Saturday followed by a kidnapping on Monday evening. Would there be another Mrs Entwhistle incident, with bodies tumbling from cupboards and only narrowly avoiding falling on piles of pristine shopping?

"Doesn't bear thinking about." Yip was accustomed to James's habit of making comments which were unrelated to the conversation and he ignored him, finished eating, wiped his hands with a hot towel, called for the bill and dismissed the move James made for his wallet with a *please James, my staff would be appalled if I permitted a guest to pay.*

"Should I lend this money to Dennis Childs, James?" Yip signed the chit and looked squarely at James, who, looking rather astonished, was wondering, whilst trying to avoid counting on his fingers the others he was familiar with, just how many restaurants Yip owned. "I can afford to do so and Mr Childs will hardly fail to repay the debt, but I have to keep in mind that it is to satisfy a ransom demand for the return of his daughter, which the police have advised him against doing. Do I support the determination of a father to preserve his daughter's life or do I respect the wishes of the law? James?"

"I'm no moral philosopher Yee Koon, but if I were in Dennis Childs's position this morning, I dare say that I would do exactly the same thing. As you say, a man of his wealth is hardly likely to renege on the debt. He'll have it settled by the time he can organise an international transfer into a new account or do something equally spry in the money department. I think I *will* pay Tommy Smythe a visit. I may get a handle on this Shaw chap and he may confide something to me about the Belinda Jones case that will help you make a decision about the loan."

Yip again allowed himself a small shudder. He had no wish to re-open his acquaintance with the Chief Superintendent or even appear in the man's mind if he could possibly avoid it. James saw the gesture and said, "I won't mention your potential involvement in the matter, of course. I have no dilemma with moral philosophy there – nothing's happened, yet."

Yip dipped his head towards James confidentially. "As ever, my dear friend, your deliberations are very well balanced. I shall be at home if you wish to telephone me later this afternoon. Good luck. Please give my regards to Pearl." They shook hands and parted, James for Central Division HQ Police Station and Yip for home and perhaps the indulgence of another cup of jasmine tea with Mrs Yip, if she was of a mind to share her afternoon treat with him – but not until he organised Mr Child's loan.

*

The air was chilly outside when James left the hotted-up drama of the yum cha palace and stepped into a taxi cab. But the trip was in vain. Chief Superintendent Smythe was in a meeting with the Chief of Police and would be unavailable all afternoon. There was nothing more James could do except catch up on some sleep. During lunch he had persuaded himself that he should break confidence with Pearl and spill all about the new note that Childs had received to the Chief Superintendent, so perhaps it was better that Smythe wasn't available. Pearl would have had a chunk of him if she had found out that he had welshed on her.

*

By five o'clock the usual line-up of arty types and young professionals were filling Carlo's Bar. The music was mostly 1960s folk and rhythm and blues remixes – wallpaper music that went down well with the oddly assorted crowd. Tony Yip had not been to Carlo's before. It was well outside his home turf and he felt a little ill at ease, but in truth he looked like any other prosperous Hong Kong businessman out for a few drinks after a hard day making money. That was exactly how Tony's day had been, although his business would be highly illegal if conducted in this part of Hong Kong, whilst in the Walled City it had been just another day where business sometimes included murder.

Mr Shaw arrived at ten past five. "Sorry I'm late, Mr Yip. Traffic."

"Hong Kong is little else *but* traffic, Mr Shaw. One allows for it. Whisky?" Terry nodded, worried that his unpunctuality had already caused him to fall from favour. He smiled nervously as Tony pushed a glass into his hand. "Well Mr Shaw? Have you made any progress?" This was the moment that would determine his future in Hong Kong, or if indeed he had a future in Hong Kong. He drank a mouthful of the strong, malty spirit. Was he in or out? Up or down?

He decided to tell the truth. "I haven't been able to contact my client."

"Is he in jail?"

Terry made a line of his mouth. "No, but he's gone to earth. I do apologise Mr Yip, but I think The Celestial Harmony Machinery Company is not going to get off the ground." He looked at the floor.

"Mr Shaw." Terry looked at Yip. "This is indeed unfortunate but perhaps you have rushed to this decision. Why don't you simply take more time to find your *client*. It is a sound idea. We can make a lot of money. I can expand my operational boundaries and you can become a wealthy manufacturer of non-existent goods."

Tony laughed, and although it could not be said to be a pleasant laugh, Terry felt immensely relieved. "Perhaps you are right. Could we discuss it some more? – I was planning to invite you to dinner by way of an apology, at Stormy's. Perhaps we may devise another project together, but, if you are willing to wait... How long will you wait?" – Tony held up two fingers. – "Two weeks?" Tony nodded. Terry said, "That would indeed be a great help. Will you be my guest tonight? Tony had heard of Stormy's and because his mood was expansive, because today he had given his brother a lesson he would not forget, why not celebrate? Besides, Tony needed change in his future prospects almost as much as Terence Shaw needed money.

"Very well, Mr Shaw. Eight o'clock." Terry was about to lean across the table and offer Tony Yip his hand when he saw a man of very particular appearance enter the bar: a tall man with brown skin, overlain with the same winter rose tones shared by Mr Browne and Sol. This man was almost certainly Browne's cousin. Yip avoided the offered handshake and left. He had not failed to notice that Shaw's attention had been taken by the exotic features of the newcomer and he nodded his second bodyguard over to his waiting car. "Weng. Follow Mr Shaw."

*

It was dark at five thirty when Mrs Yip's personal maid Polly stepped outside the gate of the Yip family mansion. It was Polly's night off. She had a taxi booked and intended to accompany her friend Melody Pang to see the newly released movie *Meteor*, starring Mr Sean Connery and Miss Natalie Wood. Polly particularly admired Mr Connery, but Melody warned Polly to be prepared to be very frightened by the film. Melody had already seen it once and said that the scenes showing Hong Kong being devastated by a tsunami were very confronting.

Polly shivered a little in the cold, despite being well wrapped up. She saw the headlights of a car enter the quiet cul-de-sac where the Yips lived, her taxi no doubt. But there were two cars and one was Mr Yip's brand new super luxurious black Ford Fairlane. Polly frowned. But surely Mr Yip was at home? Polly drew back into the shadow of the ornate front gate. The car came to a halt and a man she did not know got out. A second car, possibly a European model, pulled into the kerb and the driver of the Fairlane jumped into the passenger seat. Without even coming to a full halt, the second car swung around and was gone in a second.

Another set of headlights appeared. Polly was discomfited. Perhaps she should inform Mr Kim that Mr Yip's car had been left parked outside by a stranger. The second car was her taxi and she motioned to the driver to stop and spoke to him rapidly. "I will be back in two minutes. There is something I forgot to tell my employer. Can you wait?" The cabbie nodded. Of course he could wait. He turned the meter on.

Polly couldn't find Mr Kim. She thought of knocking on the door of Mr Yip's study but was too intimidated to do so. Instead, she knocked on the door of Mrs Yip's personal sitting room and reported what she had seen to her mistress. "Thank you Polly, I will deal with this. Now go and enjoy your evening." Polly blushed and withdrew from the room and, remembering that the taxi meter would be ticking away, trotted through the large house to the gate. The taxi driver had turned off the vehicle's lights but even in the dark she could see that his face was very pale. There was panic in his voice:

"That car. I got out to take a look at it. There is a man lying across the back seat. I think he is dead." They looked at one another a little wildly. Did he expect her to look into the car? She could not do such a thing.

"Wait here," she said. "I will fetch my master's manservant." But Mr Kim still could not be found and Polly had no choice but to knock on the door of Mr Yip's study and tell him what the taxi driver had seen. Mr Yip was kind, urged her to compose herself and asked Mrs Yip to give her water. He calmly walked outside and nodded his head grimly when he recognised the man in the back of his car. It was indeed Mr Kim.

He asked the taxi driver to wait in the kitchen where some tea would be prepared for him. "This is a matter for the Hong Kong Police, you understand. They will need to interview you," said Yip to the taxi driver. The man looked frightened at the mention of the police and Yip quietly empathised. "Do not worry, your role in this matter is above reproach, but this man has not died naturally."

Yip's duty was clear. He had to ring the Central Division of the Hong Kong Police Service. He did so and followed up with a call to James at the Hilton. When there was no reply he rang Pearl. "Pearl, Yip Yee Koon here. I wondered if, by any chance, James is with you?"

"Mr Yip. Not a family matter this time I gather?" The unintended irony in her words was not lost on Yip and despite the circumstances he permitted himself a very small smile. "You and my father are up to something aren't you? Dad isn't here – really. He's dining with Peter Benson at Stormy's at eight thirty, but where he is now, I've no idea. Probably having a few drinks somewhere. I'm moving back into my old apartment tomorrow and James is going to stay on for an extra week and help me get organised. I rather imagine he needs a drink, there's a lot to do and he keeps pleading jet lag, which frankly I doubt. Mr Yip? Are you going to tell me what is going on?"

"Pearl, I will talk to you at another time. The front door bell has just rung. It will be the police."

*

Dennis Childs left the house carrying a small suitcase and a briefcase which accommodated fifty million dollars in British pounds and US dollars. The delivery had arrived promptly at four o'clock by courier, courtesy of Yip Enterprises, with both the briefcase and its contents crated up in a wooden box. The Bentley was still parked in the street where it had been since the previous evening, and this morning the instructions about how and where to deliver the money for Belinda's release had arrived. He was careful to tell no-one of his movements, least of all his chauffeur, who would find it unusual if his boss did not use the Bentley.

He booked a cab and it arrived as he stepped through the front gate of the house. He briefly caught a glimpse of Jane watching him from the living room window with an expression of open curiosity on her lovely face. For her part, Jane found it unusual for her boss to leave the house without telling her of his movements and it was the second time this week that he had done so. She shrugged. It was a small point, and there was correspondence and the dinner menu to sort out.

Dennis kept the bags with him. "Hong Kong Yacht Club, please driver," and sighed as he hefted the suitcase into the back seat of the taxi. There was a lot to think about. Pearl's part in this, for instance. Dennis Childs had always had a type of grudging respect for Pearl which he had demonstrated in very material ways, whereas Belinda, well, Belinda was very different. Dennis Childs had raised Belinda. He smiled, a small smile, of content.

*

It was seven o'clock and Pearl sat at the window and watched the harbour spangle itself with lights, slipping with easy familiarity into its nocturnal routine. She was uneasy. The police, Mr Yip had said. Knocking at his front door! He sounded quite calm about it, much more so than the night Pearl remembered so clearly, at even this distance of years, when James despatched Yip to fetch the Water Police to Sharp Island to remove the body of the man who had murdered her mother. The memories of the events of that night were still strong and Pearl could even remember how the colour had drained from Yip's elegant features at the suggestion he should fetch the law.

James, for his part, reckoned that he still dined out on the story of how he had persuaded Yip to accompany him to Central Police HQ when the story surrounding the killings in a case dubbed by the press as the *Red Bird Summer Killings* began to unravel and Yip's part in stopping two death contracts issued on Pearl and Kaz became known. The contracts were issued from within the Walled City by the former Archaeological Museum Director Albert Ho during a psychotic episode that ended his own life. Yip had succeeded in stopping the contracts and was later interviewed at Division HQ. The case never went to court but it almost had and the lead-up was the most publicly visible that the mysterious Yip Yee Koon had ever been. The press had a field day photographing him going about his business. Since those times, he had become even less visible and ran his business empire from home, an empire which never lost the faint odour of corruption. Even so, Yip Yee Koon remained one of Hong Kong's most powerful men.

Pearl addressed herself to a passing ocean-going yacht. "I don't like this mood. I think I'll join Dad and Peter at Stormy's. They'll find a spare place for me. Dad's not getting away with this latest Mr Yip mystery." She hummed as she drifted about the room. Now, what to wear?

*

Belinda, blindfolded, was hefted from her prison, led to a toilet and without reference to anything that resembled modesty, was informed that she would be watched and was not to try anything tricky. She was given some water and her hands and face were sponged. She was then told to open her mouth. She did so, expecting something repulsive to happen. It did. Cold custard. Disgusting, thick, sweet and no doubt yellow. Cold custard. She choked and spat out as much as she could. "You bastards," was all she managed to scream before her mouth was bound and she was pushed back into her cell or box or whatever it was that she had occupied since – since when? She had lost touch with time but had been taken to the toilet three times which meant it could be Wednesday or even Thursday. She must have been drugged, because within half an hour of drinking the water they gave her – simply because she had to – she would lapse back into a state of half-sleep.

She begged, each time before her mouth was bound again, "What day is it? What day is it?" But no-one spoke beyond issuing monosyllabic orders. Then the narcotic would kick in and she would slip away. But on this occasion, her head seemed clearer for longer. The toilet. Whoever took her there, and she was sure it was two men, pushed her head down as she went through the door, which meant there were space constraints, which could mean that she was being held on a boat....

*

Yip Yee Koon saw Chief Superintendent Smythe to the door. Mr Kim's body had been removed, the car impounded and Polly and the taxi driver were on their way to Division HQ to make statements. Yip wondered, when his turn came to make a statement, should he reveal knowledge of Mr Kim's movements? He did not know where the day's events had led his manservant, although he had his suspicions. He decided simply to tell the truth. He had no idea why his house was being watched, but it was, and he had put his own measures in place. Beyond that, he was unable to shed any light on where Mr Kim had met his end.

Chief Superintendent Smythe was not surprised that the man he considered one of Hong Kong's major criminal forces was so clearly up to some sort of covert rubbish, and it was some time afterwards, back in his office, that he realised that contempt for Yip had clouded his thinking. This event could be the beginning of a triad struggle. But Tommy Smythe was wrong. It was the beginning of internecine warfare.

Yip was restless and paced his study. Mrs Yip heard the unfamiliar sound coming from her husband's private sanctuary, knocked on the door and offered jasmine tea. "My dear, I think more than jasmine tea is required." Whisky was also refused. "I need to see James. He is dining at Stormy's Restaurant this evening. I am sure he will forgive a brief intrusion." He almost asked Mrs Yip to summon Mr Kim. "Will you – no, of course not – I will take a taxi, I wish Mr Lam to remain here. Do not wait for me my dear, I may be some time."

*

Marcus looked around the softly-lit, smartly-furnished apartment that Pearl had found for him, taking in its modern lines with satisfaction. He was hungry and needed to find somewhere to have dinner but discarded almost immediately the fleeting thought that it would be pleasant to eat out with Pearl. She was charming and clever but her head was a million miles away, that much was clear. For all that, Marcus still felt confident that he was on a winner with his idea of a joint collaboration. He had seen enthusiasm for it growing in her eyes and he had watched her friend Kaz's face gradually relax and then beam with pleasure as she watched Pearl *going off,* as she put it.

This morning when they had met, Pearl had told him bluntly – which he realised was a warning that they were brushing a delicate subject – that her absence from Hong Kong for so long was due in part to a lack of direction with her work but now she hoped that their shared endeavour might be the way for getting that direction back. They had even had some serious discussion about how it would work at a day to day level. She had initiated dozens of projects over the years and once she realised that the only real difference between them and the Seminole's venture was that a material product was to produce a philanthropic result, she felt happier with the ethical side of it.

Before going out for a walk and to check out the local eateries, he called Sergeant Thornton to leave his contact number, but the Sergeant was off duty. He left a message for the Sergeant. He could do without spending another night banged up in a remand cell.

*

Derek's day had its successes too but they came late and after a frustrating start. If he had remained at the Mandarin for a little longer, taken his time and had some breakfast or read the morning papers or watched the news, he would have been there when Marcus rang. But Derek checked out and hit the streets of Hong Kong early, only to learn Shopping Lesson No. 1: Nothing happens until at least 10.00am.

He stopped for coffee and breakfast, bought a newspaper and forced himself to concentrate on the business section. There were plenty of hotels available and he found a telephone box and called a few, but they were either right out of budget or the hoteliers didn't speak English. He wondered if seeking the advice of a travel agent was the answer but as the day wore on and he rejected suggestion after suggestion of accommodation from several agencies, Derek began to weary of the task, and diverted himself by buying some more clothes from Lane Crawford's Store, where he also acquired a small suitcase.

As the afternoon drew in he became tired and hungry. He still had nowhere to stay and the suitcase was getting heavier. He decided to try one more agency but that yielded nothing of any assistance either and when he saw Carlo's Bar flashing a flattering turquoise and flamingo pink neon invitation to enter, Derek was beckoned over the threshold with the promise of something to drink and eat. The bar was pleasantly appointed and the buzz was friendly. He ordered a Coke and sank gratefully into a soft leather banquette. He re-ordered, a whisky and soda this time, something he could nurse. The bar started filling with people and the music shifted between folk and blues – Otis Redding's "Sitting on the Dock of the Bay" was playing at the moment. The song made him feel homeless, just like poor old Otis. Just then a voice spoke to him.

"I say, mind if I share your spot there?" Derek nodded his head, said something like "Sure thing, man," and continued listening to the music as Terence Shaw sat down beside him. *It had to be one of the best songs ever written.*

Terry glanced at the suitcase. "Looking for somewhere to stay, by any chance?"

"I am," said Derek warily. "But the better hotels are too expensive and the cheaper ones are just that. But as I may be here for a week I think I'll have to go back to where I stayed last night and just wear the cost of it."

"No no no, that's not at all necessary old boy, plenty of good guesthouses on Hong Kong side, you just need a few names and addresses. Give me a couple of minutes and I'll jot a few suggestions down for you. You can grab a taxi and do the rounds, plenty of time, night's young. Terence Shaw's the name, by the way. Businessman. Local manufacturer."

"What sort of manufacturing are you engaged in, Mr Shaw?"

"Machinery. Call me Terry. I build machinery to spec, old boy. Own a little set-up called The Celestial Harmony Machinery Company and take on tailor-made jobs for clients with specific design needs. What brings you to Hong Kong?"

"A project. A particular project. I'm Derek Wong, Finance Director for the Seminole Council of Florida." Terry handed over a sheet of notepaper with six addresses on it, all around Kennedy and Robinson Roads. He shook Derek's hand. Terry made quite sure he didn't shake too enthusiastically. He felt that his luck had turned at last.

"Good luck with those. Only two of them are rooms to let. The others are apartments and I looked over all of them recently. They are reasonably priced, clean, fully fitted out and a much better deal than a hotel. You're bound to find one with a vacancy but you probably should get going if you are to organise yourself tonight. My card. If your particular project is anything to do with machinery, I'm your bloke. My premises are currently going through a re-fit. We're setting up for a special run of gambling machines for one of the Macau casinos. We're not fully operational yet but will be by this time next week. My client has a particular theme in mind which I am to finesse. You could get an idea of how we work if you care to visit."

Terry hesitated. Had he gone too far, too fast? But dare he risk losing the chap? He was hard to read with that impossibly handsome face. "If you are really fed up, you are welcome to come back to my place. I'll ask the Building Manager if there's another apartment available. They are a good price – I'm not a chap to spend money on fripperies either – and if there isn't one available, you can sleep on my couch tonight and set off and look at the other places tomorrow. What do you say? I'm going out to dinner, won't be back until late, won't be a bother to you at all."

*

The card Terry handed to him confidently stated that Derek was talking with Terence Shaw, owner and operator of Shaw's Manufacturing Pty Ltd., trading as The Celestial Harmony Machinery Company, with an address somewhere in Kowloon. What was he to say? Derek remembered the suggestion that Mr Childs had made to him yesterday when they met at the police station, to ring him if he had problems. He had problems but this man had just dropped into his life and solved the immediate ones – was that too much like good luck? Was it wise to accept an offer from a stranger in a strange environment? After all, he was hardly in the Everglades here … He looked at Terry carefully but there seemed little odd or suspicious about him. He looked just a regular guy.

"I'm very grateful to you Terry. We could also have more to discuss than my accommodation. When do you plan on leaving here?"

"Now, if you're ready. May as well get you settled in before I go out again."

"Just one thing. I need to phone the police."

Terry didn't miss a beat. "Make the call from my flat, dear chap. Not in any strife, are you? Don't want the police swarming around my place, good chaps though they are, hah?"

"No, I'm not in strife, but my cousin had a problem of sorts. Shall we go?" Terry tried hard to keep his smile casual but he felt fluttery, that familiar old shaky ground feeling. When they reached his apartment he excused himself whilst Derek made his call. The building manager had Apartment Seven available and by eight o'clock Derek was sitting on a very comfortable couch in a neat one-bedroom apartment downstairs from Mr Shaw's place and considering going out for a bite to eat.

He rang the police again to see if Marcus had been in touch but this time, the desk clerk fobbed him off with the statement that such information could not be given over the phone. He decided to leave it until morning, thinking that he might as well have stayed in the remand cell at Central Police HQ himself as he seemed to have spent most of his time in Hong Kong doing nothing but speak to the police. He leant back in the armchair and tried to relax. Today had yielded a worthwhile result after all. He had an appointment with Terry Shaw tomorrow and Shaw was going to put in some work before then on setting out the framework of a business plan for the Tortoise Universe Project.

*

It is a journey of just over 800 kilometres from Hong Kong to Taipei, where Dennis was bound in the ocean-going yacht he had hired to organise Belinda's payout. The money was to be deposited in an account set up in his name at the Bank of Taiwan. Once the kidnappers confirmed that he had deposited the money, Belinda would be released, which just left the matter of Pearl Green to deal with. He had tried to speak to her several times during the day and she had finally called back with the assurance that she was fine and that either her father or a friend was with her at every moment. At the time in fact, Pearl was quite alone in her hotel suite and she lied glibly and without apparent conscience. "I think the second demand was a bluff of some sort, Mr Childs," she had said to him. "No doubt it seemed like a good idea to someone at the time."

*

Dennis ate his solitary meal on board and drank a last glass of whisky. He had left Jane a note letting her know that he had to make an unexpected journey. She would have found it by now. Things were going to run differently in the Childs household when he got back. His employees were a complacent lot and Dennis wanted fresh faces to run the show. He wanted to re-invent his empire. Jane and the other staff would receive generous severance payouts upon his return, but they had to go.

He wondered what Belinda would do after she was released. No doubt her first priority would be to get to Smut's concert in

New York. Would she make it? Dennis found that he didn't much care. He hadn't seen her for years until she announced that she was turning up this week and apparently it required something as extreme as his supposed death before he drew a visit from her. She would not be his concern after this was over. He summoned the yacht's Skipper. "I'll be back two hours after we dock in the morning. Make sure you are ready for the return journey. I want to be back in Hong Kong by tomorrow evening. Understood?" The skipper understood his role as well as he understood his debts to Mr Childs. He nodded courteously and left the cabin.

*

James and Peter Benson finished their drinks at Sunny's Bar and climbed the steep steps to Stormy's at precisely half past eight. The restaurant was crowded with diners occupying a jumble of square, dark wooden tables and hard, rack-backed chairs. The furniture, combined with bare, neutral walls, gave a stark air to the space, unlike most Asian restaurants that set out to please the eye as well as the stomach. Stormy's was only about food.

"I'm looking forward to this" said James and actually rubbed his hands together. On the one other occasion that he had been to Stormy's, other events had banished any thought of eating and James had missed out on an experience that no-one in Hong Kong who appreciated the very best in modern Chinese food would ever deny themselves.

"Can't think why I've never managed it," he said to Peter as they waited to be seated. They were shown to their table. Peter knew that other diners would soon be seated with them which meant that their conversation either needed to be to the point before that happened, or they would need to conduct it allusively. Peter was not sure if he could conduct an allusive conversation with James Gates. "James, this place will be roaring by nine o'clock. Whatever it is we have to discuss, we should do so now, whilst we have some privacy."

James smiled benignly at his former colleague. "Peter, we both know what my concerns are regarding Pearl, but when I arrived yesterday and bearing in mind our conversation on

Saturday, I was met by a woman more resembling the old Pearl…."

"You have my interpretation of that."

"And that's why I'm worried. If she was as low as you say she was on Saturday, if her only plan was to go off hare-brained and buy back her old apartment – *for God's sake* – why did she so cheerfully pick me up from the airport three days later, stuff me into a taxi-cab with Karen and a lovely chap called Marcus Browne and proceed to reel off a long story of dodgy events that appear to have been happening?"

"It's obvious, James. Pearl is in danger."

*

Tony Yip was not happy as he laboured up the steep staircase into Stormy's. The restaurant entrance was no more than a doorway between a bar and a shoe repair shop in a part of Kowloon where Tony had no influence. He felt even more uneasy as he stood in the tiny reception area and waited to be seated. There was only one way in and one way out. He insisted on being put at a table where he could at least see the door, and by the time Terence Shaw arrived five minutes later, another diner had already been seated beside him.

Tony was not a master of small talk and when the elderly tourist smiled at him and wished him a very good evening, he glowered at her. She failed to take the hint and gabbled at him about how her son-in-law had discovered this place several years ago when on assignment in Hong Kong and had insisted that if she ever travelled that way, she wasn't to miss Stormy's, almost over and above all of Hong Kong's other attractions. Tony squirmed. Why did this woman not shut up and keep her place? He gestured to the waiter, "Whisky!" Thankfully, Terence Shaw appeared at the door before he had to acknowledge her next observation that she would have expected that Hong Kong restaurants would be altogether more glamorous sorts of places.

"Traffic, Mr Shaw?"

"Something else altogether, Mr Yip. Business." Terry arched his eyebrow in the direction of the woman and Tony gave a small shrug of indifference. *This dinner was a mistake.* Shaw sat down, clearly in a cheerful mood, and ordered a whisky. "Good business, Hong Kong style, straight down the middle as we planned it. Different investor." His drink arrived and Terry raised his glass, "We're on. Cheers". The tourist raised her glass of tea and reiterated the toast. Tony Yip looked at her, his expression one of undisguised disgust. Why *do* these foreign women have no sense of place?

*

The sea urchin poached in a light stock and garnished with seaweed sent a shiver down James's spine: surely this dish not only invoked the sea, it was the sea, served up in one delicious mouthful. The two men ate in silence. The first course – there was no menu – arrived within five minutes of their being seated. "That dish was amazing, Pete. I have to say that your predictions are sometimes amazing too. You are quite right. Pearl could be in danger. Let me tell you what has happened."

Peter, with one eyebrow frozen into an arch, listened to the story of how Belinda Jones's kidnappers had not only demanded that Dennis Childs pay for Belinda's release but wanted Pearl as part of the exchange, and he was sure that James was correct in surmising that it would be an easy opportunity for the kidnappers to dip into the considerable fortunes of two well-known Hong Kong citizens, without too much effort required on their part.

"Police?"

"She refuses," said James. "And another thing, Childs has borrowed Belinda's ransom money from Yip Yee Koon but other than that is keeping very quiet about what he plans to do next. It's possible that he's waiting for more instructions. I wanted to call the police of course, but just getting on with things is what Pearl intends doing – and speaking of same, it is the deity herself ...." If James had been eating at that moment he would have spluttered. Pearl walked into Stormy's, beamed at the maître d', waved to her father and Peter, and made her way towards their table.

"Dad. Peter. Gate-crashing. Do you mind? I'm bored. Excited."

"Do stop gabbling and sit down, Pearl. You promised that you would stay put," James hissed at her. Pearl's smile faltered, but only a little.

"You are understandably excited about tomorrow's move back into your home, Pearl," said Peter, sipping the last remnant of sea urchin stock.

"Yes. Damn. I missed the sea urchin course. I love that soup."

"How can you describe something so exquisite as *soup*?" said James. "And by the by, Pearl, Peter and I are discussing you. It is the reason for this dinner. It is not *de rigeur* to have the gossipee show up. Stifles the gossipers' styles.

"I may sit down though, mayn't I? I decided to pay you a visit because Yip Yee Koon is looking for you and you know as well as I, dear father, that when Mr Yip comes looking for Sir James Gates, it is usually because things are getting pretty bad somewhere. *N'est-çe pas le cas?*"

"Your French is atrocious, Pearl," said Peter. "Please refrain."

"It's not as bad as Dad's Japanese. I expect you speak perfect French, Dr Benson?"

"Naturally. I have inimitable oral and written command of fourteen languages. That is how I managed to have a perfectly good career as a Linguist until the British Home Office came along and wrecked things by turning me into a spook." He was serious. Pearl was impressed. James was amused.

"Righty-oh children, enough. One, Yip knows where I'm staying. We lunched together and I will certainly call on him again if I am granted brief respite from furniture moving duties. Two, the matter of the note received by Dennis Childs, the eye for an eye thing: Peter and I were about to discuss if it is a double-dip kidnap attempt or merely bluff. I know you think it a bluff, Pearl, but perhaps there is a different objective altogether." Peter nodded.

Pearl said, "But what different objective? And why is it mixed up with what happened to Belinda? I don't get it. If it's true, it's just about money."

"Well," said James, "we have toyed with the idea that Belinda was taken instead of you, and that you were the original target. Let's say that she showed up in the lift at an opportunistic moment and was nabbed, rather than the kidnapper going to your room and nabbing you. You are both feisty, wealthy women. Perhaps you were the original target and she was a serendipitous alternative. After they successfully removed her from the scene, it encouraged them to have another go at you. Not only *just about money,* Pearl, but easy money too." He felt uncomfortable, aware as he spoke that he hadn't really been taking this business seriously enough either and Pearl had swanned over here in a taxi by herself and it was so dark outside ....

"Saturday...," she fell silent as the second course arrived. The waiter asked her if she would like the sea urchin dish as the final course and she smiled her thanks. "Saturday and everything that happened with Marcus. Do you think the two events are related?"

James had to scratch his head, an irresistible action when he was genuinely puzzled. "Peter? It crossed my mind in a passing sort of way, any thoughts?" Peter looked vague. Pearl was about to start on the deep fried oysters, her second most favourite food in the universe, when her eyes lifted from contemplating the delicious morsel and widened. Pearl was seated adjacent to Tony Yip's table, her back to it, facing the door. James had his back to the door. She and Peter both saw Yip Yee Koon at the same time – weaving quickly through the room, looking not at them but over their heads and at the same time Pearl swung around and recognised Terence Shaw sitting with another man and a woman.

The tourist smiled at Pearl and said, "Is there something wrong, dear? Oysters off, do you think?" She looked a little worriedly at her untouched serving.

Peter murmured to James, "Don't turn around James. Yip Yee Koon is powering across the room, looking like hell itself, glowering at the chap you are facing at the back table." James swallowed his oyster and reached for the table napkin and as he unfolded it he took a quick look at Tony Yip.

Pearl hissed to her father, "the Caucasian bloke is Terence Shaw, the man I asked you to check out. He's the one who's supposed to be a diplomat."

James smacked his forehead and Pearl creased her mouth at him. Yip knocked Peter's chair in passing and managed to say smoothly that he was sorry, at the same time that Tony Yip stood up and moved around the table to avoid Yee Koon. The two men came to a halt on either side of Pearl's chair.

Talk in the room stopped and James saw the gun before anyone else. In a flash it was pressed against his daughter's right temple. It happened between breaths. Tony Yip pulled Pearl to her feet. James remained still, his mind registering everything in the room. The tourist's mouth dropped open and the fried oyster she was about to eat ended up on her lap, and although Shaw's eyes flickered at the movement, they never left Tony Yip. A waiter clutched his apron and wrung the fabric as though it were wet. Cutlery drooped from hands, forgotten, or was dropped in the clutch of fear that took over the room. The hiss of woks in the open kitchen was the only noise.

Yip Yee Koon was the first to speak and it was his usual calm, level voice that reverberated around the room. "Leave her out of this. This is between us. I will go with you."

Tony Yip gave a short bark of laughter. "I think not. Move," he said to Pearl, and then said to the room at large, "If anyone else moves, I will kill the waiter." James watched his daughter walk through the restaurant as gracefully as though she was being escorted onto a dance floor, the gun pressed into her cerebellum. She said not a word. The room remained frozen and footsteps, one of high-heeled shoes, the other of flat-soled leather replaced the dying hiss of the woks as the dominant noise in the crowded space.

James wanted to scream, to yell, to chase and push the man down the stairs but it was Yip who reached the small landing at the top of the steps first. Another man standing at the bottom produced a revolver and barked at him to stay where he was whilst Pearl was bundled into a car. By the time Yip and James reached the footpath, the vehicle had gone.

"I said Pearl was in danger, James," said Peter when James came back and slumped into his chair.

"Shut up, Pete."

CHAPTER NINE

Wednesday 5 December 1979: 8.45pm

Marcus sat as still as stone, thoughts of the meal he had just enjoyed gone, thoughts of everything else that had seemed important five minutes earlier, all gone. Chief Rolling Thunder had cried. Marcus's grandmother, Granny Browne, had just been buried without Marcus having any idea that she had died. They couldn't wait any longer for his return and the Chief was full of remorse that he hadn't told Marcus when they had spoken on Saturday night. "Derek wanted to tell you in person, my son, and we all thought that was the right thing to do. If we had been able to contact you, we could have waited a little longer, but you know our customs ...."

Marcus knew his people's customs. He knew that it would have been hard for Chief Rolling Thunder to make the decision about the funeral without Granny Browne's only grandson being there, without even knowing that she was gone. It was all as he would expect. What he couldn't get a handle on was that his grandmother was dead.

"Why did she have to go now?" he asked the kitchen clock. Granny Browne had been his last closest living blood relative and had died in her sleep. *Your grandmother died peacefully, my son* the tribal elder had said and Marcus wanted to believe it. Chief Rolling Thunder hadn't heard from Derek and was worried about him too. "He knew there was no time to lose. We now know where you are, but Derek? Where is he"? Marcus had put down the phone without answering. He wished he knew.

*

Pandemonium broke out among the diners. Three men, Terry Shaw one of them, bolted, food unfinished, bills unpaid. James took control when the fourth diner was about to make his escape. "Quiet everyone. I said QUIET. Sit down sir. Remain calm, madam. No-one else is to leave this restaurant. Is that understood?" He turned to Yip Yee Koon. They could hear the howl of approaching sirens. Yip stood by Pearl's empty chair, arms hanging at his side, no more than a slight frown altering his usual demeanour.

"Yee Koon?"

"James. I did not expect this."

"What did you expect?"

"To talk to you, my old friend, about an outbreak of violence within the Walled City. That is why I came here tonight, to talk to you. This is all-out war James, nothing less. The man who took Pearl is my brother."

*

Five minutes after bolting from the restaurant, Terry was still running, hard, trying to put as much distance between him and Stormy's as he could. His dinner companion had kidnapped another diner without any more pause than most people would give to batting away a mosquito. What was he to do? The entire Hong Kong Police Force would be after Tony Yip and it wouldn't be long before they came after him too.

He finally slowed down, in case his fleeing form attracted attention. Not that it mattered. He was ruined. The Celestial Harmony Machinery Factory was doomed and not only that, but he had organised for the bloke he intended to scam to rent the apartment below him. He lit a cigarette and his head began to clear a little. Perhaps he could cut a deal with Tsiu Wah-Heung and do the business in China after all. And if he could keep Derek Wong happy with an altered game plan whilst Tsiu found satisfactory premises, perhaps they could launch it in Shenzhen. Shenzhen was growing fast as a manufacturing centre: deals could be done almost on the instant. He started formulating how the new business plan would look, mindless of the beauty of the Hong Kong night as he took a seat on the deck of the Star Ferry. The wreath of lights adorning the neck of the Peak, the city's skyscrapers aglow, and the lights from the endless skirmish of boats that criss-crossed the water...the entire nocturnal parade passed him by.

He glanced at the door of Apartment 7 as he climbed the stairs to his flat. At least he hadn't paid out any money to Yip, so his stake was intact. *Why* had the man so brazenly kidnapped that woman when that other man came at him through the crowd of diners? Who was that other guy? Terry gulped a whisky and lit a cigarette. The obvious explanation was, that if Yip was a triad member, then the other chap, who obviously wanted a very big piece of him, was probably a triad too. He sipped on. Perhaps the deal with Tony Yip wasn't such a failure after all.

At least by working with Tsiu Wah-Heung, one could have a reasonable prospect of staying alive.

*

Yip Yee Koon joined Peter and James at their table. There was no further prospect of dinner and the chef had taken up guard duty with just a glimpse of an impressive cleaver evident. When the sirens stopped, James saw Yip tense. He watched the door and when five Hong Kong Police Officers stamped up the steps and filled the small dining space with their considerable presence, Yip's face became pale and pinched. The Officer in Charge was Detective Inspector Robin Fairweather. James flashed his Home Office badge and when he understood the situation, the Detective Inspector radioed to base. He needed authorisation to mount an all-out rout of the Walled City, something no Hong Kong Police officer ever relished doing on their beat. They would need at least forty officers.

*

Tommy Smythe felt a little smug. He had been learning to play contract bridge in a very desultory manner for some months to satisfy his wife's desire for them to play socially. Tommy couldn't believe how challenging a mere game of cards could be – privately he looked down on card-playing – but bridge left him feeling reduced not only in enthusiasm, but reduced also in basic intelligence as he bumbled and stumbled his way through a world of complex bidding and card play. Not to mention the protocols. – It was almost worse than the Police Service for that. – But tonight they had played well and he and Melanie had just made their contract against Jane and Gary Burnside. Burnside was big in the bridge world – a bridge-playing equivalent of a great white shark, winner of international competitions, a grand-master.

"Well played, Thomas. Excellent bidding, you two. I can see you both playing a good game of bridge yet." Tommy felt patronised despite the win and was relieved when the phone rang and Tommy Smythe, indifferent bridge player, was required to be the authoritative Chief Superintendent Smythe.

"My sincere apologies, an emergency. Melanie, best not to wait up for me, my dear. I think I shall be some time."

He certainly hoped so.

*

"What is it, Yee Koon?"

"James, I came here to tell you tonight of something very bad that has happened in my household. Mr Kim, my head man, was transported to my door early this evening, in my new car. He is dead. I have already encountered Chief Superintendent Smythe this evening and to think about what is now going to happen, well it is too much. I am sure my brother is responsible for Mr Kim's death. Now he has your daughter."

"Bad spot we're both in here, old man." James's voice sounded a lot steadier than he felt. He forced the image of his daughter walking from the room with a gun at her head out of his mind. He needed to be able to think.

"I can already see how it will appear to the police, James. I pray it does not make the Chinese language newspapers. Mrs Yip will not be able to bear it." He lowered his head and thought about his father. Yip's elderly academic father and mother were long dead but had lived out their lives in peace after Yip paid bribe after bribe to stop them from becoming victims of the anti-intellectual revolution that swept through China during the mid-sixties. Yip enjoyed financial success and always met his obligations to those on the mainland who continued to bribe him for his services and his power until his father died. In the intervening years Yip built an empire but lived like a hermit. He had never shaken off the whiff of criminality that stalked him, due in part to the parallel career of great wealth that his brother Tony Yip had built by illegal means and, it is true, also due to some of Yip Yee Koon's more unsavoury businesses such as money-lending. To many, there was always the sniff of triad links about

Yip Yee Koon and in a fashion, this was also true. "My brother is the leader of the Wo Luen Shing Triad, James. He effectively governs the Walled City of Kowloon."

"Oh," said James, feeling foolish. "Yip, I know you've done business in the Walled City on behalf of other's interests in the past, but I never imagined that your influence was familial. I'm sorry, old man. I'll help you in any way I can, of course. Now what do you say? After we have our turn here being interviewed, shall we trot off into that City of Darkness and get my little girl back? She's looking forward to moving into her old home tomorrow." Yee Koon looked at his friend. Such an action, for himself, was clearly not possible. He even wondered if he would be leaving here except in the company of a police officer. He and his brother were at war now and Yip wouldn't last ten minutes in the Walled City and it was also possible that Tony wasn't even there. Perhaps he had taken Pearl somewhere else.

"It is possible, James, that my brother may avoid his own patch. He will be alarmed when he considers what he has done with such a high profile person as your daughter as his victim and he may take Pearl to the factory where Hua Leung saw him on Monday. He will also surmise that the police will enter the Walled City in great numbers once they know his identity – and even though he knows the city better than anyone else alive, it may be politic to keep this particular matter away from it."

Yee Koon knew too well that because his brother was a triad boss, he could never place himself in a position where he lost respect. Yip Yee Koon was a threat to Tony Yip now and Tony's reputation in the Walled City had to be inviolate. If he lost a dispute to his brother he would lose respect, and with that he would lose his power, his fortune and perhaps his own miserable life.

"Oh, and James, another thing. The man sitting with my brother…"

James's expression lightened and he interrupted Yip. "You're quite right my old mate. Pearl wanted me to look up his diplomatic status. He gave his card to that lovely American chap who also dined here on Friday night, Pearl's new friend Marcus. He also offered to vouch for another chap who shared their table. Pearl thought he looked familiar. I forgot about it, unfortunately."

"He is the man Hua has been following. He moved out of 6, Ong Hing Terrace this morning. And James?" James exhaled loudly again. What *was* this longing for a cigarette?

"Yee Koon?"

"I know where he went."

Peter Benson had been listening, sifting and sorting the information flying between James and Yip. He said, "If you and James are going to endeavour to find Pearl, then I shall put Mr Shaw under surveillance. See what he does and so on."

"Careful how you go, my old linguist," said James, "that almost sounds as though you are operational again."

*

Pearl was of value to Tony Yip only as his passport out of the restaurant, away from the roiling look of hatred on the face of his brother Yee Koon. War was declared, however it was perhaps unfortunate that he had abducted a woman of considerable local fame. He was tempted simply to stop the car and push her out, but he couldn't be seen to be weak, which is how such an action would seem to his men – getting rid of the woman because of her own power. She was involved in this whether he liked it or not. She was a problem he had to deal with.

Tony passed gun-wielding duties to his bodyguard and had the driver cruise the dark back streets of old industrial Kowloon, not far from the Walled City. When the vehicle slowed down near the southern gate and after giving curt instructions to the driver to keep going, he said to Pearl, "Three and a half years ago death contracts were issued on you and one of your friends." Pearl ignored him. "They came from within the Walled City. I had them extinguished. I did so because it was my brother's wish. He paid a fee and your life was saved." She didn't so much as glance at him. "I saved your life," he said.

"Are you trying to be subtle?" Her tone was scathing. "If so you're damned awfully bad at it."

"You are of no use to me, yet I have to decide what to do with you. Because once before I saved your life, in my world that also keeps me in your debt. You see my difficulty?"

Pearl held her ground. "I have a difficulty too. The only reason I wasn't killed at that time is because my life was saved by my husband. Your cancellation of the contracts was too late to stop the gunman taking a pot-shot at me. The result may have been very different, so of course I don't see your difficulty you malicious little ...." She strained to remember an insult she had heard once. It came back to her and she spat it at him in Cantonese, "You malicious little turtle face". Tony's face tightened. She had insulted him, called him a bastard in front of his inferiors, in language they understood. This would spread like a fire throughout the Walled City. People would snigger. It may even become his nickname. He would have to demonstrate his power over her or he would be ruined.

"You have just solved my problem." He gave the driver new instructions. He knew exactly where to put this foreign upstart and in addition, perhaps there was another way in which she could be useful to him. He would ransom her to his brother. That would morally square the debt between them in language they both understood – money. As for saving her life on this occasion, well, he would, if it was convenient to do so.

CHAPTER TEN

Thursday 6 December 1979: 3.00am

The Yip household was in quiet tumult. Yip had been questioned at Central Police HQ over his role in the kidnapping of Pearl Green by Chief Superintendent Smythe for more than four hours before the Chief Superintendent was sufficiently satisfied with his explanation of events. Yip gave a full statement and as he signed it, he also signed over the revelation of his relationship to Tony Yip. Yee Koon felt diminished as well as exhausted, and by the time he arrived home, it was after three in the morning. The house was ablaze with lights and there were extra security men patrolling the grounds.

Mrs Yip reported that she had been so distraught that she had taken a small glass of brandy. Yip folded Mrs Yip in his arms. Indeed he had only known Mrs Yip to imbibe alcohol once before in her life and that was after the funeral of her much loved mother-in-law. The phone rang and he sat his wife down gently in a chair before answering. It was James.

"Yee Koon. Everything tickety-boo at your end?"

"Yes, relatively so, James, if I understand you … but, James?"

"Mmh?"

"I don't know what to do."

"Can't believe I'm hearing that my old china. The police are still swarming through the Walled City if that is of any assistance to you, and of course they haven't found a sign of Pearl. Peter kept watch at Shaw's apartment until the lights went out at about two, I think. We don't know if he returned home directly from the restaurant of course and it is possible that by the time Peter gave his statement to the police and went to Caine Road, Shaw could have had time to go somewhere else. But Yee Koon, I don't think Shaw's connection with Tony Yip had anything to do with the events at Stormy's."

"The factory, James?"

"That's why I'm ringing, old boy, as well as to see how you and Mrs Yip are faring of course. I left you without getting the bally address of the thing. Not like me to skip details, Yip, must have been more overwrought than I thought. I tried your home but of course you've been the guest of Her Majesty...."

"I know where the factory is, James." Yip cut him short. He preferred not to think about Her Majesty in that particular context. "Shall we go together?"

"More than generous of you."

"I'll pick you up outside the Hilton in half an hour."

*

Yip was in his old Fairlane, the model superseded by the new vehicle that had been impounded as evidence relating to the death of Mr Kim. Apart from a muted greeting, they were silent. The car drifted through the dark back streets of Kowloon until they reached Tony Yip's factory in deserted Beecham Street. Three steps led up to a set of double doors flanked by two windows. Similar buildings abutted the factory on either side.

"There must be a rear entrance – there has to be some way of making deliveries," whispered James. But there was no rear laneway, nothing but adjoining buildings on all sides. Both men knew that this was not Tony Yip's style. He would not limit himself to one entrance – they had seen the result of that tonight – "must be through the building at the back," said James.

Yip nodded. He had an odd look on his face. "Perhaps. James, I am going to break the window."

"But what if...?"

"We must rule out the possibility that Pearl is here and do so quickly." He nodded to his chauffeur who produced a tyre lever and at another nod from Yip the man neatly smashed the lowset window. He cleaned away the shards of glass as though performing a delicate household task, and climbed inside. He offered his hand to Mr Yip, who in turn helped haul James into a large, square, empty space. Yip turned on his torch and spun the beam around the room and ceiling.

"The ceiling, James." James saw what he meant immediately; it was too low for the age and height of the building. They moved silently across the concrete floor. There was a doorway which led to an annexe at the back, in which was a basic kitchen on one side and a toilet on the other. In here the ceiling soared to its true height of about twenty-five feet but there was no back door and still no obvious way of accessing the adjoining building. They saw a ladder propped against the back wall. He and Yee Koon looked at one another. Yip arched one fine wing of an eyebrow at James. "Are you confident on ladders, James?" James said that it didn't matter if he was or not. He would be on this one. They scanned the dividing wall between the main factory floor and the annexe and saw immediately that it was only partitioning, plywood squares held in place by thin wooden battens.

"Look at that one." Yip looked. There was a slight gap between the panel and the battening. They moved the ladder as quietly as they could. Yip whispered to Mr Lam to keep watch outside and then lithely climbed the ladder and shone the torch into the ceiling cavity through the gap. There was something in there, propped against the wall.

"Good evening, Pearl, or rather, good morning. Your father and I have been wondering where you are. Yip Yee Koon here!" James shook the ladder. Yee Koon jiggled the panel and sure enough, it was loose and easily removed. He passed it carefully to James. "Do not damage it, James. We do not wish to inconvenience my brother further," and he ably manoeuvred himself from the ladder into the ceiling space. James followed, not so lithely.

*

The sight of his daughter, tied, gagged, and propped against a partitioning wall was a sight that would never be erased from James's mind. In a flash they covered the distance to her, worked loose the ropes that bound her and removed the gag. James massaged her hands and forearms and helped her straighten her legs, which had been bent and bound so tightly that she could not move. She cried, she laughed, she kissed them both and Mr Yip did not flinch, although he was not a man to welcome overt affection. James hugged her until Yip wondered how the woman could still breathe.

"Sshh. We have to get you down. Can you manage it?" She nodded. She would jump to the floor, if necessary. Both men helped her, placed her feet one by one on each rung and tried to ease the pressure on her arms as she painfully descended. Yip replaced the panel. It did not occur to him until later in the morning why he had bothered, after having broken the window. He even put the ladder back where he had found it. James continued to massage Pearl's arms and hands, warming her, hugging her, murmuring into her hair. She leant against him and he felt her tears soak into his jacket. Her legs were badly cramped and after the effort of getting down the ladder, she found it hard to take even a step.

"We have to get out of here and quickly. We will carry you." She didn't object and in a minute was handed through the window like a baby and carried to Mr Yip's car. The street remained quiet apart from the soft purr of the car's engine.

Pearl looked at Yip. "Mr Yip, that man explained to me that he owed me a debt for saving my life once, but he also said that he had decided to nullify that debt in another way. I think he was just going to leave me there to die, Dad. Dad, Mr Yip: how? How did you know where to look for me?" James and Yip glanced at one another: it was time, Pearl had to know.

"That man, Pearl, is my brother," said Yip quietly. "My brother likes to be clever and he would think this a clever move. Everyone else would expect him to take you into the Walled City." Yip waited for Pearl to say something but her face very still and she did not take her eyes from him. "This building is a recent acquisition for him I think, and very few people would know about it. But because I have had my brother under observation this week, I knew he had been here recently. Neither James nor I really expected him to bring you here but we decided to rule it out before considering our next move. I am very glad we decided to break that window."

Pearl smiled at them both. She was glad too. The car slid through the oily early morning streets. At Division Central Police HQ the Sergeant on duty at the night desk looked closely at her as she walked slowly through the door, flanked by her father and Mr

Yip. He glanced at a copy of the photograph of her that had been distributed as part of an All Alert. "Lady Green!"

Pearl found a smile for him. She knew what was coming next.

"Lady Green, this was taken just last week, wasn't it?"

Pearl took the copy of the photograph reproduced from one that had appeared in last Saturday's *South China Morning Post*, the one in which she thought she looked dazzled and wary.

"It's me all right, but not anymore, Sergeant. I'm not that frightened-looking little rabbit. Is Chief Superintendent Smythe around, by the way?"

*

It was just after four thirty in the morning when Yee Koon and James had found Pearl but in Florida it was early afternoon and one Florida resident had Hong Kong on his mind. Terry's phone remained unanswered. Sol Lewis had handed over half a million in US dollars to his step-brother and now was being forced to consider the possibility that Terry had scammed him.

Sol knew Terry was doing it tough in Hong Kong. Would a man rip off his own step-brother? He didn't even bother to second guess the answer. Terry would. He would if he needed to.

*

Thursday 6 December 1979: 4.00am

The yacht reached port before dawn and an hour later Dennis Childs was in the sealed 24-hour security drop-off office at the Bank of Taiwan in Taipei City. He produced the deposit box key, lodged the cash and headed back to the yacht without attracting any curiosity or even interest from the security officer who let him into the sealed overnight banking facility. The skipper was looking out for him and gave the order to sail as Dennis walked over the gangplank. By eight o'clock they were powering along, assisted by the swift south flowing currents. They would probably make Hong Kong by late afternoon.

Dennis tuned into several radio bands, trying to find an English language broadcast that might have news about Belinda's release. There was nothing until just after breakfast when the Skipper picked up a breaking story: the kidnapping of the famous

Belinda Jones was world news and among the excited tones of the announcer Dennis heard his daughter's name.

"What's the story, Skipper?"

"Mrs Jones has been found at Taipei Airport, Mr Childs, quite well, but shaken and dehydrated. A moment please ... she has refused hospitalisation and is insisting that she be put on the next flight to New York. The announcer is telling the story of how your daughter is her husband's good luck talisman and that he will not appear at a concert without her ... the Taipei Police have refused her request to leave and insist that she is hospitalised before being permitted to fly."

"Well, thank God that's over. Mission accomplished. Smut will have to cancel his concert if he daren't take the risk of appearing without her. Seems small beer to me." The Skipper did not respond. "Good work, Skipper, step up the pace now, I've got lots to do," said Dennis. He would call Belinda when he reached home, but now that she was safe, his thoughts turned to Pearl Green. As for being interviewed by the police when he returned – as he was sure would happen – he would simply say that he had decided to meet the ransom demand and as the transaction was not to take place in the Colony of Hong Kong, he did not feel as though he had shown disrespect to the Police Chief's request that he should not co-operate with the kidnapper's demands.

*

Terry woke, jerked from sleep by a dream he lost straight away. His head hurt. He should not have polished off that bottle of whisky so quickly. He turned on the radio just in time for the eleven o'clock news, which was dominated by an account of the spectacular kidnapping of Lady Pearl Green from a well-known Kowloon restaurant the previous night in a stand-off between a prominent Hong Kong businessman and another, unknown, Asian male. Terry made a coffee and wondered if he should leave the apartment. What if he had been identified as one of the people who fled Stormy's before the arrival of the police? Did the police want to talk to him? More importantly, why was Tony Yip described as an unknown male?

He moved over to the window and tweaked the blind just enough to see what was happening outside. All of a Hong Kong morning was out there, the non-stop rush-hour milling of vehicles and people and three of those people in the crowd saw the blind twitch. Hua Leung watched from his taxi, Peter Benson was reading the *South China Morning Post* as he apparently waited for a bus and one of Tony Yip's men lounged against the inner door of an old office block, smoking a cigarette.

He closed the blind. Perhaps it was best to stay put at present. Who knew who was out there? After the events of last night, Terry had crossed Tony Yip off his list of possible business connections, but had Tony Yip crossed Terry from his?

*

At the request of Chief Superintendent Smythe, the Hong Kong Police Chief issued a suppression order on Pearl's release and the first editions of the daily papers went ahead with the story of the scene played out at Stormy's, and were rife with speculation about Pearl's whereabouts. When the news broke about the release of Belinda Jones, the press went wild. Two prominent Hong Kong women kidnapped in the space of three days! What was happening in Hong Kong? Rapidly compiled articles summarising the lives of Pearl and Belinda appeared like magic from many busy typewriters – the friendship between them that dated back to their teenage years and the fact that Belinda was kidnapped when she was on her way to visit Pearl provided endless scope for speculative stories.

Upon his return to Hong Kong, Dennis Childs authorised a brief statement, "I am relieved and grateful that my dearly beloved daughter has been released and I will make arrangements to see her as soon as possible." He refused further information and the press compensated by going into hysterics about whether Dennis had paid a ransom for Belinda's release and if money would be demanded to secure Pearl Green's safety.

Tony Yip listened with interest to one broadcast claiming to have inside information that fifty million Hong Kong dollars had been demanded for the release of Lady Green. The young reporter who was carried away enough with the drama to write the piece lived to regret it when the police came to the broadcasting studio and removed him for questioning. In addition to repressing news of her release to the press, her appearance at Division Central HQ in the early hours of Thursday morning was also kept quiet throughout police networks and the factory where she had been held was put under surveillance. Chief Superintendent Smythe wanted to see what or who he could force out of the woodwork if it was widely assumed that Lady Pearl Green was still missing.

*

Yip Yee Koon was thankful that his name did not appear in any of the publicity around the incident that must surely, food or no food, be Stormy's most spectacular production – an actual armed stand-off and kidnapping. Mrs Yip listened to the reports with rapt attention. She moved quietly past her husband's study more often than necessary and each time, glanced in on him. Even Mrs Yip was not aware that Pearl had been found. Yee Koon had no intention of telling her anything that could compromise her safety if there were further moves against him by his brother.

*

After leaving Division Central for the second time in the space of three hours, Yip had sat at his desk, motionless. The factory window had to be mended. It was important that Tony's suspicions about Yip's actions last night be held at bay for as long as possible and it was barely daylight when the Maintenance Manager from Yip's racing stables stumbled into his van and made his way to an address Mr Yip had given him in Kowloon. The instructions were to proceed with replacing the window as quickly as he could.

This done, Yip put his mind to thoughts of revenge and whether it would be more satisfying to deliver it from a distance or pounce immediately. He could mobilise an army of his own and go on the attack, or he could be more subtle and find a way to erode his brother's power within the Walled City and force him out. During none of these musings did it occur to Yee Koon that he could also speak to the police and leave it to them to deal with Tony Yip. This was personal and it was not until the long slow Hong Kong dawn began to shiver light on the peak of Tai Mo

Shan that at last Yip abandoned the creeping unhappiness that had frozen his thoughts in hatred – and finally slept.

*

James and Pearl were finishing off a late breakfast when the phone rang. Marcus had read the story about Pearl three times before fully absorbing it. She had been kidnapped whilst dining at Stormy's Restaurant and removed at gunpoint by a man unknown to any of the other diners during a stand-off with a local business tycoon who remained un-named. Marcus's reaction was purely reflexive: he phoned the Hilton and asked for Room 569. James had begun to stack their breakfast plates onto the room service trolley and was horrified when Pearl picked up the phone and said, "Hello?"

"Pearl?"

James flapped his hands at her in panic. "Oh. No?" She pushed her voice up an octave, "You have the wrong number." James grabbed the phone from her.

"Who is this?"

"Marcus Browne."

"Marcus," he said, "Get around here immediately. Don't talk to a soul on the way."

*

Dennis Childs got off lightly with an extremely fatigued Chief Superintendent Smythe. He described the final instructions he had received for the payment of the ransom money, that he slip out of Hong Kong undetected, place the money in a nominated deposit box in the Bank of Taiwan and leave immediately. Whether Belinda would be released or not was a risk he was prepared to take, but the journey had paid off and whilst Belinda was still in hospital and her fitness to fly in doubt, she was essentially safe and well. He rang Bobby and reported the news of her release.

Bobby seemed almost as distraught as when his wife was first missed but once again, as the conversation progressed, his distress seemed as much related to the coming concert as to his Belinda's condition. He was torn – should he cancel the show and rush to Belinda's side or go on as a tribute to her strength and his love for her? Again, Dennis decided that it was an indelicate moment to mention the idea of money to the man, some compensation perhaps for the time, money and ingenious effort Dennis had put into the scheme perhaps? Perhaps not. Dennis followed up this unsatisfactory conversation with a call to the hospital where he spoke with the Hospital Registrar. The medic was naturally guarded but when Dennis said that he was about to drop everything and fly to Taipei, he was advised that apart from being dehydrated Mrs Jones was quite well, her release had been authorised and she was at that moment on her way to Chiang Kai Shek International Airport. Dennis was relieved. Belinda was fit enough to travel and clearly, she intended making it to New York in time for the concert.

*

Derek's spirits had lifted by the time he returned to his apartment. At last, Central Police HQ had given him Marcus's address but he arrived at Causeway Bay too late – Marcus had already gone out. Derek borrowed paper and pen from the concierge and left a note. He had the meeting with Terry Shaw at mid-day lined up and couldn't afford to hang around, but when he knocked on Terry's door spot on twelve, there was no reply. He had some lunch, but there was still no sign of Shaw when he returned and by two o'clock, Derek was fuming. He bounded downstairs to the Building Manager's office and a couple of minutes later, banged shut the door of Apartment 7.

Shaw had checked out at 11.30am. No forwarding address had been given. The concierge at the apartment at Causeway Bay had refused to give him Marcus's telephone number earlier and there was no choice but to wait in until Marcus phoned him. If he didn't, the charade of chasing his cousin around Hong Kong Island would go on until they were both old men. Derek had things to do before he became an old man. Marry and have children for a start. He made coffee and slumped into an armchair with the morning paper and read about the overnight kidnapping. It was the second such case in a week, and the two women were old friends and well known in Hong Kong. He turned on the television to find that programming had been interrupted for some breaking news. The wife of Smut Jones from The Froth and the daughter of well-known Hong Kong businessman Dennis Childs had been found wandering dazedly around Chiang Kai Shek International Airport in Taipei ....

Derek was transfixed. The man they were talking about would have to be the same Dennis Childs who offered to help him if he got stuck looking for somewhere to stay wouldn't he? The brother of the other guy found dead in the Hilton? He began to feel a little uncomfortable as he watched the broadcast. Hong Kong could sure be a small island, it appeared.

*

Marcus listened intently as Pearl and James described the events of the previous evening at Stormy's. Pearl looked tired but otherwise seemed perfectly calm and steady. He wished he felt the same. He had been in Hong Kong only six days and from his perspective the place seemed to thrive on violence, which everyone seemed to accept with an almost airy resignation. Pearl confirmed his opinion when she said that the experience had not left her with any traumatic aftermath, so far at any rate, and in fact she said that she felt more like her old self. "It's brought me back to earth in no uncertain fashion. Very grounding experience, especially getting down that ladder with my calf muscles seized up." She saw that Marcus didn't get it – maybe her humour was too dry for the Everglades, so she said, "I've been self-absorbed for too long. Belinda has been released too. Isn't that just amazing? We've more in common that I thought."

James laughed absently, his mind on other matters. Young Marcus had to be added to the number of people sworn to secrecy over Pearl's release and not only that, but as soon as she heard about Belinda's release, Pearl had rung the Childs's residence and left a message with his PA for Dennis to call her. She seemed surprised when James had angrily gestured at her to hang up and when Childs phoned back James had all but ripped the hair from his temples when, after congratulating him on securing Belinda's release, she proceeded to tell him that she had succeeded in re-purchasing her former apartment. He literally shook his fist at his daughter when she said she was moving in immediately, but she had just held up her hand, laughingly, and said, "Oh, and Mr

Childs? The police want my little adventure kept quiet for a while longer. Not a word to anyone, please. Love to Belinda from me when you talk to her, oh, and by the way, anything more about me being a trade-off? Mind you, I'm second-hand goods now. Perhaps they've lost interest."

At this last comment, James thought he would explode. He did. "Pearl. Get off that phone NOW." The cohort of people in the know about her release had grown from their inner circle to include Marcus and now, one of Hong Kong's most powerful business barons – and that was without forgetting Chief Superintendent Smythe and the handful of officers who had been on duty at Central Division HQ in the small hours. James suggested that they may as well invite in *Hello* magazine and do a full feature spread complete with photographs and a possible short description of the décor of Pearl's apartment, but he forced himself to simmer down and far more sensibly suggested that Marcus should leave further discussions with Pearl about his project until the following day, when her release would no doubt be public knowledge. In the meantime Marcus could help evacuate – Pearl thought it rather melodramatic of James – *evacuate* Pearl from the Hilton.

She gave Marcus the address of her apartment and the phone number and asked him around for lunch at one o'clock the following day. James could but sigh. He hung a "Do Not Disturb" sign on the door of the suite, patted the large slab of fine looking young man on the shoulder and with a *don't worry Marcus, we'll get your project going yet*, the two men carried Pearl's suitcases to the foyer. As they parted James said, "obviously young man, mum's the word." Marcus did not think the comment obvious at all but he nodded, wondering what James's mother had to do with it.

James summoned the Floor Manager, one Kenneth Ward, who openly scowled at the departing Mr Browne. James produced his Home Office identification and after observing its customary effect of raising eyebrows and causing mouths to purse or gape at the unequivocal authority it carried, he said, "Mr Ward, would you tell me exactly what you know of my daughter's situation?" His hunch was right. Mr Ward knew only as much as the newspapers had to tell about it and nothing more. James held up his hand to stop the tirade of sympathetic comments that followed. The only person around when James and Pearl had returned to the Hilton in the early hours of the morning had been the night clerk, who was slouched across the front desk, fast asleep. They had made it to Pearl's suite without seeing anyone else and now, James could see that there was not even a blink of suspicion from the Ground Floor Manager that Pearl may have returned to the hotel.

"Thank you for your kind words," said James. "My daughter's first week back at home has been rather eventful. I'm advised by the police that the less talk about it the better; good advice, don't you agree? I'll settle up Lady Green's bill now, please. I intend taking her luggage to a friend's house." James was quite shocked when he went through the billed items: Pearl had spent $HK2,800 on a tub of caviar and $HK850 on a bottle of champagne and that was without the cost of the suite *and* on top of spending $HK50,000,000 on an apartment .... He smiled weakly and handed over a wad of traveller's cheques. Perhaps Pearl would think to pay him back for settling her hotel bill, however after paying out fifty million, perhaps she was a little short ... James pushed a familiar, persistently faint concern about money to the back of his mind. He was rather fond of money and liked to keep it.

Whilst the transaction was being finalised, a woman wearing a large black hat, scarf, beige topcoat and dark sunglasses strolled from the lift through the foyer. James pocketed the receipt and picked up two of Pearl's suitcases. Floor staff followed with the other two. A taxi was summoned and the luggage hefted into the boot. James tipped the bellboys, gave the taxi driver an address and as the vehicle started to move away he said, "just one moment driver, please". The driver paused, the passenger door behind him opened and a woman wearing a big hat smoothly slid into the seat. "Connaught Road driver," said James, "I've changed my mind. The old Fire Services Building. Do you know it?" He turned to Pearl and grinned.

She beamed, "Thanks Dad. Top marks for daughter smuggling." She kissed his cheek. He patted her hand. The Thompsons had agreed to hand James the apartment keys, ostensibly so he could have things ready for Pearl upon her release. She waited in the taxi whilst James did the business. As he told her later, Nell and Brian Thompson were visibly distressed by what had happened. Nell Thompson said that she had even confessed to Brian as they read the papers at breakfast that morning that she felt guilty about how they had pushed Lady Green so hard on the price. Brian agreed but privately thought that Nell's distress would have been far greater if the financial settlement had not been completed the previous day. The money was already in their bank account.

The Thompsons left without a backward glance. James made a vague huffing sort of sound when they were out of sight. There was something unpleasant about them and he knew what it was when he examined the ostentatious rosewood bar they had installed in the main sitting room. They had money but ghastly taste, always such an unfortunate mix. He allowed ten minutes for them to be well gone before fetching Pearl. She was confident, and James reluctantly agreed, that she would be safer in her own home than anywhere else. The place was like a mini-fortress thanks to the security lift, but for all that James organised not only to maintain the existing security service but he bumped it up with an extra guard on permanent duty at the front door and with additional patrols by the two other security staff.

Pearl had planned on spending her first day at home stocking up cupboards and generally fussing around and being domestic, but the shopping expedition she planned to include clearly was out, for her at any rate. Shopping was not James's forte but he bravely volunteered, "Not too much though Pearl, shopping distresses me, especially having to buy things I do not understand, for example" – he consulted the list – "Gumption and sponges. What the devil is Gumption?"

It was just after four o'clock. Pearl had moved one of her sofas back into its old position and was reclining on it, her back firmly turned on the over-ornate bar. She sighed and stretched contentedly. James looked at her indulgently as her eyelids drooped. She was home and safe and once he got this damned nuisance matter of the shopping out of the way, Yip and he could get to work.

*

Belinda Jones was well used to getting her way. Dirty, hair uncombed and greasy and without a skerrick of makeup, she effortlessly commanded attention at the first class desk of Pan American World Airways. The next passenger flight out of Taipei to New York was not scheduled until the following day, but a Pan Am cargo flight was to leave in an hour. She presented her passport. There was swift discussion between the receptionist and a manager and in no time Belinda was writing a cheque for twelve hundred US dollars after which she was led to a door at the rear of the terminal. From there she was transferred to an airport van and delivered – an exotic piece of cargo indeed – to the aircraft.

The Chief Pilot assured her that she would be made as comfortable as possible in far from optimum conditions for a paying passenger but Belinda, still wobbly on her feet, was almost breezy. "Compared to where I've spent the past few days Captain, it will be first class." (She eventually quoted that comment in her memoir of the whole event in a chapter entitled, 'First class is a state of mind.') There were seats on the plane at the forward end and she was the only non-crew passenger. She was comfortable enough and by the time the Junior Radio Operator brought her a coffee with some biscuits, she was asleep.

*

Marcus could hear the phone ringing. He fiddled with the apartment key and sprinted across the parquet floor.

"At last man. I've been looking for you ever since I arrived. Marcus, I've got some…"

"Bad news, I know. Brother, if you're going to tell me about Granny Browne, spare yourself. I phoned Chief Rolling Thunder and he told me everything that's been going on at home. I knew you were here too, man, I just couldn't find you. Do you want to come on over?"

"Do I? Don't move." Derek gathered up papers and his briefcase and caught a cab to Causeway Bay. The first thing that occurred to him in the taxi was that maintaining two separate apartments whilst they were in Hong Kong, even if only for a few days, was an extravagance that Granny Browne, not to mention the Seminole Council would not smile upon. Either he or Marcus would have to move.

*

"And that's it." Derek could only shake his head. Marcus's six days in Hong Kong was a saga that would go down in the annals of tribal history. "But that's not all. I've left out the proposal for getting the project up and running." He grinned at his cousin. "I've been multi-tasking, you could say."

"That's a woman thing, cousin, men can't multi-task. I read it in a book."

"Was it written by a woman?"

"No, a man."

"You mean a con-man. Women have been conned into thinking that multi-tasking is some sort of unique genetic attribute which renders them superior to men, when all it really means is that women push themselves to do even more work. But this particular piece of multi-tasking could pay off, cousin. Listen...." He stopped. He should have thought about Pearl's position before opening his mouth. One, he had agreed not to mention her at all at the moment and two, what if she got miffed about Derek being invited into discussions before being consulted about it? He should have kept his mouth shut.

"I'm listening."

"When are you going home?"

"Thanks brother, it's nice to feel welcome. I made this trip for only one reason and that was to tell you in person about Granny Browne. I intended to go home immediately if you wanted to stay on. I only brought one change of clothes with me and not only have I had to buy more but I've also had to rent an apartment. The hotel tariffs here are..."

"Steep, very steep. I know. When did you say you are going home?"

"I'll wait a bit. Make sure you're settled in and doing okay, first, I think. We don't want to have you going through another *Midnight Express* episode." Marcus smiled. So. Derek had taken that part of his story in at least. The old tit-for-tat was on again.

"That's kid's stuff compared to the film about the tsunami that hits and decimates Hong Kong and Kowloon. It's supposed to be predictive, could happen any minute. Now that is scary, brother." They smiled at one another, opened a beer each and made a respectful toast to Granny Browne. Derek knew there was something Marcus was keeping back. He'd find out what it was, he usually did.

*

Kaz hung up for the second time. There was still no reply from James's room at the Hilton. She had been at the hospital day and night since Drew's collapse, isolated, concerned with nothing but the state he was in. She hadn't heard a radio broadcast, watched television or so much as glanced at a newspaper for days. When the early evening edition of the Hong Kong Times arrived in the hospital cafeteria at five o'clock, she was having a short break from her vigil at Drew's bedside.

Her hand hovered at her mouth as she read the two most sensational stories to hit Hong Kong in a long time. The headline was, "An Heiress for an Heiress?" Photos of Belinda Jones and Pearl Green were set side by side immediately above the lead story. Kaz could hardly read it. She knew about Belinda. That had happened before Drew went off the rails. Belinda had been released and mercifully was safe and on her way to New York to be re-united with her husband, but Pearl....

She read the story again – the details about Pearl's kidnapping at gunpoint on Wednesday evening was no longer the major media focus, because everyone in Hong Kong knew about it with the exception of Karen Henderson and Andrew Pierson. The evening story was more speculative. – Had a ransom demand been issued for her release? What were the odds that two consecutive kidnappings would result in the safe return of both hostage victims? By the time Kaz caught up, the story had developed a more sinister slant than the straightforward account of Pearl's violent removal from Stormy's Restaurant. The front page story insinuated that the incidents had a common source and a possibility of triad involvement was hinted at.

There were many people in Hong Kong who had already guessed that one of the men involved in the standoff the previous evening was Yip Yee Koon, even though he had not been named in the press. Gossip implicating him was already gently circulating throughout Hong Kong's many-layered networks. Yip could read it between the lines in both the English and Chinese editions of the *Hong Kong Times* where he was described as "a prominent businessman, owner of Hong Kong's richest racing stables" – not much scope for guesswork there. He made sure that the papers went no further than his study. Mrs Yip need not know about this. He was due to meet James and he needed to focus on what they were about to do. They would need their wits about them.

*

Terry Shaw still had the key to Number 6, Ong Hing Terrace and with the two hot showers he had taken at the Caine Road apartment already a memory, he moved back in. The tiny house only cost HK$200 a month to rent – something had happened here and it was rentable only to the desperate. Terry felt desperate. His plan to relieve Mr Browne of many millions of dollars had fizzled, leaving him without any other prospects for making some quick cash. He squirmed as he thought of the colossal error of judgement he had made in impersonating Browne's cousin – and if that wasn't enough of a balls-up, he had been Tony Yip's dinner-companion when Yip decided to abduct one of Hong Kong's better known citizens. Wonderful!

He looked around the squalid house. Where was left for him to go? He was *persona non grata* with his family in England; had scammed his American relative; was AWOL from the British Army; and although he had taken the precaution of ridding himself of his true identity, his photograph could pop up anywhere. If he stayed in Hong Kong he would have to lie low and that meant staying put in Ong Hing Terrace. He couldn't do it. The telephone rang. The only person who had the number was Sol. The sound intermingled with a firm knock at the door. Terry flopped into the room's only chair. The ringing was as persistent as the knocking. His head spun and his stomach did a 360 degree flip.

"All right, *all right!*" He wrenched the door open. Peter Benson smiled at him benevolently and said:

"Good afternoon, sir. Have you heard the word of the Lord today? By the way, your phone is ringing."

*

Hua Leung watched the tall foreign man stroll along Ong Hing Terrace and knock on the door of Number 6. Mr Shaw had only just returned and already had a visitor. Hua puzzled over Peter Benson. He had seen him somewhere before but could not quite place him. Hua wondered about Mr Shaw too, who had moved his accommodation for the second time within the space of twenty-four hours. His suitcases looked heavy as he had hauled them into the house and Hua surmised that he had not returned to Sheung Wan in order to remove more of his possessions to the apartment in Caine Road. What did it mean? He would report to Mr Yip. *Ah.* The door opened. He could see that Mr Shaw looked very angry with the tall *gweilo* who stood there and Hua could even hear one or two shouted words although he did not know what *bloody rot, rubbish* meant. The other man took absolutely no notice of him but somehow angled himself through the door and picked up Mr Shaw's phone. Hua could see that Mr Shaw was almost bouncing with rage.

"Hello?"

"Terry?"

"Yes," said Peter Benson. "Who is this?"

"Sol, of course."

"Ah. Sol. So sorry," said Peter in a very good rendition of Terry Shaw's clipped military tones. Shaw made to grab the handpiece from Peter but Peter applied pressure to a particular part of his neck and Shaw's knees buckled. "Just a moment, Sol." Peter applied more pressure and was satisfied to see that he hadn't lost his touch. Shaw's features relaxed. Peter lowered him into the chair. He would be unconscious for some time.

"I'm here. What's happening?"

"I've changed my mind, that's what happening. This scam is too risky, much too risky. If the Council ever found out that I'd moled them, my life would be over. I must have been crazy to think I could outwit an entire tribe of brothers. I want my money back."

"Ah."

"Don't tell me you've already spent it."

"That's right."

"So the factory scam is set up?"

"'fraid so."

"And the money's been sunk into it?"

"You got it."

"Fuck. Can you get it back? Or don't those triad guys do refunds?"

"I'm sorry. They tend not to."

"That was my life's savings. Our dad always told me to save even though I'm never short of a buck from my day job. That money was legit. Terry, you're breaking my heart."

"It wasn't for legit purposes Sol. Maybe this is karma." Peter hung up. Sol stared at the phone. Terry would never say anything like *this is karma*. Who had he been talking to?

Peter removed the leather straps from Terry Shaw's suitcases and bound him hand and foot. He needed to contact James.

*

A small van cruised along Beecham Street in Kowloon and turned left into Beecham Lane. From his observation point in a rundown apartment building on the other side of the street, Detective Sergeant Wing Li-Fat noted the vehicle movement and the time but when the van disappeared, he lost interest. Unseen by the Detective Sergeant, the vehicle stopped not far from the corner and two men alighted, an Asian and a Caucasian. They unlocked the side door of the building in Beecham Lane and closed it quietly behind them. It was already deep dusk outside and black as pitch in the abandoned factory. James flicked his Dunhill lighter on for just long enough to establish that the space was empty, as was its neighbour, and that it had the same smooth concrete floor and a ceiling height that was low for its age and size.

Yee Koon saw James smile faintly as the flame went out. They were both right. James whispered, "What a team, eh?"

*

Pearl hummed "We are family".... She had promised James that she would not leave the building or contact anyone, including Kaz. The appointment with Marcus for tomorrow could be managed though, even if her release was still a secret, but all Pearl really wanted to do was phone Kaz. Kaz would have heard the news and she would be frantic, and after the week she had been through .... Had James thought about that? Certainly Pearl hadn't before she took a nap but as she pushed and pulled furniture around the apartment, her head cleared and with it, her mental worry beads started working overtime. She made up the bed in her bedroom, before attacking the bathrooms, which she scrubbed thoroughly even though it was obvious that the place was spotless. It wouldn't be when that hideous bar came out. That would be quite a job and would create chaos. She flopped onto the sofa. She was mortally tired and her muscles ached. *A drink. Gin and tonic.* After the second, she thought that perhaps she should have had something to eat first. The alcohol's effects had kicked in a little too readily. Damn it, no, she would ring Kaz. How could it hurt? Would she ever forgive Kaz if their positions were reversed? Kaz's housekeeper, Mrs Chan, informed Pearl firmly when she rang that Miss Karen was not at home, she was at the hospital with Mr Drew. Pearl rang and asked for Drew's room. A nurse picked up the phone.

"I'm a friend. Is Dr Henderson about, please, Sister?" She wasn't. Dr Henderson had become distraught earlier that evening, so Pearl was informed. Visitors and patients alike had witnessed her break down in the hospital cafeteria. The Hospital Registrar had been called. Kaz had been admitted and was in Room 32.

"Who is speaking please?" Sister Roberts remembered her confidentiality protocols a little later than she should have done.

"I'm a friend. Tell her," Pearl cast around for something that Kaz would recognise as being clearly and only from her. "Tell her that a black tortoise winter is here, Sister. Tell her to stay put, in her shell. She'll understand." Pearl twirled a strand of hair and finished her second drink. An hour. She'd give it an hour and then decide what to do.

*

The configuration of the two factories was so precisely identical that James was sure that the two buildings had originally been one. He and Yip were in the ceiling cavity, but on this side there was a steep wooden staircase which provided easy access. No need for a ladder here. James was relieved. The door also had identical panelling to that in the building next door and it opened easily.

They walked silently across the vast room. The door that linked the two buildings together was more obvious on this side than on the other, where they had found Pearl lying trussed like a piece of poultry ready for market. On this side an architrave framed the doorway and the lock even had a key in it. Yip's face was mask-like as they carried out their small investigations. The factory was under police observation and had been nearly all day. James assumed that the observation team was accommodated in Beecham Road with a good view of the factory. He also assumed that if Tony Yip did turn up, Yee Koon had his own ideas for what might happen before the police descended on the building, which is why James had decided to accompany him – there was little doubt in James's mind that Yip intended to kill his brother, to avenge his family and his friend's daughter.

James again thought of how they had found her, her poor cramped and stressed muscles, her distress, her bravery. If Yee Koon and he hadn't discovered Pearl in the early hours of the morning, what state would she be in now? Would she still be alive? His mouth tightened. Tony Yip had had all day to decide his next move. If he didn't turn up tonight, it meant he had decided to leave her to die in this place. But Yip was more of a mind to think that his brother would turn the whole thing into a money making venture and during the day, hourly, he had expected either a telephone call or a note of demand slipped under the front door. Yee Koon was equally sure that Tony wouldn't approach James, he would want every drop of poison he could extract from the situation to affect his brother.

"Shall we see if the lock works, Yip old boy?" Yip's expression became even more set and although he said nothing, James knew his thoughts. *What if there is someone next door, keeping guard? Watching? Waiting? Armed? What if Pearl's disappearance was discovered before the surveillance team arrived and my brother has planted an assassin in the roof, knowing that I will not let the matter rest? He wouldn't care whom he took out, anyone connected with me would be a worthwhile sacrifice.* Yip suddenly nodded to James, abruptly, and they walked silently towards the door that led into the adjoining building.

*

Upon regaining consciousness, and even while working out that he was very firmly tied up with his own suitcase straps, Terry realised that he felt remarkably rested and serene, as though something odious had been twitched out of his system after a long and healing slumber. There was none of the usual tension in his neck and his inner nervous tic had vanished – as had his visitor.

*

Hua Leung watched the tall man close the door of Number 6. Should he follow this man? They were not his instructions and if Mr Shaw left the house and Hua was not there to follow him, he doubted that he would see the bonus in his pay packet promised to him after his inspired piece of detective work at The Perfect Picture Sign Writing Company. He let the idea go and resumed reading a review of Mr Jackie Chan's latest movie, *The Fearless Hyena*. Hua read so avidly – he had yet to see his hero's latest action movie and looked forward very much to another cinematic extravaganza that would showcase the formidable martial arts skills of Mr Chan – that he did not see the *gweilo* take a small notebook from his pocket and write down Hua's vehicle registration number.

*

Dennis dined alone. When Jane came into the dark-panelled, quietly-lit study to remove the dinner tray, he said, "I have a letter for you. It is your letter of release from my employment. There is a generous severance cheque with it and a reference as to your capabilities. I am willing to corroborate what I've said about you verbally to any future employer. However I am not prepared to discuss the matter with you further. Send in Chef will you? Oh, Jane, forgive me, one last thing. I want you to leave immediately. I have made a booking for you at The Florence Weir Guest House in Kennedy Road. I think you will find it satisfactory. The rent is covered until the end of next week. Goodbye."

Jane Franks had been Mr Childs's Personal Assistant for two years and she knew better than to argue or second-guess him. He was a cold, polite man, an engineer who started off his climb to wealth with the purchase of a run-down London dockyard and now ran a vast financial empire. Theirs had never been other than a formal working relationship. She was a worker bee and she knew it. She went back to her office near the kitchen, had a word with Chef and sat down at her desk to read the letter. It was brief and set out that a restructure of the company was about to begin which would re-configure many positions in the organisation. The cheque was indeed generous, and quite adequate to see her through a period of unemployment or re-settlement. She read the reference which was a brief but complimentary tribute to her competency and pleasant manners.

She placed the documents back in the envelope and went to her bedroom in the staff wing. Two suitcases were enough to hold her possessions – her life outside the Child's household was almost non-existent. Perhaps that would change. She heard Chef shouting. There was a scuffle. Jane knew exactly what was happening. Chef would have protested against his dismissal and Mr Childs would have summoned a security guard to remove him. Lord. It was a massacre. And there were still the outdoor staff who would no doubt be told their fate tomorrow and *not* to forget the day help and what about Gibson, the Chauffeur? He had been with Mr Childs forever.

It was a good time to leave and she did so without a backward glance. Dennis watched her close the front door from his study window and wondered if he had made a mistake in letting her go.

*

Tony Yip lived richly in the Walled City of Kowloon. High above the original paved alleyways and mud-brick houses, his penthouse was as big as three generous houses, complete with a roof terrace with enough armoury emplacements to provide protection not unlike the original fort which had occupied the site. A recent addition to this area was a lift well that descended fourteen floors to open into a ground floor shopfront. There was only one stop, ground to fourteen or fourteen to ground. Within the penthouse, the internal doors could be shut and locked until it seemed like just another warren of rooms – albeit well furnished rooms – perched precariously above the original city footings. There were many panels that gave unexpected entrances and exits into different sets of rooms, the most useful being a panel in the hallway that gave access to the "fourways", a series of spoked corridors that terminated in a circular lobby and offered a different route to the city's heart from each of the four cardinal compass points. Tony was the only person versed in how all of these escape routes worked.

Tony wasn't married and cared little for what others thought of as usual family values. His family had stronger ties than those of blood. He had power and money and was the patriarch of the most densely populated urban area in the world. He could turn this whole place upside down in an instant if it suited him, and everyone knew it. Tony Yip was a man who enjoyed much respect.

He did however have a housekeeper and as evening settled in and he dwelt on what to do next, she entered the room with a tray of food. He waved it and her away. "Go. I will send for you." She bowed her head silently and left. It was unusual for Mr Yip to order food and then reject it. He enjoyed his meals. However, on other occasions when he had instructed her to go, trouble had soon followed. She hurriedly removed her apron and left.

*

Tony did not have other arrangements. It was approaching twenty-four hours since his bodyguard and driver had hauled the woman into the ceiling space of the Beecham Road factory and still he hesitated about what he should do with her... Ransom her to his brother or leave her to die? Whatever course he chose, he was safe from detection, and while he lived in the Walled City always would be, even if Yee Koon plastered his likeness over every building in Hong Kong. However, there were exceptional circumstances to consider – last night he had not only operated outside of his usual territory but had removed and now had under restraint an extremely high profile person! Why did it have to be her he had seized in that restaurant when he made his escape from Yee Koon?

For all his swaggering confidence, Tony had begun to feel more vulnerable by the hour during the day and as he examined the unfamiliar sensation from all angles, his hunger for food left him and anger set in. He took a large gulp of whisky and brooded. It was all Shaw's fault. If the stupid man had not invited him to that restaurant, none of this would have happened. Shaw and his fine plans, which had come to nothing so quickly, despite his big talk. Perhaps Mr Shaw should pay for last night's events. Perhaps Mr Shaw should be implicated in Pearl Green's kidnapping. Or perhaps, instead, to pay him out – Tony's expression softened a little – Mr Shaw should be given a personally guided tour of the Walled City. Tony's people would arrange for him to meet some interesting characters. After that, he would make sure Yee Koon paid a high cost for the release of the Green woman. If it all worked out, he might yet finance Mr Shaw's operation, if he was still alive. Who knows how things could work out? He called out to his bodyguard who was watching television in the next room.

"Fetch Mr Terence Shaw. Now. You and Ng. No, wait. I will go with you."

III

Black Tortoises & Turning Turtle

CHAPTER ELEVEN

Thursday 6 December 1979: 7.00pm

The door that divided the ceiling area of the building into two attics was hinged to open inward, towards them. They gave one another the nod and Yee Koon turned the key firmly, pulled the door open and stepped into the adjoining space. James saw the snout of a revolver in his friend's hand. He was not surprised. James remained poised on the other side, behind the door. Had Yee Koon seen James's weapon? It was a ladies revolver, a sentimental piece from his old operational days, a legacy from the time before he became the shadowy leader of a government department's shadowy side. Would Yee Koon be surprised that James was armed? James thought not, but he found the sight of a gun in Yip's hands unsettling, even given the circumstances. The torch beam flashed. James stepped through the door.

"It is as we left it last night, James."

"Good. Then we have the jump, old boy."

It was as though Yip had suddenly woken up. He said, with something like surprise in his voice, "James? Should you be here?" *James certainly shouldn't be here* thought James. *James should be with his daughter, but how in the name of a thousand deities can Yip do this alone? Surely the apartment security at Connaught Road was ramped up sufficiently to keep a marauding of Martians out of the damned building.* His eye twitched. It was always a dead giveaway, that twitch, and it told him that, of course, he should never have left Pearl by herself.

*

Detective Sergeant Wing Li-Fat yawned. He was tired, hungry, and he wanted to go to the toilet. It was 7.20pm and Detective Sergeant Carruthers should have taken over at seven. Detective Sergeant Wing felt distinctly uncomfortable, he really had to visit the toilet. Then he would radio Division Central and find out where Detective Sergeant Carruthers had got to.

*

For Tony Yip to be surprised by events at any time would be an achievement, but within the past twenty-four hours surprise had confronted him twice – if having his brother hurl himself at him across the dining-room of Stormy's hadn't been bad enough, now, as his men easily forced the door of Number 6, Ong Hing Terrace in Sheung Wan, there was Mr Shaw, neatly tied up with leather straps, as if waiting for them. Mr Shaw seemed serene, not at all taken aback to see Tony and his men. The room was overcrowded with four people in it and Tony stood back to give the bodyguards room to hoist Mr Shaw to his feet.

"It appears someone else has a grudge against you too, Mr Shaw. They will be perplexed when they return. You are going on a guided tour this evening." He jerked his head at his offsiders who hauled Shaw into the street. Tony opened the rear passenger door and the bodyguards placed Terry on the back seat as if he were a parcel. His eyes never left Tony Yip's face but he said nothing.

From his taxi, Hua saw what was happening and even though it was dark, he slid down as far as he could under the steering wheel. Mr Shaw was being bundled into a car by three men! A Mercedes car, very new. Clearly, this was no social outing. He raised his head sufficiently to peer out of the window at the same time that one of the men gestured towards his taxi and said something to another man – *and aiyah!* – that man was Mr Tony Yip! Hua wasted no time. This was not a good place to be. He turned on the ignition and ground the gears into reverse and the vehicle skewed backwards awkwardly. He had the advantage. He was nearer to the adjoining lane than they. He swerved, still in reverse, into Sparrow Street, shoved the gears into first and accelerated so hard that the engine screamed and the tyres gave off a hot tarry smell of indignation. His employer would hear of this matter immediately.

*

The conversation with Terry still bothered Sol. Maybe he called too early, Hong Kong time. Maybe Terry had a hangover. He should try again. Tony was about to get into the front passenger seat of the car when the telephone rang. He went back inside and picked it up.

"Wai?"

"What's with the *way* stuff, man? You going off your nut? *Karma? Way? Which way?* I want my money back, okay? And for your personal information, brother, I'm coming over to get it. Nobody, including my step-brother makes a fool of Sol Lewis. Understand?"

"Your brother is not here, Mr Lewis; but take down this address: 6, Ong Hing Terrace, Sheung Wan. When you arrive in Hong Kong you will find him there. Understand?" Tony smiled as he replaced the receiver. Mr Shaw would have a relative to help him out after his tour of the Walled City was completed. Family should help out in times of trouble. This was good, unless Mr Shaw was not at home or was unable to answer the door when his relative called by.

*

James heard a vehicle approach followed by an engine cutting out. Both he and Yip tensed. Had they made the wrong guess about how Tony would enter the building? What if he knew about the Beecham Lane entrance? They strained to hear footsteps or a door being opened or the rattle of keys, but there was nothing. Soon after, the vehicle – they assumed it was the same one – started up and the noise of its engine faded away.

"Ah, I've got it. That would be the observation turn-around shift, Yip old man."

*

Detective Sergeant Carruthers was late and Weng, Tony Yip's number two bodyguard, had watched him hurry into the building where Detective Sergeant Wing had been on duty for the past twelve hours. Weng, under instructions to watch the factory, had been drinking at The Emperor on Wednesday night and recognised Detective Sergeant Carruthers as one of the police officers who had come into the bar, looking for his boss, Mr Yip. What was he doing here? Soon after, another man ran down the stairs and stepped into the plain black Ford vacated by the other officer. He too was one of the police officers involved in the raid, he also had come into The Emperor Inn and questioned customers, Weng among them. The car drove quietly away. The bodyguard mounted the stairs and listened outside the door of unit 1. He heard the faint flush of a toilet. He knocked.

"Are you back already, Detective Sergeant Wing?" came the hearty tones of Detective Sergeant Carruthers as the door swung open. Weng threw himself against it and as Detective Sergeant Carruthers lurched back against the wall he was seized and expertly garrotted. The bodyguard waited until he was confident that the man was dead, before he left, closing the door behind him very quietly. He would have to tell Mr Yip what had happened. He was sure Mr Yip would approve of his actions. He might even pay a small bonus for the service.

*

Pearl woke with a start. She had fallen asleep and it was already after seven-thirty. Where was James? Surely he should be back from his chat with Mr Yip by now? Surely they weren't doing anything stupid like trying to catch Tony Yip on his own turf? She felt a cold streak of worry. Had she reached the point in life where she had to worry about a parent in the same way that parents worry about their children?

Kaz! She rang the hospital again but nothing had changed; Kaz was still asleep, sedated, and her husband Dr Pierson was stable. Pearl stopped dithering. She would go and sit with her friend, as she should, and show her support properly.

She put on her beige topcoat – she was feeling the cold and already remembering how icy the big old apartment became during winter and she made a mental note to have another heater installed in the big sitting room. It could be part of the remodelling work when the bar was removed. But outside there was an almost balmy edge to the night with no wind and a certain dense warmth on the surface of the harbour waters. Pearl crossed Connaught Road and stood near the harbour walls, waiting for a taxi.

She turned to face a light breeze that began to drift in from the south. Damn. She'd forgotten to tell the security guard that she was going out and she should also leave James a note. She dodged traffic and crossed the road again and let herself into the lobby, rang the security buzzer. But there was no reply. She rang again and again. The rapid clack of her high-heeled boots on the marble tiles of the foyer reflected her impatience as she strode across the vast space towards the security office, which soon would once again be the offices of the June Bowen Foundation. There was no light on in there and when she flicked the switch, nothing happened. She became aware that the building was very still, but it still took her a few seconds to work out why. She had left the front door open and the roar of the Hong Kong night which had followed her into the building had gone.

Someone had closed the door.

*

"Yip old man, every aching muscle is yelling at me that I must get back to Pearl. Are you coming?"

"I think not, James. I do not see how my brother can fail to come back here tonight, or send one of his people to check on Pearl. I will stay."

"I think we should leave it with the police, Yip. I implore you, *do* leave it with them. It was a mistake, coming here. If this is a matter of revenge, Yee Koon, hold on to it until another time. The police will most likely apprehend one of your brother's minions, and that will be that. Your brother is highly unlikely to risk his hide coming back here. Don't stay here alone, Yip, I beg you."

"You are a wise man, James, and quite correct in what you say. Pearl has to be your priority, as my family is mine. On this occasion unfortunately, that includes my brother. I cannot let this rest. Leave. We shall speak tomorrow."

It was a bad moment for James. But Yip had made his choice and there was no point in trying to talk him back from it. James patted his friend on the shoulder and whispered, "sorry old man but we have a worse dilemma. We have only one vehicle." He wished he could laugh out loud. Life's more serious decisions can swing on amusingly small hinges sometimes. Yip permitted James a small smile of surrender.

"Very well. I will drive you back. And perhaps you are right about the other things too, James. Let us go."

Marcus and Derek bickered about who should move apartments. "This place is attractive, there's a second bedroom and it's cheap," said Marcus.

"Mine is more central and you can walk to the main business district. Look." He produced a street map but Marcus just muttered something about what use was there in being near the CBD because as far as he remembered they weren't here to buy an office block.

"You'll only be here for a few days Derek, so I don't see why I should move out. It's comfortable and I like the aspect of the place." Derek felt the sting of being pushed aside again.

"You win, but the more secretive you become, the longer I stay. Understand? I know you're hiding something. It's oozing out of your pores."

Marcus nodded. "You are absolutely correct, cousin and I swear that I'll tell you everything tomorrow. Until then I'm on a promise man, and you just have to trust me. Now let's go eat. I saw this restaurant with the most amazing looking ducks hanging up in the window. I love duck...."

*

Kaz hovered for a time in a place where she thought she was awake but the giveaway was that hospital rooms generally do not come equipped with koalas sitting on the end of the bed – this one gently scratching its rump and staring vacantly into the middle distance as it munched on a cluster of gum leaves. She had a way to go yet before she was fully awake and by the time she got there her mind was quite clear – she had obviously experienced one of her rare but debilitating vertigo attacks, during which she would have collapsed. It happened rarely; a trick of her brain which unfortunately immobilised her limbs. Stress-related, she had been told time and again, and as she drifted into full wakefulness, she acknowledged the likelihood that the diagnosis was correct after all. She pressed the nurse call-bell.

"Hi, Nurse. What happened?" Nurse Roberts saw that whatever it was that had struck this woman down so violently, it was all over. Her voice was clear, her eyes were focussed and she got out of bed without so much as a wobble.

"You had a moment, dear. I'll get the Registrar. Oh by the way, I took a message for you whilst you were sedated – from one of your friends – here it is." She handed Kaz a slip of paper. It was from Pearl, and it told her as clearly as though her friend was in the room that it could be from no-one else. She read it twice.

"Was the caller a man or a woman, Nurse?"

"A woman. She didn't leave her name but she said you'd understand."

"Yes. Thank you." The nurse looked at Kaz curiously. It was an odd message, something about a tortoise and the winter which obviously had meaning for her patient. Kaz understood so well that she went pale again. Pearl was reaching out to her, she was alive, Pearl was safe. But safe *where*? Kaz hopped back into bed adroitly. If there was any chance that she might ring back.... "I think I will rest for a few more minutes after all. I'll wait for the Registrar." She picked up the phone and dialled the Hilton. "Is Sir James Gates available?" He wasn't. "Is, is Lady Green there?" The voice on the other end of the line sounded a little shocked. No, Lady Green was not there. Kaz was asked to hold. A man's voice came onto the line. "May we take a message to pass on to Lady Green?" Kaz banged the phone down. *God. They probably think I'm connected with the kidnapping.* Holding on to the side of the bed, she reached for her handbag and extracted her address book. She found the number, one she hadn't had cause to ring for a long time, but the phone in Pearl's apartment in the Fire Services HQ building rang and rang, until it rang out.

She's not there either. Kaz got out of bed. Drew would know what to do.

*

Belinda fumed her way onto the flight deck. "How much longer are we going to sit here?" The Captain turned and eyed her up and down. Mal Flint had an eye for a pretty woman but this one went beyond pretty. She was spectacular, even though she was filthy dirty and brought the faint meaty odour of unwashed flesh into the cockpit with her.

"We'll be here for at least another hour, Mrs Jones."

"I have to get to New York."

"So do we ma'am. After Japan and via New Zealand, Fiji and Honolulu. Didn't anyone explain that to you? This is a cargo flight ma'am and it's a twenty-four-hour trip to New York. We won't make JFK Airport until ten o'clock tomorrow.

"Too late for me. Where are we now?" They were at Tokyo's Narita Airport. Belinda's dash to her husband's side had detoured sharply north and she had just very neatly put her arrival in New York more than twelve hours after Bobby's concert was due to begin. "There must be something that can be done. Can I transfer to a commercial flight from here?" The Captain shrugged. Mrs Jones could no doubt do whatever she wished but it still wouldn't get her to New York in a moment, unless she could hi-jack a Concorde. Even Belinda had to accept that the situation was beyond her influence and she returned to her seat, resigned to the fact that she was about to find out if her husband's famous prediction would be realised. But there was more on Belinda's mind than Smut's safety. The events of the week had made her think hard. They had been together for eleven years. She was very aware of her role: she was his muse, his good-luck charm. But there were times when she wondered if she meant anything more to him. If he wasn't playing concerts, he was off playing elsewhere more and more, leaving her with the children in one of their houses.

What if he did leave the stage in one piece after the concert? He would be free to leave her, to find someone else. Or worse, what if he'd taken precautions against Belinda letting him down one day and already had an alternative, as back-up? She settled back into her seat and smiled at the young crew member who brought her yet more coffee. She really should say something civil to him. "Would you like my autograph?" came to mind but she decided against that. There might be no more "Blessings from Belinda Jones". She wished that she could speak to her father. She had left Taipei as fast as she could without giving Dennis a second thought, but she did now. No doubt he would be at home, alone in his study. She was always first in his thoughts, Belinda knew that, and hadn't she taken it for granted! She would go back to Hong Kong as soon as she could – she wasn't going to be of much use to Smut in any event now – and she would see her father. They hadn't had time together, just the two of them, for years and years and he deserved more, much more than a visit from her which was originally necessary only to identify his body! She felt full of something that could have been guilt and returned to the flight deck.

*

Yip Yee Koon talked non-stop on the return journey and James was quiet, a reversal of how conversation usually flowed between them. "I have to think more clearly, James. These feelings of confusion and hatred are most unpleasant. We know the factory is under observation and perhaps I put the police-work at risk by going back there. I need more than revenge on my brother. I need..." He left the sentence unfinished.

"James. My brother has gone into the heart of my household and has changed it forever into a place where fear now stalks instead of peace and safety. He has stuck a long bony finger out of the wretched heap of humanity he tyrannises in the Walled City and has pointed it in my face."

James listened to the words, so disconcerting coming from his friend whose spoken thoughts usually sprung from more gentle streams of observation. One particular side of his own nature had been beckoned out, so it appeared, enough to subsume Yip's cultured reserve. There was no point in going back over the conversation they had had at Tony Yip's factory. When they had left, there was no sign of any activity anywhere in the street, not a glimmer of light from the buildings opposite, not so much as the purr of another vehicle engine.

He grunted softly. "He didn't manage to point the digit in your face for very long, Yee Koon. Your intelligence found Pearl, don't forget that, and as for Mr Kim, well perhaps you will find a way to redress his death. If there is any finger waggling to be done, I think you can take the trophy, my old china plate." Yip's shoulders relaxed, just a little. The streets were still full of people coming and going through the long Hong Kong day that gobbled up some of the next and Yip needed to concentrate on negotiating the traffic.

"I will accompany you to Pearl's apartment and pay my respects to her if you don't mind, James. Seeing Pearl whole and well may be the elixir I need to get this bitter taste from my mouth. If, when we opened that door into the other building tonight my brother had been there, in all truth, I think I would have shot him." James looked at the bulge in the breast pocket of Yip's jacket and wondered. He couldn't help imagining the level of Chief Superintendent Smythe's delight if he finally had something substantial to pin on Yip Yee Koon, but James decided not to mention that just at the present time.

When they came in sight of the Fire Services building James saw that the blue security light above the front door was off and there was no sign of the extra security guard he had hired. In fact, the entire building was in darkness. He waved his hands flappily at Yee Koon for him to keep driving as Yip began looking for a parking-space and, his voice eerily balanced compared to the jangling sensation in his head, indicated they should drive on until well past the building. Yip frowned and did as bid. James thought fast, not about Pearl, because this was so obviously about Pearl, but about the side door access into the building.

He examined the bunch of keys she had given him: front door; security office; lift keys; safe key – ah, what was that? *That* was an old fashioned key made to be inserted into an old fashioned keyhole to open an old fashioned lock and the only old fashioned keyhole James knew of was in the side door, hidden from street view by the façade of the market stalls that were supported by the northern wall of the Fire Services building, right at the entrance into handbag alley. Pearl had told him once that it used to be her secret key into the apartment – into her own castle when she was a kid. She would run through the ancient bookbinder's shop into a hidden corridor and let herself into a downstairs lobby that wound up to the penthouse via a staircase. It was her "Secret Princess' Staircase".

"We'll use the Princess' Secret Staircase, Yip old boy." Yip nodded, oblivious to what a Princess' Secret Staircase could be, but confident of James's ability to negotiate it. The bookbinder's shop had long gone, as surely as the bookbinder himself. In Pearl's recollections of him he had always been an ancient. The alley shops were all closed and James hunted around, probing the end of the northern wall where it met the flimsy wooden shop façade. He pried the material back enough so that he and Yip could squeeze through. Between the shop and the building was a small square of space that disguised a stoutly built square timber annexe, fixed to the main building. The key fitted the door and it swung open – so noisily! – on hinges that hadn't been used for many years. James inched it shut. He found himself wondering if the Thompsons knew about this exit. Probably not. They were definitely the types who would want to be seen framed in the impressive double entry doors facing onto Connaught Road. It was totally black and for the second time that evening, he and Yip literally found themselves in the dark. James groped for the staircase banister and kicked his shoe against the bottom step. He tapped Yee Koon on the arm. "We're in business again, old man."

*

The meal was not a success. Privately, Marcus thought that with Derek's Chinese ancestry, he could have shown a little more interest in the local cuisine. True, using up all of the animal and displaying its various parts was perhaps not very appetising to someone unfamiliar with local food customs, but Derek had only managed to nibble a few pieces of spiced duck breast, declared the greens that went with it to be 'stringy' and poked his serving of rice around the plate until the bulk of it ended up on the table. Most of his dinner consisted of Tiger Beers. Marcus finished off his own serving and the rest of Derek's portion. It was delicious. The chestnut-coloured glaze on the duck hinted at spices that built up into a flavour he had never tasted before. Perhaps he could get the recipe for it before he went home....

Derek was still brooding. Marcus's promise to give a full account of himself tomorrow satisfied neither his curiosity nor his superior professional status. He was used to having the upper hand over Marcus in job seniority, knowledge and responsibility. Marcus may be the tribe's financial wizard but Derek was the

Chief's delegate, the one who saw the big picture for the community. He was the planner, the go-getter. Now he was on the outer. Marcus paid for the meal and when they started to leave Derek turned to him and said, "I'll go back to Caine Road tonight, and bring my things over tomorrow. What time?"

Marcus didn't meet his eyes. "I don't know. I have an appointment at one o'clock and after that,"

"After that you'll tell me the *whole* story. Right?"

"Guess so. I'll certainly tell you *a* story. I've got to get the green light on what is currently a delicate situation."

"Personal?"

"It's a promise, that's all."

"We've never held secrets back, bro."

"And I'm not now, Derek, I'm keeping a confidence. That's different. You'll understand soon enough." They walked side by side, uneasily, the silence between them unfamiliar, uncomfortable, unable to be bridged by their usual talk. Derek turned to hail a taxi and Marcus turned with him. A taxi was right there, just behind a big, luxurious car. The vehicle, a Bentley, slowed with the traffic and the two men looked at it admiringly.

Derek sounded excited and said, "I've met that guy, see, the guy driving the Bentley. That's Mr Childs, the father of the woman kidnapped from the Hilton earlier this week. I came across him at the police station when I came looking for you. I nearly called him …."

"*Why* did you nearly call him?" Marcus was right in Derek's face and Derek knew it wasn't little cousin Marcus talking.

"He offered to help me man, that's all. I think he was embarrassed by the treatment that bastard at the Hilton gave me. I thought, when his daughter was released, that I would express my thanks for the offer and congratulate him on getting his daughter back safely, you know…what's it to you anyway? You got your own agenda man. I'm outa here." He walked away without a further word.

A cab came by and Marcus hailed it. He had just kept something else back from his cousin – *why didn't I just say that I also know who the man is?* The answer was simple: it would complicate things between them even more; and right now, he had a lot of work to do in preparation for meeting Pearl tomorrow. He had to make sure that his people came out of this deal with what he'd been sent over to achieve ....

*

Peter Benson realised that James and Pearl had done a bunk from the Hilton when his third phone call to James's room went unanswered. Pearl had been determined to move back to her old home as quickly as she possibly could, despite the events of the previous evening, and it seemed she had done exactly that. Peter strolled back to the office. There was plenty of time to check the late mail before locking up, after which he would pay them a visit at Connaught Road. Leaving Mr Shaw to his state of bliss for an hour or two would not inconvenience him very much. Benson was very pleased with how successfully he had applied pressure point fighting techniques to Mr Shaw, after such a long absence from practice. Mr Shaw would benefit from a rare martial arts experience – restraint combined with healing.

James and Pearl would no doubt be enjoying some time settling in together, but Peter had no qualms about intervening. Anything he did usually managed to irritate James. Pearl would just carry on doing whatever it was she was doing. In fact they would both be fussing around, Pearl folding linen with the same, concentrated look she had inherited from her mother and Peter could see James sorting cutlery and glassware, washing and stacking plates and saucepans. There had always been something indisputably domestic about James.

*

"Welcome to Sin City, Mr Shaw." Tony Yip laughed heartily. A number of men appeared from the shadows beyond an archway between two shopfronts and two of them unstrapped Terry. They all laughed and two of them advised him to keep up. "Otherwise," said one, "you will not be a happy man". Even before the forced march into the Walled City began Terry was already far from happy. He vaguely recalled a few stories about the place, of violence or even death being the penalty for many who had gone in there for thrills or just to sight-see, but the accounts were invariably fuzzy on detail.

Tonight Terry was to have a unique view of the wire-tangled city, tangled not only in its in architecture but in its soul. As he walked, painfully at first, he found that despite the discomfort, he could think very clearly. In fact, he hadn't felt so clear-headed for years. It was almost as though a different man was doing the thinking for him. What did Tony Yip want with him now? Had the bible-bashing lunatic who appeared at his front door bound him up on Yip's orders or was that about something else entirely? Yip knew his cash reserves were limited and the seven million Hong Kong dollars in his bank account would hardly be a temptation for someone like Yip to kill him, surely?

His limbs served him better than he could have expected and before too long he kept up without difficulty, weaving through lanes no wider than a corridor. The quiet was deep until the scream erupted, a scream that could not possibly be human. Yip's number one bodyguard and Yip muttered something to one another and Yip laughed. "Perhaps too soon for that, Li. Mr Shaw needs to be eased into the Forbidden City, not thrown in at the deep end."

Silence descended again with even the tread of their shoes upon the aged cobbles muffled by the thick, stifling air, until a low whistle came out of the darkness. It was Yip's second bodyguard. He pushed his way to Yip's side and whispered to him. Yip smiled and patted the man on the shoulder. "Well done, Weng. Anything else?" Weng shook his head; apart from the sound of a car engine that had come and gone so quickly there was nothing else the boss needed to know.

"No, nothing else, boss."

Tony's thoughts were less generous than his appreciative words to Weng. So. There were police in an apartment across the street from his factory, waiting for him, which meant that Pearl Green had been discovered. He had to find out what had happened, for he liked the idea of her being liberated even less than her escaping by herself. He ascertained from Weng when the police change-over had taken place and estimated that there was plenty of time to go to the factory and work out for himself what had happened before the officer Weng had despatched was missed.

He barked a general order. "Keep Mr Shaw company, take him to The Emperor Inn and give him something to eat and drink. Let him come to no harm. You two" – he gestured at the two bodyguards, Li and Weng – "We are going out again." Things had changed swiftly for Yip and Mr Shaw was of no further interest to him at present, but there was no need for Mr Shaw to know that. Let him feel uncomfortable for a time.

*

Hua Leung was informed that Mr Yip Yee Koon was unavailable when he arrived at Yip's house at seven-thirty. He pleaded to leave a note and when the manservant returned with a notepad and pen, Hua wrote, "Mr Shaw taken from Number 6, Ong Hing Terrace at 7.00pm by Mr Tony Yip and his men. With respect, Hua Leung." He folded the piece of paper and gave it to Mr Lam with a slight bow, but when he returned to the taxi he decided to wait. Perhaps Mr Yip was out rather than merely not receiving anyone and would soon return. Hua found the thought of returning to his room in the Walled City more unappetising than usual. In fact, there would never be a good time to return to his lodgings, now that Mr Tony Yip knew who he was and would soon no doubt realise what he had been doing. It would be nothing for a man like that to snuff Hua's life out on a whim. He smoked and bided his time, totted up the extent of his possessions and came to the conclusion that it would be wiser to forget that he owned anything at all. Mr Yip Yee Koon might advise him. Hua was due to earn a bonus this month and could start afresh somewhere else.

*

James and Yee Koon reached the top of the staircase which terminated in a cupboard at the service end of the apartment. It had been built as a fire escape and was a genteel replacement installed by Pearl's mother to replace the original pole exit that had connected the penthouse to the old truck storage bays at ground level. The cupboard door opened into the far end of the apartment's pillared entrance loggia. Neither Yip nor James spoke whilst they conducted a rapid search. Nothing had changed since

James had come back with the shopping, except for the bottle of Gilbey's Gin and one empty glass on the coffee table. They took the lift to the ground floor, a smooth and efficient machine and a far cry from the iron-caged monster that it had replaced when Pearl had inherited the building after her mother's death sixteen years earlier. The doors opened and they peered out into the gloom of the lobby, and Yee Koon, still clearly ill at ease, patted the gun he carried in the pocket of his suit. Even at a distance it was clear that the security office was empty. The two men walked carefully to the office door and James swung it open and switched on the lights noisily. Nothing. No-one.

"What has happened here, James? It resembles – what was the ship found at sea, perfectly preserved but with not a soul on board?"

"The *Marie Celeste*, old boy. If it wasn't for that glass on the coffee table upstairs, I would think it too much like that for my liking. They began to walk back towards the lift. "I'm sorry my old gun-toting friend, but I'm going to have to call Chief Superintendent Smythe again."

Yip was beyond pain. "So be it, James."

"No need for you to hang around, old man. I shall simply tell him that I came back from an engagement to find the entire building empty and decided to place the call. Off you scurry, Yip. You and Chief Superintendent Smythe have had enough of one another's company for one day, don't you agree?" But James had not reached the lift and Yip Yee Koon had taken only a few steps towards the front door when they heard a knock. "Perhaps it is someone for the Thompsons, Yip. I'll get it."

CHAPTER TWELVE

Thursday 6 December 1979: 9.30pm

Tony's number one bodyguard unlocked the factory door, stepped inside and conducted a swift search of the premises before giving the all clear. In the rear annexe the ladder rested against the far wall, just as they had left it the previous evening. Yip nodded curtly to Weng, who set about the task of climbing the ladder and wrestling the thin wooden panel from its timber frame. Weng shone a torch into the space and uttered a low *aiyah*. It was as empty as it had been before he and Li had so awkwardly dragged the *gweipor* up the ladder last night. Tony scrambled up to see for himself. There was nothing about the woman's release in the newspapers, which meant that the police had suppressed the news in order to lure him back here. But the police could not know that Weng had stopped the surveillance, at least for a time. But had he? Or had Li and Weng taken the woman for their own purposes and had Weng lied about the police presence?

This woman had caused him to lose respect. *The great Tony Yip*, they would say, *is as helpless as a stray kitten when he ventures outside of the Walled City.* He knew from Smith, the barman at the Emperor that already there were sniggers about the insulting remark she had made to him in the car, a remark which she had not hesitated to make, even when a gun was at her head! The bodyguards replaced the ladder and as casually as extracting a wallet from his pocket, Tony took out a gun and ordered the two men over to the far wall. "One of you is a traitor," he said. Bodyguard number one, Li, knew his boss better than his colleague and he saw Mr Yip's thoughts flow as clearly as if he was thinking the matter through himself.

He and Weng were in big trouble.

*

James opened the door. He had seldom been genuinely pleased to see Peter Benson but this was one such time. He exhaled heavily and beamed at him. "Peter my old sleuth, to what do I owe the pleasure?" He drew him through the door and explained the situation quickly – no security, no daughter. "All done a bunk." He tried to sound casual when he said that there could be a perfectly good explanation for all of it, but all the same he was just about to call Central Division and report Pearl as missing. "It's all too much, Peter, all too much. I flounder. For a mad second I thought it might have been her when you knocked and that she had simply gone out and the security guards had accompanied her. No. Chief Superintendent Smythe it has to be."

Peter cleared his throat. "Before you do, there is something else you should know, James. Terence Shaw. I have immobilised him. More than that, his telephone rang whilst I was, ah, unburdening the poor man from his worries and I spoke with an American male, who would appear to be a relative of Mr Shaw. The man, Sol is his name, seems to be under the impression that Mr Shaw is involved in a business deal which does not seem to have gone terribly well ... no surprises there perhaps, but it seems there is a triad connection involved and that could mean that Tony Yip is involved, seeing he and Shaw dined together last night. I have left Mr Shaw tied up in the house at Ong Hing Terrace. Given last night's events, perhaps you could mention this to Chief Superintendent Smythe as well."

*

After taking the call from Sir James, Tommy sat in his office and pushed his fingers in a highly irritated way through his thick hair, worry and fatigue clouding his thinking. Where the hell had Sir James gone that evening, apparently on a mission so important that he thought it worthwhile leaving his daughter alone? "Well," said James, stalling for time when Chief Superintendent Smythe arrived at the apartment and asked the question, "We – rather I – kept vigil...if I can put it that way, Chief Superintendent."

"*Vigil?* Not at the warehouse in Beecham Road, surely! Don't tell me you went back there, Sir James." James had the grace to look shame-faced. "The police are conducting surveillance on those premises."

"I realise that, Chief Superintendent. We – I – parked around the corner." It was obvious that there was more, much more to this than Sir James was letting on. Either Detective Sergeant Wing or Detective Inspector Carruthers would have spotted him entering the building and reported it unless he had found another way in. He told James in no short order to cough up his story and his florid complexion whitened in patches around his mouth when he heard that the two warehouses were connected through the attics.

"I'll have this information radioed through to the officer on duty, and I need to put another officer on duty in the street, as well as having officers go to Sheung Wan to pick up Shaw. May I use your phone?" Tommy wondered about the *I – we –* that Gates had kept tripping over in his story. No doubt, Yip Yee Koon was in on this. But that could wait until later.

*

When he reached home, Yip could not remember ever having felt more tired and drained. He left the car at the kerb for one of the staff to garage. He simply did not have the energy to negotiate the steep driveway. As he closed the door he heard the click of a car door opening. He turned, quickly, and reached for his gun. Of course! His brother would try to have him assassinated. How stupid of him, how careless of him, to believe that he could casually make his way back to his own house safely, any more.

"Sir, it is I, Hua Leung, sir." Hua's eyes widened as he saw the handle of a small revolver appear from the side pocket of Mr Yip's suit jacket. Yip's shoulders slumped and Hua observed the movement and wondered about this display of vulnerability in his boss, such a departure from his usual upright carriage. Yip listened attentively to Hua's story about the removal of Mr Shaw from Ong Hing Terrace. Hua even ventured to tell his employer that he had been seen by Mr Tony Yip and was known to Mr Tony Yip due to Hua being a long term resident in the Walled City of Kowloon and did Mr Yip Yee Koon think it wise for Hua to return there?

Yip patted Hua Leung on the back. "Hua Leung, it is obvious that you should not return to that place, tonight or any other night. Have you family there?" Hua shook his head. He had not. "Then you shall become a member of my house staff and live here. Tonight you will share Mr Lam's room and tomorrow we shall make other arrangements. Mr Lam is taking over Mr Kim's duties and my chauffeur will manage the day staff. I will need a new driver. There is a small apartment above the garages that comes with the job and you will be provided with uniforms and I will give you an amount of money to buy any other personal items you will need. You are not to return to the Walled City. Understood? Hua more than understood. He beamed with pure pleasure.

"As of now, consider this to be your new home. Tonight, put the car in the garage and then go to your rest. I must think what to do about this situation and you may find your rest is short. Go now."

*

The barman of The Emperor Inn was known as Mr Smith, but no-one knew why. It was presumed he lived in the Walled City but was never seen beyond his familiar territory in the shabby little bar located in an alley off the main thoroughfare to the northern gate. The area was at the smart end of town. In times past, adventurous *gweilos* would often smoke opium in the upstairs salons before making a visit to one of many brothels in the area but these days *gweilos* rarely visited and the business survived on the custom of locals who did their drinking in this safer part of the city. Few outsiders smoked opium anymore.

Mr Smith observed two of Tony Yip's men enter the bar, in company with a foreigner. Yip's men could have taken him into the salons through one of the upstairs entrances but they felt like treating themselves to a bit of swagger with the boss being well away. They pushed the man so hard that he should have fallen flat on his face, but Terry's entrance needed no embellishment – his presence was spectacle enough. One ancient customer known as the Skunk quaked. He recalled seeing a *gweipor* in here once before, a foreign woman, a devil witch. Nothing but bad luck had followed him since. Terry didn't fall but recovered from the violent shove and stood upright, feeling strong and even in control among the madness of his current predicament. Regardless of what had happened to him he felt as though he could take on the whole bar, but he took care to keep his eyes to the floor as the thugs each grabbed one of his arms.

"Tonight, my friends," one of the thugs said to the gathered company in a voice charged with drama, "You will hear much and perhaps even see things you should forget in the morning. After he takes some food, this man is going on a special tour of our city." The gathering of customers remained perfectly still and silent. They all knew that whatever the foreign devil had done, he had earned the penalty of a night out in the deeper reaches of the Walled City. He would not see daylight.

*

A call from Division Central informed Chief Superintendent Smythe that there was no answer from Detective Sergeant Carruthers. A car had been despatched to Beecham Road. Smythe barked into the phone that there should be back-up of another three vehicles and all officers were to be put on arms alert *and* he would be there as quickly as possible. He dampened James's hopeful look with a *forget it Sir James* and left James standing rather irresolutely at the lift.

"Might it involve Pearl, d'you think, Chief Superintendent? I *should* come with you, you know..." But he was barked down without the usual deference Tommy Smythe paid him on the basis of his status as a high ranking public servant, the father of a prominent Hong Kong citizen and perhaps, not least of all, because he was a Knight of The Realm.

*

Weng and Li risked a glance at one another. Li had worked for Mr Tony Yip for twenty years and could usually read his boss's moods, but not tonight. Tony paced the annexe, sometimes waving the gun at them, and all the while muttering. Weng caught the word *turtle face* and as Yip said it, he cocked the trigger of his revolver and held it to Weng's forehead. Weng closed his eyes and waited, but the cold metal barrel was removed and Mr Yip was again pacing and muttering.

Weng would not look at Li again. Each man must face his own destiny tonight. If they had known one another better, perhaps their eye contact could have advised each other what to do – jump the boss? Dive for his legs? Disarm him and stun him? Both knew that an attack on Mr Tony Yip was unthinkable unless they were willing to risk their lives, or take his. A wail of sirens forced a solution to the stand-off. Weng's eyes widened. Not only was it dangerous in here, there was nothing to look forward to outside. The body of the police officer must have been found! Tony reacted to the siren blast a blink later than Weng and in that blink Weng took the advantage, threw himself bodily at Tony's legs and felled him. The gun slid across the floor and in a step, Li had it.

Weng and Li looked at one another and this time they were clearly of one mind. There must be many police vehicles approaching the area. They could hear tyres screaming as brakes were hit and blue patrol lights made shadow and light play on the men's faces for a second before the gunshot sounded. The bullet went straight through Tony Yip's head and left a neat hole, rimmed in black, on his forehead. The merest spot of blood oozed from the wound. An acrid smell filled the annexe.

Li heaved the body over Weng's shoulder and between them they painfully made their way up the ladder and stuffed the dead weight of Tony Yip into the attic.

The attic in the Beecham Street factory had yet another visitor.

Li crossed the room to the door, took keys from Tony's pocket and smiled at his colleague. "Mr Yip never uses premises from which there is only one entrance and exit. That is why last night was such a stuff-up. He panicked in a situation in which he had never been put before." He found the key he wanted and unlocked the door and together the two men dragged the body into the adjacent attic, where earlier in the night James and Yip Yee Koon had stood vigil, waiting for the appearance of the very man who was now being dragged, dead, across the room.

It was Tony Yip's turn to wait.

Li replaced the panel and returned to Weng, who stood uncertainly beside the dead body of his boss. Would Li kill him? Again the two men read one another's faces and as another siren wailed Li knew that this was his last opportunity to deal with Weng. He fired the gun and Weng, who had always longed to be closer to his boss, finally had his wish fulfilled when he collapsed across the body of Tony Yip, the wound in his temple gushing blood.

*

The two men left to guard Terry were fed up. They had followed orders and had fed and watered their guest. They waited and waited. Surely the boss would return soon. Their guest sat calmly in one of the room's shabby chairs and breathed deeply, as though meditating. This increasingly annoyed Yip's youngest man, Tsiu. When would the boss return? When would the fun begin? Where would they go first? Usually such antics started off with a dental appointment, moved on to a specialist manicure and pedicure parlour and ended up in a day clinic for minor surgical procedures. These were for medium-core visits of course, visits that were designed to demonstrate Mr Yip's power.

How had this man offended Mr Yip? No-one had ever seen or heard of him before. Perhaps the boss would merely drug him and leave him somewhere nasty, somewhere difficult to escape from, somewhere like Beggar's Hall. Tsiu shivered. He had been to Beggar's Hall only once and hoped never to have to return. He looked at the man they had found trussed up in the Sheung Wan hovel. Perhaps he was a fetishist. Perhaps that is what Mr Yip had planned for him. Tsiu's eyes glowed with anticipation. He had heard of the specialist parlour towards the southern gate, a notorious venue for the serious fetishist, known as *The Turtle's Back*. He remembered the scream that had rung out earlier in the evening as they brought this worthless *gweilo* through the city; it would certainly have come from there. Tsiu had personally never been to *The Turtle's Back*, had always been told he was too young, that such experiences suited more mature tastes.

Tsiu had been Mr Tony Yip's driver on the previous night's adventure and he sniggered a little as he remembered what the *gweipor* had called Mr Yip. He had made sure word of that had got around quickly and people were already dubbing Mr Yip *Mr Turtle Face*. Tsiu felt a small shudder of fear thinking about how Mr Yip would take revenge if he knew he had gossiped. One brave wit had even said, "It would be more accurate if she had called him *turtle breath*. He could imagine how Mr Yip would react to hearing that said to his face.

Yip's other more senior man was impatient for some action too. "A little introduction to the city cannot interfere with Mr Yip's plans too much, Tsiu. Send for the dentist. We can have a little fun and no-one else need know."

*

At 11.30pm, one of the patrol car drivers thought he heard a shot as he pulled the vehicle into the kerb at the surveillance site. His Sergeant barked "where?" The Constable pointed. "Wait here." The Sergeant ran into the apartment building to find the Detective Inspector in charge of the crime scene and met him on the stairs. The Detective Inspector's face told it all.

"Sir. Constable Choy heard a shot. Other side of the road." The Detective Inspector grabbed the Sergeant's arm.

"Lock up, Toby, have two officers stand guard until the scene of crime team arrive and give the go-ahead to seal the place up. Constable, Detective Sergeant, come with me. Sergeant, take two men with you and see if there's anything going on in the building around that corner." A fifth car arrived and Chief Superintendent Smythe hurried towards the cluster of officers. Detective Inspector Lim gave the Chief Superintendent a quick debrief; Tommy nodded approval and took the steps to the apartment two at a time to view the crime scene.

*

Li looked around frantically. The attic lay-out was the same as on the other side, even the panels that sealed off the attic from the main factory were in the same style. It stood to reason that they were just as high above the concrete floor too . If so, he could not jump even if he could easily push out one of the timber partitions. No. His boss would not have considered that an ideal exit. He locked himself in with the two dead men, taking care to pocket the key and Mr Yip's gun. There was no choice but to wait this out. Then he remembered that the panel of wood that gave access to the attic was propped against the wall and the ladder was a sure indicator to anyone who came into the building that something had gone on in the upper level. It was a dead giveaway.

Aiyah, what should I do? He unlocked the door and crept down the ladder and peered through the doorway, across the expanse of the vast factory floor. On the opposite side of the street many lights lit up a scene where police officers hurried to and fro. The lights in an apartment two levels above the street were also blazing. Weng's handiwork of earlier this evening had clearly been discovered. How long before the doors to this building were battered down? The answer was at hand. He saw three police officers begin to cross the street. One of them carried a tyre lever.

Li fled up the ladder, replaced the panel and ran back into the room where he had dragged the two bodies. There was nothing for it. He would have to remove a panel from the attic wall on this side of the building, jump to the floor and escape into the laneway, if his legs weren't broken first. There was a high solid paned window on this side of the building and lights from the apartment opposite spilled dimly across the floor and in the corner he saw a square of something opaque and darker than the surrounding floorboards. He felt around in the semi-darkness. It was not a staircase but a cavity in the floor and he could feel, if he fully extended his arms, that it appeared to be a chute. Li turned and carefully lowered himself into the blackness, clutching each edge hard, just in case the blackness was a void that led to eternity and was not an escape route at all ….

*

After Chief Superintendent Smythe left, James rang the hospital. He spoke to a very chatty nurse, Nurse Roberts. Yes, a lady had called to speak to Dr Henderson and was upset to learn that she had collapsed and was under sedation. James let one eyebrow crawl a little with surprise but no such emotion was evident in his level voice. The woman hadn't left her name, no, but she did leave a message that Dr Henderson seemed very happy with. Would Sir James care to speak with Dr Henderson? She was quite awake again and at her husband's bedside. Her husband was still under sedation and may have to be moved to another – ah, facility – tomorrow, if his condition remained the same.

"James! Good to hear from you." Kaz was more cheerful than circumstances dictated she should rightfully be. "Yes, apparently a woman rang whilst I was sedated, and no, James, before you ask, she didn't leave her name. Apparently I went off to la-la land after reading about Pearl's kidnapping. The caller left a fairly understandable message: want to hear it?" James didn't have to let the skin on his forearm prickle, it did it all by itself. Pearl and her bloody tortoises! She had taunted Tony Yip with a reference to turtles or tortoises or some such equally smelly, testudinarious thing last night and now this evening she'd been on the blower to Kaz ranting on about it being a bleak tortoise winter or some such. And, he remembered, Pearl, Marcus and Kaz had given the project they were talking about sharing some bloody tortoise-y name as well.

"Kaz, what time was this? Was she drunk?"

"Really, James, how would I know? All I thought about when Nurse Roberts gave me the message was relief. Clearly, Pearl wanted to let me know that she is free. Why shouldn't she be a bit drunk? If it was me, I'd be stocious."

"She's gone again, Kaz. She's not here. She said she would wait for me. I should never have gone out again, I can't think why I went out." He waited for Kaz to speak but there was silence on the other end of the line except for what could have been a smothered sob. "Her release hasn't been publicised, so not a word, swear? The only sign of her in the apartment since I left is a Gilbey's Gin bottle and an empty glass. The police are putting out an All Alert. Anything may be relevant. Kaz?" The line was still silent. Damn and blast it if the woman's fainted again he thought, but her voice came back, strong and silvery.

"James. Do you think – think she's been kidnapped again?"

"I pray to the gods of all tortoises until the end of time not, Karen, but I just don't know. The best thing you can do is to stay with Drew, close ranks. If you hear from Pearl and it doesn't sound quite like her or anything at all seems odd, don't be lured away. Get as much information as you can and call the police. And call me. Yes. Pearl's old number."

*

Midnight: Marcus tossed until the top sheet was wound around his body so tightly that he broke out in a chilly sweat. He got out of bed, smoothed the crumpled mess back into place and got back in. The more he thought about seeing Dennis Childs earlier that evening the less real it seemed. Here they were, he and Derek, two strangers to Hong Kong, who simultaneously saw a man they both recognised! What were the odds on that for a couple of strangers in such a highly populated city?

It was no good. He got out of bed again and went to the fridge for a beer. The sight of Dennis Childs had been a shock, one that he couldn't share with his cousin, who was almost exhilarated by the recognition, but for Marcus it had been like looking at a dead man walking. The events of the past week heaped up in his mind. Should he confide in Derek after all and take him to meet Pearl tomorrow? A very definite voice in his head said *no* and Marcus knew why. Seeing her so recently after what she'd been through was a pretty special privilege and he had no right to flout it. If Dennis came along uninvited, she might see it as a betrayal of trust and refuse to negotiate any further.

Or worse, because Derek was so damned good-looking, she might negotiate something else altogether that he knew he had no hope of competing with.

*

Terry was very aware of what was happening but he felt no pain. None at all. He saw the instruments, hideous, antiquated instruments – and felt no fear. It was as though someone else had taken over his faculties entirely, including his sensory responses. Terry Shaw hated anything to do with dentistry but he watched the man set out various probes, pliers and finally, a manual drill. He saw anxiety and dread and anticipation on the faces of Yip's men. They had obviously witnessed this sort of thing before.

Terry said nothing. He reasoned that this would pass, as everything passes. He let his fear go, so much so that when the first probing with a sharp object resulted in the instrument slipping off one of the molars in his lower jaw to sink deep into his gums he merely noted the taste of his blood as it oozed from his mouth. Yip's senior man looked worried and spoke sharply to the dentist. He wanted no visible marks, just a bit of simple drilling and filling. The man shrugged. Terry smiled. Young Tsiu looked at him with an expression not far short of admiration. This *gweilo* had courage. On the other few occasions when Tsiu had witnessed similar events, the recipient of the attention was usually reduced to tears and pleading just at the sight of the instruments. This man was very different.

*

"I apologise for disturbing you, James. Yip here." James slumped into one of the armchairs in the big sitting room: *this night was endless.* "James?"

"I'm listening, Yip. What news?"

"Mr Terence Shaw is the news James. My brother, ah, removed him from Ong Hing Terrace earlier this evening." At the mention of Shaw's name, James realised he hadn't told Chief Superintendent Smythe about Peter's intervention – what was it about that man? Things he said just seemed to slip James's mind.

"Don't say, Yip. Any ideas?"

"I would imagine Mr Shaw is presently somewhere in the Walled City. The question is: why did my brother take such an action? Mr Shaw was bound, according to Hua, with leather straps. My brother's men carried him out of the house as though he was a suitcase. Have you any news of Pearl?"

"Not yet. Is old Hua all right? And Yip? Your brother is not the man who restrained Mr Shaw. He no doubt had his reasons for removing him, but Peter Benson immobilised him. Apparently Mr Shaw became abnormally upset when Peter arrived on his doorstep. Your brother had an easy time of taking Shaw away, he was literally trussed up and awaiting removal." Yip was sufficiently startled to hold the telephone away from his ear and stare at it. *This night, would it never end!*

"We are in accord then, James. We can do nothing about this matter."

"Not a sausage, old man. I had intended to inform Chief Superintendent Smythe of Mr Shaw's predicament but I must confess I forgot about him and it would seem useless to do so now. Get some rest, Yee Koon. Tonight is a case of *que sera sera* for Mr Shaw, for my money."

"And for mine, James, goodnight."

*

Li continued to hold fast to the lip of the chute. He did not dare let go for if he did, he could land at the feet of a police officer. The sounds at the front door of the factory were loud but above the noise of someone hitting the door or trying to pry it open or break the lock, he also became aware of another sound, a rustling, close by. Rats. Below him was a pit of rats. Li was a child of the Walled City of Kowloon and rats meant nothing to him except that they knew how to survive and if they could survive in here then he could too. But if there was no exit from the chute, would he be able to climb out or would he die and become food for the rats? It all depended on how deep this pit was. He began to panic. Then he heard the front door of the factory break open, followed by the noise of many leather-shod feet stamping across the concrete floor.

*

James considered pouring a whisky but thought better of it. If by any bizarre chance Pearl *had* ended up back in the factory where Tony Yip had taken her last night, it shouldn't be too long before Smythe rang. If not, well perhaps then he would have a drink, because then it *would* become a very long night. The phone went and he pounced on it but it was a wrong number. James looked yearningly at the bottle.

*

Li thought there must be at least a dozen police officers in the building judging by the noise of shoes pounding across the concrete floor. They reached the annexe at the back and he heard the ladder scrape as it was moved, followed almost immediately by the panel being dislodged. There was no more doubt. The police already knew about the existence of the attic. There were loud footsteps on the timber flooring of the adjacent room. It was only a matter of time before they would crash through the partition and find Mr Yip and Weng. He clutched the edge of the chute, desperate. Should he hold on or let go and take his chances with whatever was at the bottom of this pit – an exit – or nothing? It was lined with metal. It could be a coffin or a sanctuary. He squeezed his eyes shut, trying to judge when he would have to make the decision.

The decision was made for him. There was a brief thump on the flimsy door of the partitioning between the two attics and it burst open. Li let go and let gravity take him where it would. He did not see the four officers but they knew immediately where he was. The squeaking of rats erupted from a dark square on the far side of the room and hundreds swarmed over him. Li did not fall as far as he imagined he might. The chute ended abruptly without exiting into the street, as he had hoped, but suspended somewhere between the ground and attic floors. He was caught in the beam of a strong torch. "Ladder!" said an authoritative voice. "There's a big rat down here." Li's only thought as he was hauled into the room was that Mr Yip had made a wrong judgement about this place having more than one exit. If he had been alive he would have been most displeased. Two officers grasped his arms, took the pistol from him and handcuffed him. One cautioned him. A tall fiery-haired policeman came into the room and took in the scene. The rats had either retreated to the corners, or fled into the adjoining attic and jumped to the ground, whilst still others began to slink back to their home in the chute.

The *gweilo* with the red hair spoke to him in English. "Didn't see the other door then, what? There was no need to wait for us, jolly accommodating of you to do so, however." One officer provided a rough translation and three others smiled grimly. One walked over to what Li could see clearly in the torchlight was a door and not panels as he had assumed. One officer opened the door as if giving a demonstration and disappeared. *Aiyah.* Li was led to the staircase revealed by torchlight and escorted to a waiting police car.

Mr Yip had known his exits after all.

*

Sergeant Toby Hill took over management of the second crime scene until Detective Inspector Fairweather was free. Smythe radioed Division Central and called for another scene of crime team to come to the factory at Beecham Street and authorised continued street surveillance. He left instructions with the Night Desk Sergeant to ring Sir James Gates and inform him that the call-out the Chief Superintendent had attended did not involve his daughter, spelt out for the Sergeant the delegations he had made at the two crime scenes and headed for home. Tommy sighed. His wife had spent the evening playing bridge and Tommy would rather have been at home with Melanie playing that silly game instead of having to deal with all of this. But at least they had made an arrest.

CHAPTER THIRTEEN

Friday 7 December 1979: 6.00am

The Boeing 707 was the first landing of the day at Kai Tak. Belinda had groomed herself as well as she could; the other passengers had long ceased to look at her with curiosity and had retreated behind their various books and journals. The Stewardess treated her with the same courtesy as her other charges but Belinda noticed that she stood just a little further away than was comfortable for the service of food and drink. Belinda made short work of two vodka tonics and ate a pretzel. She had been in the same clothes since Monday and had not done anything more for her personal hygiene than have a splash wash and use of the airline's complimentary toothpaste and toothbrush.

She cared not a whit about her appearance. Her priorities had altered. Her husband might be lying dead or comatose somewhere if his prediction of doom had eventuated and if that were the case, her children would be frantic, but would not necessarily expect to be consoled by their mother. That would more likely come from their nanny or even by one of the new talismans, depending on how long Bobby had been fooling around. *If he has been fooling around...* Belinda reminded herself. During the past hours she had put herself at a distance from her family and thought only about her father and making things good with him. He had been starved of her love and affection for years and he had brought her up when her mother left them both when Belinda was twelve! These last years, unwittingly, she had been as cold as her mother toward him and how she regretted it – now – when somehow she did not feel so needed herself.

The aircraft's cabin crew instructed passengers to return to their seats in preparation for landing. She was nearly home! She beamed at the man who sat across the aisle from her and unusually, did not receive a response. Perhaps he hadn't landed at Kai Tak before and thought that the unusual manoeuvre that the pilot was conducting in the approach to the air strip was in fact the plane crashing, which was exactly how landing at Kai Tak often felt.

*

James woke, still sitting upright in one of the armchairs in the sitting room. He had finally had his whiskies and after thirty-six hours without enough sleep to support three good shots, had passed out into a deep slumber. His mouth was dry and he felt dirty but when he looked at the time it was only just after six and the sky was still the colour of dull clay-mud that marked the long approach to the breaking of a Hong Kong winter's day.

He showered and laid out clothes, smoothed his spare suit and hung six beautiful soft-washed linen shirts. In the kitchen were the few supplies he had purchased from Wellcome's Supermarket – nothing madly practical for breakfast he realised, as he perused tins of mushrooms and packets of dried herbs. Whatever had possessed him to buy a tin of Lyle's Golden Syrup? But there was tea and tinned milk and sugar and he had acquired a packet of biscuits. Chocolate coated mini-rumballs weren't *the* ideal balanced breakfast but under the circumstances they would have to do.

He dressed and ate and carried out small, comforting routines. If he went out what would he achieve by roaming the streets of Hong Kong at this hour? Would he find his daughter staggering along a footpath somewhere, swinging her high heeled shoes around, waving an empty champagne bottle and singing "Show Me The Way To Go Home"? If he went out he wouldn't be here to talk to her if she called. But if he stayed in, he would go mad.

"Hospital" he said out loud. "Hospitals are on the go early. I'll visit Kaz and Drew." He wrote a note for Pearl, gathered his keys together and whistled softly whilst he waited for the lift. He stopped at a news stall where the sleepy proprietor was stacking the first edition of the *South China Morning Post* and hailed a solitary passing cab. He settled back and unrolled the paper and had barely glanced at the lead story when he asked the driver to stop. He absently gave the man a twenty dollar note and ran back to the apartment. He huffed his way across the lobby and stamped with impatience as he waited for the lift. He flung the paper on the kitchen bench, consciously steadied himself and read the story underneath the banner headline that screamed, *Ransom Demand for Lady Pearl Green*.

The story was brief. The night editor of the *South China Morning Post* had received a call at two o'clock that morning. The voice was muffled but was definitely that of a man with a heavy although unidentifiable accent. The message was short but clear: a letter would arrive at the offices of the SCMP during the morning dictating the ransom terms for the release of Lady Pearl Green.

James rang Division Central and asked to speak to the senior officer on duty. A very weary Inspector George Wong Han-Heung took the call. He had spent the last three hours interrogating a murder suspect. The Duty Sergeant was double-checking the suspect's statement and it would soon be ready for sign-off. Even though he was tired, George Wong was quietly triumphant. It appeared that the Hong Kong Police had, albeit inadvertently and in double-quick time, solved the murder of a prominent triad leader and his number two offsider. It would be a clear triumph for the Department as the murder suspect had named his victim as leader of the Wo Luen Shing Triad, Tony Yip, who ruled over a criminal empire of immense clout within the Walled City. When his identity was confirmed, it would be a red letter day for the Department.

No, he had not seen the morning papers yet, Sir James; and yes he would listen whilst Sir James read the lead story out to him. George Wong was suddenly very awake again. "I'll have to notify Chief Superintendent Smythe immediately of this, sir. Are you at home?" He took James's number and hung up.

Tommy Smythe took the call, trying to pull the phone off the hook before it woke Melanie but as usual she grumbled, rolled over and glared at him as though she had never seen him before and said, "Really Thomas, this is too much," before going back to sleep almost instantly. This usually made him smile but after four hours sleep he was not so easily amused, not this morning at any rate. The death of Detective Inspector Carruthers, followed by the discovery of the two bodies in the factory had made it another very long night for Chief Superintendent Smythe, who had spent more than an hour on the telephone to Carruthers's widow after sealing off both crime scenes. Emily Carruthers was currently visiting family in the UK and she had been inconsolable at the news of her husband's death.

Inspector Wong gave him the news about the outcome of the interview with the murder suspect and followed that up by reading out the first edition story about the ransom note. Tommy sat bolt upright in bed. "One of the men in the factory murder was Tony Yip, did you say? Ransom on Pearl Green? What is Sir James's number? No I'll ring from here and will be at the station within the hour. George, get surveillance on the SCMP Offices immediately. Plain clothes? Yes, of course. And George? My personal congratulations. What a result. This is a real coup for the Department, apprehending the brother of Yip Yee Koon. Maybe we'll get the real McCoy yet, hmm?" George Wong didn't have the vaguest idea of what a *real McCoy* was, but praise from the Chief Superintendent was hard to earn and he did get that. Chief Superintendent Smythe did not earn any praise from Melanie however, who, now fully awake, marched into the kitchen to make a pot of tea.

Obviously something big was on the brew for her husband.

*

Stale whisky and cigarette smoke were the familiar early morning smells and the only company that generally welcomed the barman of The Emperor Inn at opening time but this morning was different. The room was full of silent, sullen-faced men and Mr Smith had to push his way to his spot behind the bar. No-one spoke. Mr Smith had authority of a kind and asked, man by man, what was wrong. Everything and nothing was the answer. Mr Tony Yip and his two senior bodyguards had apparently not returned to the Walled City. There was a *gweilo* in the city, a guest of Mr Yip, last seen at the Bamboo Manicure Parlour not long after midnight, receiving the very best bamboo inserts the manicurist could offer. Not only did he not scream in pain, he actually seemed to enjoy the experience. The consensus was that he was a ghost, beyond the realm of human feeling and thought, but with a material presence.

Mr Smith had authority from the boss to act in unusual situations. "I am going out," he said. "Attend to yourselves." He took off the apron he had donned and stamped upstairs, removed a panel at the end of the hallway and ascended a flight of concealed stairs. Weaving and winding his way through a tangle of walkways, he eventually came to the door of the highest apartment in the Walled City, fourteen stories above ground level. The door was just one of the entrances to Mr Yip's extensive apartment and Mr Smith was one of few who knew where the triad boss lived. But Mr Yip was not at home. Smith shrugged and left. He would risk going out of the city to buy a newspaper. Something told him it was going to be a long day.

*

James read the article out loud to Chief Superintendent Smythe and said, "My daughter has been kidnapped again, Tommy. What sort of idiot am I for thinking that Tony Yip would give up? He's done it again, the temptation of money, another way to hurt his brother ... but how did he know where to look for her?"

"James. Tony Yip is dead."

"How do you know that?" The story unfolded. Two men shot, one of them Tony Yip, in the attic adjacent to where Lady Green had been held until the early hours of the previous morning. James shivered. He and Yip had not noticed anything that looked like a chute in the room. "The man who killed him?"

"Allegedly Yip's number one man, name of Li. He has confessed to killing Tony Yip and another bodyguard, Weng. I'm at home, off to the station shortly and I will require Yip's brother to make the formal identification." Did James detect a glint of satisfaction in this statement? If so, at least Smythe wasn't a hypocrite. He utterly detested Yip Yee Koon.

"What are your plans after that, Chief Superintendent? At least we had some idea about how and where to find Pearl." James hastily tried to hose down the untactful comment. "Tony Yip's actions were at least possible to guess at because Yee Koon knows that the factory in Beecham Street is, or rather was, his." Tommy assured him that everything possible was being done to find Pearl, the All Alerts were to be stepped up with her photograph distributed far and wide. But the reality was that they could only wait on further information from the kidnapper or kidnappers, and who knew when that would happen? *And,* thought Tommy, *perhaps if you lot had remained at the Hilton as we agreed, this might not have happened.* But of course he could not say that, not to Sir James at any rate.

They offered one another stiff farewells after which, with the phone back on the hook, James broke down. He put both hands in his thick silvering chestnut hair and sobbed. His beautiful, wonderful, damnedly independent daughter. Where on earth could she be?

*

Dennis Childs nimbly cooked up a big breakfast. The house was empty, the staff gone. They had all accepted their dismissals gracefully, with the exception of Chef. Dennis felt remarkably free. He flipped a piece of hot toast on to a plate and deftly fried a couple of eggs. This house was too big for him. When Belinda lived here and it was full of silly giggling girls it was different. But that was a long time ago and those days were over. The house could go.

*

Mr Lam answered the phone. It was Chief Superintendent Smythe for Mr Yip. Mr Yip took the receiver as though forced to grasp a venomous snake and gave Chief Superintendent Smythe the briefest greeting he could manage without being brusque. He listened, nodded, and his face flushed. "I will be there within the hour, Chief Superintendent." He called for Mr Lam. "Mr Lam, tell Hua Leung to be ready to drive me to the Central Police Station in half an hour. Put out my grey suit please." He phoned James but James sounded odd. Could he be crying? Yip's pleasantly smooth and serious face creased and just for a moment he looked all of his sixty-four years.

"James, I have been summoned to identify a body in the police morgue. The police believe the dead man is my brother." James of course, could not say that he had already been given the news of Tony Yip's death nor did he offer Yip condolences. Sorrow did not come into it. That may come when Yip Yee Koon allowed himself to reflect on a time – if there ever was one – when he could summon up some pleasant memories of his brother. They had declared war on Wednesday and it seemed, ironically, that Yip had won without having to do anything but wait for his brother to stitch up his own fate.

"What days, Yip, old chap. What days. Do you want company?"

"Yes James, I do. Half an hour? I'll pick you up." They were familiar words between them, but unfamiliar times, unfamiliar events. James went into the bathroom and took a quick shower and pressed cool water into his face in a vain effort to wash away his grief.

*

The police went through Pearl's movements of the previous afternoon. They interviewed James and heard how he and Marcus Browne had smuggled her out of the Hilton. They interviewed the Thompsons who corroborated James's story that they had handed over the apartment keys to him, ostensibly so that he could get the apartment ready for Pearl upon her release. They also interviewed Marcus.

Chief Superintendent Smythe was not happy to find that Marcus Browne had been involved. He'd had enough of American Indians for one week. It also seemed that Pearl Green had taken some interest in him after his release. They had both caused havoc to his week already and here it was, Friday, and he had a fresh case of abduction on his hands starring the same victim. *Just wonderful,* he thought, *what next?*

*

Belinda expected to be whisked through Customs without query, but she was wrong. The Captain of the Pan Am cargo plane had organised her transfer to another Pan Am flight leaving Narita for Hong Kong. She paid the fare by cheque and had simply been transferred from one aircraft to another. Now, she delved into her handbag for the third time, looking for her passport, but her passport was obviously not in it. She showed the official her cheque book in the account name of Mrs Belinda Jones. She showed him the bracelet Bobby had given her, engraved with the words *to the amazing Mrs Jones.* The man remained unimpressed. Mrs Jones was not a Hong Kong National. She could not enter Hong Kong without showing correct identification. She would have to wait in the Customs Office until the matter could be sorted out.

*

As James and Yip left the station, James spotted Marcus on his way to register his new address with Sergeant Thornton. Yip's face was calm again, even blank, but his mind was on the Walled City. There would be chaos when news of Tony's death became common knowledge: anarchy, if the definition held in an already lawless place. "James. I am going into the Walled City. I have some authority there because of my name and the time has come to use it."

James was torn. "But Yip, why? How long since you...?" The question remained open. How long indeed since Yip Yee Koon had been into that place and what was his influence there? James knew his friend well; but in the end, how well did anyone ever know another human being? James had seen that Yip had authority in the Walled City once, several years earlier, but that was before he knew that Tony Yip was his brother. Was Tony the only source of Yee Koon's influence? Could he take on a leaderless triad? Surely Yip wouldn't put himself up for that....

*

When Mr Smith returned, the bar of The Emperor was still full and he was kept as busy as though it was a Friday night and a crowd had arrived to drink away the week's worries. At ten o'clock he finally sat down with a coffee and opened *The Daily Kowloon Times.* It was right there, a picture of Mr Tony Yip taken when he was a much younger man, with the headline, *Walled City Triad Boss Murdered.* The article was short and to the point. No-one knew much about Tony Yip beyond and even within his territorial boundaries.

Mr Smith took a visual inventory of his customers. He saw no other newspapers tucked under arms or protruding from pockets. What had brought this crowd here so early and kept them here as the morning wore on was unease about the *gweilo* who had appeared in their midst. Clearly, they had not heard of the death of the triad boss. Mr Smith gave thought to whether he should announce Mr Yip's demise. Was that within his brief? How was he to deal with the fact that, also during the course of the night, Mr Yip's two most senior men were beyond recall to the Walled City? Did anyone else have authority or would it be most likely be seized by the two more junior bodyguards?

He looked around the crowded bar. Certainly no-one here had any power that he was aware of. The announcement of Mr Yip's death and the death of his number one bodyguard would unleash chaos, but worse, the bar would empty. Mr Smith's first concern at all times was to have a profitable day, every day. His thoughts were interrupted as the door opened and Terence Shaw entered.

Mr Smith looked at him with interest.

*

Belinda waited patiently enough. It wouldn't be long before her father got her out of this. Dennis Childs was a powerful man and the mere absence of his daughter's passport would be nothing for him to deal with. The Customs Officers were unimpressed by her demand that she contact her father directly and she had to be content with handing over his number and settling down in the no-go zone waiting room whilst a Customs Officer made the call. She picked up the *South China Morning Post* and the first thing she saw was the article about Pearl. She clasped her hands over her mouth to stop the scream she knew she could so easily let loose. Pearl was still missing and a ransom demanded for her release too! She felt her hands shaking as she turned the page, looking for more detail. She wished her father would hurry.

It wasn't Belinda's morning. On page two in a small box headed *Breaking News* was a photograph of Bobby. It had been taken at last year's USA Music Awards when he took out the award for the Best Male Vocalist in Popular Music. His hair was longer then than now. She looked at the photograph long and hard before she read the story. He had been hurt in a stage collapse during the closing set of the band's New York concert.

She knocked on the glass-paned office of the Customs Officer who had her under supervision and yelled out, "Officer. My husband has been hurt. I have to go to America. And I mean, right now." The amazing Mrs Jones was back. The man leapt from his chair and referred her to a senior officer, who received the same treatment. The airport manager was summoned. Nothing stood in the way of Mrs Jones when she wanted her own way and for their part, Customs had no qualms about deporting a would-be illegal entrant into Hong Kong, particularly as she planned on exiting in some style. Mrs Jones demanded that the airport manager secure her a private jet.

*

Terry smiled amicably at the crowd of men in the bar and as if a single organism, they drew back towards the walls. Dried blood encrusted his face and his hands. Those who had never seen the results of a manicure from the Bamboo Manicure Parlour reeled. One man retched and ran into the laneway. Slivers of bamboo protruded from each side of each of his fingernails. Dried blood seemed to hold them in place. Terry held them up. "Nice, hmm?" Mr Smith's interest in Mr Shaw had turned into an idea born of desperation and he watched carefully as the crowd of men gradually inclined their heads to Shaw. This man had earned respect, which was more than anyone else was capable of doing around here at the moment.

Mr Smith called for quiet. In English he told Terry the news, that Mr Tony Yip had been murdered and the Wo Luen Shing Triad, as of the early hours of this morning was a leaderless rabble. New leadership was needed immediately or warfare would break out and result in many deaths. Other less powerful groups would be emboldened to go for the ultimate power that the Wo Luen Shing had long enjoyed and even strengthened during the so-called Triad Wars. "There is nothing else to be done: I have emergency powers delegated to me by the Leader in times of crisis. I am going to announce the death of Mr Yip and declare you leader. What is your name?

Terry smiled benignly at Smith. There was no doubt the experiences of the night had been very interesting, and, it seemed, more of an initiation ceremony than a mere medium-core torture session perpetrated by two thugs for their own enjoyment. Terry knew he had done well. He still felt strong and centred, although the bamboo protrusions from his fingernails were beginning to cause him some discomfort. "Shaw. Mr Terence Shaw. And you are?"

"Smith. Mr Smith."

"Mr Smith. By all means, I will take control of your leaderless rabble. You shall be my right-hand man. After you make the announcement I want Mr Tsiu and his offsider tied up and held upstairs, where I was held last night. Understand?" Mr Smith nodded and addressed the assembly. Not a man amongst them dared speak against him and within minutes, Mr Shaw was elevated to the leadership of the Wo Luen Shing Triad. After his hosts of the previous evening were taken away and restrained, Terry instructed his new offsider to have him taken to the day clinic where his nail job could be modified. Together he and Mr Smith would plan how they would repress any outbreaks of violence in the Walled City, what resources were available to them and so on. Terry was quite good at this sort of thing. He had been in the British Army for five years after all.

"Oh, and Smith? Find another barman. You are going to be busy."

*

At 8.00am Dennis Childs guided the Bentley up the steep drive and drove to the office. His presence was certainly going to shake things up there. He smiled. He rarely put in an appearance these days, but the New York office needed help in getting a massive tender together and the Chief Quantity Surveyor at Childs Engineering Pty Ltd was going to have to take a trip to NY as soon as possible, to make sure the deadline could be met.

Dennis had phoned ahead and asked Phillip Carrington to meet him in his office at eight thirty sharp and soon after found himself listening to what were little more than feeble excuses from Carrington about it not being a good time for him to be away from Hong Kong due to family reasons. Dennis preferred to think that whilst family may be first in a man's mind, family never came first in business. "I need people who are flexible and can respond to challenges, Carrington, not people who say they can't take on a one-off project urgently because of family issues."

Phil opened his mouth to speak but Dennis held up his hand in rebuke. "...and I don't want to know what the family problems are, but as of this minute you have ample time to take care of them. You're fired. I'll organise a settlement based on your years of service but I want you off the premises now." He switched on the intercom to the outer office. "Send in Tim Fong, have Lionel Field available and after that call me a cab. Oh, and have Ryan take my car back to my home."

*

Kaz woke up, fuzzy on detail about the previous evening. She was in a hospital bed. Slowly it all drifted back. She had gone out like a light at the shock of reading about Pearl but she thought, no, she was sure, hadn't she recovered from that? What was going on? She sat up very tentatively but her head was clear. The sedative they had given her must have hit her harder than she had first thought.

"Well well, Sleeping Beauty is back with us." It was Drew, sitting in the visitor's chair, plastered leg propped up on the side of the bed, his face alight. "My child bride. How good of you to return to us." She laughed.

"Well, I guess the sedative didn't wear off quite as soon as I thought it would. I was expecting to hear that you had been transferred to a sanatorium this morning given your loony behaviour of the past few days. I might come with you." She leaned towards him and squeezed his hand. "What the hell happened to you?" Drew shrugged. He didn't know, said it was going to have to remain one of life's puzzles, how he had lost the plot and why but at least he was aware that he had, so didn't Kaz think that encouraging? "Can we go home Drew? If we don't we'll become institutionalised. I'm dying to make my own tea."

"Not to mention downing a beer," said Drew. "The Doc's going to talk to us both, the team are on rounds now. Shouldn't be long. Try to look sane, Kaz." She gingerly got out of bed. It was all right. The world was still spinning on its axis and not in her head. She threw her arms around him and kissed him.

"Ugh. Hospital breath. Definitely, home."

*

The Chief Executive of the *South China Morning Post* prowled the corridors. The promised ransom note had failed to materialise and the staff were jumpy. Some were in preparation for a full attack, half expecting the note to be lobbed through the windows, attached to an incendiary device. Alice Yeung, the Fashion Editor who had worked long and hard to win the work station near the window with the best harbour view, announced nervously that she would attend a fashion showing of some fine Thai Silks at the Mandarin and would not be back before close of business.

Two story outlines waited on the Chief Editor's desk: one based on the ransom note having been delivered and the other designed to keep the story alive and the tension high, with speculation about how and when it might arrive at the newspaper office. The night desk staff complement had been increased from two to five and the crime reporters were out and about busy collecting story material from the rumour mills. But they didn't sniff out James. James's presence in Hong Kong had long passed the press by. His status as a high ranking English bureaucrat was not fodder for the gossip columns at any time and Pearl was only ever referred to in Hong Kong circles as being as the daughter of the late Lady June Bowen.

*

It was handed to the cooking editor, Shelley Taylor, to discover the ransom note. In the basement kitchens of the SCMP offices, a batch of angel cakes lay in paper-lace cake-cups, freshly stuffed with cream, when Shelley appeared to set up the styling shoot. The photographer waited, impatient to get on with his next assignment as she fussed with the cakes until deciding that they would look better on a tiered cake-stand than sitting prettily arranged on a plate. As she shifted the tiny morsels of sponge and fresh cream she noticed something protruding from the wings of one of them and briskly extracted it. Paper! Where had the cooking been done? Who had been so careless as to leave a piece of baking paper protruding from one of her masterpieces! She was about to throw it away when Harald the photographer stopped her. "Open it, Shelley. Maybe it's the ransom note, hah!"

It was. Shelley Taylor was not a woman easily impressed. A cooking editor's life is not easy, especially in a place like Hong Kong where most people couldn't care less about home cooking. She longed to be re-assigned to the social columns. She unfolded the rectangle of cream-smeared paper and calmly read the message to Harald. "Pearl Green will be released upon receipt of fifty million Hong Kong dollars equally converted into American Dollars and British Pounds. Further instructions will follow."

She looked squarely at Harald. "That's a lot of money Harald. Pearl Green has no family, you know. She is the money-bags. How do the kidnappers think it is going to be organised? By her ringing the bank? Well, the cakes will have to do – they look good enough, don't they? I'd better take this upstairs to the boss. It may settle some of the staff down." The Chief Executive was under orders to ring Chief Superintendent Smythe promptly with any news and he did so after taking care to have a hand-written copy of the text made by his PA. He checked it carefully before locking it away in his office safe. No-one, not even a senior policeman, was going to rob Edmund Darlington of a good story, even if he couldn't use it immediately.

*

Belinda was outraged. She waved her cheque book under the nose of the Hong Kong Airport's General Manager and shouted at him, still demanding the use of a jet, any jet, immediately. Belinda knew a lot about money but not about how airports function. The manager explained, for the third time, how an airport with the arrivals and departure schedule of Kai Tak could not accommodate an extra outgoing flight at little notice, how dangerous it would make the skies of Hong Kong and how he would not and could not risk the safety of thousands of passengers for one person. But Belinda just stamped her foot and again demanded to speak to her father, or if he wasn't available, to the Governor.

*

Belinda banged the receiver down. Her father was either not there or was not taking calls. Where was that blasted PA of his, damn and blast her? She drew a small book from her handbag and tried another number.

"I want to speak to the Governor. It is Mrs Jones here. Oh it's you, Toby. Are you still the Governor's Clerk? How funny. Put me through will you? I'm dealing with an emergency and it requires His Excellency's intervention."

Toby Blake felt caught somewhere between anger and excitement when he recognised Belinda's voice. It had been many years since they had spoken. Without so much as a backward glance she had left him for that ghastly little pop star, Smut Someone. Every time Toby saw his ex-wife's photograph in the press or a magazine he would deliberately shut the publication and dispose of it. He thought that she looked no better than a tart and now here she was, treating him as though he was a mere cipher, demanding to speak to the Governor. He smoothed his tie and took a careful swallow of water. *Call me a clerk. Indeed.*

"I'm afraid the Governor is not available. I shall leave a message for him that you called. Where can you be contacted?" Belinda banged the phone down again. *Little twerp.* She turned to the Airport Manager and demanded to be put on the next plane to New York, first class. He demurred. Could he do that? He knew she had no passport. She wouldn't fare any better with New York Customs. Was that his problem when she didn't need to go through Customs to re-embark and leave Hong Kong? His face relaxed.

"Very well, Mrs Jones. Please be patient for a little longer and I will get you on the very first available flight." It would be worth the effort to get rid of her. Her reputation might be impressive but it wasn't as powerful as her body odour.

CHAPTER FOURTEEN

Friday 7 December 1979: 11.30am

James insisted that Marcus accompany them for a coffee. The three men sat in the Blue Moon Coffee Shop near the entrance to The Star Ferry.

"I don't understand this madness, quite simply, do not understand it." Yip ignored the outburst but Marcus politely asked what James meant.

"He means nothing, young man," said Yip. "James is having difficulty seeing what is under his nose." Marcus looked into his empty coffee cup. James looked at Yip in a decidedly unfriendly way. This was a difficult situation. Mr Yip wanted to go to somewhere called the Walled City and Sir James disagreed. Sir James was fretting over how he could raise the ransom money for Pearl's release if the promised note showed up but that seemed merely to bore Mr Yip who said, in a very level voice, "Really James, please do not insult me". Yip was preoccupied by the crate of cash stashed in the vault in his basement, a little depleted since he made the loan to Dennis Childs, but adequate for this occasion, certainly. Would more of it circulate today, this time for Pearl's release? Where would it go? It could become rather like a sea container of Oxfam relief clothing that turns up at the docks of troubled nations for distribution to the needy. But is the container ever unpacked or is it just a metaphor for war and strife? *Ah, the Oxfam boat has arrived, there must be trouble.*

Marcus checked the time: eleven-forty, time to set off to meet Derek. The two older men were still at odds with one another in a mildly bickering way until Sir James said, "Very well Yee Koon, let's have it your way." Yip flung a fifty dollar note on the table and beckoned James to follow him.

"My car is over here. Young man, it has been …."

"I think he should come with us."

"Really, *this* is too much, James."

"He could be useful Yip, *if* you get my drift."

Yip considered Marcus as though he had not noticed him before. He would stand out in the Walled City, certainly, and those eyes could be very useful. Many believed that green eyes were the sign of a celestial being. Perhaps a bit of assistance from the gods might be an asset today. He said, "Are you with us, Mr Browne?" James didn't wait for Marcus to reply but grabbed his arm and started marching him towards Yip's car.

It appeared he was.

*

Detective Inspector Cullen handed the ransom note to the Chief Superintendent, sealed in a plastic envelope, the greasy heritage of time spent in the wings of the angel cake undetectable to the Chief Superintendent's long, bony fingers. From a locked drawer in his desk he pulled out the two notes that had appeared at the Childs household following Mrs Jones's disappearance. Not remotely the same, although he would get the handwriting chaps onto it.

Tommy sighed a little. Everything seemed to be demoralising him. He tapped the top sheet of a pile of case notes. Was this phase two of the Belinda Jones case or a copycat crime? What about the ransom? Dennis Childs had organised the money for Belinda's release, against police advice certainly but nevertheless … what would happen in the case of Pearl Green? Did she have that much money? Did her father?

Tommy knew who did have that sort of money – Yip Yee Koon. Tommy wouldn't be surprised if that crook ended up brokering the release of Lady Green and made interest on it. He shook his head. He really had to get a grip. Pulling the odious man into every unsavoury scenario that cropped up was not good thinking at any level. He'd damned well talk to Melanie seriously this evening about having six months in the UK. In the meantime, he would get on to Sir James and let him know that the ransom demand had turned up.

*

Kaz packed Drew's clothes and shaving-gear and dabbed at her face with a damp hand-towel. Bathing could wait until they got home, although the matter of bathing Drew at home was going to offer food for thought. The fracture to his leg was assumed to be healing within its pallid plaster casing and his mind had seemed at last to have relinquished or at least suppressed the nightmares that had so firmly kept his fear button pressed on. For all that he could have had reservations about releasing him, the Consultant Physician was of the opinion that Drew would be better off at home and had no hesitation in pronouncing that both husband and wife be discharged immediately.

Kaz phoned her housekeeper, Mrs Chan, and gave her the good news. Mrs Chan set off to the kitchen to cook a cake to welcome Mr Drew back. Kaz would always be Miss Kaz to Mrs Chan. Mr Drew loved cake, especially chocolate cake. After that she cleaned the apartment with a ferocity that suggested that a plague of mites and fleas had been through it, including all the bedding and carpets.

*

Peter Benson arrived late at the office. Judith Sung looked at the clock and wondered where the morning had gone. She had never arrived at the office before Dr Benson during the time she had been at the Bowen Foundation but he made no comment about why he was late. As for Danny Chiu, Danny hand spent most of the morning sitting at his desk, jabbing at his nails, a ledger lying ignored beside him. He pounced on Peter. "Dr Benson. Have you seen this morning's edition of the *South China Morning Post*? I thought, well I thought you may have gone to search – for Pearl." Peter read the headline and within it saw the likely truth of the matter – that whilst the kidnappings may have been conducted for different reasons, they had an objective in common. It all became clear to him: whoever had Pearl now had simply had the opportunity to take Belinda first.

Peter wondered what the kidnapper must have felt when Pearl was taken right from under his nose by Tony Yip on Wednesday night. Having a second crack at her the following night must have been like a blessing from the gods and kidnapping her when she was publicly already considered abducted must have seemed like a double blessing. "I have been telling James that Pearl is in danger ever since she arrived home but the man won't listen" he said without any further explanation or even acknowledgement of the fact that not only had James realised Pearl was in danger on Wednesday night but had taken extraordinary steps to get her out of it. Peter looked at Danny. Poor Danny had only had his boss back for a few hours before she was in trouble up to her finely-crafted ears again. He had the same look on his face that Peter had seen when Pearl had been in trouble once before, years ago. He was agonised. Peter wondered if Danny realised that he loved Pearl.

He was direct with them. "Your safety is my immediate concern. In that regard, I would like you, Danny, and you Judith, to go home. It is my intention to close the office until Pearl is found. We could all, merely by our association with her, be in danger. I don't want to alarm you..." He gestured at Judith Sung to move more calmly, as she jumped to her feet and made for the coat rack. "... But please go directly home, no diversions, take a taxi each...oh...and book them from the Hong Kong Taxi Company. They keep driver records of all bookings. I will ring you when it is time to return to work. Try not to worry about Pearl. We all know how resourceful she is. And also, don't forget that Pearl has gone off in the past, on a whim, Danny. I remember..." but he decided not to relate what he remembered. Pearl had only been a girl then.

He saw both staff safely into their taxis and returned to the office. He tried to second-guess what James would be doing right now. No doubt he was off on some mission of his own, looking for Pearl. He read the story about the ransom note again, which was appearing in every news network in Hong Kong under the storyline of *The Cupcake Caper*.

Yip Yee Koon would be called on to identify his brother's body and James would certainly accompany him. Peter's face lightened. After that it was obvious what would happen. Yip would want to go to the Walled City. He would know what was likely to happen in there – if it had not started already – chaos in a place where chaos was part of the daily side-show, but this particular type of chaos could be more catastrophic than the old city could take. It could crumble at the seams. In Peter's opinion that would not be such a bad thing. He locked up and went out into Upper Albert Road to hail a taxi.

"Dentist Street, Kowloon-side, and fast, please driver."

*

Derek Wong was also out of his usual routine and it was much later in the morning when he finally caught up with reading the news. After he and Marcus had parted so unsatisfactorily the previous evening, Derek decided to visit a few of the bars Hong Kong was so famous for. Derek was a big hit. The girls loved him: not only the bar girls, but the girls out for a laugh, out for the night, out looking for a man – everyone was out. The admiring glances he had drawn from so many women during the week became concentrated and obvious as the evening wore on. He almost felt how it must feel to be a movie star, recognised and feted by an adoring public.

Two girls had even argued about who would buy him a drink and before he knew it Derek had put away a few. He felt a sudden jolt of arousal when one of them asked him if he wanted to go upstairs for a *good time* until he realised exactly what that implied. Embarrassed, he had left that bar but soon found another, a little more informed of what to expect this time. But he had still smouldered about Marcus holding something back from him and found that the drinks weren't having any effect on the lump of resentment he was trying to swallow. Another girl approached him and this time Derek decided he'd take the bait if she cast him a line. She did. She was tall and blonde and gorgeous and the drinks they shared were the ones he should have resisted, even if he couldn't resist her.

She had been in his flat until half an hour ago and left on a promise that she would meet him for drinks and dinner tonight. Her name was Jane Franks. She had looked as good to him when she woke up as she had through his desire and drink-sated haze the previous evening. After making love again he made her toast and she made two mugs of instant coffee. "No tea?" she had said, which he thought cute. The English love their tea.

*

Terry winced as the bamboo inserts were removed from his nails. Mr Smith looked on with something approaching awe. This man showed no more pain than the ancient warriors from the old stories who could be wounded with a hundred arrows and wander across deserts with no food or water for weeks and still survive to fight another day. The Wo Luen Shing Triad leader would be followed only if he could command respect, regardless of where he came from or who he was. Mr Smith thought Mr Shaw would be a formidable leader. Mr Smith gave Terry a half bow and paid respects to his courage but Mr Shaw merely gave a casual wave of his right hand, its fingers still adorned with their bloodied inserts, and instructed Smith to take him to the residence Smith had spoken about, for a debrief.

This order worried Mr Smith. He could see the sense of it. It would be a brave assertion of power to take over Tony Yip's stronghold, but should he be seen to take Mr Shaw there? Were there other senior members of the triad he did not know, who might be watching events....men with leadership ambitions who would find this action so presumptuous on his part that they would punish him? Or would they grudgingly accept Mr Shaw's outright confidence in claiming not only the crown but also the seat of power? Mr Smith rather thought that Mr Shaw had the aplomb to take over the entire rabbit warren of crime and disease by force of personality alone. Mr Smith thought that even the fearsome rabble in Beggar's Hall would bow to him.

The last insert was removed and the young doctor at the day clinic who completed the procedure also bowed his head briefly to Mr Shaw, after which Mr Smith escorted the new King of the Walled City back to The Emperor Inn. He would however, give thought to all of the risks before he escorted the new monarch to his private chambers.

Friday 7th December, 1979: mid-day (Hong Kong time)
When Belinda stepped off the Pan American Airways flight at JFK Airport in New York, the press were out in force. It was the last flight of the day to touch down, the weather was freezing and it was four days since she had been blessed with access to fresh

clothes or a bathtub. She had piled her greasy hair into a towering chignon and put on fresh makeup before leaving the aircraft. *She was Belinda Jones. She* had influence. She might even use her new look to start a fashion revolution – something grungily urban.

She posed at the top of the aircraft steps and let the barrage of cameras do their work. There would be the familiar pictures and storylines in the morning – the prophecy had been fulfilled, the distraught wife returns home against all odds .... The aircrew had radioed ahead and a limousine was waiting for her outside the airport to whisk her off to the hospital to see Bobby, her Bobby, perhaps only just clinging to life until his wife came along to save him. Belinda could see it: Bobby, pale, his pulse dropping, eyelids fluttering, machinery slowing, emergency lights blinking, alarms bringing nurses and doctors, much regretful head-shaking until – miracles – Belinda Jones walks into the room and it is all lights, cameras, results!

Belinda had taken precautions to ensure that there wasn't a repeat of her experience with the Hong Kong Customs Office. One of the aircraft crew had radioed the skipper of the cargo flight and the tote bag she had left behind, complete with passport, was on hand for her to collect at JFK. She settled back into the limousine and was driven off at speed to rescue her dying husband.

*

As Belinda's limo sped through a cold New York night, in a chilly Hong Kong where it was mid-day, three men stepped out of a car at the northern entrance to the Walled City. Earning Yip's clear displeasure once more, James gave Hua Leung instructions: if the trio did not return by three-thirty, Hua was to report to Chief Superintendent Smythe. James handed Hua a slip of paper with the relevant number on it. Yip's expression became solemn, because of what they planned on doing next or because his name might come before Chief Superintendent Smythe yet again, who could know? Marcus, the third member of the group, had already crossed the road and was looking intently at the dental prosthesis shops that marked the northern entry into the old city, their windows full of leering mountains of dentures; a macabre display for the entrance into a macabre place.

The plan was simple. Yip Yee Koon intended to go to his brother's apartment and summon whoever he could from the ranks of Tony's senior men. Yip knew how to get there and James thought he had a bit of an idea too. James had discovered a concealed entrance at the back of The Emperor Inn more than twenty years ago when he had been on an operation in the Walled City to secure the release of one of his Hong Kong operatives and at the time he had thought it probably led somewhere important. The tricky bit was to get into and exit The Emperor Inn without being seen and apparently Yip knew how to do that. As they walked into the clasping confines of the old city, James tapped Marcus on the arm and said, "Don't lose Yee Koon or me, whatever happens, young man. Hang on to our jackets if need be. And Marcus?" Marcus turned to James, "I don't intend to alarm you, but there are rats in here and sometimes they blunder about. Try not to yell if one jumps on you, understood?" Marcus looked intently at James. What would he say if he did intend to alarm a man?

Tony Yip's penthouse was built in sections which could be shut off into discrete suites of smaller apartments. It was four years since Yip had been into the Walled City and on that occasion he had been with James. It was no family event that time. He and James shared a history of this place which neither of them had ever sought. – June Bowen, Pearl's mother and James's former wife was murdered here and it had been Pearl's girlhood fate to find her mother shortly after she had been shot. Many years on Yip and James were destined to find the bodies of two people who had been brutally murdered in the second salon of The Emperor Inn. But all of that was in the past, a past, which, to Yip, seemed almost simple by comparison to what they might have to face in here now.

Was James having the same thoughts? Yip wondered how James dealt with his own memories of this place. Perhaps it was all ancient history to him. How Yip wished it could be thus for him! Such a grasp the Walled City had on his own present! His brother was dead. Mayhem would break out, and soon. Would anyone but Mr Smith necessarily recognise him? The old barman from The Emperor, the criminal but clever old Fang Li, had retired and if he was still alive, lived somewhere in Greater Kowloon these days. A couple of ancient customers might find his face familiar. Yip had only ever met Mr Smith once but he knew that Mr Smith was neither aware of the origin of his relationship with Tony Yip nor why he had been appointed Barman of The Emperor Inn. A lot was riding on what type of man Mr Smith was below his humble status of drinks server.

Marcus tried to suppress his sensory responses to the place – the smell was unbearable, but the quality of the light fascinated him. Near the entrance, it was the colour of old ivory. The air was so opaque that he wondered how it could be inhaled, and its hue penetrated everything including the fabric of the mud-built houses and the cobbled street. It was like a deserted stage-set, or at least that's what Marcus thought until he squeezed around a corner and stepped on a rat. It squealed. He flinched. James grasped his elbow. They walked on, Yip in front, stepping lightly, until he made a sudden gesture for them to stop.

They were in front of a mud-brick wall. Yip examined it carefully and then began to push at it. A panel, plastered carefully to look like the rest of the wall and invisible to most eyes, slid open only when Yip applied pressure at certain points. Behind it was a door which opened easily. James beamed at him and whispered, "You are a sorcerer my friend." Yip put a finger to his mouth and ushered James and Marcus into a space of some sort before sliding the panel back into place and closing the door. They waited and adjusted their vision to the deeper gloom within. To the right and only just visible was a staircase. Yip led the way and James took up the rear. Marcus tried to walk as delicately as James and Yip but found it difficult and when his shoe caught on a stair tread the dull thud of leather on wood echoed through the void. It felt to James as if they were ascending in a zig-zag pattern. He thought ruefully about Pearl's Princess' Staircase. If there were any princesses in here, James did not care to encounter them.

He counted the steps and when they finally stopped he was thoroughly breathless. There were 140, roughly equivalent to climbing up the side of a fourteen storey building which meant that the rumoured thirty thousand souls who lived in here really could be accommodated, in some way at least. Although many had it that there was still a sense of community in the Walled City, James doubted it. If there was, The Emperor Inn was its last faint stronghold. People lived poorly, or desperately, or lived by crime either voluntarily or when crime was forced upon them to survive. It was too much to contemplate. How had even a man of Tony Yip's formidable power been able to keep any sense of control? Perhaps it was because those who lived here knew they could not survive unless they were supported by lawlessness.

Ahead of him, Yip held up his hand in another calm gesture of command and they halted. There was a door in front of them. Surprisingly, Yip extracted a key from his pocket, opened it and without hesitation stepped inside. James and Marcus followed him and he locked the three of them in.

James pulled his trust and faith in his friend around him much like a skirt billowing too frivolously in a spring breeze and waited to see what would happen next.

*

Belinda walked into Mount Sinai Hospital's reception area. She gave her name to one of the desk staff and demanded to see her husband immediately. The woman flicked the merest of curious glances at her. So, another one had turned up, claiming to be the famous rock star's famous wife! This one looked as if she could do with a good scrub-up.

"Floor 4, Room 17, Madam. But Madam...?" But madam had stalked off to the lift bay. Her moment to fulfil the prophecy that she would save her husband's life had arrived. She felt exultant, powerful. She swept from the lift and followed the arrows to a block of private rooms. Without hesitation she swept into Room 17 and posed at the foot of the bed, booted legs akimbo, hair flung free of its chignon. Bobby's head was bandaged and he looked more like a sad old man of sixty-five than one in his prime. His head of untamed hair was hidden and grey stubble grew patchily on his jowly, pallid face. He was sitting propped up by pillows with a tray of food in front of him and he looked more like a patient in a nursing-home than in a hospital. He was tucking into the food with relish. A lump of mashed potato was caught in the stubble on his chin.

Neither said a word, largely because of the two women who occupied the visitor's chairs, women who looked alarmingly like herself, with long flyaway black hair and black clothes. Both were painfully thin. Neither smelt as bad as Belinda. She lifted her chin and looked down her nose at her husband. "Your new backing group by any chance? Or the *back-ups* you had on tap all the time, you cowardly little runt." He quailed and sank down behind his tray for protection but she said nothing else before she stalked from the room and from his life.

She checked into The NoMad Hotel and early next morning a hotel car took her to the airport. The hotel night staff had cleaned and pressed her clothes and she worked on her appearance until she looked smooth and chic. Gone, the flyaway hair, replaced by a French pleat, gone the pallid makeup and extravagant use of black kohl pencil. She wore blusher, a light coating of mascara and coral lipstick. The change in her dress style would have to wait until she got back to Hong Kong but Belinda Jones was gone and Belinda Childs was – well not quite back – but definitely was not on the rebound either.

CHAPTER FIFTEEN

Friday 7 December 1979: 1.00pm

"I owe you an apology James." James felt a cringe coming on. Surely Yip wasn't about to tell him he was co-leader of the Wo Luen Shing Triad? That he shared this apartment with his brother from time to time? That the rumours that had followed Yip around Hong Kong for more than thirty years about his shady dealings were true? A little free market money lending or laundering James could understand but ....

"I see what you are thinking James, but thankfully my friend, you are quite wrong, although there seems to be a certain primness surrounding free market money lending these days which I simply fail to understand."

"Yee Koon old man, I simply don't know how you do it."

"I should apologise for failing to tell you that I have always known where my brother lives. We could have come here on Wednesday night and literally bearded the lion in his den instead of spending hours in that cramped attic in Beecham Street. But I did not have the courage for that, James. This is a stronghold, not a home, and it is infamous for trickery. I have had this key for thirty years. I have to assume my brother forgot that he ever gave it to me. Tony had many habits in those days that clouded his memory and if he had remembered, he would have had a new master key made. I doubt he left it with me for sentimental reasons. Few people know about this place. Come James, come Mr Browne. I will take you both on a tour."

The tour revealed a palace perched on an almost literal pile of rubbish, with a flourishing rooftop garden that had a magnificent view of Lion Rock and was free of the stench that came from the buildings below. It was the highest apartment in the Walled City and as it overlooked Kai Tak Airport, it was a plane-spotter's dream territory. Within, Yip's key opened many doors. Marcus was agog. Tony Yip was a collector and four rooms were set up as a gallery that showcased his collections of Chinese antiquities. In other areas there were sitting rooms, studies and bedrooms and in the entire web of rooms, here and there, were dotted a plethora of kitchens and bathrooms, the former basic, the latter luxurious in their use of marble and gold fittings.

The penthouse could be shut off into independent apartments, excluding the display gallery. Each had its own front door and each had access to its own web of aerial walkways and staircases. The design was about the ability to escape and disguise as well as to impress the visitor who would see only a space of unsurpassed luxury. James was fascinated by it all and saw clearly how Tony Yip had so comfortably wielded power from here. Yip had not yet said what they were going to do but James knew there was little doubt about it. He was here to end a war.

Or was it to start one?

"We will wait here. Remember the panel at the back of the upstairs hall in The Emperor Inn James? I have a notion the next move will come from there and that way leads into this apartment. Young man", he waved Marcus into a chair, "Please sit down. I have something to explain to you, as James has been so insistent on your accompanying us. This is not what James might be tempted to describe as a teddy-bear's picnic. Please listen...."

What Marcus heard was an account of Tony Yip's career and why he and Yee Koon had become such bitter enemies. It was a story of betrayal, disloyalty and treachery that ultimately led to their paths dividing. Yee Koon told it clearly and even took some of the blame for how his brother had turned out. "I am, was, older than my brother. I should have protected him from his baser instincts. Ultimately I chose not to. Our divisions were final and bitter and I cannot pretend grief over his death. I am here only because of a sense of responsibility to the vulnerable people in this place, the ones who had my brother's protection and those who will be punished as a show of power if a new Leader is not chosen with great care.

"Your role, Mr Browne, is to remain silent and use your eyes and I *mean*, use your eyes. Your eyes are the same colour as those of the ancient tortoise spoken of in my country's celestial tales: they are the eyes of ancient power and portent and they can save the world. In times of trouble, the great tortoise rises from the deep and turns over on its back and gazes at the sky with its single emerald green eye. You will be seen as having powers of divination, Mr Browne, and I urge you to appear to know how to use that power if we get into what James may describe as a spot of bother."

James made one of his more explosive expostulations. "I've never heard you utter so much rubbish, Yee Koon. Tortoises? Why do flaming tortoises keep coming into the conversation? Even Pearl called your brother turtle face."

Marcus knew. He said, "I guess turtles were on your daughter's mind, Sir James. If you remember, Pearl, Dr Henderson and I had started talking about my people's project which has been named by the governing Council The Tortoise Universe. My people see the tortoise as wise and brave whereas this tortoise that Mr Yip speaks of has only one eye and turns to look at the sky every three thousand years. To me this doesn't seem to have much of a purpose."

"The purpose," young man, said Yip, "is that during the years whilst the tortoise gazes at the heavens, the earth and the sky are in harmony and the old stories say that fortunate times and peace prevail during these interludes. That seems wise and brave enough to me."

James was fed up with all this talk about tortoises. They had to have a strategy. What if a dozen gunmen blazed their way into the apartment, all fighting each other for the right of occupancy and taking the three of them out at the same time? Flashing young Marcus's lovely green mince pies around wasn't going to do it. In truth, once again, James wondered why he had come this far with his old friend when, once again, his daughter was out there somewhere, unaccounted for and a kidnapping victim for the second time in just days. He wondered for a moment if his mind was playing tricks on him, telling him that the likelihood of someone being kidnapped twice in a week was so remote that somehow he couldn't take it in. He couldn't let old Yip take on this challenge alone, but oh when, oh Lord, would something actually happen instead of all this waiting and talking about things testudinarious?

*

Terry was anxious to act. He felt like a veteran of the city, a General about to make a historic move on his enemies, whoever they were. His two hosts from the previous evening were trussed up in one of the upstairs salons, much as Terry had been when they took him from Ong Hing Terrace. He decided to make an example of them, and thinking about Ong Hing Terrace gave him an idea. His first announcement as Leader would be that those who betrayed, cheated, lied or in any way undermined his authority would be taken for punishment to a much darker place than the Walled City of Kowloon. The Sheung Wan slums on Hong Kong side would be unknown territory to the inhabitants of Sin City but being held at Number 6, after they had been given a full account of the horrific murder that had taken place there several years earlier, would, Terry was sure, be a fine way of not only obtaining obedience but of shifting undesirables from his patch. The inhabitants of the Walled City were both imprisoned and protected by its infamy, and ironically, to feel safe in here was to feel safe anywhere. The house in Sheung Wan would challenge that. Terry felt very pleased with himself, his thinking was so clear, his resolution so sure, his physical strength blooming and blossoming, it seemed, by the hour. He issued instructions to Mr Smith to have the two men deported; Smith was to make sure people saw what was happening and wanted them to be seen being carried out trussed up, in the same way that Leader Shaw had been dragged to the edge of the city. Terry wanted to make it quite clear that these were new days and there were new ways of wielding power under his leadership.

Once again Mr Smith was very impressed and the strategy worked well. The quietness of the Walled City fairly howled as Tsiu and Ng were hauled through the southern gates to the world outside. Mr Shaw showed a subtlety of thought combined with daring actions that others would find hard to read or defeat.

*

Jane Franks picked up a few necessities from Wellcome and when she arrived at the guest house just after one o'clock she showered and changed, then relaxed and thought about Derek Wong and the night they had just shared. She stretched luxuriantly. Jane had not made love to another man since she parted from her boyfriend more than two years earlier, immediately before she went to work for Mr Childs.

There had been no opportunity or time for even a fling during the two years that she lived in the Childs' residence. Her evenings off were few and she had lost nearly all of her networks since parting from Rod. She had come into Rod's life when she arrived in Hong Kong and the only friend she had made on her own account was Chrissy Ryan. She had called Chrissy early the previous evening for a chat and was urged to view her dismissal as a good thing, which made Jane start thinking less about fear of the future and more about what she could do with it. Chrissy's short-term therapy was to get into the scene without further waste of time, so how about a few bars?

Jane hit the jackpot at the second bar the two women visited. Chrissy urged her to make a move on Derek after she had seen Jane eye off the tall, exotic looking man who had come in to the Bright Sun Bar shortly after eleven o'clock. When at about two in the morning they went back to his apartment, Jane was more than ready for a one-night stand. The next morning, when she finally gathered up her clothes and handbag, she hadn't expected anything further from Derek, but he had taken her in his arms as she was about to open the door to leave, looked deep into her eyes and asked if she would go out to dinner with him that night. Would she? She would go anywhere with him.

Jane was smitten, but didn't forget for a moment that there was a job to be found and her life to organise. The room at the Florence Weir was hers for a week and after that she wanted to be settled into a flat, preferably working or with some promising job applications in the pipeline, and that necessitated doing the rounds of the employment agencies. Jane knew her own capabilities and working for Dennis Childs had not really exploited them. She wanted to be more than a Personal Assistant to a rich man. She wanted ... she thought about Derek again. She knew what she wanted.

She forced herself to stop lounging about and began to sort through her possessions, which lay unattended in her two suitcases. As she organised the wardrobe space she wondered what Derek did – their conversation had not been of a business nature. She dreamed on about him as she unpacked her cosmetics but came to with a start when she saw the key. It was in the bottom of the case, with her perfumes and face creams. She still had a master key to the Childs' residence. She picked it up – should she send it back by courier or drop it around? She had the afternoon to herself and could take it around and drop it off to Mr Childs personally. That way she would feel that she had done the right thing by making sure that the key ended up in the right hands. When she thought about Dennis Childs she had the same niggling sense of unease she had had about him for the past days – the change in the man, his strange comings and goings – well of course everyone knew what that had been about now – he had undertaken a very daring venture to ensure his daughter's release, but then to follow that up with a mass sacking of staff, well really. Still the way people treated family and other people always varied didn't it? All that blood being thicker than water stuff.

Jane was pleased with her handiwork. It was a lovely room, with off-white furniture and heavy linen curtains that framed the old fashioned windows. Spartan but at the same time very feminine. She decided there and then to forget about Mr Childs or anything to do with work today. She would go lingerie shopping instead. Something in nude with black satin trimmings would look good against her complexion, or perhaps something in deep rose....

*

Peter hurried through the twists and turns of the Walled City with neither a glance to right or left. Right or left glances in here were a waste of time. You might see your fate leering at you around the next corner or just see yet more piles of indescribable rubbish being nibbled and gnawed by the endless numbers of rats. Or did the number of people now outnumber the rats? The compression of air in the city seemed worse than Peter ever remembered it. He paused not far short of the major mud-brick wall junction that bisects the city into four unequal quadrants, pushed open the door of one of the ground floor hovels without any hesitation and walked confidently inside.

A very old man squatted in the one-room dwelling, idly plucking a chicken. The room was empty apart from him and a bowl of bloody water and entrails. Peter wondered if it were something to do with Tony Yip's passing: the ceremony of chicken slaughter was part of triad ritual. The man appeared not to notice Peter, much as he had appeared not to notice the hundreds of people in times past who used this way to get into the back section of the Emperor Inn and although this gweilo was the first opium user to come in through this entrance in years it did not raise even a flicker of interest from the old gentleman.

There was a ladder in the corner of the room and Peter climbed it, also without hesitation. At the top was a manhole that gave entry into the building that abutted The Emperor Inn. He poked at the square of wood to ease it loose and in a single movement hoisted the panel upwards. Using it as a shield, he bounded into the concealed corridor behind the two upper salons of the inn. He let go a sharp expulsion of breath. *Empty.* All he had to do now was remove the wall panel and he would be inside the inn. He replaced the manhole cover. Would James and Yip be in either of the salons? He looked around. The corridor had two branches and Peter had never had reason to follow the left hand way, but thought perhaps he should give it a go. Gaining access into the upstairs section of The Emperor was one thing but leaving if he was discovered was another matter. He would have a look around to see if he could expand his escape options.

*

Tsiu Wah-Heung was concerned. Two months without income was not good, and worse, the lack of activity was making his brain slow. But he was still curious about Mr Shaw. Even if Mr Shaw was not interested in pursuing any further business with him Wah-Heung had come to a decision: he would speak with Mr Shaw, even if it meant confessing that he had been following him.

The smell of money that Wah-Heung had sensed last week at Stormy's Restaurant was still with him, but if Mr Shaw kept their regular appointment at the *Half Moon Café* next Tuesday, Wah would be very surprised. Business had not been so slow for many years and he did not understand why. He needed to create new capital and fast and so he returned to Sheung Wan and lingered at the corner of Ong Hing Terrace and Sparrow Street. Not long after arriving there he heard a vehicle enter the street from the eastern end. He peered around the corner. Three men emerged and one unlocked the door whilst the other two manhandled what appeared to be a large parcel out of the boot.

Wah-Heung stifled a gasp. They were carrying a man between them, a man bound with leather straps. They threw him bodily into the house and then repeated the exercise with a second, also bound in the same fashion. In an instant they had locked up and the car took off at speed.

Merciful heavens what can this mean? Tsiu's first thought was to get away from the place as quickly as possible. This neighbourhood was far from healthy, but as the panic brought on by what he had seen subsided, a new thought occurred to him – what if Mr Shaw was one of the men thrown into the small house like so much baggage? Mr Shaw's business activities might have rebounded on him badly. Tsiu waited and waited but saw nothing more. At last he walked hesitantly and openly into the street, and finally rushed to the door of Number 6 and knocked loud and hard several times, surely enough time for Mr Shaw to answer if he was there and able to. He pushed at the door. It was an old door and the lock rattled. It could probably be forced. He tried the window but it was curtained. Was there a back entrance? He would try to find one. Should he place an anonymous call to the police? Would that be a better action, or, should he simply walk away?

Wah-Heung was an honourable man in his way and his conscience did not let him ignore what he had seen. He walked back and followed Sparrow Street downhill, looking for a back alley entrance that might lead to Number 6. It was not so difficult after all. There was a path, albeit no more than a metre wide. It was full of rubbish and he picked his way carefully through mounds of rotting cardboard boxes and obscure, rusting pieces of machinery.

Each house in the terrace had its own back gate and the gate to Number 6 opened easily. The tiny back courtyard was a surprise. It was overgrown with vegetation but had once clearly been a very special place. There was a small pavilion, a pond and a reclining statue of The Buddha just visible through a tangle of vines and weeds and there was a path that wound through the growth to the back door.

Terrifyingly, the door opened easily to his touch. There was no time for a change of mind after that. The house was only one room deep and before him, barely three paces away, two men lay on a piece of old carpet, their hands and feet bound together, their legs bent and strapped high up their backs. Their faces were covered with loose black cotton hoods.

Tsiu knew what the hoods represented. These men were traitors to a triad. The hoods marked the death sentence. One of them arched his back and made some semblance of noise – they were no doubt gagged underneath their execution garb. Wah-Heung feared approaching them even in their helpless state, but he could not leave them like this even though he was well aware that triad members were to be feared unless they were dead and these men were not dead.

He spoke to them in a voice not much more than a quaver and said he had seen them being taken into the house and would do his best to release them. The straps were cruelly tight and there seemed nothing in the house that could help him but he finally managed to work the bonds of one of them loose and together they released the other man. Wah-Heung quaked. Would they kill him now? Was his useless assistance of no further interest to them? His fears were quelled. "I am Tsiu", said the first man he released. "You will be rewarded richly for what you have done today. Your name and where you can be contacted," he barked. Mr Tsiu Wah-Heung bowed his head. He was not sure he wanted to be *contacted* by these men but they seemed ordinary enough as they rubbed their limbs and he found water and a bowl in the small pavilion in the back courtyard and they drank and splashed their faces until they were revived.

"Now leave, Tsiu Wah-Heung." It was the same man who had spoken before. The other had remained silent. "You will hear from us again, but until then you are warned to say nothing. This has not happened. Got it?"

*

Peter had no idea where the paths he followed were taking him except that he was gradually climbing higher and higher into what felt like the centre of the city. He was disoriented. This cheered him up immensely. He was one of the city's outsiders most knowledgeable about its layout, so clearly his ignorance of this path suggested that it might end up somewhere interesting, perhaps even at the heart of the triad boss's famed but poorly known sky castle.

His attention was caught by an odd irregularity in the bamboo wall of one of the structures he passed. He noticed too that the number of rats had diminished and even the air seemed clearer. He stopped and studied the slightly raised area in the middle of the wall. It was a door of course, but where did it lead? He ignored it and followed the walkway for another minute or two but had to come back. The path curved and simply ended in a burnt out shell of a former dwelling high on the perimeter of the city.

Peter stood before the bamboo door. His internal compass told him that he was facing north-north east, and the building in front of him should overlook Kai Tak. He listened for planes coming and going and was puzzled not to be able to hear anything until he realised that there must be insulation smothering any noise and if someone had gone to the trouble of sound-proofing this area it could only mean one thing. He was about to enter the lair of Tony Yip's infamous palace. He opened the door and found himself in a sort of lobby. There was some muted natural lighting and different and ornately carved doors marked the four compass directions – it was a case of pick a door, any door.

What had been Tony Yip's favoured celestial symbol? The tiger defending the west, or the phoenix, ever looking south? Perhaps the warrior Tortoise guarding the north or the Dragon that oversees the east? The eastern door was closest and it had an old-fashioned ivory handle above which a small plaque was mounted on which was a small enamelled sky-blue dragon dancing on a cloud and emitting forks of red hot fire. He opened it and stepped into another lobby that was more affluent eyrie than entry space. Dragons in varying depictions and poses abounded on wallpaper and statuary. As he turned to close the door he heard voices approaching from another direction. He left the door open a chink and saw Mr Shaw and Mr Smith from The Emperor Inn enter the main lobby. They did not seem too concerned about being stealthy and the fact that Mr Shaw walked with a marked swagger made Peter realise that, whilst his ministrations had not yet worn off, Shaw was close to the end point of the treatment where confidence and feelings of well-being and power either aid or destroy the intentions of the cure. Peter was more interested in the man with him.

Mr Smith, The Emperor's barman, was old Fang Li's replacement. Traditionally, the barman performed the dual function of running the inn as well as being middle-man for the Leader of the Wo Luen Shing Triad. The role of barman was complex: they were never part of the triad family, nor were they mentor, advisor or servant. They were granted no favours but they took part of the profits from the inn and had the power of influence and exercised a certain level of control over what could happen within the city's walls. Perhaps most oddly, they were paid a stipend by the owner of The Emperor, a shadowy man who also had influence, if not power, in the city's environs.

Mr Smith had excelled in the role which he had held for four years without anyone ever learning much about his personal background, except that he had appeared in the Walled City several years earlier, well before being appointed to the job. Whether Mr Tony Yip had known anything about Smith's background was immaterial – Tony Yip cared nothing for his minions. They were mere tools and were readily expendable. His presence here today, however, suggested that perhaps Mr Smith had ambitions. Perhaps he wanted more tangible power than behind the scenes influence.

Peter pressed close to the door, listening. "Are you ready, Leader?" said Mr Smith in excellent English. Peter allowed himself a small smile – *well well, Mr Shaw has used his time efficiently since our encounter.* Terry asked Mr Smith to tell him about the four doors. This also served as extremely useful information for Peter: the western door led to nothing more than an empty room which exited to a staircase which terminated at the main thoroughfare. The southern door entered the apartment adjacent to Mr Tony Yip's gallery of antiques. Terry asked a few rapid-fire questions about the collection and said *excellent, excellent.* The northern door led to two other, less opulent apartments.

"And this, the eastern one?" Peter closed the door and stepped back.

"This is where we will have our meeting, Leader. This is the meeting room and the master apartment is in this wing, to the right. Once inside, there are two other exits in case this one is blocked off for some reason. It is the ultimate escape route." Terry voiced his approval.

Peter saw the handle of the door start to turn and pressed back against the wall. A mechanism was activated and the wall opened seamlessly outward as the main door opened inward. Even Peter was surprised. Perfect escape routes indeed. He found himself back in the main lobby whilst Mr Shaw and Mr Smith were in the dragon's entrance to the eastern wing – this lobby with its four doors was the centre of the apartment complex and from the centre all exits were accessible. Had James found it?

*

3.00pm

Chief Superintendent Smythe puzzled over the second ransom note which arrived as promised, addressed to him and marked *Personal and Confidential.* It simply said: *the arrangement is to be as before.* Before what, exactly? Was this a reference to Belinda Jones's kidnapping and her father's maverick action in sailing off to Taipei with a crate full of cash or was there another meaning he was missing?

He had two of his staff go through all recent reported kidnappings and their results and the task didn't take long. The last formal kidnapping in Hong Kong happened in 1976 when an Australian who posed as a tour operator, but who really ran a drug running business from his spruced up tourist junk, held an American woman hostage for six hours as he tried to escape pursuit by the Water Police. His last-ditch effort had been to try to exchange her for money. He was still in jail. Hardly a parallel case. Or did it simply refer to the first note, found in that wretched cake display at the *South China Morning Post*'s offices? Fifty million dollars stuffed into cupcakes? Surely not.

*

Silence had fallen in the room in which James, Yip Yee Koon and Marcus sat. Marcus had paced around Tony Yip's gallery of antique ceramics, porcelains and bronzes for half an hour before he at last sat down in a black leather chair, which was a combination of executive chair and an armchair. It had an ashtray built into one of the arms and idly, he flipped open the lid.

"All deities!" shouted James and even Yip jumped. Marcus reflexively pushed himself back in the chair as a panel in the floor slid back. Confusion was followed by a simultaneous gasp of comprehension from James and Yip. "Sit still young man," commanded James and stepped carefully around the edge of the cavity that had opened up before them; a pit as deep as a tall man's height. He reached Marcus, closed the lid of the ashtray and soundlessly the panel closed. He opened and closed it a couple of times. The perfect trap took up so much of the floor space that the average person would simply topple in on their first full step across the threshold.

"My brother's taste for exotic entrances and exits continues to educate us in how he survived here for so long, James." Yip's face had softened. Was there a morsel of admiration in his face for the cleverness of his brother in protecting himself with such endless guile and attention to detail?

"Sshhh" said James, "Noise." There was a sound, but it was more like the whisper of change in an evening breeze than footfalls and it was not close. James waved Marcus out of the chair and said, "Behind that bookcase – go". He gestured to Yip to stand behind the door. James took up his position in the chair. The door did not open. But on the opposite wall two paintings appeared to move upward at alarming speed as the panelling slid away and a man stepped into the room. James raised the ashtray lid and Peter Benson fell forward, the floor literally pulled from under his feet. James leapt out of the chair. Peter landed in the pit in a crouching pose and swivelled around quickly, arms raised to his face in defence.

"Peter, it's you old boy, I am so so very sorry. Wouldn't harm you for a king's ransom. Got a bit twitchy with the old ashtray lid. Here, give me your hand. How the devil did you know that was a door? Damned clever." Peter had no choice but to let James and Yip haul him out.

"I expect you enjoyed that, James. Very spook stuff. This place is full of it. Now, regarding entry, why did you choose the Tiger's Den when clearly the assault is going to erupt from the Dragon's Lair to the east?"

Yip said, "It seems that you are speaking about the fourways, Dr Benson. Have you found it? It has always been more of a rumour than fact. How did you...?"

"It was obvious really, Yee Koon. You follow your intellect. I follow my instincts. I dare say there's a pit in the middle of the fourways too, if one could find the trigger mechanism. I didn't, thankfully. Your brother was a cunning sort of chap but he made one mistake in the layout of this place." James did not feel like discussing Tony Yip's architectural or interior designing mistakes but he did feel a familiar bristle of irritation towards his old colleague, mixed with a degree of envy at the way his mind spiralled off on tangents and produced solutions that a perfect application of logic could rarely achieve.

"I am fascinated, Dr Benson. Please enlighten me." Yee Koon could be damned irritating too sometimes, if the truth be known, James thought. But Peter shook his head and said,

"Later. The new Leader of the Wo Luen Shing Triad has just arrived in the meeting room with Mr Smith. I am not sure if there is anyone else left who will join them and confirm the leadership, but in any event I rather fear it is going to be a short-term appointment...."

*

Derek had idled his way through the day, and instead of going out spent the time considering what to wear when he took Jane out for dinner. Formal clothes had been far from his mind when he bought a few basics from Lane Crawford's Department Store and now he needed to be outfitted properly. Like Marcus always was. The thought of their disagreement lay more lightly with Derek now. Marcus would probably still be at his mysterious appointment and no doubt things would sort out between them. That could all wait. He needed lunch before anything else. Derek was suddenly starving.

By four-thirty he was back at the apartment. He hung up his new clothes which were not unlike Marcus's usual choice of charcoal grey suit, pale grey shirt and charcoal tie and he spent some time walking around the apartment in his pair of new leather shoes that felt just a bit tight. He went through the business section of a financial journal that he had also purchased, which further reinforced his belief that right now was a perfect time to initiate business in Asia. The place was ready to roar with the industrial development promised by economic change in China.

He yawned, poured a beer, drank half of it and swished the remainder down the sink, shut his eyes and pretended to doze. But it was no good. He was bored. A sight-seeing tour perhaps? It was probably too late to organise something at this hour. He still had an itch to ring Mr Childs, and why not? Maybe ask him out for afternoon tea or whatever the go was with the English at this hour on a Friday afternoon.

"Mr Childs? You may not remember me sir – Derek Wong – you..."

"Of course I remember you, Mr Wong." Dennis was annoyed at the interruption. The issues at the office had been sorted out and he was comfortably enjoying a cup of tea in his study. The last person he would have expected to hear from again was this Mr Wong chap.   But Mr Wong only wanted to say how glad he was that Mr Childs's daughter had been safely restored to her family

Black Tortoise Winter 250

and to express gratitude for the help Mr Childs had been ready to offer to a stranger, "And when I saw you last night it jogged my memory to ring and thank you ...."

"Really, Mr Wong; you saw me last night? You should have said hello. Oh, in traffic was I? I must have been on my way to the club. Later? Going home then. I don't keep late hours. Mr Wong, if you are at a loose end this afternoon, why not pop around and have a cup of tea and a chat. Six o'clock? We'll make it a G&T in that case. Got a pen? Goody-o. See you at six."

*

Yip Yee Koon was quietly rattled about the pit and the entrance into this room that Peter Benson had discovered! Regardless of the luxury surrounding him, clearly his brother had become obsessed not only with power but being able to wield it in many ways. His face became perfectly passive but without any sign of relaxation or calm. James saw and read it as a bad sign. Yip was suppressing much anger and it seemed they had no choice but to entrust their next move to Peter, whose remarkable mind had emerged differently patterned after a serious nervous break-down in the mid-60s and who, with extraordinary leaps of instinct and insight, could produce magnificent triumphs or...

"Exactly where is this meeting room Peter?" said James, uneasily.

Peter was busy consulting his internal compass. "...Not sure, unless we return to the fourways."

James began to feel rattled as Peter led them to a narrow spoke of a corridor that ended in the central lobby, indicated the door decorated with the little ceramic dragon and whispered, "In there. I don't know if everyone has arrived but there's an interesting way of getting out which will save us if we aren't the last to drop by." James shook his head jerkily in lieu of one of his outbursts. They were in the real inner lair of the lord of the Walled City at long last. Marcus looked at James and could almost smell his concern. This matter no longer seemed to be in the control of either Sir James or Mr Yip.

He only hoped this Dr Benson guy knew what he was doing.

*

Hua Leung looked at his watch again and was not cheered to see that, although it was still not quite three-thirty, it was definitely three twenty-nine and more than three quarters. His orders were clear: if Mr Yip's party did not return to the taxi by three-thirty, he – Hua – was to ring the number that the high ranking *gweipor* had given to him and report that Mr Yip, the *gweilo* Sir Gates and one other man of alarming colouring, whose name he had forgotten, were missing in the Walled City of Kowloon. Hua had spent the past four hours crouched behind a newspaper, terrified that someone would emerge from the northern gate, who knew him, who might....Was it only last night that he thought he had seen the last of this place? Mr Yip had offered him a new start, a good future; and the first job connected to his change in destiny brought him back to his old life. Could his good luck have turned sour already?

He looked at his watch again. No doubt about it, it was now past three-thirty. He peered into the semi-gloom of the Walled City's northern entrance but there was no-one about so he started the taxi's engine as quietly as he could and pulled away from the kerb. He would leave the message and hope that it reached the famous Chief Superintendent Smythe. Hua wondered if Chief Superintendent Smythe was related to the barman of The Emperor Inn, Mr Smith. Their names seemed similar. The Emperor Inn would be the only feature of the Walled City that Hua Leung would miss of his old life, but he also knew that it was time to take more exercise and not to drink so many whiskies each night.

*

Chief Superintendent Smythe looked at the note handed to him by Constable Chua. It said, quite clearly, that Sir James Gates, Mr Yip Yee Koon and another man were in trouble in the Walled City of Kowloon and would the Chief Superintendent kindly send some officers to assist them?

*

Peter opened the door. James was like a dog gnawing on an old bone or at least, gnawing away at something he should have seen earlier but hadn't. This door opened to the east. Just a few minutes ago he and Yip thought they were in the extreme north of the building. Where in fact were they? They looked around and Peter demonstrated how the doors – one obvious, one apparently no more than a panelled wall – worked in synchronicity. Marcus was very impressed and saw instantly how it could work to the enormous advantage of someone wishing to leave unseen as someone else entered the lobby.

All of the dragons poised in paint or statue within the small lobby were in positions of guard or defence, their reputation as peace-makers far from apparent on carved or savagely moulded visages. James told himself not to be ridiculous, that of course there wasn't a camera mounted in their eyes to track the progress of all comers – was there? In front of them was the second of four spoke-like corridors, just like the one Peter had led them along from next door. At its end was a narrow, single door. James didn't like this at all and whispered, "A single door? Not the chap's style, think you, Benson?" Peter nodded in agreement and James announced that he and Peter would go ahead, with Yip and Marcus to stay near the escape door and bolt if he and Peter didn't reappear. Yip and Marcus looked at one another and each broke out into a smile. *As if* thought Yip. *As if* thought Marcus.

The corridor was only about five metres long. When they were near the end, James tugged at Benson's shirt and pointed to a slim black stand that stood against the wall. On it was the carved head of a particularly odious looking dragon. Peter pointed at the dragon's stubby, foreshortened nose. It was a different colour to the rest of the ceramic work and was very smooth, as if use had worn the colour away. The two men nodded. This was no doubt the real entrance into the room, but did it lead into the meeting room itself or into yet another lobby?

They stopped and listened but the silence was as it had been. James beckoned Yip and Marcus to join them and as he did so the door that gave access from the fourways began to open. James pulled at the dragon's nose, pressed it, hit it. He and Peter were going to be on full show in a second. Yip and Marcus disappeared without detection as the paired entrance door worked its magic and expelled them from the lobby just as the dragon's nose finally yielded its secret and a door adjacent to the stand not only opened but dropped a screen across the narrow corridor, screening James and Peter from the view of the incoming guests. Although ingenious, it was not possible to see who had entered the fourways or where Yip and Marcus had ended up.

James and Benson found themselves in another tiny anteroom where the walls were papered with the same dragon motif that decorated the lobby, but there was no furniture, no statuary. Was this a room for pausing in, making choices in, perhaps outwitting others in, hiding, taking refuge in? Benson found the first door. There was a small metal circle attached to the nose of one of the papered dragons and James found its twin on the panel next door. Was this a rotating door set-up too? James looked skyward in supplication. Peter looked at his shoes. He whispered, "It could be another pit. Take half a step to the right. The door will open to the left. Armed?" James nodded. Of course he was armed. "Mr Shaw will be near his time James, and I can't predict how he will emerge from his recent experience." James nodded again. They were wasting time. Hua Leung would already have reported their absence to Tommy Smythe and the police could already be on their way, though a lot of good that would do them, perched this high above the entire damnable place. Tommy Smythe would have to demolish the entire city before he would ever find Tony Yip's eyrie.

"Let's get this over with, Pete." Peter opened the door and took half a step to the right and James followed. They triggered nothing, nor was there anyone in the room to thwart them. It was yet another well-furnished room, empty of people but equipped as in the Tiger's Lair with a luxurious executive-style armchair that had an ashtray set in the left hand arm-rest. The two men took in the situation and moved on, keeping to the perimeter of the room just in case the chair had a mind of its own. They could hear voices, raised voices, but from this room, unless they retraced their steps, there appeared to be only one way forward, and that was towards those raised voices.

*

Yip and Marcus swivelled out of the fourways entrance and as they entered again by the adjacent door they were just in time to see the two men they had avoided disappear through the narrow door at the end of the corridor, apparently hard on the heels of James and Peter Benson.

*

James and Peter were on familiar ground. Have your weapon ready but not visible. Surprise was the thing. Get them to pull one another's hair out if at all possible. The door was hinged to swing inwards, which made a sudden appearance potentially awkward. James had no doubt the door had some other function. Tony Yip would not disadvantage his own entry. The meeting room held a long table with curved corners and it was made of black stained wood with a dozen heavily carved chairs set around it. There was nothing else in the room except for the human tableau playing out: at the head of the table sat Terence Shaw and to his right stood another man. The two men Yee Koon and Marcus had seen enter the fourways were there and both Shaw and the other man looked shocked.

"Tsiu. Ng. How did you...?" squawked Mr Smith. Terry's shoulders slumped. His plan had failed. His torturers of last night had returned from Sheung Wan. He would not earn the respect he needed to run this place after all. They may even shoot him. Or worse. How good was Smith at defence? Terry felt sweat break out on his forehead and his damaged hands began to shake. Was there no-one else to help? No other supporters for his leadership? He tried to speak but his voice failed him. Tsiu and Ng would have sniggered, except that they saw James's gun. Then another *gweilo* spoke to them in immaculate Cantonese and told them not to move or they would lose what they had left of their brains. Then, horror of horrors, he walked towards them and reached for their necks like a vampire. But the touch was gentle and because neither man had thought to re-arm – they agreed that dealing with Mr Shaw and Mr Smith would be like picking off fleas – any defence was too late. They sank to the floor, smiling as though they had fallen into sweet sleep rather than being rendered unconscious, and before Mr Shaw and Mr Smith could show some gratitude at the removal of this threat to their safety, James joined them and smiled at both, pleasantly, his gun firmly in evidence. Peter had been careful not to employ any healing techniques with his latest application of passive martial aggression. They would merely wake up without feeling that they could rule the world let alone this heap of maggots. James snapped at Shaw and Smith to give up any weapons they were carrying. They had none.

"As you see, James, the effect of my treatment of Mr Shaw has now completely worn off. Mr Shaw, you should be grateful that we are here to help you. Your end in here would not have been pleasant." Terry Shaw wept as he thought of what he had endured the previous night and at last screamed out the pain he had suppressed – the infernal drilling, the sizzle of hot metal against exposed nerve endings, that hammering, the heat of the tongs as the bamboo slivers were inserted into his poor tortured fingernails. Would he ever sleep again?

"As for you, Mr Smith ...." Benson turned to him and Mr Smith acknowledged his name with a curt nod but his mind was whirling: *Who were these people? How did they know so much?* Peter continued, "Go back to the bar."

James indicated which exit he should take. "You are in no danger and your position has not been compromised," he said. "The real Leader of the Wo Luen Shing Triad is in the room next door. He wants you to resume your usual role until he sends for you. In a way you are yet to understand, you have much power. Do you understand what I am saying to you?" Smith managed a very small smile and ran. But he didn't run through the door to which James had directed him but headed for the other side of the room. Peter looked peeved. James looked smug.

*

When Yip and Marcus glimpsed James and Peter before they disappeared, seemingly straight through the wall, Yip studied the dragon statue and figured out the entry. Now they waited in the room which James and Peter had so recently vacated. The clues about how the place worked were becoming easier to read. He took up residence in the armchair and was patting the concealed pocket of his suit in which his small pistol rested when the door was flung open. Yip did not hesitate and with a smooth action flipped the ashtray lid open and the floor yawned as it received Mr

Smith. He lowered the lid and Mr Smith disappeared from view in an instant. Yip remained in the chair and called through the open door, "James, what is Mr Smith doing, running in here like a startled hare?"

"Yip old man, so glad it is you. We have Mr Shaw here with us and Mr Shaw is looking forward to meeting Chief Superintendent Smythe. By the way Yip, did Mr Smith see you before you ditched him? If so, he thinks you are the new Leader of the Wo Luen Shing Triad."

"As of course I am, James" said Yip Yee Koon.

CHAPTER SIXTEEN

Friday 7 December 1979: 4.00pm

In Tommy Smythe's opinion another raid on the Walled City was a waste of police time and resources, but Sir James and Yip Yee Koon being bailed up in there made it a different and somehow more enticing matter. Chaos would be abroad as news of Tony Yip's death spread and there was the further enticing thought that perhaps Yip Yee Koon would openly take over his brother's role. What good fortune it would be, *balm to the soul* thought Tommy, to enter the Walled City and find Yip doing something that he could legally be nabbed for.

But Smythe's ruminations on how he might finally get the goods on Yip were paltry compared to what James was going through. "Of course Yee Koon is the new Leader, James," said Benson, inadvertently in accord with the Chief Superintendent's sentiments. "He is the only man with enough clout to carry it off. Right, Yee Koon?" Yip nodded. James was apologetic. How could he have thought for one second that his old friend did not aspire to the role?

"You will remain here, Yip?"

"Until I find a solution to this, James. James, a favour?" A nod. "My wife, my household, can you possibly...?" James could more than possibly look after the good Mrs Yip. "A story, James. Tell her a good story. She must know nothing, nor should any member of my household and most particularly, Hua Leung is not to come in here under any circumstances. Mr Shaw..." Yip turned to the unfortunate man whose sobs had at last subsided and who sat disconsolately in the chair he had occupied as Leader of the Hope Sun Wo Triad for such a brief time. "You will surrender to the Hong Kong Police and account for your recent behaviour during the kidnapping of Lady Pearl Green and you will include in your account your full association and business dealings with my brother."

Terry quailed. So this man *was* Tony Yip's brother. Older, probably more vicious than the man who, Terry assumed, had organised his torture. This man probably taught his brother all he knew. He nodded assent.

"I will look after Mr Shaw if I may. I have a couple of questions of my own for him," said Marcus. Marcus had recognised his dinner companion from a week, no, a life-time ago.

"We Seminoles have a few tricks of our own when it comes to disabling enemies. I assume that Mr Shaw may know something of our practices." Terry shuddered. Scalping. Indians scalped people.

It was time to leave. Mr Smith was extricated from his prison, unharmed but terrified. For James, there was no choice but to trust his old friend in doing whatever it was he had to do in here, and if Hua Leung had carried out his instructions, the police raid would happen soon. "Yee Koon? What will happen to Mr Smith?"

"Mr Smith will continue as barman for the moment, James. After you leave he and I will have a little chat. There are things I know about Mr Smith that it is time he knew. As his uncle, I owe him an explanation." James and Peter both arched an eyebrow, James in another bout of disbelief, Peter in understanding.

"Matters need to be very clear between us." Yip still sat in the black leather chair. "I appreciate, James, that there are many matters that are not clear between you and me at present and I ask you again, please keep your trust in me."

James could only nod. It was time to leave this madness. Were all families mad? He crossed the floor to Yip and grasped his hand. "When will I see you again, my old friend? Will you still be my old friend?"

"It depends on how long this matter takes, James. I have to show strength in here, otherwise there will be mayhem and my strength would be diminished without your friendship. Mr Browne? Mr Browne, I wish you success in your venture. It has been a pleasure to meet you and Doctor Benson it has been my great joy to meet you again. We seem to be destined to meet in this place. May this be the end of it." James visibly gulped. Damn all deities, what did the man mean, *May this be the end of it?* He wasn't going to cry, was he? He felt Peter tug at his arm.

"Come James, there is much to do." James saluted Yip Yee Koon, who bowed his slim and elegant head in response. But Yip wasn't quite done.

"James. Why not use the lift?" James gave him one of his ferocious looks. Yee Koon had feigned ignorance about this wing of his brother's penthouse. "It will terminate behind the corridor that leads to the panel that gives you access to the main thoroughfare through *The* Emperor. Push the 'close' button twice when the doors open and the panel will slide back and you will know the way from there. My engineering company installed it and I made the mistake of believing it had been installed in the other meeting room adjacent to my brother's own quarters. It was very clever of him." James shook his head sadly and asked himself for the second time that day: *Did one ever really know people?*

*

When just after five-thirty Chief Superintendent Smythe and Inspector George Wong entered the bar of The Emperor Inn – their least favourite watering hole – they were greeted by the sight of Sir James Gates and Dr Benson taking their repose in a corner of the bar. The scowl on Tommy Smythe's face deepened when he saw Marcus Browne. There was a fourth, dark-haired man with them whose face was familiar to him from police files. He looked to be at the end of his tether. In fact they all looked exhausted, particularly Sir James, who nursed the remains of a small glass of evil-looking whisky. Sir James introduced Shaw.

"Think you may find a chat with him illuminating, Chief Superintendent. My colleague here" – Smythe nodded in Peter's direction – "will come to the station in due course and make a further statement." Tommy looked perplexed.

"You are not stranded, clearly, Sir James. I have officers poised to conduct a raid that has been specifically mounted to find you and your colleagues – result of a report received that you had gone missing in here. This looks like nothing more than a criminal waste of police time and resources."

"Pure luck, old man, that we weren't thoroughly stranded."

"Yip?"

"Ah, we did lose Mr Yip, unfortunately." Tommy's face brightened. Was this loss a euphemism for something cheerier, such as Yip's demise? James read the look wearily. "Mr Yip will find his own way out of here. He has some family issues to attend to and there is no need for a police presence. This city is in better hands tonight than it has been for more than thirty years, Chief Superintendent. I suggest we leave it at that for the time being."

*

Jane threw a pile of parcels and bags onto the bed and started pulling the contents out and hanging or folding them. She set aside a set of new underwear and carefully shook out and hung the simple but beautifully-styled dinner dress she had bought especially for her date with Derek. She hurried into the bathroom. They were supposed to meet at The Urban Hub bar at six-thirty and she couldn't wait to see him.

*

James moped and barked if Peter or Marcus spoke to him. He refused to leave the bar. "It's not a very stylish drinking venue, James, although, grant you, it does bring back memories, doesn't it?" Peter gazed around at the bronze light that was the best illumination on offer in the mud-floored, mud-walled structure with something approaching fondness. "It has a certain savage charm. Memories, James, you and me, and particularly Pearl," he said and, when he saw that James was about to bark again said hurriedly, "You'd be much better off waiting for news of her at home. Come away, James."

"I wasn't thinking about you or even Pearl, oddly enough, Pete, my old bon vivant. I'm simply trying to order my thoughts, but perhaps you are right. We should move. Righto then, on on." There were times when the bar worked on an honour system – a rare concept in the Walled City – that when the barman was absent, everyone helped themselves to drinks and left payment. James left a tip. This impressed the other customers and it was quickly scooped up.

*

For his part, Marcus knew that his time in the company of these men was running out and he kept close as they wove their way back towards Dentist Street. He had been through an experience not many people would have in their lifetimes and he chewed over it, thought about the sights he had seen, the squalor, the odd sense of people knowing how they fitted in – or didn't – and decided that the Walled City was a community of sorts. It just didn't have the same sort of glue that more conventional communities have. It seemed to work because of a lack of shared interests or goals, in precise opposition to how his community worked so successfully. He knew what Granny Browne would have made of it. She would have had the Walled City gleaming in a day, with everyone knowing precisely what they had to do and when they had to do it. She would have been the triad boss and saved Mr Yip the bother of shouldering that task. He felt overwhelmed for a moment. He had seen and done things in the last week far from anything he could ever have imagined himself ever doing and he had picked up more knowledge and information about Hong Kong in that time than many would in years. He snatched another look at James. Should he risk being barked at again and see if he could still tag along once they were out of here? But James was not with them. His walk had become disjointed and jerky. He kept putting his hands in his pockets, taking them out and shaking each one as though he had been bitten by something. Marcus decided not to say anything, perhaps they would all share a taxi somewhere ....

*

Derek arrived at the Childs residence promptly at six. Mr Childs greeted him cordially and invited him into the study. There was silence whilst two gin and tonics were carefully prepared. Derek had never had a gin and tonic before. He was strictly a beer or bourbon man and the taste surprised him. Dennis Childs laughed. "New taste sensation, I see, Mr Wong. Very British, G&Ts. Be warned though, they can have a sting in the tail! Deceptive, a couple can have more of a punch than one sometimes wishes for. Now tell me all about how you are finding Hong Kong and also about seeing me out and about last night. I gather you must have seen just me in my dear old Bentley?"

*

Marcus accompanied James and Peter Benson back to Pearl's apartment without their even seeming to notice that he was still with them and he joined in as they made another search for signs of any outside contact – messages, notes, the answering machine – and drew blanks.

"I have to think about how to raise the money for Pearl's release," said James. "I don't have it, you see, without selling up assets in England, and there isn't time for that. Old Yip is the obvious answer but he's got enough on his plate. The police don't approve of ransom demands being met. They say that it sets up a culture of success for potential kidnappers. But, hang it, I'm going to do it. I'm going to see Dennis Childs and ask him for a loan."

Here we go again, thought Marcus. *Dennis Childs.* "Sir James, about Mr Childs, did I tell you that Derek and I saw him last night?" When James absently asked *where* and Marcus said *Causeway Bay* and James said *what time* and Marcus said *about eight,* he did not expect the response he earned, any more than two weeks earlier he could have imagined that he would be banged up in jail or spend the good part of a day in a triad bosses lair in the most infamous quarter of any Asian city. James rounded on him and barked, "Causeway Bay? Pete, old seer, tell me what I'm thinking...."

"The only reason that someone of Dennis Childs' social calibre would be seen in Causeway Bay, of course, James, is that he was on his way to the Hong Kong Yacht Club. I have a notion that he wasn't dining there. Cab! Now! All of us!" said Benson smoothly.

"Are you sure you haven't been operational for the past thirteen years?" said James. "Maybe you should take up spooking again old chap, I know a chap who can give you a job...."

CHAPTER SEVENTEEN

Friday 7 December 1979: 6.30pm

Mr Tang had been the Hong Kong Yacht Club's Restaurant and Bar Manager for as long as anyone but the very oldest members could remember. He knew James and beamed with pleasure at the sight of him and even remembered the last time he had been a guest, four years ago, when he was in the company of the wealthy tycoon, Mr Yip Yee Koon. James was impressed with Mr Tang's memory and said so whilst Peter wondered if James ever went about with anyone but Yip whilst in Hong Kong, and if not, how did he manage to attract the big welcomes from the maître d's, whilst others in Yip's orbit often received the opposite treatment?

Mr Tang said that Mr Childs had not made a dinner reservation at the Club restaurant tonight and no he hadn't dined the previous evening either, but he could ask the marina staff if his boat had been booked out, if that would be of any assistance.

James assured him that it would be of wonderful assistance, as he wanted to see Mr Childs on a matter quite urgent. They waited, with James looking longingly at the elegant dining-room already filling with early diners, the candles, the long-stemmed wine-glasses glinting purple and gold light into the eyes and across the cheekbones of beautiful women, who held the gaze of their dining companions as they sipped their wine. He could stand a feed but perhaps not here tonight, perhaps when Pearl was back, perhaps ....

"Ah, Mr Tang, prompt as well as gracious. Any news?" There was. Dennis Childs had not been seen at the club today but had taken his own yacht *The Belinda* out for a moonlight cruise the previous evening. He said he would be away for a few days and the marina staff helped him load a large cabin trunk, but he returned only a few hours later and had said to one of the night staff that he had to come back because he didn't feel well.

"I suppose it made him feel even worse having to carry such a big cabin trunk back with him then," remarked James. Mr Tang bowed his head and returned to his tables.

"If he bought it back with him, hmm?" James said to his companions. "Fancy a stroll along the wharf, anyone? What better thing to do on an evening that promises moonlight than look at a decent boat or two, d'you agree?" *The Belinda* was moored in its usual berth and there was no-one about to see James deftly jump on to the deck whilst Peter and Marcus, in a very leisurely way, took up positions on two nearby bollards and exchanged pleasantries about the quality of the rising moon and the graceful lines of the many moored boats. James reappeared wearing an expression that Peter had never seen before. He was drawn and pinched and looked murderously angry. He extended his hand. In it was a button, a large pearl-beige button, a button from Pearl's top coat.

"We have the evidence. Do we call the police or go to his place and sort it out ourselves, Peter? I don't know how or why but Dennis Childs has taken my daughter. I have to further presume that it was he who set up the whole business surrounding the ransom notes as well. Any clues as to why, Peter?"

Peter said, "This whole thing has always been about Pearl, James, we know that. But think! You can't go to his house knowing about this." He pointed at the button. "Can you speak to him knowing..." he took the button from James's still outstretched palm "...knowing what this may represent?"

James's face lost some of the colour it had regained but he nodded and said, "Of course I can. It's what I'm trained for."

"Good," said Benson, "I'll go to look for Pearl." He nodded vaguely in the direction of the harbour.

"Using what to float upon, Pete, a used sardine tin?" But Peter Benson, expert sailor and fully paid up messer-about in boats, merely pointed at *The Belinda*.

"Nothing but first-class, James. I have an idea. And, James? Take care. This man is dangerous. Take Mr Browne with you. I think you will find that he is invaluable in a panic."

*

Jane waited until six forty-five before leaving the bar. Anyone taking the trouble to look at her lovely face closely would see that she had been stood up. Her shoulders drooped and she clutched the small evening bag she carried tightly, her knuckles white with anxiety. She had ordered a glass of white wine and when she finished it and saw the time, decided in a quick burst of irritation that she wasn't a woman to be stood up, even though obviously she had been of no more interest to Mr Derek Wong than a one-night stand after all.

*

James rehearsed what he would say to Childs. It was confidential, father to father stuff, need for the money, how he planned to repay it, etc. etc. He reminded himself that Childs ran a veritable financial empire and was probably worth hundreds of times the ransom demand, could pluck it out of the air, tip it out of a piggy bank, write a petty cash docket.... The cab stopped outside the house and James pondered if he should have the driver wait, in the event he needed to make a quick exit. Finding a vacant cab at the Peak could be a nuisance sometimes. He leant in through the front passenger seat window. "Can you wait? Thanks." He put Marcus on surveillance duties, charged him with keeping a discreet eye on the place whilst he talked to Dennis, made his way to the front door, knocked, and was surprised when Dennis himself opened the door.

"Staff night off, old man?" Childs looked at him oddly.

"In between staff at present." He looked quietly furious and bluntly said to James, "How may I help you?"

There had been many times in James's career to thank various favourite gods and goddesses for the ability to keep a straight face. It had been invaluable in the field, beyond riches at the level he occupied in the highest ranks of the British Public Service and was paying him back in spades right this minute. He allowed himself a mild look of surprise. "This is Kevin Eburn's house, is it not? Invited for dinner, running a bit late for drinks …."

Childs jerked his head and said, "Two doors up. Goodbye." James nodded his thanks to the firmly closed door, smiled pleasantly at it and left. He checked up on young Marcus who was doing a good impersonation of a stroller enjoying the quiet of the evening. Another cab pulled up and a young woman alighted, and she too walked towards the Childs residence. *I don't think so*, thought James and he hurried towards her, talking affably so as not to startle her.

"Hello there! Good evening, lovely night isn't it? Not off to Dennis's famous impromptu formal dinner by any chance?"

She nodded vaguely but said nothing.

"I'm late too. Drinks will be over soon. I'm James Gates by the way. May I escort you?"

She stopped, looking uncertain. James noted her appearance. Clearly she was on her way to dinner somewhere and looked ravishingly dishy in a wonderful black frock.

"No. Thank you all the same. Mr Childs is hosting a dinner? I shan't go in then. I'm Jane Franks, Mr Childs's former Personal Assistant. I am returning my house key. I found it when I got back to the Florence Weir this afternoon, that's all. Never mind, another time."

James gallantly offered to pass the key on for her. "Won't be a problem at all unless you wish to hand it over personally." She dropped her head and clutched a little purse she held very tightly. This young woman was upset, that much was very clear. "You said you *were* Dennis's PA? Had a falling out, did you?"

Jane looked at James's kind smiling face and told him how Mr Childs had dismissed the entire household staff and to her best knowledge his three key Hong Kong executives just yesterday, immediately following his daughter turning up in Taiwan after the kidnapping drama. James listened and nodded his head and tut-tutted.

"That's very tough luck. Seems as if old Den has taken a bit of a turn over Belinda's ordeal, although he is determined to celebrate its successful closure tonight." He accepted the key she proffered. "I'll pass this on with your compliments. Good luck with your next employer. I hope you receive better treatment. I'm sure you are a very competent as well as a lovely looking young woman." He managed to win a small smile from her before she returned to her cab.

James fumbled for his wallet, dismissed the cab, signalled Marcus to keep doing what he was doing and appeared to stride confidently through the front gate, but he pulled up short in the deep night shade of a bougainvillea vine that shrouded the covered gateway. He might have a key but he also had a quandary. Dennis Childs had not recognised him, in fact, had obviously completely forgotten that they had met one another at functions several times over the years, the last one being a fundraiser for the June Bowen Foundation.

Why would old Dennis not recognise old James? He slipped back to the footpath, taking care not to pause or seem indecisive and made his way firmly down the steep driveway towards the garage. James intended to see if the key was a master key and if so, where might it lead him?

*

Yip Yee Koon was alone in the meeting room when Tsiu and Ng regained consciousness, without apparent damage, but restrained in an interesting cell that Yip had discovered in one of the wall panels. Initially he thought the room empty apart from its oversized table and twelve chairs but the walls were panelled in oak, each panel delicately inset with bevelled timber beading which gave the room a grave, library-like air. It was obvious to Yip that there were bound to be more of his brother's contrivances built into the panelling and he found, in no short order, a well-stocked bar complete with a small refrigerator; another panel slid back to reveal an equally well-stocked gun and knife cabinet complete with handcuffs and other restraining devices, whilst the final one swung out to reveal a cage-like structure, higher than a man and complete with lock and key.

Yip gave up his exploration of the room. If he uncovered its full contents he might be tempted to call Chief Superintendent

Smythe himself. Persuading the errant triad members into the cage was an easy task: his name, his calm voice and steely gaze – not to mention a gun and handcuffs – were sufficient to persuade them to follow his orders. Yip was quietly pleased. He had their respect and they would be comfortable enough until it was prudent to release them.

"Tell me what has happened during the past twenty-four hours," he said in his formal way, which let loose a garbled and contradictory stream of explanations from Ng who talked over the more junior Tsiu. Yip listened, punctuating his silence with small nods to encourage them. There was nothing new to hear. It appeared to have been a rather nasty but not unusual night in the Walled City. Yip looked at the remaining untested panels in the meeting room and felt nothing but loathing for his dead brother. By the accounts of the two men and Mr Smith's account of the silent presence of so many people in the bar early that morning, it was clear that the city's residents knew that something beyond their own understanding of things untoward in that black place were happening and if they had known about Tony Yip's death at that time, chaos would most certainly have erupted. It also became apparent that Weng and Li, Ng and Tsiu were Tony Yip's only senior men. Tony Yip had gradually centred his power by locking out other senior triad members over the years by killing, buying, or expelling them from the Walled City until he was not only the Leader but also the city's Dictator.

To Yip Yee Koon this was good news. It meant fewer knives to come out of the darkness when one least expected it and as for allaying chaos, there must have been relief when Mr Smith announced the elevation of the man Mr Shaw, who was said to be strong as a tiger and brave as a warrior tortoise. Those who had not been impressed by his courage were terrified of his appearance and thought he was a ghost and by late morning he had the city in his hands. Ng related with shame how Mr Shaw took power without hesitation, and made an example of both himself and Tsiu by making them outcasts, left bound and gagged somewhere on Hong Kong Island. As Yip listened, he hoped that ultimately the day's events would make the job of maintaining some sort of order easier when it was learned how easily he had deposed Mr Shaw, restoring the Wo Luen Shing Triad leadership to the Yip family without further challenge.

"Explain how you were freed."

Yip considered what they said carefully. Tsiu Wah-Heung was in the picture once again. He had difficulty with the thought of the small-time conman freeing these two men. He must have had a strong reason, or perhaps he had a conscience. It was not how Yip Yee Koon thought of the elderly Tsiu, with his ill-fitting shiny suits and marked limp. He was an opportunist, but today he had displayed something else. He would be rewarded, as Ng and Tsiu had promised. Perhaps it was time for him to take up another occupation.

Yip allowed himself a small sigh. If he remained here for even a day, let alone the weeks and months he saw ahead, he too would have to make an example of Ng and Tsiu in order to exert his own power. After that would come other challenges. He, Yip, had insufficient knowledge of how strong or weak the other triad groups in the city were these days. Perhaps there were cells of power that had escaped his brother's influence as he became more isolated and who were merely waiting for an opportunity to seize control. He flexed his shoulders as he stood. There was another answer and it lay with family. It was time Mr Smith knew that he was family. It had been a long day, a day in which much had changed. His household was safe again, no longer in danger of being randomly garrotted by any whims of evil that may issue from this place and that raised a further question in Yip's mind: why not simply walk away? He had asked himself the same question times before in the past and it worried him that he could not *simply walk away*.

*

The driveway terminated in a carport and James found himself sharing space with Dennis Childs's Bentley. The parking bay was adjacent to a lift, obviously the functional entry into the house and the control panel showed that it was currently at the second floor. He wondered about having a lift placed so that anyone at all could walk down the driveway and summon it, before remembering that the property was sure to be security patrolled or at least had been until the staff were sacked. James considered using it; at worst case scenario if discovered, he could make a banal comment about having mistaken the house for the Eburn's residence. *Perhaps not.* A bare electric light bulb hung from a long cord which shed inadequate light in the concrete-lined space. It had been a day for concealed doors and such things and James examined each concrete panel carefully. Ah! Was he on to a Yip-ism? He tapped on one panel which was a slightly different colour to the other slabs of material. It was painted wood, rendered lightly to look like concrete. He pushed at it. It didn't budge but he could feel give in it. He flattened his hand and eased it sideways until a mechanism clicked and it slid open, easily. In front of him was a door. With a lock. *This is it James, old boy. Here we go again.* He fitted Jane Franks's key into the lock and turned it slowly. The door was hinged to open inward and James pushed it open sharply, having gone too far now to back off; he was already trespassing on private property and mistaking old Den's place for the Eburns with old Den's master key wouldn't wash.

The door opened into blackness and James put one black leather shoe across the threshold and slid his foot forward, but the floor was solid – no tricks here, so far. He took a step inside, reached out, and as expected, found a staircase railing to his right. He reminded himself that it had also been a day for secret staircases, in fact the island was fairly rippling with them: for princesses, triad bosses, and now? A simple, run-of-the-mill kidnapper? There was a certain air of surrealism about the situation, and but for the evidence of Pearl's coat button, James could never have even contemplated that Dennis Childs was capable of kidnapping his daughter.

*

Back in Hong Kong at last, Belinda was too tired to quibble when the Customs Officer recognised her and took an age to examine her passport and inspect her handbag, nor did she raise so much as a squawk when he insisted that his supervisor examine the documents too. She submitted to a second round of questions, sat patiently as her passport photograph – all wild hair and overdone eye makeup – was given careful scrutiny against her new, pared-back look. Not one of the men doubted it was the same woman who had given them grief the previous day. She smelt and looked a bit better but still wore the same grubby black clothes and when at last she came out alone into the biting air of a sudden burst of winter evening weather, she quietly hailed a taxi and settled into the shabby vehicle to be driven to what was again to be her home.

Part IV

Falling From The Stars

CHAPTER EIGHTEEN

Friday 7 December 1979: 6.30pm

During the eleven months spent living in a village adjacent to a temple that she thought of as Peter's monastery, Pearl devoted long periods of time to achieving some calmness of mind. She trained herself to breathe rhythmically and slowly learned to unburden herself sufficiently so that she could almost see her thoughts depart. She had learned how to meditate.

Once again there was little choice but to sit and wait as the tide slapped into the cave in which she had spent the last hours of daylight, retreating further and further into its depths as the waters lapped then leapt over the rock shelf on which she had woken during the afternoon. Too weak to walk far, she had waited, hoping to see a boat, or perhaps hikers on the peninsula on the bluff on the other side of the narrow channel, until the waters finally scrolled across the platform and those hopes faded. Now, small waves were beginning to toss up against the walls of her sanctuary.

She started drifting again, half asleep, fuzzy, still drugged. Kaz was with her, talking: *Pearl, your tickets. Are you sure you have your passport?*

It took a big effort to speak but I needed her to remind me where I was going.

You're supposed to be flying to London, but I think you should go home. How can you go off like this if you've even forgotten your destination? Pearl? It's me, Kaz, please speak to me. I'm half mad with concern for you ....

The muscles in her right arm jerked her awake and this time she felt more alert, and for the first time she remembered the rest of that day clearly: hugging Kaz and Drew, scooping up everything and stuffing it into her cabin bag, running away.

I'm running away. I don't want to have to pretend that I'm capable of living a normal life. I'll write. I love you.

She even remembered her friend's face, distraught, dear Kaz, always unable to dissemble, unable to hide her loves and her hates.

She had forgotten everything else but the tears streaming down her cheeks, and for the next two years that was one of the only real things she did remember, of things that meant anything to her that is, until even that faded in a grief for her lost husband so intense that it consumed everything.

She shifted position as the memory of that day crashed in on her and for the first time Pearl saw herself as Kaz and others had seen her then and in that instant forgiveness came and she cried and laughed and wiped her cheeks until she was brought back into the darkening cavern by something caressing her left foot, which dangled over the edge of the stone shelf on which she sat. She screamed and recoiled from the contact but almost instantly too realised that it was the head of a large tortoise. The animal rose from the water that lapped near her feet and regarded her – head turned on one side – from one large and watery eye. She sat very still as it slid back under the water. The small waves that kicked and reared against the shallow stone shelf flicked her with foam as the tortoise swirled its body around and for a second she saw the outline of its entire shape as it swam from the cave on the tidal outwash.

Pearl wiped her face again and smiled at the dark departing form. If the tortoise was somehow an omen of good luck then she had just been unabashedly singled out of the crowd for a dose. "About time too" said the more familiar and steady Pearl to nothing more receptive than the roof of the cave, before another swish of incoming water broke over the shelf and sloshed over and well past her. "Sorry," she said to the roof of the cave, "a bit premature about the luck was I"? She wriggled backwards until the space between floor and roof became so tight that she felt like a tinned sardine, and debated whether she should return to the cave's entrance and take a chance that the water wouldn't fill it entirely – when she saw a speck of light. There was just room enough to prop herself up on her elbows and when she peered upwards she saw a narrow slice of moonlit sky. And miracles, she could even see a star.

The cave was connected by a vertical tunnel to another, higher in the rockface.

James felt around and found a door. *There we have it, James old son, staircase to the right, door to the left, access into the garage behind. The full triage of exits and entrances. This door must lead to the cellar.* He felt around for the lock. Good old Jane Franks, the key she had returned was indeed a master key. Another inward opening door, another tentative feel about with his right foot – "Yip has a lot to answer for, I'll never casually step into a room again" he muttered, closed the door and groped around for a light switch. It was now a case of having come so far, why not go further?

Yip Yee Koon paused long enough in the entrance of The Emperor Inn to create a lull in the buzz of drinking and conversation. He walked easily through the crowd of men who drew aside for him. Mr Yip Senior was here and everyone knew that things would be all right now. Mr Smith stood erect behind the bar, ready to salute him. Yip took two keys from his pocket and addressed Mr Smith in clear tones, tones so clear that an hour later the announcement he made had carried effortlessly to the extreme edges of the Walled City.

"I want you all to know that Mr Smith is my nephew and I appoint him Leader. From this day on he will be known by his birth name of Yip Wing Li." Mr Smith was no less impressed than those present to hear his name and family connections announced so publicly. He bowed his head respectfully as Yip Senior handed over a key, whilst making sure that everyone saw him pocket the second. He addressed the younger Yip directly. "I recommend that you seek the services of Mr Tsiu Wah-Yeung to be barman of this establishment, to take up the role that the barmen of *The* Emperor have traditionally filled for The Family."

He lowered his voice and added, "You will need to do this quickly as there are one or two matters in the meeting room that require your attention this evening." Mr Smith bowed his head again, apparently unable to speak. There had after all been a reason why he had been taken from his school in England so many years ago to be dumped so unceremoniously in this place, a place he could never leave because, as he was told again and again, he was an illegal immigrant and would be thrown into prison if he ever reached out beyond the confines of the Walled City. He had been young enough to believe it but also young enough to develop ambitions to do more than the menial laundry work he was assigned to for the first three years before being appointed to the role of barman of The Emperor. That role gave him access to the city's most powerful man, Mr Tony Yip, and slowly his knowledge of how the city operated was only surpassed by him. It seemed that he had been groomed for the role of Leader and today, Tony Yip's turtle child had come into his inheritance.

"But first, Wing Li, a round for everyone if you will. I like to keep my customers happy." Yip smiled his rare smile and left. He had left everyone with enough news to occupy the gossip mills throughout the night and it was anyone's guess which was the most sensational: the revelation of Mr Smith's birthright, his elevation to Leader of the Hop Wo Sun Triad or the bets that were settled with the discovery that Yip Yee Koon did in fact own The Emperor Inn.

*

Marcus continued his easy stroll and put his hands in his pockets as he walked the street with apparent casual enjoyment of the young moonlit night. There was something in one of the pockets and he drew it out and looked at it whilst he walked. It was the tiny ornamental pin that he had found on Saturday. He had forgotten about it. The detail of the work was so fine that even by moonlight it looked exquisite. "Where in the...." He didn't finish the sentence because he had walked too far and found himself – against James's explicit orders – outside the Childs's residence. He glanced in at the house and like a snapshot he saw through filmy curtains the figure of Dennis Childs bending over another man, as if handing him a drink. Marcus assumed the other man was Sir James, but Childs moved away and Marcus recognised the long frame of his cousin. He was slumped in a chair with his head hanging so that his hair fell across his face like a sheet of black silk.

Marcus stepped into the shelter of the hedge. Where the hell was Sir James? He walked back to the driveway where he had last seen him and peered into the gloom, but only the dark shape of a car was evident.

*

Peter made a few preparations before he eased the yacht from its moorings. No-one had seemed interested in its departure and he had taken the time to find rope, a grappling hook and a small canvass bag. The kitchenette yielded biscuits, a bottle of water and a torch. He packed it all up and set his course, cruising north on the low hum of the yacht's powerful engines and when he was settled in the skipper's chair he let his thoughts roam. They roamed to Drew. He had paid Drew a visit on Wednesday, the day when he had fallen into a state of muttering despair interspersed with nightmare-spattered sleep. Kaz talked to Peter about him, saying, 'He keeps shouting out Pearl's name. Just that. Then he mutters other things I can't make out and ends up screaming. It's terrible, Peter.' He wondered if Drew had experienced a premonition and could almost hear James snort with poorly contained derision. But to Peter Benson it was obvious now where he would find Pearl.

*

The connecting tunnel between the two caves was just wide enough to accommodate her but was longer than her five foot ten inch frame and it would be a push to make it. Pearl didn't think about what could be up there, it was good enough that it was higher than the waterline. She starting inching her way up and made good progress until the cavity narrowed and she could go no further. She took a deep breath, pulled back and with both arms raised above her head, scrabbled at the rock and pushed. It was revolting and she felt like a cork being dragged out of a bottle of wine, or maybe it is how birthing must feel to a baby .... In an anguish of memory-blotting strength, she pushed harder and twisted her body to an extreme of pain in striving for a firmer grip on the sides. *God.* One of her feet slipped. The water had arrived. She jammed one leg behind the other and with the extra purchase it gave her she pushed for all she was worth until, with her upper torso fully extended and hips and legs twisted in crunching discomfort, she knew she was getting there. She remained still for a moment to recover but the image of some archaeologist finding her remains one day and hypothesising about her death pushed her forward again. Would they wonder if her presence here was the result of a ritualistic offering or a punishment, perhaps? It would not be a kind death. She grunted as she managed to gain some more purchase higher up on each side of the tunnel until at last she straightened her legs, pushed again and with a final thrust, she was through.

She fell forward, arms extended. There was enough light to see that she was on the steeply sloping floor of a cave much wider than the one below. She could only crouch at first and she eased forward until with something like a sigh of luxury she felt the floor begin to level out. With each step – she had long been deprived of the boots she had been wearing last night – she struck hard, knobbly objects, again and again. Stones, or *perhaps,* a small voice whispered, *bones.* At last she could stand fully upright. She was in a dry cavern that had a level floor which was scattered with the remains of human or animal occupancy. The roof of the cave was domed at the entrance, and moonlight was pooled there.

She laughed out loud before she knelt and then crept towards the light. To anyone looking on, she might have been praying.

*

James found the cellar light switch. There were racks of wine, boxes of books, all the usual kit people stored – old bicycles, a freezer, refrigerator, an open box spilling teddy bears, another full of clothes, no doubt Belinda's old clothes, all very posh and, James thought as he carefully shook out and re-folded a somehow very familiar looking nubbly pink tweed jacket – probably *haute couture* – but apart from a vintage Ducatti motorbike stored in a corner over which he quite violently lusted, there was nothing of interest to see and he returned upstairs.

There was the matter of the other staircase that no doubt led to the servant's quarters and the kitchen. Jane Franks said that Childs had sacked all of the household help and if that was correct … he heard a noise, ducked back to the cellar landing and pulled the door to. An oblong of light appeared on the stairs that led to the higher levels of the house. With the light came a sound, the sound of someone labouring, grunting with exertion.

It didn't take long for James to see what the problem was. A man of Marcus's height, perhaps even taller and with a good set of muscles on him, was being half carried, half hauled down the stairs by Dennis Childs. A lack of resistance on the part of the large-ish chap suggested that he was either out to it or acquiescent. James rather suspected the former. Dennis Childs is a bit stringy, *a bit like I'm getting,* thought the still-lankily framed James, *getting on a bit, not as muscled up as previously.* In any event he was making jolly hard work of it and James wondered if he would like a hand, but decided no, chap hadn't earned much in the merits department, what with kidnapping his daughter last night, and clearly setting about something else tonight. Problem was, did he intend storing the bloke in the cellar with his other unwanted goods? Because if he did, old James was in a bit of a spot.

*

Marcus stepped easily through the gate of the house next door as another vehicle approached. It stopped outside the Childs residence and a woman emerged and began fossicking around in her handbag. The internal light of the cab was on and the driver's expression became more and more irritated as the woman rustled around, obviously having not much luck finding what she was looking for. In the end she shouted loudly, "Wait here. I'll get some money from my father. Wait." The driver did not understand the shouting, took offence at the overdone miming, and started shouting back.

Marcus absently pocketed the little clip. The woman was about to go into that house where his cousin was – was what? He had to find out.

"Ma'am. May I help you?" Belinda turned and saw a tall man walking towards her, obviously on his way out, beautifully dressed, good looking.

She said, "This is the last straw, really. It has taken me two days to get home and now I don't have any bloody money. I'm trying to make this man understand that I'll get it from my father and bring it back out to him, but he's being damned uncooperative about it." Marcus took his wallet from his pocket and handed her a one hundred dollar note.

"Is this enough? Small price for peace, ma'am." Belinda looked at him with more interest. American. Tall, fabulous skin. She pulled at her jacket and patted her pleated hair, said *awfully kind of you* in her old plummy Hong Kong-Brit accent and gave the driver the cash, waving away his attempt to return her change. Peace broke out.

"Thank you so much Mr...?"

"Marcus Browne at your service, Ma'am."

"Belinda Jones." She felt the small rush of adrenalin begin when she saw that he recognised her name.

"Pearl's friend?" Belinda's face sagged just the tiniest bit. In the past twenty-four hours she had handed in her passport to fame and now she was only recognisable because she was Pearl's friend, not the magnificent Mrs Jones. She nodded and with a *quite, now please excuse me* she offered her thanks again. This was a different home-coming to the one she had planned on Monday. This was beginning to feel more like what real life would be like from now on.

But Marcus had not finished with Mrs Jones. "No, Mrs Jones, *excuse me.* I'm coming with you. My cousin is very likely with your father and I want to see him, right now."

*

Peter wished things were different and that he was sailing this beautiful craft through the moonlit waters on a nocturnal excursion, rather than navigating the hallucinations of a sick man in a desperate guess at finding Pearl. He sailed further seawards to avoid the sharp out-jutting of rocky cliffs south of the Sai Kung Peninsula before veering back and hugging the coastline as much as he could. As he adjusted his navigational path he thought about how the old sailors had found their way through these seas; recalled the inspirational writings of Jorge Alvarez, the first European to sail to China in 1513, who recorded his observations at landfall at the mouth of the Canton River. The academic Peter, who had studied the southern trading routes from China, envied

Alvarez, who would have talked with traders from Canton and the Fukien coast as well as from Luzon, Borneo, Cambodia and Siam. From his anchorage he would have been able to see south to Lantau island; perhaps even as far south as Lo Man Shan and he would even have had a glimpse of the great water basin to the south west at the mouth of which stands Macau. The array of boats on those waters too would have been wonderful. Alvarez would have seen junks from Swatow, Amoy, Quanzhou, and other provincial ports of Kwangtung, Fukien and Che Kiang, all jostling with Imperial war junks sporting great banners as well as Cantonese and Fukinese cargo ships, river boats, fishing junks and sampans ....

He looked to the north, where the dark outline of the Sai Kung Peninsula was beginning to dominate the nightscape. It was time to get down to business. He cut the engine near Po Pin Chau, put up the mainsail and called Pearl's name as he started the circumnavigation of the small sheer-cliffed volcanic island.

*

Dennis Childs and James both heard the loud knocking coming from upstairs. Childs froze even as he was reaching for the handle to the cellar door, behind which James was hiding, praying to as many saints as he could muster at short notice to preserve him from detection. The last thing he wanted to do with Dennis Childs was to have to use a weapon. There was too much for Childs to explain, all of it, James was sure, of an interesting nature. The knock came again and the other man swore, lowered his unconscious guest to the floor and went to answer it.

James exhaled softly and opened the door a crack. The oblong of light at the top of the stairs had vanished and he was alone in the dark with – he lit his cigarette lighter – with a man who resembled young Marcus remarkably well, not so much in features but certainly in colouring and hair style. *Well damn me* said James under his breath, *this fellow would have to be young Marcus's cousin or I'll waive that hot tip Yip gave me for the 2.30 at Happy Valley tomorrow. How the devil has he got mixed up in all of this?* He knelt beside the prone form. He was breathing at least. Now what had that beastly little excuse for a father used to sedate the chap? And what was this chap *doing* here? He listened for some noise from above but all was deathly quiet. James took each stair tread with infinite care and infinite hope that the door above didn't open again. Yes. The lock was a two way deal and oddly there was a bolt on his side. *Now what the dickens?* mused James. *Why is there a bolt on this side?* The hidden staircase lobby and cellar set up could be used as a holding cell but could also keep people in the house from getting out that way. James thought that interesting too, particularly in terms of controlling the entrances and exits. *Damned entrances and exits again. I wish the door would shut on this day, it is starting to feel a trifle long. Now I wonder how Peter is getting on finding that girl of mine?*

*

Belinda belted on the front door again. All her former calm was gone and she radiated high octane anger. Yep, thought Marcus, this is one cross babe.

"I'm coming, I'm coming" snapped an irritated voice and Marcus recognised the form of Dennis Childs through the door's etched glass panels. He clenched his fists, ready to throw a punch if necessary at the man he had seen stooping over the prone form of his cousin. The door was wrenched open and Childs looked at Marcus, ignored Belinda, and demanded, "What do you want? Am I part of some sort of bloody mistaken address trail tonight? If it's the Davidsons you're after, they are two bloody doors on, up the hill. Good night." He lowered his gaze to Belinda and said, "I can also tell you both that you are running very late. That other damned cove was here more than half an hour ago, so you had better get your skates on if you want to eat." Before either of them could react, the door was slammed in their faces.

*

"That man is not Dennis Childs, is he?" Marcus said very reasonably to Belinda. Belinda would often recount the story of when she fell in love with Marcus, because, as she delighted in relating, he said it exactly as she turned to him and saw his wonderful eyes and at precisely the moment precisely the same thought occurred to her. Except that her thoughts went more like,

That horrid man is not my Daddy. However it went, it was a moment full of karma, deliverance and opportunity.

"That man is Dennis Childs's twin brother, isn't he?" Marcus said to Belinda even more reasonably. Belinda was not quick enough to have made the same connection of thought with any degree of synchronicity on this occasion, but in retrospect she was sure she had. What Belinda did have was a way of knowing the truth.

"Watch this," she said, "this will sort it out," and she thumped on the door again, hard.

*

Pearl settled back far enough from the cave's entrance so that she wouldn't topple down the cliff if she drifted off to sleep. She was comforted by being dry and safe and the calm she had fought for whilst she watched the water rise higher and higher in the lower chamber of the cavern came to her now, unbidden. The sky was star-full and the moon was high enough above the eastern horizon for its light to dance on the waves that clipped the base of the cliff. She estimated that she was possibly ten metres above the waterline. Was the tide also higher tonight because it was full moon and if she had remained crouched at the back of the lower cave, would she have drowned? No matter. Luck had been with her tonight after all and for that she was grateful.

She thought about James, who would, no doubt, be tearing his hair out over her disappearance by now. Had he thought through every possible scenario and drawn a blank this time or would he work it out? Would he realise that she had been scooped up from her own home turf, and if he drew that conclusion, would he remember the very few people who knew that she had returned to her apartment? Would he put it together? But *how* could he know that she had left the apartment voluntarily, without having any idea that she had been followed when she first left and when she went back to notify security that she was leaving? Would he believe how stupid she felt when she noticed, too late, that the security office was empty? Would he know that she went cold when she realised that someone had opened the door behind her? How could he know her fear when she had heard those footsteps clipping across the marble tiles towards her? And if he had known all that would he, as she had been last night, convinced that Tony Yip had tracked her down and had vengeance in his heart?

But it wasn't that at all. It had been Dennis Childs, full of apologies for dropping around unannounced and obviously giving her such a fright. He had decided on a spur of the moment that they should all share a toast to a successful ending to what had been such a dreadful week and he had spotted Pearl going in through the front door as he drove up. He had a bottle of champagne tucked under one arm and when she explained that James was out and she was on her way to visit Kaz, he offered a lift to the hospital instead of the drink.

It had all seemed so natural, so understandable – fathers reunited with their daughters after the ordeals of the week – but apart from recalling the leather-new smell of the interior of his Bentley she remembered nothing else until that afternoon when she had woken up, cramped and sore, water to her right, sheer cliffs to her left, stranded on a narrow rock platform somewhere in Hong Kong's waters where she had never before been.

She stared at the night sky from her perch high above the waterline, marvelling at how good it all was. She felt so alive, so very grateful to be alive. She could not remember feeling grateful for anything for a very long time and all the fears about coming home and taking up her old life at last seemed so insignificant. The events of the week had forced people to extremes: Kaz, Drew, Mr Yip, James, Marcus, Belinda, herself, *My god* she thought as she remembered with a twinge of guilt how intolerant – was that the word – impatient perhaps, she had been at finding her friends so contented and settled when they had dined together at Stormy's last Friday night. How she had been almost yawningly bored that they had failed to inspire her as to what she should do next, as if it was even remotely their role.

She had come a long way since last week but had to wonder if it was the events themselves that had finally pushed her back into some sort of world-consciousness or the shock of the violence involved that jolted her back to reality? She was slumped against the wall of the cave and becoming uncomfortable with the hard stone and with her thoughts. Drew's accident happened on Po Pin Chau Island. She called out into the night, "Is that where I am? Is this a great game? If it is, who's playing with us?"

A voice floated through the still air, calling, "Pearl, is that you? Pearl, can you hear me? Pearl!"

She shook her head and muttered, "I must be hallucinating, no food, no drink, definitely hallucinating." The hallucination returned, but this time it was visual as well as audible. She saw a white yacht in the east, back-lit by the moon. She watched it move closer until she recognised the familiar, elegant lines of *The Belinda*. She moved back, well away from the pool of moonlight.

The voice came again, "Pearl, it's Peter. Peter Benson. Pearl. Can you hear me?" Relief at hearing Benson's voice did not fully dispel the familiar clutch of anxiety that it also brought with it; a sense that she could not quite trust its owner, combined with a frisson of nostalgia and hope and something else all mixed up, which was all about her past, that old haunted past part of her that never quite knew who or what he was or where he was supposed to fit in her life.

"Peter!" She took a deep breath. "Up here!" she said, but her voice didn't carry. She shouted, "UP HERE!" The boat was close now and she could make out his slender form standing on the deck, hands cupped to his mouth.

"I'll get help."

"I can jump into the water and swim."

"Don't be ridiculous, woman. I'll fetch Water Rescue. Wait for me." Pearl said that she didn't seem to have much choice and felt a bit more normal for taking an acerbic snap at him. The boat was drifting and he worked the sails and turned so that he could see her, sitting at the mouth of a cave above the waterline, the moon outlining her hair in a great halo of silvered gilt. He called out again, "I'm going to throw up some supplies and a torch. I'll be back in an hour or two." He sailed as close as he dared to the rock-face, said *stand back* and threw the canvass bag of supplies with smooth confidence to her. He backed the yacht off and when a minute or two later he turned it starboard, she was sitting there, grinning at him.

"Peter? This *is* Po Pin Chau Island isn't it? Guess what is up here?"

"It certainly is Po Pin Chau, but really, Pearl, I couldn't possibly begin …."

"It's Kaz's cave. This place is an archaeologist's dream. It's her Neolithics up here." She shone the torch so that she could see down the face of the cliff. "I can see steps too and lower down there's a narrow platform. I can climb down and jump into the boat or the water, easily."

Peter felt something he hadn't done for a very long time, a knot of anxiety around his navel, but she made it sound so possible that he found he could say nothing except, "If you are sure. When you reach the ledge, jump into the water. I'll fish you out." Pearl smiled. There was no doubt. Of course he would fish her out.

*

There was a thump followed by loud steps stamping through the house. James peered around the cellar door. The young man in the lobby had not moved. James thought it was time he did. He slipped out of the cellar and shook him, whispered reassurances, shook him again... nothing. This bloke really was out of it. He felt for a pulse and it was there, and strong.

He tried to lift him but it was impossible, but, determined that this young man was not going to endure further ministrations from Dennis Childs, there was no other choice but to drag him outside and put him in the car. *All saints alive, what now?* thought James a little wildly when he finally wrestled the prone form into the parking bay. The car was locked. The lift was still parked on level 2. If only he could be sure that he had a minute or two to act he could fetch Marcus and together they could get this bloke up the driveway and wait for the police to take care of Mr Childs. But he didn't know how much time he had and clearly something else was going on upstairs. *Time to beard the lion, James lad.* Bearding lions in dens seemed to have been quite a feature of his week. He half hauled and half carried – much as Childs had done – the dead weight of Derek Wong to the lift. James had his small lady's revolver handy when the doors opened, but it was empty. He pulled Derek inside and propped him against the wall and when he started to moan James very badly wanted to join in.

As James pressed the button for level 2 Dennis Childs was running to the front door, anger blurring his vision. He hurled it open but before he could say a word, the woman he thought he had sent packing leapt at him in a burst of pure fury that equalled his own. Standing behind her was the same man he had also seen off earlier, now effectively blocking the door.

"You are not my father," screamed Belinda. "You are Uncle Bloody Ronald Jug Ears Childs. You killed my father didn't you, didn't you didn't you and now I am going to kill you." She had a nail file in her right hand and was making pretty impressive stabbing movements at the air with it. Her voice rose to a screech, "Kill you, I'm going to kill you!" Childs saw that she meant business and he turned and ran to the lift and frantically pressed the button.

*

It was dashed bad luck for Ronald Childs that he, old James, was there to greet him as the lift doors opened, gun nicely poised. Ronald sank to his knees, pushed his fingers into his hair and let loose a tide of invective. With his hair pulled back, his large ears were very evident. Marcus very coolly relieved Belinda of the nail file and just as smoothly picked Childs up by the back of his shirt collar and held him up in the air, much as a fisherman may hold up a catch for closer inspection.

"We Seminoles have a well-documented history of not taking kindly to attack, Mr Childs." He shook him and dropped him. Belinda clapped her hands in childish delight. Childs screamed and later inspection revealed that he had sustained a nasty twist to his left ankle, which the police physician pronounced must have occurred when he dragged Derek Wong downstairs from the first floor to the cellar.

"Very impressive stuff, young Marcus, very well done." James was very admiring of Marcus's style: *chap didn't so much as displace a cuff link in all of that.* "Now if you would help me assist Mr Childs to the cellar – we'll use the lift – he can remain there until the police arrive. Dashed efficient locking systems in this house. Perhaps we had better help your cousin out of the lift first. Belinda. Keep your uncle under supervision for just one moment if you would." Belinda would. Marcus looked at her as she took a very deep breath. She saw the look from those emerald eyes and it was enough to steady Belinda for a very long time. She would do what she had to, and after that, she would weep for her father and begin to live with the knowledge that she would never see him again.

*

Chief Superintendent Smythe waited until the police Physician had dressed Terry Shaw's hands and a Dentist on emergency call-out tended to the terrible wounds in his mouth. He would need all of his ruined teeth removed but that would have to wait until another time. He needed immediate pain relief and careful nursing to ward off infection. Chief Superintendent Smythe had already recognised Shaw from one of his routine browsings of police notification records and whilst a crimes list search for Terence Shaw paid no dividends, half an hour in Records did. He matched the description and photograph of one Corporal Stewart Moore very neatly, absent without leave from the 1st Battalion of the Argyll & Sutherland Highlanders, who had been on border duty north of Hong Kong during the summer. Moore was briefly brought to the Charge Room, to hear the charges against him as far as currently known: Stewart Moore absent without leave from his military unit; procurement and use of a false identity to enter Hong Kong; a possible charge of fraud and another for leaving a crime scene.

That would do to hold him until full statements were taken, after which, as Tommy was sure, his Battalion Commander would be very anxious to provide Moore with alternative accommodation. Tommy yawned. It was almost eight-thirty, he had missed one of Melanie's carefully planned dinner parties again, but the cheery part was he would also miss the bridge game to follow. He returned to his office and started methodically clearing his desk. *What a week* he thought. *I'm glad Pearl Green doesn't flit in and out of Hong Kong more often. Perhaps we will have some peace now.* The phone rang and Constable Chua, who sounded very animated despite being at the end of a twelve-hour shift, announced that Sir James Gates was on the line and needed to speak to the Chief Superintendent urgently.

"A moment, please Constable. Ask Sir James to kindly wait." He removed his cap and police issue winter overcoat from the coat rack, donned both and picked up the handpiece. "I imagine you require my immediate presence, Sir James? I'm on my way. Where to this time, might I ask?"

*

Pearl manoeuvred her way along the narrow ledge. She wondered briefly what it signified to the people who once lived in the cave. Perhaps they fished from here or made offerings to their gods. There was a curve in it that followed the natural jutting of the basalt outcrop and she was confident she could make an easy jump of it into the water. She said to Peter, "Back the boat off and I'll swim out to you." He had taken down the mainsail and started the engines to gain better control of the boat in the near-shore swell. He reversed and turned so that the yacht's flank lay parallel with the cliff face. Pearl looked at the water, all concentration. He looked at her. The wave that slapped the side of the boat took him by surprise, the vessel lurched towards the cliff and Pearl jumped at the same instant. Steady as a rock but with his eyes closed, he held out his arms and she fell into them as smoothly as if they had planned it.

"I knew you would fall into my arms again one day." He opened his eyes. Pearl was so amazed that she stayed quite still, quite comfortable, the familiar little twist of anxiety in her neck muscles that pinched up whenever he was around quite gone.

"You're talking about my mother. You *did* love her didn't you, Benson, you all time shyster!" Then she continued, less pragmatically, "And I always wanted to fall from the stars. Guess we've both had a near-truth experience tonight. Look at this." She opened her hand and in the clear moonlight he saw a small disc of stone on which was carved a simple image of a turtle in the act of turning over, the eye in its abdomen half revealed. Beside it was a star. "I think Po Pin Chau is a turtle that was turned to stone, and I think I was sitting in the turtle's eye up there. Peter?"

"Hmm?"

"Are you going to put me down?" He lowered her to the deck. "Did you really think that I was my mother just then?"

"I certainly hope so, Pearl. Otherwise I've caught more than an armful of trouble." She looked at him but found she had nothing to say.

*

Really, James thought, the young fellow had gone too far. Derek, having refused medical assistance, sat on a metal chair in the Division Central waiting room, waiting, at 10.15pm, as were Marcus, Belinda and James, to make a statement. His chin was on his chest, his hair was dishevelled and now the damned man had started moaning. *No,* thought James, *he's not moaning. He's keening.* Marcus sat next to him, the supportive hand on his cousin's shoulder long removed, and the vertical line which had appeared between his eyebrows so deep it could have been ploughed. Clearly Marcus had had enough as well.

"Seems to be taking it a bit hard," said James by way of conversation.

"This is unnecessary." Marcus was curt. "Derek, you're making a fool of yourself. Pull yourself together, man." It had no effect.

James turned to Belinda. A change in conversation was possibly the go. "Dashed good luck that Jane Franks came along and gave me the key, eh Belinda? Lovely young woman. Did you ever meet her?"

"I've only ever spoken to her over the...." Derek leapt from his chair with a howl before she could finish the sentence, and before James could even so much as think *all adjurations,* Derek was kneeling in front of Belinda – who seemed not fazed by the gesture at all – after all, she was still the fabulous Mrs Jones even if she was about to become the fabulous ex-Mrs Jones. The same could not be said for Constable Chua, on duty at the enquiry desk. James saw him quiver.

"Do you know where she lives? I have to see her." Again there was a slight sag around Belinda's mouth. He wasn't interested in her either, just bloody Jane Franks, just as Marcus had been more interested in Pearl than her. Well, she would see to that ….

"She is staying at the Florence Weir Guesthouse, young man," said James. "Now will you kindly get to your feet, straighten yourself up, sit down and shut the blazes up? This keening and howling is beginning to ruffle my feathers."

Derek did as he was told, in sequence, and beamed at them all. "The Florence Weir Guesthouse. Do they have a honeymoon suite?"

Marcus's frown smoothed away. When Derek fell in love he didn't go in piecemeal. Whenever or however he had met this Jane Franks – it had to have been last night – she would need a good set of legs on her if she planned on getting away from him. Marcus smiled and looked at Belinda. She had a good set of legs on her too, although he wasn't too sure about her clothes. But what was going on between them had nothing to do with what she was wearing. She looked at him and they held the look. *Yep*, thought Marcus, *definitely nothing to do with clothes.*

*

James also looked at Belinda, although his glance was speculative in a different way. As they had waited for Chief Superintendent Smythe to arrive at the Childs residence, he had asked her how she knew Ronald was not her father and the answer that she gave was that it was because of his ears. But more to the point and before she even thought about that, it was obvious that Ronald hadn't recognised her. *As indeed,* thought James, *he didn't recognise me and that is why we are all spending the evening in this delightful place.* Belinda said she knew for sure when he failed to recognise her, because Ronald would have seen her photograph in the media only in her persona of Mrs Jones. He couldn't see *her*, beyond the hair and the makeup and the clothes, as her father would have done. And then of course, later, when he was caught and she looked at his ears, well …. James nodded kindly, omitting any comment about the matter of Ronald's ears not becoming evident until after Belinda attempted to set about him with her nail file. That lapse would be disregarded in anything he had to say to the police.

Chief Superintendent Smythe entered the waiting room and beckoned to James, "A quick word, Sir James?" The quick word stretched into forty-five minutes and when James came back, Marcus was off giving his statement and the other two had completed theirs. There was relief on the faces of Belinda and Derek when advised they could leave. Belinda had booked a suite at The Peninsula whilst the Childs' residence underwent a scene of crime examination and Derek, even given that it was well after eleven, intended to go to the Florence Weir Guesthouse, where he said, in what James thought a somewhat poor impression of someone on the verge of homelessness, he hoped to find a bed for the night.

James took a seat and waited for Marcus. Young Marcus could come back to the apartment with him and together they would wait and see what else the night would yield. But Belinda had other plans for Marcus. She needed someone to support her, she explained to James quietly, and the Chief Superintendent's suggestion that a policewoman accompany her was not what she had in mind. Mr Browne's protection of her in what Belinda would at all times after assert was *her darkest hour* was needed further. Belinda had lost her father and her husband all at once and there was no way she intended her green-eyed hero to slip from her grasp and most certainly not when she considered the alternative – her own company.

James nodded sympathetically. Her own company must be somewhat interesting and in any event it would be some time before the shock of her father's death at the hands of his own brother fully impacted on her, so of course she should have someone supportive with her when that happened. It had been a hellishly long day and it was time for him to leave the young to their endless devices and energies. He would go to the apartment and digest everything Tommy Smythe had told him and heavens knows that would be enough to keep him occupied as the night wore on as he waited, still waited, for news of Pearl. So when Marcus emerged from the interview room James offered him his hand, and, on firm instructions to himself about not dithering, he said, "Marcus dear chap, be a sport and look after Mrs Jones will you? She's going to need a friendly presence. Call me tomorrow. Should have news of Pearl by then, I dare say. Cheerio all." He kissed Belinda on the cheek and offered her his number which she took a little absently, *a bit like her smile really,* he thought kindly. He had the feeling that Mrs Jones's recovery would be swift.

Ah, the delights of living in the present!

*

The taxi pulled into the kerb outside the Fire Services HQ and after paying the fare, James stood wearily on the pavement and fiddled with his bunch of keys. He didn't see Yip until he was at the front door and his friend emerged from the deep shadow created by the thick columns of sandstone that framed the street-front windows. James jumped. He could have jumped for joy. His friend was here which meant that his friend was back, another stitch in the tapestry of this eventful day that didn't need to be pulled out and fretted over; an old familiar pattern that did not need to be re-embroidered. Yip was smiling too, which meant...?

"Means what exactly my old china plate?" he said. "You're smiling."

"Come, James. Let us have a whisky together. I can see you have much to tell me."

*

"If Chief Superintendent Smythe had any idea that we are sitting here like a couple of old village gossips with me putting you in the know about very hush-hush information, he would have conniptions, Yee Koon, my oldest and most favourite triad boss. However, he doesn't. To your health." Yip toasted James in silence. James put his glass on a side table and leant forward in the chair, willing himself to stay awake. He had to stay awake, any second Benson might return with news of Pearl .... "Ronald Childs killed his brother Tuesday before last," he blurted out. "He knows the layout of the house; let himself in through the kitchen, sent Chef off to market and the PA into head office with the Chauffeur and took the lift to the second floor and strangled his brother. He dragged him down the back stairs off the kitchen and stashed him in a chest-freezer in the cellar.

"This is very sordid, James." Yip was not amused. He had a freezer in his own cellar but it was for the storage of orchids that were brought in from the New Territories. Mrs Yip was very fond of orchids. "Have barely started, old man. So far so good. But what was he to do with the body? Ronald is bright enough but he's like a hurdler, can jump a hundred hurdles then out of the blue, baulks at one. He dithered about disposing of the body, went to dinner at Stormy's last Friday night – what a week, Yip, that was only a week ago – where he overheard Shaw and Tsiu doing their number on poor old young Marcus here." Yip had to look around. Mr Browne was not with them of course. James could be so irritating.

"The point, James?"

"It was a turning point, my dear chap. He saw Pearl in Stormy's."

"I don't understand."

"Ah, Yee Koon, Pearl has been central to this all along as our dear Doctor Benson would happily remind us he has known from the start, were he here. All saints alive, I wish he were here." Yip arched an eyebrow, unaware of Peter's mission and very surprised to hear James wish for Dr Benson's company, to Yip's best recollection the first time he had ever done so. "Ronald recognised her which is odd because he didn't recognise Belinda." Yip remained silent. Hopefully James would get his thoughts ordered soon. "He met her at Dennis's house once when Pearl was about sixteen and was like that" – James crossed his fingers – "with Belinda. Pearl hasn't changed that much with the years." Yip nodded. This was true if one omitted the fact that Pearl Green had changed from an attractive girl to a stunning – many said beautiful – woman. "Belinda knows the physical difference between her father and her uncle and when Ronald recognised Pearl, he became worried – did she also know how he differed from Dennis; something that ordinarily would be a minor piece of information but in this context could have exposed him?"

"And what could such a secret be, James – a mole, a birthmark, a hairline?"

"Ears, old man, ears. Ronald has jug ears and Belinda used to scoff at him and call him Uncle Jugs and his ears were the only two features that could differentiate the twins. But that's not all of it, Yee Koon. Ronald had three days after killing Dennis to go through his business papers, which is when he discovered the reason why he decided that Pearl had to be sidelined." James faltered, took a gulp of whisky and started again. "Those papers revealed something to Ronald about Pearl." Yip raised an eyebrow, waiting for an explanation, but James glossed over it and related how Ronald had taken in enough of the conversation at Stormy's to know that Marcus was staying at the Hilton and was being set up to be scammed. He had an idea – Dennis owned the linen company that services the Hilton. Ronald had access to a company van, a key to the hotel basement and another key to the service lift and the linen room.

"All he had to do was plant the body at the Hilton, set Marcus up to be on the scene and bingo, there's an arrest and Ronald was free to concentrate on disposing of his brother's financial empire without anyone coming near the Childs residence, and with the crime scene focussed on the Hilton."

"He went to a lot of trouble, James, when he could simply have deposited his brother's body in the harbour," said Yip. James ignored this; it was definitely one of Yip's comments better left ignored, he thought.

"Anyway, back to Saturday morning. He had poor old Dennis stashed in a linen trolley. He phoned Marcus first and arranged to meet him in Room 676. With Marcus out of the way he would have time to dump the body in his room. But it didn't go well because he saw Pearl. He did not of course, realise that *she* was staying at the Hilton until then. According to Chief Superintendent Smythe, Ronald insists that she saw and recognised him in Marcus's room, even though he was wearing a staff uniform.

"He panicked, pushed the linen trolley out of Marcus's room and jumped back into the service lift which was summoned to the sixth floor before he could hit the basement button. He really had the panics up then; he went into Room 676 which was supposed to be empty, according to the room-cleaning schedule. Marcus wasn't there but he heard a hairdryer going full belt in the bathroom. He was out of time and stuffed poor old Dennis into the cupboard and fled back to the basement. From that point on, Marcus was in trouble.

"You know what happened after that, Yip?" said James. Yee Koon did not bother to even shake his head. James was barely speaking to him, after all. He was making sense of the business himself. James said, "When Childs rang Belinda the next day to assure her it was Ronald and not Dennis who had been done in, he was taken by surprise again when Belinda insisted on coming to see him even though it would be a flying visit. She would expose him immediately so he set up her kidnap before they came face to face, simple as that, old man. He went to the police station to identify his brother which happily also gave him a near dam-perfect alibi because when Belinda arrived at the airport he was at the Station and even mentioned that Belinda had arranged to see Pearl before going home to spend the evening with him. This was a gift to old Ronald. He had time to forestall her and he already had a tested method of getting her out of the hotel.

"When Belinda took the lift to Pearl's floor, Dennis, togged up again as linen staff, waited and ushered her into lift 7. Lift 7 has two sets of doors because it doubles as a service lift and staff can use it as an express lift by double locking it. The door was open and ready to go. He knocked her out, took her to the basement and over to Causeway Bay to the marina.

"Initially he was going to abandon her on Po Pin Chau Island but that meant she would probably die and even Ronald had reservations about that. He kept her on board *The Belinda* and overnight decided that the whole thing could be an instant earner for him as well as give him a back-stop if he had to get out of Hong Kong quicker than he'd planned on doing. He had his skipper hire a yacht and moved her from *The Belinda* the next day.

James became very still. *She would have been in the same metal chest as Pearl, probably. How could he endure another moment of this?* He gulped a very large mouthful of whisky and Yip quietly admired how he was able to keep talking without spluttering on it. "He had the second ransom note ready and he used a Taipei bank account he had set up in Dennis's name years once before when he was going to try a different scam out on his brother. All very efficient and no-one suspected a thing. The police this end merely assumed that finding Belinda near the airport meant that the kidnappers made sure they got the money deposited by him after which they released her. The hired yacht will be fingerprinted now of course for evidence that Belinda was held there.

"Worried about something, Yip?" Yip shook his head, but of course he was worried. The money he had lent to that man, the worry it had caused him – had James, always so acutely aware of his own finances – forgotten that? What would become of it? Would he ever get it back? To do so, would it require even more interactions with Chief Superintendent Smythe? Yip surreptitiously did a sum on his fingers. He was heir to his brother's estate and the sale of Tony's collection of antique pottery would more than cover the money he had lent to Ronald Childs. His brow smoothed again. He could live quite well without thinking about that money, and who knows, perhaps it may come back to him without him having to be formally involved in its retrieval.

James was still talking, although in Yip's opinion all was clear except for one or two details. "The motor yacht was skippered by a chappie who has done some leg-work for Ronald's various little schemes in Hong Kong in the past. The police have him in custody too, conspiracy and kidnap charges laid, so I believe. While Ronald went to the bank and deposited the money, the skipper took Belinda to the airport and dumped her. By the time Ronald returned the whole job was done, and very neatly too."

James stopped speaking but only for a second. "And then of course there is the trifling matter of *my* daughter …."

"... who is here and fully in one piece. Hello Dad. Hello Mr Yip. That all sounds pretty riveting stuff, what I heard of it anyway." Pearl and Peter Benson were at the door, both looking at James very intently. James tried to get to his feet but fatigue and emotion caused him to stumble. Yip and Pearl moved forward but he regained his balance and composure just long enough before bursting into very uncomposed sobs. She held him and for the second time in a week, cried into his good tweed jacket.

Yip and Peter shook hands. It seemed the only thing they could do.

*

"Go on, Dad, finish telling."

"I can't, Pearl, I – Peter?"

"As we assumed, James, Pearl was deposited by Mr Ronald Childs on Po Pin Chau Island where I found her yelling her head off at the mouth of a cave set high in the rock face, whose last apparent inhabitants were Neolithics. Pearl looked a bit Neolithic herself, perched in the mouth of it, high above the waterline. She jumped," he said in answer to James's anxious questioning of how he had got her out. "But," he said as James looked faint, "she is quite all right, the boat lurched and I caught her."

"He did too, Dad. It was magic. I fell from the stars."

"Straight into my arms," said Peter.

James hook his head. He was hearing things now.

*

James and Yip were alone again. Pearl had phoned Kaz and was now taking a bath and Peter was in the kitchen heating up a tin of buttered mushrooms, flavoured with the mixed herbs James had purchased from Wellcome. James heard him whistling as the smell of toast crept tantalisingly into the living room.

"Whisky, Yee Koon? And do have a rum ball." Yip accepted the drink and sipped it with deep enjoyment, but declined the rum ball.

"Brother versus brother, James. Two such tragedies in the course of one week. Did Pearl know?"

"No, Yip. She didn't notice Ronald in Stormy's. If she had, would she have gone over to say hello? Probably not. Pearl always felt uncomfortable around Dennis Childs. But Ronald didn't know that. Anyway he had his back to her and left as soon as he decently could after spotting her. Seeing Pearl really put the wind up old Ronald, according to the Chief Superintendent." James was striving to remain calm. Perhaps he had misinterpreted those silly remarks Pearl and Benson had made.

He clasped his fingers together to stop his hands from shaking: the fabric, the very roots of the relationships between Peter, himself and Pearl had depths he preferred not to think about too much. James had gone through much in the years since he had discovered he was Pearl's father. She hadn't gone off and fallen in love with the mad monk now, had she? He sighed deeply and slowly became aware that Yip was looking at him with concern. He raised his hands in a sharp gesture of denial and said, "Surely not, Yip!"

"James?"

"Perfectly all right, old man. Just overcome by a thought. Anyway, where was I? Ah. Ronald failed to do his homework, particularly in regard to Belinda. He wore a wig and a uniform when he kidnapped her from the Hilton and she didn't recognise him. He knew her, however, because at that stage she was still in her Rock Wife get-up. Of course he didn't go below deck of the yacht whilst he had her held there either, so he didn't recognise the real Belinda when she arrived on his doorstep. He was only familiar with her media image. He didn't recognise me either, not that Dennis and I were great mates, but we were on familiar terms. Dennis Childs, well, Dennis Childs..."

"...James is having difficulty saying that Dennis Childs fell in love with Pearl's mother when they had what was for June just a casual affair." Peter was at the sitting room door again, gently stirring the pot of mushrooms and with a tea towel slung over one shoulder. He looked deeply content and deeply non-meditative. James nodded. Dennis Childs was yet another man who had fallen in love with his ex-wife and, moreover, stayed in love with her. Benson was the only man whom June had never fully captured and was the only man she had ever seemed to love. James shook his head regretfully. Yip leant towards him, frowning. Whatever was bothering James, it was not doing his health any good.

Peter continued, "After June's death, Dennis changed his Will, in which he had left the bulk of his fortune to June, and divided it between Belinda and Pearl. Not equally, mind. Belinda inherits the business and his personal fortune and Pearl inherits his property holdings, which are considerable both in Hong Kong and abroad. Pearl has known about this for a long time and it was the cause of some awkwardness between them, but she accepted it in the spirit Dennis intended. Pearl more than likely will donate her share to the foundation.

"Ronald worked fast after he killed Dennis, shifted millions into his Taipei account after sacking all of the senior people in the company who might pick up what he was doing. In another week or two Belinda's share of Dennis's estate would have been heavily stripped back."

Suddenly James exhaled very loudly and relaxed his fingers from around the whisky glass. By coming into another fortune, Pearl would be able to refund him her hotel-bill money without difficulty and he could still plan on retiring next year without being too pressed about money worries. However, Yip was not so diverted and said, "And in the event that Pearl, ah, passed on before Dennis or his daughter? I'm sorry, Pearl, but this is a most curious matter. – Dr Benson, who would inherit Pearl's share of the estate? Would it go to the Bowen Foundation, for example?"

"Now that is interesting, Mr Yip," said Pearl. "No. Dennis stipulated that if I pre-deceased Belinda before the Will was finalised, my share simply defaulted to the family. That includes Ronald I guess. Dennis was either sloppy about that or had his own reasons for not wanting Belinda to have the lot and, doubtless, he thought it a remote possibility."

"And that is why Ronald decided that Pearl had to go. It also ties up with some other information kindly provided by Chief Superintendent Smythe" said James. "This is in confidence of course." They all nodded. "Ronald got himself in a bit of a mess by swapping identities because of course he knew nothing of how his brother had distributed his wealth until he started going through Dennis's personal papers. Initially he planned on mining Dennis's assets and disappearing from Hong Kong as quickly as he could in case his cover was blown. He intended to leave selling off the property until later on. But when he read the terms of the Will, well you can imagine how he felt – not only was he blocked from accessing the property assets whilst Pearl remained alive but with her off the scene he would be assured of both the legal right and the time to cash in on them when he resumed his own identity, as he planned on doing, eventually, with the help of a faked Death Certificate and a dodgy lawyer or two. Disposing of Pearl became a necessity." James's mouth set in a hard line.

"It was all going well for Ronald until Belinda announced that she was coming to Hong Kong. He panicked. He had to get rid of her before they met but he baulked at killing *her*, knowing that he would never be able to escape the world-wide attention that would focus on him if she was killed on her home turf. By kidnapping Belinda he removed the immediate threat of her returning to Hong Kong again, at least in the short term. Her husband's new concert tour is a full program for the next year and she never left his side when he was on tour. Furthermore, Yip, he made an unexpected cool fifty million courtesy of your contribution" – Yee Koon raised an eyebrow – "but he needed to work fast on cashing in assets just in case Belinda did come back earlier, although he expected that by the time she jumped off her merry-go-round lifestyle and decided to visit him again, he would be long gone. If she came back earlier, well, I think we can all presume that he would have killed her too.

"Incidentally, kidnapping Belinda gave him a double bonus because of Belinda's intention to see Pearl at her hotel. He phoned her after he'd disposed of Belinda and wormed his way back into Pearl's life, enough for her to confide in him when she was moving back to her old apartment, when he pulled the security guards off duty. Dennis owned the company of course.

"But the whole scheme went wrong before that, when he realised that, after Pearl heard about Dennis's death, she might also remember that Dennis was a twin and might think it worth a mention to the police. He was put on the back foot with Pearl returning to Hong Kong so unexpectedly and sure enough Pearl did raise the issue with Chief Superintendent Smythe, who called the Childs mansion. Old Ronald had to act fast and he did, fuelled by greed and fed by anger at how vulnerable his precious scheme had become."

There was silence. Peter flicked the tea towel from his shoulder and made a snapping noise with it. "And it all fell apart, just like that, on one simple piece of knowledge," he said, flippantly, in James's opinion. James glared at him, Peter shrugged and left the room only to find Pearl walking along the corridor looking as though she had just emerged from a beauty parlour, wrapped in a plush bathrobe, her skin glowing. He wondered what he had to offer her. He felt pleased when he remembered there was something.

"Mushrooms, Pearl?"

"Mushrooms would be lovely, Peter."

CHAPTER NINETEEN

Monday 24 December 1979

Yip's yum cha palace in Central Hong Kong had a private dining-room which Peter considered too unnecessarily luxurious to justify the mere act of eating food and in addition, the crowd of old friends, allies and occasional competitors who met there, in company with some new chums, were clearly not happy. Kaz was sulky and Drew jostled his crutches as he struggled to pull out a chair. He ignored a hovering waiter and said, "Kaz you could give me a bit of a hand here, I'm not good with these things you know." Kaz sighed very loudly, which told the entire room that such was self-evident. "You're a rotten nurse, Kaz."

"Which is irrelevant seeing that I'm an archaeologist," she said flatly, leaving her husband to struggle on alone. James took stock of their unhappy faces...what was happening with those two? He watched Pearl as she smiled and hugged Belinda, who had Marcus firmly in tow. James thought Marcus looked a bit dazed. He nodded to James but James noticed that he avoided looking at Pearl.

The Yips were the last to arrive and Mr Yip sat Mrs Yip between himself and James. She would feel at ease with James. The Yips' daughter Annie had refused the invitation to visit Hong Kong at their expense; she was in Paris and the prospect of a reunion with her parents and her old friend Pearl was not sufficient enticement to lure her home. Yip patted his wife's hand. Mrs Yip had been so disappointed when Annie refused to come that she had privately threatened to drink brandy again.

Pearl began talking animatedly to Jane Franks but she could feel Derek Wong's compelling eyes on her. *He must be the jealous type,* she thought: *either that or he thinks I'm talking shop out of turn.* Derek and Jane had been a hot item for the past two weeks and apart from interviewing her to manage the Tortoise Universe Project, to be administered by the June Bowen Foundation, this was the first time Pearl had met Jane socially. She was to start her new job after the Christmas week break and would have a handover with Judith Sung and Danny Tsiu. Judith was only coming back for one or two days to familiarise Jane with the workings of the foundation. She had never returned to her duties since the day she was sent home in a taxi because Dr Benson thought it was too dangerous to remain at the office – *too scared,* she had said, *such awful things happening, life is too short* ....

James saw the glance Derek gave Pearl too: it was hostile, no doubt of it. James crisped his mouth into a line; he had tried to like this young man but could not quite bring it off. He had nothing of the stamp of young Marcus, although there was no doubt he was smitten by the lovely and talented Jane. Perhaps he had wanted to spirit her off to the Everglades when he left Hong Kong until the job offer with the June Bowen Foundation came up and tempted her more than any plans that Derek might have in mind.

James dropped his glance and studied the menu of twelve courses rounded off with a spectacular Christmas pudding, Bombe Alaska style. James loved Christmas pudding and he would have been quite happy to skip the rest of the food-fest and just concentrate on dessert. The conversations around the table were halting and when the menus were delivered, the silence that followed had relief in it as thirteen pairs of eyes studied the feast on offer. James also felt relieved when the first of three iced bottles of champagne were brought to the table. "I think we need a little something to get this started, don't you say so, Yip? Seems to be a bit of tension in the room." He stood and tinkled a fork against his champagne flute. "Attention all, please. As you know, twelve courses make up this monumental feast and I am instructed to inform you that Chef will be delighted to provide other dishes of your choosing should you so desire. Our host – he turned and bowed slightly to Yip Yee Koon – is anxious that there are dishes to suit everyone, even crumbed and deep fried chicken legs – although I'm not sure who eats crumbed and deep fried chicken legs." He stopped. Derek was glaring at him.

Crumbs, thought James, *it must be a Seminole dish, damn and blast it; I thought Marcus said they ate turtles....* "Tonight we are together to share not only a seasonal feast but to celebrate the fact that we *are* all together: Pearl, Belinda, Drew, Kaz and Yee Koon have all been through extraordinary events, and by association, each and every one of us has been affected by them." There was no response except from Kaz, who made an unfortunate slurping noise as she took too large a mouthful of champagne.

James felt a prickle of impatience bead his forehead. "But I see you do not share these sentiments." He banged his champagne glass down rather more severely than intended and lost some of the contents.

"James, there is little doubt about what is wrong here." The torch that could fuel James's impatience at any time was lit. Peter Benson stood up and announced firmly, "Allow me, please. This entire matter is unresolved for many here tonight, James. We had a week that began with the demise of Belinda's father, followed by Drew's truly appalling accident and a sprinkling of kidnappings. That summary excludes mention of several other deaths including a member of Yip Yee Koon's household, his own brother and a police officer who died whilst on duty.

"Into this mayhem, a turtle literally swam into our lives and challenged how we think about altruistic behaviour. It has to be said that we witnessed severe limitations in human altruism during that week, and whilst a murderer has been brought to book and the case effectively closed, some of us," Peter emphasised *some of us* and James scowled, "some of us need time to think about this some more, to reconcile the generosity of a mere animal with the savagery we have seen within our own species, and for many of us, within our own families." There was total silence.

"Marcus for example," he continued. Marcus stopped studying the little finger of Belinda's right hand – such a gorgeous finger – "Marcus came to Hong Kong to launch a project for his people; his grandmother died and he was caught up in a case that led to him being held on remand for two days as soon as he arrived here. His part in the week's drama saw him transported from a world in which he knows how to operate to one in which he felt not only alien but I am sure, abandoned. But as I am now aware..." Belinda looked at Peter crossly, wondering if he was going to gazump *her* announcement "...that Marcus has just accepted the position of Hong Kong Executive Finance Director of Child's

International Enterprises, I imagine he will feel at home in Hong Kong in no time." Belinda threw her napkin onto the table petulantly. No-one, including Marcus, took any notice. "Although," said Peter, "no doubt he will have issues surrounding this decision that he needs to come to terms with."

Marcus looked at Peter vaguely. The only thing he seemed really to have to come to terms with was an apparently permanent state of mild distraction.

"Derek Wong followed Marcus to Hong Kong to give him the news about his much-loved grandmother, and returns with the role of managing the American end of the new project. As this was initially to be Marcus's job, I imagine Derek has some issues of his own to resolve before he leaves Hong Kong next week." Derek looked pointedly at Jane, who avoided the look and rather studiedly folded her table napkin and placed it on her lap.

"And of course there are Kaz and Drew." Kaz took another swig of champagne and plonked the glass on the table. She reached for a beer. "Kaz," Peter said, "Well, Kaz started this week with the drama of Drew's accident and if that weren't enough she also had to cope with what happened to Pearl. Kaz endured many sleepless nights during the years Pearl was away because she, perhaps more than any of us..." he looked pointedly at James who was looking at the bottom of his empty champagne flute, "...she more than any of us knew how fragile Pearl was during those years. As for Pearl..." Peter decided not to dwell on Pearl's escapades since arriving home "...suffice it to say that even during her various trials during the week in question, Pearl took a little time out to discover a rare archaeological site on Po Pin Chau Island, the possible existence of which has intrigued Kaz for some time ...."

Pearl looked at Peter with gratitude that he had not delivered chapter and verse on the events of her week. James saw the look and frowned. "Yes, and," said Kaz unexpectedly, "Pearl removed an artefact from said site without permission from a qualified archaeologist." James whistled softly – that was a low blow. Everyone knew how Pearl had dabbled with the idea of studying Archaeology and here was Kaz taking an academically snobby shot at an amateur. Pearl stood up, clearly bristling. James wanted to duck under the table.

She barked, "Said artefact doesn't seem to be damaged by its unexpected and unauthorised removal. You've got it safely tucked away haven't you? How bloody small-minded of you Kaz. I thought your karmic moment with the turtle had cured you of concentrating on trivialities."

"Ladies and gentlemen..." In Danny Tsiu's opinion James didn't intervene a moment too soon. Danny had begun nervously to tie and untie his shoelaces, hiding from the room's acrimony as far under the tablecloth as he dared. James motioned to Peter to sit down. "...Peter is quite right to acknowledge the tension in this room but tonight is intended to be a celebration, not a back-biting session. However as there clearly are issues that need to be resolved before this becomes a celebration, I feel I must contribute. Peter, I very much disapprove of what seems to have developed into an attachment to my daughter on your part …."

Oops! Everyone around the table twisted their table napkins. Yip Yee Koon dropped his and as he bent to retrieve it he saw Danny's face peering anxiously at him from underneath the folds of the damask tablecloth. He winked and Danny banged his head on the edge of the table.

"And I very much object to being your nursemaid, Drew," said Kaz. "You are so bloody ungrateful for everything I try to do for you. How can I be expected to know how to bathe someone who has one leg in plaster? It's not as though it's summer and you stink...."

"Maybe not from where you're standing, which is on the other side of the room most of the time...."

Peter interrupted, "My attachment, as you put it, to your daughter goes back many years and has had many guises, James, but it ends, as it began, with her mother, your former wife, James." Only Pearl understood the meaning behind the last few words, which were inconsequential and confusing to everyone else.

James sat down, pulled his handkerchief out of his pocket and twisted it around his fist. He was still trying to come to terms with Pearl having at last told him about the child she had borne, the circumstances and the sad aftermath of it all – her inability to bear another child. That crack Peter made about Kaz being the only one who knew Pearl's real state of mind in those days had hurt, but even Kaz hadn't known about the baby. What hurt James was that she had told Peter, before anyone. Why? In the days since Pearl and Benson had returned from Po Pin Chau Island, James had seen the altered dynamics between the two of them and had even begun to think that a twenty-year difference in age was inconsequential if they had somehow developed at attachment ... how could he say, even under his breath, *if they had somehow fallen in love? Did they not see what he saw?*

Pearl took James's hand. "I have had difficult feelings for Peter ever since I was very young – Dad knows this, as most of you do – but when I had to jump from that rock platform below the cave onto the deck of *The Belinda*, well, my whole life was in that moment. That was not only luck, it was trust. And trust was always my door-stopper with Peter. I'd never trusted him, but I do now. And please, let us all please, please, stop bickering and fighting and..."

"Ah, ladies and gentlemen, the first course has arrived." Yip ushered in the first round of dishes with some relief. Jane Franks kept her eyes on her plate. What sort of crowd had she bought into? Danny's hands shook. So, Pearl, his Pearl was back, but did she love Dr Benson or did all these words mean something else? He could not tell. But he could tell that there was love in her face again, the face he loved, the face that he would give everything to have look at him with such love.

*

Marcus fossicked around in his jacket pocket. He had remembered to bring along the little brooch thing he had found at the hotel and wanted to ask Sir James if he would get into further trouble by admitting that he had forgotten to hand it over to the police. "Lost something, darling?" Marcus smiled at Belinda absently and her petulant expression returned. The old lines didn't seem to be working as well as they had once, or maybe it was Marcus.

"Sir James? Remember I mentioned this little clip to you? Here it is. I'd forgotten about it." He unwrapped the tiny object from a film of tissue paper and excused himself to Pearl as he reached across her to hand it to James. Pearl screamed, very loudly. Peter looked at her with interest. He had never heard Pearl actually scream before – Kaz yes, many times, but Pearl was quite capable of raising her voice without losing verbal coherence. – Kaz screamed too. No-one took any notice of her, least of all Drew. James went deathly white.

"So," he said, "we have this object in our midst again. I am loath to suggest to you that *this* is why this room is full of bickering inanities, ladies and gentlemen, but please indulge me...." His chair scraped as he rose to his feet again, his voice full of the authoritative tones of Sir James Gates. He held the object out for all to see. "This pin has turned up at times of great trouble for more than fifteen years among various members of this group. We recoil from its seeming ability to place itself in our midst. We have let ourselves come to believe that its appearance heralds times of conflict and that it has a power, a power that sweeps our horror of the unknown and incomprehensible before it. But now: *we* have *it*. We no longer have to harbour our superstitions about it. Charge your glasses please. If this object does represent a circle of evil, it is complete and its time of influence is past.

"To your health, ladies and gentlemen!" He hoped they would buy the sentiment. *What the devil was he to do with this bloody nuisance piece of metal? Bury it in one of Tony Yip's penthouse mantraps? Send it back into outer space from where the metal it was made of had originated? Take it out to sea on The Belinda and sink it along with this sulky lot?* The company drank deeply. Did the tension really leave the room at last or was it the second glass of wine that caused everyone to relax or was it merely that they had something mutually unsavoury to focus on? Pearl Green and Peter Benson made a silent toast before turning to James, who had adopted a decidedly prunish look around the mouth as they drank one another's health.

Pearl said, pointing at the object, "Dad, I think there's still more to it. Look at the animals carved on each of the cardinal compass points. The east-facing tiger reminds me of events in Hong Kong in October 1964, when this object first turned up. You could say *that* was a classic tiger autumn." Who else saw her hand shake? "The phoenix: it occupies the southern point and celebrates the rebirth of summer; and who can forget the summer of 1975 when this clip was stolen from the museum and everything that happened, especially to dear Kazzy? She turned and beamed at Kaz. And here" – she pointed to the northern compass point with a long, pearl-painted fingernail – "here sits our warrior tortoise, guarding the northern skies: the magical tortoise whose time is winter. All of us here today have just gone through one hell of a start to winter; but I have to say apropos of the supposed divination power of tortoises ...."

"And finally..." Peter interrupted her smoothly when Kaz bristled "...There is the dragon: The dragon guards the east and its time is spring. We are not done with it yet, James. One day there will be another cycle to complete, and even if you did jettison it, who is to say that its influence will die? No. It will be returned to the museum where it belongs and no doubt, time will inform us." James took a thoughtful sip of wine. It did not escape him that Peter had read his thoughts yet again. The silence in the room had become total, but he felt no further need to referee it; the bickering was over, competing interests forgotten. Pearl, Karen, Drew, Yip and Peter leaned forward a little at the same time.

James watched them. It was almost as though they were united by a single thought, and he could read it as clearly as though some vaporous presence had scrawled a message across the tablecloth: in just a few moments they had become one, they were a collective; they were there for each other, despite all their differences.

Notes on the Seminole Native Indian Tribe of Florida, USA

The Seminole Tribe has its roots in Florida where it remains today, a nation of American Indians that has set itself apart in taking on conflict in order to retain traditional lands; by the strategy of adopting entrepreneurial responses to invasion and in the 1970s, devising an innovative use of legally-won land rights. As a nation, the Seminoles put up effective resistance to being removed from their own lands; demonstrated great resilience in response to changing times, and not only survived conflict but emerged as a thriving nation in the latter half of the twentieth century.

In the early 1970s the Seminole people won a landmark decision to have their lands officially recognized as their own and a year or two later also won the freedom, through the federal court system, to make use of those lands for whatever purposes benefitted their people. The decision the Seminole Council made about how to apply that jurisdictional freedom was nothing short of astonishing – to establish a gambling outlet which eventually became a full scale casino. Following the Seminole's example, other Native American Indian tribes followed suit.

The days when the only way for Native Americans to earn money was from tourist gimmickry or agricultural work were over and as the money flowed in and gambling moved from simple games such as bingo to more sophisticated gaming, the Seminole nation continued to look to the future. With more and more casinos being built on Indian-controlled lands, the way ahead for the clear-sighted was very clear indeed and this story, although fiction, *may* have been possible.

Note on Po Chin Chau Island

Readers who are interested in the geological history of Po Chin Chau Island and the nearby East Dam (part of the High Island Reservoir) will find that an excellent internet site to visit for further information is www.geopark.gov.hk

Reference

Donald A Mackenzie. China and Japan Myths and Legends. Bracken Books (1986).

ADVANCE RESPONSE TO *BLACK TORTOISE WINTER*

Murder, kidnapping and intrigue with a Hong Kong backdrop! *Black Tortoise Winter* is a fast-paced thriller set in 1970s Hong Kong. The novel suggests the tortuous complications of life under the then British administration, and introduces a wide cast of unusual characters. From the American Indian, Marcus Browne, in town on a mission from the Seminole reservation, to the whimsical Mrs Entwhistle, subject to that well known Hong Kong pastime, a shopping frenzy; all the protagonists have their part to play in an intricate web of politics and deceit, juggling their parts with aplomb. Expats, including the runaway heiress Lady Pearl Green, and local residents, represented by the mysterious Mr Yip, are thrown together in a heady buck's fizz, bound to cause a few headaches at day's end.

Black Tortoise Winter will satisfy readers interested in diving into Hong Kong's history via a mysterious, intricate story.

The turtle/tortoise image surfaces throughout the story in many different guises – an intimate and pleasurable conceit for reader and author to share.

—**Patricia Grey**, author of *Death Has a Thousand Doors*, the first thriller in English to be set in Andorra in the high Pyrenees.

WRITE TO US!

We are interested to read your comments on
Jan Pearson's *Black Tortoise Winter*.
Please write to our email address, proverse@netvigator.com,
giving us a few sentences which you are willing for us to publish,
describing your response to this book.
If your comments are chosen to be included
in our E-Newsletter or website,
we will select another title published by Proverse
and send you a complimentary copy.
Please include your name, email address and mailing address
when you write to us, and state whether or not we may cut or edit
your comments for publication.
We will use your initials to attribute your comments.

NOVELS, SHORT STORY COLLECTIONS
AND OTHER FICTION
Published by Proverse Hong Kong

If you have enjoyed **Black Tortoise Winter** by **Jan Pearson**, you may also enjoy two other books in her series of thrillers set in Hong Kong: **Red Bird Summer** (2014) and **Tiger Autumn** (2015).

You may also enjoy the following (all titles in English unless otherwise stated):

A Misted Mirror, by Gillian Jones. 2011.
A Painted Moment, by Jennifer Ching. 2010.
An Imitation of Life, by Laura Solomon. 2013.
Article 109, by Peter Gregoire. 2012.
Bao Bao's Odyssey: from Mao's Shanghai to Capitalist Hong Kong, by Paul Ting. 2012.
Bright Lights and White Nights, by Andrew Carter. 2015.
cemetery miss you, by Jason S Polley. 2011.
Cop Show Heaven, by Lawrence Gray. 2015.
Death has a Thousand Doors, by Patricia Grey. 2011.
Hilary and David, by Laura Solomon. 2011.
Instant Messages, by Laura Solomon. 2010.
Man's Last Song, by James Tam. 2013.
Mila the Magician, by Zhang Jian 章簡. 2013. (English / Chinese bilingual)
Mishpacha – Family, by Rebecca Tomasis. 2010.
Odds and Sods, by Lawrence Gray. 2013.
Paranoia (the Walk and Talk with Angela), by Caleb Kavon. 2012.
Revenge from Beyond, by Dennis Wong. 2011.
The Day They Came, by Gérard Louis Breissan. 2012.
The Devil You know, by Peter Gregoire. 2014.
The Monkey in Me: Confusion, Love and Hope under a Chinese Sky, by Caleb Kavon. 2009.

The Monkey in Me, by Caleb Kavon. Translated by Chapman Chen. 2010. E-book. 2010. (Chinese)

The Perilous Passage of Princess Petunia Peasant, by Victor Edward Apps. 2014.

The Reluctant Terrorist: in Search of the Jizo, by Caleb Kavon. 2011.

The Shingle Bar Sea Monster and Other Stories, by Laura Solomon. 2012.

The Snow Bridge and other Stories, by Philip Chatting. Scheduled 2015.

The Village in the Mountains, by David Diskin. 2012.

Tightrope! A Bohemian Tale, by Olga Walló. Translated from Czech by Johanna Pokorny, Veronika Revická & others. 2010.

Tightrope! A Bohemian Tale, by Olga Walló. Translated by Chapman Chen. 2011. (Chinese)

University Days, by Laura Solomon. 2014.

Vera Magpie, by Laura Solomon. 2013.

OTHER GENRES

We also publish in other genres, including autobiography, biography, children's illustrated books, educational books, Hong Kong educational and legal history, memoirs, poetry, teenage / young adult books, and travel. Other genres may be added.

ABOUT PROVERSE HONG KONG

Proverse Hong Kong is based in Hong Kong with expanding long-term regional and international connections.

Proverse has published novels, novellas, fictionalized autobiography, non-fiction (including biography, history, memoirs, sport, travel narratives), single-author poetry collections, children's, teens / young adult and academic books. Other interests include diaries, and academic works in the humanities, social sciences, cultural studies, linguistics and education. Some Proverse books have accompanying audio texts. Some are translated into Chinese.

Proverse welcomes authors who have a story to tell, wisdom, perceptions or information to convey, a person they want to memorialize, a neglect they want to remedy, a record they want to correct, a strong interest that they want to share, skills they want to teach, and who consciously seek to make a contribution to society in an informative, interesting and well-written way. Proverse works with texts by non-native-speaker writers of English as well as by native English-speaking writers.

The name, "Proverse", combines the words "prose" and "verse" and is pronounced accordingly.

THE PROVERSE PRIZE

The Proverse Prize, an annual international competition for an unpublished book-length work of fiction, non-fiction, or poetry, was established in January 2008. Unusually for a competition of this nature, it is open to all who are at least eighteen on the date they sign the entry form and without restriction of nationality, residence or citizenship.

The objectives of the Proverse Prize are: to encourage excellence and / or excellence and usefulness in publishable written work in the English Language, which can, in varying degrees, "delight and instruct". Entries are invited from anywhere in the world. Long-listed writers to date include writers born or resident in Andorra, Australia, Canada, Germany, Hong Kong, New Zealand, Nigeria, Singapore, Taiwan, The Bahamas, the PRC, the United Arab Emirates, the United Kingdom, the USA.

Summary Terms and Conditions
(for indication only & subject to revision)

The information below is for guidance only. Please refer to the year-specific Proverse Prize Entry Form & Terms & Conditions, which are uploaded, no later than 30 April each year, onto the Proverse Hong Kong website: <www.proversepublishing.com>.

The free Proverse e-Newsletter includes ongoing information about the Proverse Prize. To be put on the eNewsletter mailinglist, email: info@proversepublishing.com with your request.

The Prize
1) Publication by Proverse Hong Kong, with
2) Cash prize of HKD10,000 (HKD7.80 = approx. US$1.00)

Supplementary publication grants may be made to selected other entrants for publication by Proverse Hong Kong.

Depending on the quality of the work in any year, the prize may be shared by at most two entrants or withheld, as recommended by the judges.

In 2015, the entry fee was: HKD220.00 OR GBP32.00.

Writers are eligible, who are at least eighteen on the date they sign The Proverse Prize entry documents. There is no nationality or residence restriction.

Each submitted work must be an unpublished publishable single-author work of non-fiction, fiction or poetry, the original work of the entrant, and submitted in the English language. School textbooks and plays are ineligible.

Unpublished first translations into English (including those already published in the writer's mother tongue) submitted by the author are welcome. The submitted work will not be judged as a translation but as an original work.

Extent of the Manuscript: within the range of what is usual for the genre of the work submitted. However, it is advisable that novellas be in the range 30,000 to 45,000 words); other fiction (e.g. novels, short-story collections) and non-fiction (e.g. autobiographies, biographies, diaries, letters, memoirs, essay collections, etc.) should be in the range, 75,000 to 100,000 words. Poetry / poetry collections should be in the range, 5,000 to 25,000 words. Other word-counts and mixed-genre submissions are not ruled out.

Writers may choose, if they wish, to obtain the services of an Editor in presenting their work, and should acknowledge this help and the nature and extent of this help in the Entry Form.

KEY DATES FOR THE PROVERSE PRIZE IN ANY YEAR
(subject to confirmation and/or change)

Receipt of Entry Fees / Entry Documents	[No later than] 14 April to 31 May of the year of entry
Receipt of entered manuscripts	1 May to 30 June of the year of entry
Announcement of Semi-finalists	July-September of the year of entry
Announcement of Finalists	October-December of the year of entry
Announcement of winner/ max two winners (sharing the cash prize)	December of the year of entry to April of the year that follows the year of entry
Cash Award Made	At the same time as publication of the work(s) adjudged the winner / joint-winners of the Proverse Prize
Publication of winning work(s)	In or after November of the year that follows the year of entry

FIND OUT MORE ABOUT OUR AUTHORS AND BOOKS

Visit our website
<www.proversepublishing.com>

Visit our distributor's website
<www.chineseupress.com>

Follow us on Twitter
Follow news and conversation: <twitter.com/Proversebooks>
OR
Copy and paste the following to your browser window and
follow the instructions: https://twitter.com/#!/ProverseBooks

"Like" us on www.facebook.com/ProversePress

Request our E-Newsletter
Send your request to info@proversepublishing.com.

Availability
Most titles are available in Hong Kong and world-wide
from our Hong Kong based Distributor,
The Chinese University Press of Hong Kong,
The Chinese University of Hong Kong, Shatin, NT,
Hong Kong SAR, China. Web: chineseupress.com

All titles are available from Proverse Hong Kong
and the Proverse Hong Kong UK-based Distributor.

We have stock-holding retailers in Hong Kong,
Singapore (Select Books),
Canada (Elizabeth Campbell Books),
Principality of Andorra (Llibreria La Puça, La Llibreria).
Orders can be made from bookshops in the UK and elsewhere.

Ebooks
Most of our titles are available also as Ebooks.